Kinklife.ca

Lord Chelant

THE BDSM FACTOR

A Madame Claire Crime Trilogy

By Lord Chalant

Book One

"Kinklife.ca"

Part I – Alternate Values

Part II – Flowers for Gennifleur

Book Two

"Predicament Bondage 201"

Part III – The Face of Evil

Part IV – AfterWords

(Sundry Stories from the Times Dispatch)

Book Three

Is a stand-alone story

that takes place six years later

Due for publication Oct 2017

Kinklife.ca

Lord Chalant

Disclaimer

Readers should not attempt any of the BDSM activities described in these pages without experienced supervision.

Neither the author nor the publisher assume any responsibility for the exercise or misuse of the practices depicted herein.

Violet wand play, flogging, whipping, fireplay and knife play, among other BDSM pursuits portrayed, can be expressly hazardous and may have serious health consequences. Tattoo drumming is relatively safe if the impact is not overly enthusiastic.

The key to successful BDSM is Safe, Sane and Consensual. Imposing any sexual or BDSM activity on un-consenting parties is morally offensive and constitutes a criminal act.

ISBN -10 1517290074
ISBN-13 978-1517290078

Table of Contents

Dedications & Acknowledgements

This BDSM trilogy is dedicated to the Lady of Chalant, who didn't just help with the research, she participated in most of it.

...And to the large number of kinksters in the Ontario BDSM Community who honoured us with their friendship and trust. You know who you are and we respect your privacy.

Importantly, a word of thanks and congratulations to some of our written inspirations - LT Morrison for his 'Devil in the Details – the Art of Mastery – a Mentoring trilogy'; Desmond Ravenstone for his informative book on 'Ravishment, the Dark Side of Erotic Fantasy' and Lady Joan for "Ask Lady Joan" and so much more.

Also a tip of the riding crop to Muriel Lennox for her rousing biography of Northern Dancer, F00Dave for his Cosmological constant, Kat for the sushi layout, CherrysLola for sundry statistics and WaywardWoman for her ravishment workshops.

It goes without saying that this is essentially a work of fiction. Situations and even seemingly familiar characters bear no resemblance to actual real people or events. Not much, anyway.

Chapter 1 A Man of Many Names

He is a Predator. A sociopath in his late twenties. Good-looking, well-spoken when it suits his purpose or fits his chosen role.

His online name is Richard, - or Rick or Rickie, as his mother calls him, or so he says with a fetching smile. Or Edward, Ed, Eddie. Or James, just James - no Jim or Jimmie, a cautious, calculating engineer.

He has as many names, as many identities, as he has sock puppets. Separate, distinct puppet profiles specifically designed so that he can prey on women. Women of all ages, but he prefers them to be young girls, Eighteen give or take. The more innocent and naïve the better. He thinks of them as young meat. His meat. His prey.

He is also known as Henry or Hank. Or William, Bill, Billie, again, only by his Mom he says, with that easy boyish smile of his. Such a sweet, cute smile, he thinks, in his sweet, cute, slightly oily way. Like Paul and Karla Bernardo, he muses. And now he has his own Karla as well. A slave nicked SorryBitch. He had found her on Kinklife.ca in the early spring.

He plays every angle. Admires his own cleverness. He boasts to acquaintances that he was in the Canadian Forces, in Afghanistan he says. He doesn't add that he was dishonourably discharged, fortunate to avoid imprisonment for sexual assault.

In civilian life, social media is his stalking ground. He prefers the free BDSM sites: Kinklife.ca, Bondage.com, Ravnet.net, Fetishworld.com, Forcefantasies.com, and Fetlife.com. Sites that include rape fantasies among their stock in trade, articles and stories that feature ravishment and the not-so secret yearnings that hide in numberless fanciful female hearts. Here, he finds his victims. Primed and waiting for his adroit and masterful touch.

His experience of actual BDSM is limited. A short-term drop-in at a single major Munch. Banned from another after a brief visit. Any knowledge he has is mainly gathered on-line, made up as he goes along. He has different histories on each site he frequents.

Different photos. Different myths. He sees himself as the consummate juggler, always with half a dozen pain-wracked bodies in the air. He marvels at his own dexterity. “You’re a smart bastard Hank, Eddie, whoever the hell you are. Tell ‘em what they wanna hear and they’ll flash their pussies just about every time. Fuckin’ beg you for it, they will.”

Like this Dawn bitch from Marybourne he was gonna meet at Tim Hortons soon enough. Thigh-high skirts and pert breasts. Eighteen if she was a day and just asking to be raped. “In so many words,” he sniggered, always in awe of his chosen M.O. “Well you’re gonna get it, bitch,” he crowed gleefully. “You stupid cow!”

His eyes glazed. They are alternately empty and disturbing. As Richard, he affects small wire-framed lightly-tinted sunglasses, from which his dark black eyes peer out like a fathomless sea with the merest hint of cold blue steel within. He daydreams in colour. The predominant colour is red. Great blotches of red, splattered and dripping. Surrounded by black. Swirling banks of sooty black and foggy greys. Dark, sombre colours, shot through by blood.

He was not misled or mistreated into his world of pain. His parents didn’t beat him. His teachers did their best. The NCO's and officers in his unit tried to counsel him without success. He chose to be what he is. Pulling out a kitten’s whiskers came naturally to him. Butterfly wings were passé at four. At five his favourite storybook figure from history was Richard III. Richard, Dick, Dickon. Dickon Crookback, killer of the Princes in the Tower.

He calls himself a Master, the Master.

He is not. He is evil.

And his evil is still growing.

One rape at a time.

Chapter 2 The Madame Claire

Claire Faversham had kept her own surname when she married Walter Black five years ago. With all her various business cards it had seemed the sensible thing to do and Walter had said it was entirely up to her. He had no insecurities about such things.

The six p.m. CBC news was just starting and Claire was in the kitchen at Walnut Cottage, baking up some of her special tea biscuits in case anyone came home with her after the Kitchener Munch later that evening. She had a reputation as a good hostess and was rarely caught short. “In anything,” she murmured to herself.

Right now she was in what Walter had been wont to call her domestic mode. She had mixed flour, salt, baking powder and shortening in a ceramic mixing bowl and was kneading the dough vigorously. Her leopard rolling pin would come into play next.

The early summer sun was streaming through the cottage windows and giving the kitchen a warm, golden glow. She was wearing her favourite leopard apron and had absently brushed hack her hair with one floured hand, giving her short auburn hair a white streak across the front.

"Fifteen minutes at 450 and they'll be done," she said, talking to herself as usual. "And I better get me a new dog or I’ll turn into that dotty old Claire-what’s-her-name up at Black Walnut Cottage....'

Not that forty-two, okay forty-four, was old anymore, and she still had her figure. Five foot eight, and nicely rounded. Always well-dressed too, even if she did go a bit overboard on the trademark leopard. A warm, friendly woman, if she said so herself. A mentor to many.

The doorbell rang as she was putting the cookie sheet in the oven. Young Matt Llewellyn came in without undue ceremony.

"Hello, lovely lady," he said cordially in his faintest of faint Welsh accents. "Still working, I see."

She flashed him an amiable smile and blew the hair off her forehead. "You're early tonight?"

Matt deposited his knapsack on the counter. "Got out of the stables by 5:30 for once. Figured you'd be off to your Munch by seven. Can't have Lohengrin not starting on you."

She grinned back and took off her apron. Matt was the boy from just down the Marybourne hill. 'Man,' she corrected herself. He was a truly good-looking young fellow. Handsome, even. Twenty-three, she knew. On the short side, no more than five foot eight, but slim and clean cut with an easy smile and close-shaven head. An exercise rider and aspiring jockey at Francis Dickie's Avalon stables.

"She's only acted up a couple of times," Claire told him.

"Probably just being temperamental. BMW's are noted for that. Just like racehorses."

Claire said "Mostly she runs real smooth"

Matt took a bottle of Niagara wine from his knapsack. "The Major said to give you this. A good Shiraz he said. And I've told you a hundred times, Claire. Lohengrin is a male."

"Walter liked German opera," she protested. "He had a Schwartz family story about Lohengrin. What better name for an old BMW he always said."

"Gertrude, I told him," Matt responded, long-suffering. "Heidi, Wilhelmina, Gretel. He was as stubborn as you are. And it's a 'vintage' BMW, not old." Matt had worked with Wally on the restoration.

Claire smiled fondly. "Hey, he always got vintage right." She and Matt were good friends and had enjoyed this conversation many times.

"What time do you have to get to the Smuggler's Den?" he asked.

"Seven-thirtyish. You won't be coming, I take it?"

Matt shook his head. "Not my bag, as you very well know." He picked up his knapsack. "Okay, let's mosey on outside."

She tossed him the car keys. "Don't let me forget my bickies."

"Be honest, Claire, you never forget anything. Mind like a steel trap."

They went into the backyard parking area. He unlocked the car. "Vintage," he said, smiling. "And you always lock it, don't you? Even on your own property."

"Once bitten..."

Matt tried the key in the ignition. Lohengrin started right off.

"She always does that when you're around," Claire said. "Showing off I guess."

Matt turned on the ignition again. The BMW purred into life. "We should have time for a quick spin before the Munch. How long will your 'bickies' be?"

"Ready now, I'm sure." She popped back into the cottage. "Won't be a moment."

"And Claire, wipe that flour off your hair," he called after her. "You might be mistaken for my mother"

She returned almost immediately, laughingly brushing off the flour. "I'd have to bone up on my Welsh."

"Just say 'Look you' a lot," he said, switching to the passenger side. “You drive and I'll listen."

Claire batted her eyelashes. "Oh Matt honey, you're so masterful," she said coyly. "A natural Dom."

He did up his seatbelt. "And all this time I thought that was your role. A dominant, I mean. Leeza certainly thinks so."

"Dear Leeza," Claire said. "Such a beautiful girl."

*

It was a perfect evening for a brief but leisurely drive. The rural side road from Marybourne to the slightly bigger Tilverton was largely downhill through Ontario Mennonite country. Small, neat farms nestling close together. The occasional horse and buggy on the gravel shoulders. Lots of straw hats and old fashioned bonnets with dark overalls and plain dresses. Children for all the world like miniature editions of their parents.

"They really school their horses from a young age," observed Matt. "Some of them could do real well at the trots."

"Did you ever get into trotting?"

Matt shook his head. "I gotta tell you, Claire. It just ain't the same." His manner changed and the youthful enthusiasm tumbled out. "There's nothing quite like the sensation of being on sixteen hundred pounds of racehorse galloping all out, responding to every touch. That's when I feel truly alive."

"I get the same feeling topping a good sub," said Claire with a smile.

Matt nodded his head in understanding. "To each his own, I guess."

"So how about Lohengrin? She sounds fine to me."

"Me, too. Not a clunk or a whiz or a muted whine."

"Why did you think she had a problem starting?"

Matt shrugged. "Could be the starter itself. Or maybe the alternator. Could be the solenoid. You need a diagnostic I'm afraid."

Claire raised her eyebrows. "I do?" she started to say.

His voice cut in sharply. "Watch it, Claire! Pedestrian."

Claire expertly swung the car out into the road a couple of feet. "Saw her, but thanks."

There was a girl standing on the side of the road, partly obscured by overhanging bushes.

"Hitchhiking, I guess," Matt said.

Claire braked to a stop a few yards past the girl. "I think I know her. Seen her at a Munch, I believe. Yes, and she works in the Tilverton Mac's Milk."

"Thanks for stopping, guys," the young girl said gratefully, coming up by Matt's now open window, She was an attractive, bouncy blonde. Eighteen or so. Dressed all in white and carrying a tennis racket. "Tennis, anyone?" she said with a charming smile

Matt reached back and opened the rear door. "You're the chick from Mac's Milk, right?" he said warmly, with a sly wink at Claire and a soppy grin on his face. "I'm Matt Llewellyn."

"Leeza's big brother," put in Claire helpfully.

"Dawn Gretsko," the blonde said brightly, settling into the back seat. "And you're Madame Claire. The Madame Claire. I've seen you at Munches." They were moving again. "My bike got a flat." Dawn went on. "I'm heading for the arena in Tilverton. The Tim Hortons there." She looked appraisingly at Matt. "Haven't run into you at the Munches. I would have remembered."

"Not my scene," Matt said shortly, colouring slightly. "I'm into riding and horseracing."

"That's great," said Dawn, giving him a smile to remember.

Claire managed to get in a word. "So I guess we won't be seeing you at the Kitchener-Waterloo Munch tonight?"

"I plan to get there late," Dawn said. "First I got a meeting with this guy Edward from the Guelph Racket Club. Eddie, as his Mom calls him. We'll have a quick game so he can see how good I am. I'm hoping to be an assistant pro with the club."

Claire frowned. "You know this fellow?"

"Not personally. We met through Kinklife.ca. Calls himself Sir Edward. He knew all about my second place in the Southwest Ontario tennis finals."

Claire was thoughtful. "The hockey arena must be closed in summer. The tennis courts are sort of out back, aren't they?"

"That's why Eddie suggested we meet at Timmie's. Better safe than sorry, he said in his last email."

"Do you have a backup?"

"Huh?"

"Someone on call. Knows where you are and who you're with. You phone in at a pre-arranged time, say ten o-clock."

Dawn laughed. "I expect to be at the Munch by then, complete with job offer. And there's such a thing as being over careful."

"Here's the Sports Complex now," broke in Matt. "And Dawn, if you ever want to do any horseback riding, I can set you up at Avalon Stables."

"Gee, thanks, Mattie, "she replied, opening the car door and getting out. “I'll take you up on that. Thanks for the lift, Madame Claire. You're real sweet." She waved cheerfully and turned into the Timmie’s beside the hockey arena.

"I should have been firmer with her," Claire said, shaking her head. "It can be hairy out there."

"Super chick," said Matt enthusiastically. "Hey, maybe if I can't keep the weight down, I'll take up tennis."

The Jockey Club limits were 5' 9" and 135 lbs for a jockey, meaning he cut it pretty close at 5"8" and 131. Most jockeys were much smaller.

He grinned at Claire. "Better get you home, luv. Wouldn't want to make the Madame Claire late for her evening show and tell."

"How's about Lohengrin, Mattie?" Claire ribbed him back.

"Don't think there's any rush. I'll borrow a diagnostic tester from the stables for the weekend. Francis has one in his garage. Fully equipped he is."

Claire turned serious. "How is the Major?”

"No flare-ups recently. Desmond says he has a new neuroplasticity programme. Smooths him right out."

"Give him my regards, though I guess I'll see him at the Munch. You know I worked with him once on a doping scandal."

Matt nodded. "Saved the stables a fortune the way I heard it."

Claire smiled sweetly, as if a sudden thought had just struck her. "You know something, Matt? That Dawn would be an ideal submissive for you if you weren't so dead set against the Lifestyle."

"Like Leeza for you, is that it?"

Claire seemed a trifle awkward. "A bit... Will she be at the Munch, do you know? We do have a sort of date."

Matt looked her full in the eye. "It's her first BDSM Munch, Madame Claire," he said punctiliously. "And I happen to know she bought an expensive new outfit for the occasion."

They stared at each other very seriously for a moment. Then both burst out laughing.

They were back at Black Walnut Cottage well before seven.

Chapter 3 The Smugglers' Den

It was the first Tuesday evening in June. Time for the once secretive Walter Black Munch, held monthly in the legendary Smuggler's Den at the historic Siebert Hotel in downtown Kitchener, Waterloo Region, Ontario.

The Walter Black, commonly referred to as the Black Wally, was where the BDSM community in K-W, Kitchener-Waterloo, came together for a relatively vanilla evening of socializing, carousing and lively war-stories from the front. It was where lifestylers hooked up for the numerous parties, private and semi-public, held throughout the Region. Where eager newbies to the still expanding Scene made their way, most often hesitant and nervous, to discover for themselves what the grand mystery was about.

The Siebert Hotel was a stately old edifice of a building, with about a hundred imposing bedrooms and a dozen tastefully furnished suites, dating back to Victorian times, when Kitchener had been known as Berlin. Then it had been a small town of mainly German immigrants, some four kilometers, two-and-a-half miles in those days, from the Anglican/Presbyterian township of Waterloo. That changed in an outburst of Canadian patriotic pride during the First World War, though the two towns had stubbornly preserved their own identities and sense of direction. In Kitchener the principal shopping street supposedly ran east and west from downtown. In Waterloo the self-same dead straight street allegedly ran north and south from Uptown. Even newly-minted cab-drivers were confused at times. Many a bewildered visitor wound up at 600 King West when their destination was 600 King South.

The storied Smuggler's Den took up the entire 12,000 square foot basement of the Siebert. The massive support pillars of the hotel had all been enclosed in smooth ornamental brickwork, with a vaulted ceiling and gleaming terrazzo floors. The name went back to the Jazz Age Twenties and Prohibition in the States. Back to the time when Samuel Seagram and his sprawling distillery in wet Waterloo utilized the basement space as a storage and staging point for the vast quantities of spirits he exported to Buffalo, Detroit, New York and the Chicago of Al Capone.

Appropriate to the changing times, the current Lifestyle activities were more or less legal in Canada but decidedly less so south of the Border. But where great fortunes had once been made in liquor, even unto the third and fourth generation, this was not yet the case with BDSM. Nor was it remotely the case with Sammy Seagram, the long-time manager of the Smuggler's Den bar and restaurant. His original given name had been Joe, but he had adopted Sam to go with the job description and it had stuck. Unfortunately for him his salary had evidenced a similar lack of upward progress. He was not a happy man.

"Okay, you lot," he was saying in the kitchens as he marshalled his servers. "Smarten up and keep everything you overhear to yourselves. You'll have a hundred, hundred-fifty head in the Den tonight. Half of 'em will wanna eat; most of 'em will wanna drink; all of 'em will wanna rattle on nineteen to the dozen. You guys jest wanna stay busy. Don't get involved and for Christ's sake keep the orders straight. I'll be out there watching you like a hawk,"

Sammy was a small, birdlike man with thinning ginger hair and prominent teeth. He had an oily, ingratiating manner with customers and was a martinet with his minions, as he called them sarcastically. The turnover in staff was constant, with most of the good ones graduating upstairs to the hotel's posh Breithaupt dining room with its sparkling Victorian crystal chandeliers. He regarded his wait staff as the dregs and rode them incessantly.

"This bunch calls themselves the Black Wally Internet Social Club," he told them. "Take 'em with a full salt cellar and like I said don't get caught up in the chit chat. Polite and efficient, that's all I want. Use your legs and not your ears. If the service stinks, you're outa here. Pronto!"

*

A sweeping brick passage curved from the bar and kitchen area into a capacious archway leading into the restaurant and conference hall proper. Like the rest of the Siebert lower level the passage and arch were finished in smooth sanded brickwork that gave a mellow and old-world ambiance to the surroundings. The main hall was steadily filling up, with more kinksters arriving every minute. They were of all types and ages and everyone was given a name tag as they entered, promptly filled out with their online names.

The hall featured a dozen large round tables, all of them with a differently coloured flowered centerpiece. Ten matching bucket chairs sat around each table, supplemented by deep couches against the walls. A functional small stage stood just inside the archway. Two additional fair-sized banquet rooms led off either side of the central hall. Beyond those were several smaller, more private dining rooms. The hubbub of voices was already loud, echoing off the gold flecked ceiling. The guests were laughing and talking as they circulated from one table to another to greet and hug their friends. It was a very huggy, welcoming community.

"Always makes me feel I should do a program on the art of hugging," Madame Claire was saying good-naturedly to Bertie Stanislav. Claire was wearing a lightweight leopard-patterned smock and had a smart leopard fascinator perched on the very front of her head. "Though I guess radio isn't the ideal medium for so tactile a show."

Bertie was the official host and organizer of the Walter Black Munch and the least threatening Dom in the Ontario lifestyle. He was usually ready with a compliment or bon mot. "Dear Lady", he said with a smile, "I'm sure you'd have the audience eating out of your fascinator."

"You could always do a workshop at FatMan," offered Sir Robert Challenger, holding out a chair at the red table for his wife, Lady Grace. "We had a delightful Japanese tea ceremony with Missy Alexis a fortnight ago." He and Grace ran the twice monthly FatMan private parties at Challenger Manse. The respectful English titles were part of their online avatars, routine in the community. Though Robert's plummy Oxford English supported the rumour that just maybe his knighthood might be real.

Claire tilted a red chair into the table before sitting next to it. “I’m expecting a special guest,” she said simply. “I think you’ll find her intriguing and quite lovely,” she added, with a secret and very attractive smile. “I know I do.”

“That’s a high recommendation,” teased DarkMaelstrom, claiming a seat across the table. “And I see you’re sitting close to the entrance. Taking no chances, eh, Madame Claire?”

She smiled at him sweetly. “I know how swiftly you Doms can move,” she said. “Though it seems you’re already set for the evening.” She was referring to the tawny-haired young woman he had installed beside him.

DarkMaelstrom grinned “Like you, Claire, I try to make our newbies feel at home.” He introduced her pleasantly. “This is Froken Julie, folks,” he said. “Miss Julie to those of you who don’t speak Swedish.”

“Or are not familiar with the playwright August Strindberg,” chimed in Celeste Baron, also at the red table. She was an actor from nearby Stratford.

“Marie-Celeste, our Shakespeare luminary,” he introduced her to Miss Julie. “And the leopard lady with the cute hat is the moving force behind 'Ask Madame Claire', our internet radio podcast.”

Claire pretended to be mildly horror-stricken. “Don’t let the Man-in-Black catch you saying that, Roger. He’s the moving force; I just occupy the hot seat. Your first Munch?” she asked the Swedish girl, who nodded self-consciously. “Leeza’s too. She should be here shortly.” She glanced at her wrist watch. It had a leopard strap. Her friends always knew what to give Claire for her birthday, or as the fancy struck. Her home, Walnut Cottage, was a Serengeti paradise.

*

At the pink table on the far side of the hall Dana Gennifer Van Lith was chatting with ex-Major Francis Dickie and tall, slim Desmond Trout. Dickie was the short, stout, forty-five-ish horse trainer who owned the Avalon stables near Weissenberg, just past

Claire's cottage in Marybourne. Des Trout was his way more boyish lover; a slight Catholic school-teacher just turned thirty.

"So, Francis," Dana Gennifer asked. "Are you running a nag at Fort Erie? The Prince of Wales stakes?"

"Haven't missed in seven years, Fleur de Lys," the major replied boisterously. Fleur was the online name Dana was better known by. Gennifleur, as it said on her name tag. She was the local representative of the American NCSF, the National Coalition for Sexual Freedom. There was a neat story attached to her choice of aka. Many kinksters had stories behind their online names. They were still necessary cover for anyone who valued their privacy and didn't wish to be outed in public. Francis was listed as OddsOnFavourite on his name tag.

The Manager of the Smuggler's Den, Sam Seagram, was bustling around the pink table with a pasty wait-girl delivering four heaping plates of steak dinner. "Mind me enquiring who's riding, Major sir?" he asked obsequiously.

A touch of irritation flit over Dickie's distinctly florid countenance. "I'm planning to give the youngster his chance, Seagram," he said brusquely. "Young Matt Llewellyn."

"He's very inexperienced," demurred Sam. "Hope he can handle the pressure. It's a $300,000 purse, right?"

Desmond Trout chipped in. "He was a champion scrum-half at Lester Pearson Collegiate," he said loyally. "He's done well in a couple of claiming races."

Francis Dickie snorted. "I gave you a tip on Leopard Damsel, Seagram," he said bluntly. "You should have backed her." He cut the horse racing discussion short. "And bring me some HP Bold, man. You know I take it with Filet Mignon."

Sam was instantly overly deferential again. "Of course, Major, sir. Right away, sir." He snapped at the tiring waitress. "Bring the Major some Bold, girl. And toute suite about it."

"Slimy little pest," growled Francis, as Sam shoo-ed off the girl and started to turn away. The Major was not noted for his diplomacy.

"So Gennifleur, dear girl, did you hear about the cross-dressing Mix and Mingle fuck up?" he wanted to know. "Missy Paulette came home from Thailand after her gelding and they can't decide whether she belongs in the group any more. Moot point, I s'pose."

Fleur laughed. "I haven't a clue where the coalition stands on that," she admitted. "And we're supposed to be the least judgemental people on earth."

The Major shook his head lugubriously. "A regular judgement of Solomon, eh, what?"

"Eh, what?" she mimicked him, straight-faced. "That's Canadian/Brit military overkill even for you, Francis."

They grinned at each other. They had been friendly acquaintances for many years.

*

The spacious conference hall was getting packed. The echo of plates and cutlery and conversations was almost deafening. Kinksters were continuing to arrive in twos and threes. Flamboyant Lord Muckety-Muck swept in with his angelic Lucrezia. Statuesque DasUberdomme with her diminutive submissive FrauleinPussylapper in tow. Young GeorgyBoy, GeorgyGirl and PuddenandPie, a comparatively new threesome, only recently, and earnestly, into poly. Polyamory, Greek for many and Latin for loves, as Georgyboy helpfully told anyone he could buttonhole.

The earnest threesome was followed by a striking young girl with long raven hair, awesome lilac eyes and a very classy appearance. She was wearing a short creamy white Greek tunic trimmed with violet piping, and a saucy white cap. Her slim legs were long and shapely and her pointed white ankle boots had five inch stiletto heels. Coming in through the passage way she moved gracefully and confidently, yet somehow conveying a sense of innocence and vulnerability. When she paused in the archway, she was framed by the tan brickwork like a pre-Raphaelite painting of a young goddess emerging from the Augean caves. She was in a word unbelievingly stunning. Leeza Llewellyn, scene name Lisa Labelle, had made her grand entrance to the Walter Black Munch.

She gazed around the hall, her lilac eyes keen and searching. Then her face lit up in a lovely smile as she spied a relieved and expectant Madame Claire advancing to greet her.

"Leeza Darling," gushed Claire, who knew a thing or two about playing to an audience. "I'd almost given you up. Your very first Black Wally." She enfolded the glorious girl in a welcoming embrace. It was a special patented Madame Claire caring hug. Subtle pheromones were flying.

"Madame Claire," responded Leeza, who knew a thing or two herself. This was a significant moment in her young life. Momentous, even. "I apologise if I'm a few minutes late. I simply couldn't decide what one wore to a Munch." Her voice was perfectly modulated and deliciously husky.

Claire held both her hands gently and gazed deep into those arresting eyes. "You look transformed, my dear," she said sincerely. "And don't worry your lovely head about all these unfamiliar people. They'll be as bowled over by you as I am. You're breathtakingly beautiful." She turned to Bertie, who had witnessed Leeza's entry and made his way over. He was quick like that. "I've been begging Leeza to join us for months, Bertie," Claire said. "I've watched her and Matt grow up. They're my neighbours."

Bertie glanced questioningly at Claire and then extended his arms toward Leeza. In the community you asked permission before hugging a submissive. Not that Madame Claire was Leeza's dominant - yet, she would have said - but Bertie was a stickler for Scene protocol. Claire smiled at him graciously and he wrapped his arms around the girl in the friendliest of hugs. "Pleased to meet you, Bertie - Sir," she said, picking up on the courtesy title. She was a quick study. It helped that Claire had prepared her.

"Come sit, dear girl," Claire said, steering her to the red table. "I want to show you off."

*

At the yellow table in back of the hall Sir Galahad, Lance McComber in real life, had an overflowing circle of listeners for his vivid recountal of a sadistic scene he had recently played out with his red-haired slave OrphanAnnie. Even Francis Dickie and Des, at the pink table close by, had tuned in. Lance's wife Ruthenia, mother of his three children, had kindly made some space for the Major. She was pregnant again. She didn't make it out to as many Black Wallies as Lance and Ann, but she was fully content with the arrangement. Galahad was happy to share Ann with Ruth, or Ruth with Ann if it came to that.

"Anyhow, next I strung little OrphanAnnie up to the St Andrew's Cross by her thummie-thum-thumbs," he was saying, with a great deal of boyish relish. "Then I used my Japanese clover clamps to fasten her boobs to the Vee. Couldn't twitch, let alone move. Oh, and did I say I had her on tippy-toes, with a homemade pointy caltrop under her heels?" He was pleased as Punch as he continued. "Then I laid into her back with my seven foot singletail. A good and proper beating I gave her"

"That sounds like Predicament Bondage," the Man-in-Black intoned in his deep bass voice. He was the producer and announcer of the 'Ask Madame Claire' internet radio show.

"Nah, that's just common or garden S&M," laughed Ann, her eyes glowing like hot coals. "Sir is a sadist. I'm a masochist... We go together like the Marquis de Sade and the Story of O."

Ruth looked pleased with herself. "While Momma stays home and raises the kids," she crowed. "I don't play half as much as when we were first married." She was quite happy with that too.

"You guys are way out of date," observed the Man-in-Black, whose secondary fetish was helpful information. "Sadism and masochism have been struck from the D.S.M., the American Psychiatric bible of mental diagnoses. You're not even an aberrant condition anymore."

Galahad shook his leonine head dolefully. "I grew up knowing I was different," he said. "A clinically insane deviant. Now they tell me I'm just another shade of normal."

"Only in Psychology Today, honey," Ruth consoled him. "The general public still thinks BDSMers are dangerous sex-crazed monsters."

"Which we're not, of course," said the Man-in-Black. "Monsters, anyway."

*

By now there were close to a hundred kinksters congregated in the conference hall. The tables were full. Laughter was constant and increasingly well-oiled. Amusing anecdotes and a fair degree of hooking up were the order of the evening. One of the topics which often came up when newbies were present was exactly how the regulars had gravitated to the lifestyle to begin with.

"I was tricked into it," said Celeste Baron, who had driven in from nearby Stratford, where she ran the local boutique Munch in tandem with her long-time domme and girl-friend, Supermoll, an assistant director at the Shakespeare Festival. "Claire's former husband Walter conned me into attending the Naughty Night Out party. He insisted I'd be shocked out of my wits."

"You, Celeste? Shocked." exclaimed Leeza, sipping a Pinot Grigio. She seemed right at home.

Celeste glanced at Claire, who shrugged. "Walter was a mentor to many of us here," she disclosed to her guest. "He was the most subtly dominant man I've ever known. He told Celeste a play party might be just too real for a girl of her theatrical tastes.

There was general laughter, which a table hopping RubyThursday came in on. "Me, I saw a dominatrix flogging a black boi in a French porn movie," she said to Leeza, smacking her lips sexily. "Chinese chopsticks in her hair, tight corset and the cutest leather skirt I'd ever seen." She laughed. "I can do that, I said, and baby, look at me now. Lady Ruby, flogger to the stars." And she leered at Celeste, who played the submissive role in the lifestyle.

Claire downed her Cosmopolitan and waved the glass at Sam Seagram, lurking watchfully nearby. "Right away, Madame," he said and glanced questioningly at Leeza, who put a hand over her wine glass. "I can't stay much longer," she said regretfully to Claire. "Tuesday is really Matt's night out with the stablehands."

"He mentioned that, darling." said Claire. "But you must hear how Sir Robert and Lady Grace got involved. You see you don't have to be twenty to discover the Scene. You were seventy plus back then, right Robert?" Claire had a well-honed interview technique. She was well aware that 'back then' was at least ten years ago.

"Seventy-four," said Robert. "And Grace was fifty. We'd always been too busy running a chain of retail stores even to recognise the existence of BDSM. Then I came down with prostate cancer. I was a survivor, but our sex life pretty well went tit's up. That's how come we went to the Everything About Sex Show in Toronto."

Grace offered a brief clarification. "We tend to be rather open in the lifestyle, Leeza," she said. "Fifties, seventies, we still like lots of sex. Of which there's plenty in BDSM,"

Leeza's lilac eyes were shining. She thought Robert was a wonderfully dignified elderly gentleman and considered Grace charming and warmly maternal. "I'm not sure I fully understand," she said slowly. "How did a Toronto sex show morph into the lifestyle?"

Grace gave a dazzling smile. "One whole corner of the CNE Automotive building was curtained off. ENTER AT OWN RISK, the sign said. "BDSM DUNGEON"

"It takes place four times a year," added Claire. "We get a lot of new blood from the sex shows. I'm sure you'll get to visit one before you're much older."

Sir Robert summed up. "It was like walking into a set from Game of Thrones," he said, shaking his head at the memory. "There was a Gorean Post, a couple of St Andrew's Crosses, Spanking benches.... Oh, and a tall, auburn-haired woman in full BDSM regalia with a long sinuous leather whip in her gloved hands. It was the best theatrical presentation I've ever seen. And guess who?"

"Madame Claire," chorused everyone at the red table, and some from the nearby purple and white tables who had heard the tale before. Claire did the theatrical bit with her eyelids. Grace finished off the story. "She said hello, introduced herself and told us she was what was called a Domme, pronounced Dom, but spelled D.O.M.M.E. She had us on the hello."

Claire picked up where Grace and Robert had left off. "You know, Leeza," she said. "That really makes me wonder what you'll say in, oh, ten years' time. About your first exposure to the Black Wally."

Leeza went her one better in the provocative eyelid department. She turned up the tip of her nose as well. "Maybe that I made my older brother late for his night on the town," she said. "And why? Because I met this Domme, spelt D.O.M.M.E, but pronounced generically, who had blithely decided that I needed a - what did you call it? Ah yes, a mentor. Which I almost certainly do." She was learning fast in this company.

Most everyone at the red table laughed. Sir Robert smacked the table loudly. DarkMaelstrom whistled.

Claire was playful but serious. "And as your anointed mentor, darling," she said, "My job is to persuade you to stay a few minutes more. Coincidentally, dear Leeza, your first Walter Black Munch is also the twenty-third anniversary of the first one."

"There'll be a cake, ice-cream and our own Braveheart to pipe it in," said Grace at her cajoling best.

"How can Matt blame me?" asked a most innocent Leeza with the dancing lilac eyes.

"Great Scott, girl" said Sir Robert felicitously. "You'll fit right in."

Chapter 4 The Girl in White

Vijay Puri was having a beer with two of his boyhood Tilverdale high school friends. In actual fact, they were having a beer; he was drinking a coke. Vijay was a first year constable with the Waterloo Regional police.

They were sitting at a wrought iron table on the front patio of Crazy Joe's, a dilapidated bar and grill near the corner of Main and Highway 8, in the very centre of the sprawling township. Vijay was officially off duty but had a patrol car to deliver a package from his staff sergeant to Mort Rothstein, a Kitchener lawyer who lived out on Main Street.

The boys were talking sport. It was a common interest. "The Blue Jays are plain loaded this year," said Bernt Sjostedt, who was a born optimist. "They figure to repeat Ninety-two. Ninety-three."

"So they win the World Series again," said Izzy Rothstein scornfully. "All that proves is that our Americans are better than their Americans."

Vijay grinned. "Unlike hockey, where our Canadians always win the Stanley Cup for Anaheim or Pittsburgh."

The three boys, young men really, had been on the same forward line when the Tilverdale Timberwolves came a surprise second in the local high school championships. That had been one of the biggest things ever in the sleepy township.

Tilverdale was your typical Ontario small town. Main Street South was largely residential, though many of the grand old Victorian houses were spruced up as 'antique' shops in the summer months when weekend tourists from Toronto descended in search of bargains. Main North had Crazy Joe's, a Thrift shop, a Food Basics, a Chinese restaurant and, farther out, Tilverdale Sports Complex, which was the somewhat grandiose title for the Councillor Shewchuk hockey arena, the football field and, tucked away in back, the blacktopped tennis courts.

Vijay was peering down Main North. It was dusk, dark almost. The traffic lights at the Highway 8 intersection gave Crazy Joe's an alternating red, yellow and green glow. "Some chick coming our way," he said, frowning. "Can't seem to decide whether to walk or run."

Bernt was more explicit. "Kind of early for a drunk and disorderly," he said dismissively.

"She looks sort of familiar," said Vijay.

They watched the distant figure looming out of the darkness. It was a woman for sure. A youngish girl most probably. She was wearing white shorts and a half-open white shirt. She did seem to be staggering a little.

She slowed to a dead stop in front of the Food Store. Stood perfectly still for a moment, her face in shadow. Then she moaned aloud and burst into tears, burying her face in her hands. The guys could hear her sobbing.

Vijay rose to his feet. "That looks like...what's-her-name? The Dawn girl."

"Dawn Gretsko?" said Izzy. "Nah, she don't drink. Her Mom's real strict."

The uniformed police officer straightened his tie. "I don't think she's drunk," he said thoughtfully. "More like she's in some kind of trouble. “Is that you, Dawn?" he called out to her. "Dawnie Gretsko...? Are you okay?"

The girl in white reacted like a scared rabbit. Her head shot up and she peered around in fear, the traffic light turned green and bathed her in an eerie glow. They could see now that her white shirt was torn and dirty. Her long hair was hanging untidily over her face, partly hiding it. She seemed ready to take flight.

The girl saw a cop standing behind the railing at Crazy Joe's. She thought she remembered him from high school. Her first thought was to rush over to him for help. The second thought stopped her. She had a vision of police and teachers and community members staring at her in consternation. She could almost hear their tongues wagging. Mom will never forgive me, she thought, panic stricken.

"I'm not Dawn," she called back and crossed to the far side of Main to hurry past Crazy Joe's. She didn't wait for the light to change. Highway 10 was the through street but there was no traffic at this time of the evening.

"You could ticket her for jaywalking," said Izzy helpfully.

Vijay grunted. "Not my bailiwick," he said. He was plainly unsatisfied. "I could have sworn it was the Gretsko girl. I remember her figure."

"Big tits," Izzy said, enjoying the memory. "They really stuck out at the tennis courts."

"Best serve in Tilverdale," agreed Bernt, with a lecherous leer.

"That would account for the white outfit," said Vijay, still thoughtful. "I mean if it was Dawn. Can't help wondering what happened to her."

Izzy was still on his own track. "With those bazooms she probably got herself assaulted," he said. He wasn't noted for political correctness.

"Not our business anyway," said Bernt, signalling for another beer. "And not your bailie-whatever-it is," he added, adopting an accent from the Deep South. "This heah is Ontario Pro-vincial Police country."

"Some things are everybody's business," Vijay said, a touch sententiously. He picked up his cap from the table and tried a few words of Southern himself. "The Gretsko plantation is about four klicks up Main, eh?" He grinned. "Roughly two-and-a-bit cotton-picking miles, I should say."

Bernt could see that his friend had made a decision. "Watch out for her Ma. She's a hard-nosed old cow."

Vijay laughed. "Caught us pinching apples as I recall." He started to head to the parking lot. "I won't be long. Keep the bugs out of my coke, will ya."

Izzy shook his head at Bernt... "Sherlock's on the scent," he said in amusement. "A natural do-gooder, our Vijay. Makes me feel real safe having him around.

They grinned at each other. Vijay had always been the responsible one. "Even if he is out of his...territory," said Sean.

"His bailiwick " Izzy corrected him smugly, as they clinked glasses in the direction of Vijay's departing back."

It was unfortunate, and very bad timing, that when Officer Puri got to the police cruiser it had a flat. "Shit," he said wondering what he should do now. Should he walk very fast in the hope of catching up with Dawn, if indeed it was Dawn? Her hair hadn't been that long, he remembered.... Or should he spend eight or ten minutes changing the tire?

He decided on the latter course. "Give her time to get home and clean up," he told himself.

It was a fateful decision. Life might have unfolded very differently if he had walked fast.

*

"Raped?" said Sophia Gretsko, "You was raped?"

She had gone as pale as her daughter. There was a note of disbelief in her voice. This wasn't the Balkans. This was Canada. Canadians were always so polite.

"Raped," she repeated, and beaten...?" She couldn't believe it. She didn't want to believe it.

"At the back of the tennis courts," Dawn said, tears streaming down her face.

"What you doing behind tennis court at night?" Sophia demanded. What you was thinking?"

Dawn was trying desperately to make her mother understand. "He tied my wrists to a bush. A lilac bush. He tore down my shorts."

It was almost too much for Sophia to take in. Too horribly familiar. It couldn't be happening again. Not here. Not now.

"Who he?" she said numbly, her voice cracking. She had been baking in the kitchen when Dawn burst in, only minutes ago. She was still wearing her yellow apron, the one her daughter had given her on her thirty-eighth birthday. She rarely stopped working, regardless of the hour.

"Edward. His name was Edward, Eddie." Dawn said. "He wrote he was a tennis pro at the Guelph Racket Club. A good one he said." Her voice quavered. "Momma, he hurt me."

"Edward. You are knowing him?"

Dawn shook her head. "We met on line." Her face puckered up and she broke down. "He punched me, Momma. In my face. On my breast. He hurt me, down here." She flung herself on the sofa, burying her face in the colourful flowered arm.

Sophia Gretsko stood rooted to the spot, waving her hands in tiny incoherent circles. "Men," she said bitterly. "Is all animals. Not human."

Dawn looked up at her mother, her face stained with tears, her right eye swollen shut. "I'm bleeding, Momma. My shorts are all wet. He raped me, Momma" She turned her head back to the couch, sobbing pitifully.

Mrs. Gretsko wanted to help, to comfort the girl. But it just wasn't in her nature. Not anymore. She sat on the edge of the sofa behind Dawn and patted her back, feebly. "This Edward," she asked. "Is local boy?"

"From Guelph, he said in his emails," Dawn mumbled. "Forgive me, Momma," she pleaded with her, brokenly.

Sophia awkwardly patted her daughter's back again. It was difficult for her to show affection. She had lived a hard life herself. She had been younger than Dawn during the horrors in Croatia. Now she was having to come to grips with a new disaster.

"Folk can be terrible cruel," she said, as much to herself as to Dawn. "Even our friends will say you bad girl. Shorts too skimpy. Bare legs." She got up from the sofa and moved away. "Always they say girl lead man on."

"Momma," protested Dawn. "I thought we were gonna play tennis."

Sophia was working her way to a decision. "They not care what you say," she said tautly. "You just woman." She was thinking about what would be best. "From now on we not talk about this. Never again. It not happen. You know what I mean? This rape not happen."

Dawn's mouth dropped open. "I was so afraid you'd be mad at me, Momma," she said.

Her mother had become practical now. She knew what had to be done. "We go in bathroom," she said. "You get all clean. Throw away clothes. We burn in woodstove." Sophia had made her decision. She would protect the girl in the best way she could. The terrible experiences in her own life would help her daughter now.

"You must wash yourself out," she said without hesitation. "Down there. Inside."

Dawn looked at her dumbly. She had never even considered that her mother would talk about such things. "Use that spray thing on the showerhead," Sophia bade her. "Wash inside like you never wash before. Even if hurt, you wash and rinse. Rinse two, three times. You understand what I say? Is like to flush toilet."

They started toward the bathroom. Then froze. A siren was coming along Main in their direction.

"Go bathroom and strip," Sophia said. "This man, this Edward, he not human. He monster."

The siren cut out and a car's headlights shone into the living room. Mrs. Gretsko hurried to the window and peered out. "Is coming here," she said, blanching visibly. "A policeman." The car lights went out.

"No, Momma" cried Dawn, distraught. "It must be that Vijay. I can't talk to him. I know him from school." She was growing incoherent again. On the verge of breaking down."

Sophia knew what Dawn was feeling. She knew she must be strong. "You go get clean. Brush hair. Stay in bathroom." She was thinking quickly about what to say. "I tell him you sleeping. You not been out."

There was a knock on the door. Sophia looked briefly out of the window again. "I handle this Wijay. He very young." She shooed her daughter away. "Move quick now, Donja. Close the door. Wash your private part."

After the girl had gone, Sophia composed herself. She took off her apron and patted her hair. Her lined face grew set and stern. She became Mrs. Gretsko, mother, ready to defend her daughter against all comers.

The second knocking was with the door knocker. It was loud and peremptory. It sounded like what it was. A policeman, demanding response.

There was a small speakeasy-type grille high up in the door. Sophia took a deep, juddering breath and opened the small viewing door. "Yes?" she said, with no hint of nervousness. "It late. What you want?"

"Vijay Puri, Ma'am. I used to swipe apples from your tree. I'm a Waterloo police officer now."

"Why you come my house? It gone ten."

Vijay was very polite. "Ma'am, I thought I saw Dawn over by Crazy Joe's." he said. "She looked in a pretty bad way."

"My daughter not drink," Sophia replied curtly. "Beside, she in bed. Good night." She snapped the little door over the grille tightly shut. It echoed.

He tapped the door knocker lightly. "Ma'am," he called, his voice deeper. "Please, Ma'am, open up."

She tightened her lips and opened the security door again. The grille had shiny brass deer-heads where the bars crossed each other. "Why you not stop being rude?" she asked aggressively. Her heart was pounding in her chest, but there was no sign in her face, which was fixed and severe.

"I need to see your daughter, Ma'am," said Vijay stubbornly.

"I say already no. Donja not well."

He was patient. "Ma'am, this is police business. I really must speak with her."

"She take sleeping pill. She out like light."

He was very firm. "Ma'am, this is official. Kindly open the door."

She frowned, slammed the small security door shut and opened the front door a meagre four inches. A silvery chain stopped it opening farther. Her voice was very dour and bossy. "I tell you, she not well. I not let you in if you God Almighty Himself. Now leave us be." She went to close the door. The tip of his boot foiled her for a moment. But Sophia was having none of it. She was defending her daughter.

"Good night, Officer Wijay," she said stonily and slammed the door. This time it worked.

Vijay stood stock still for a moment. He was nonplussed. It was a silly word, but it summed up his chagrin. He was taken aback. He didn't quite know what to do for the best. He angrily went to knock again, but stopped himself "Damnit," he muttered in frustration, and retreated unhappily down the concrete steps to the car.

He was fairly sure the girl in white had been Dawn Gretsko. Dirty white clothes, soiled and green with grass stains. It had to have been Dawn. She had been the Tilverdale High School tennis champ two years in a row. Top heavy, the guys all said. And for sure Mrs. Gretsko was hiding something. "Double fucking damnit!" he swore, taking off his cap and putting it on the dash.

Okay, so he accepted the old witch had beaten him off. He had no idea how to handle the woman. He regretfully realised that he wasn't going to get his chance to interview Dawn tonight. Anyway, it was out of his jurisdiction. But he wasn't at all satisfied with his performance. He was too inexperienced. He should have been able to overcome Mrs. Gretsko's objections. First year or not.

He headed the patrol car back to Crazy Joe's. "I should call in the OPP," he said to the clown air freshener dangling from the rearview mirror. Of course it was all speculation, he thought realistically. Nothing tangible.

Another thought popped into his head. "Horatio Bellingham," he said aloud, to the clown again. "Detective Horatio Bellingham at Western Division in London Ontario." The clown nodded up and down as the car hit a pothole. Vijay grinned, his sense of humour returning. "Haven't seen him since we lost to the Marybourne Knights."

He was so relieved and deep in thought that he missed the turn-off into Crazy Joe's parking lot. The police cruiser seemed to have a mind of its own. He realised he was driving north on Main Street. Out toward the Tilverdale Sports Complex.

"Wouldn't do any harm to take a look," he said breezily to the grinning clown and let the car take him to what he already thought of as a possible 'crime scene.' "I'll make a fine investigator some day," he said, feeling much better about himself.

The cruiser led him over a bump into the tennis courts parking. The clown danced. Vijay knew his instincts were on the right track.

*

Sophia had felt all the combative strength drain out of her body as the police officer drove away. Her squared shoulders slumped. She held on to a plant-stand for support. For a moment she was back in the Yugoslav war, in Croatia. The murderous Orkhan irregulars were outside in the moonless night, setting a torch to the village.

With an effort she shook the fiery scene from her head and put the yellow apron back on, tying the strings methodically behind her back. She was Mrs. Gretsko again.

"He gone," she said to Dawn, tapping on the bathroom door and going in.

Dawn had finished her ablutions. She was wearing Sophia's maroon chenille bathrobe from the back of the door. "You did it, Momma," she said wonderingly. Her face was pale and drawn. Her long hair brushed back. But the tears started again when she saw her mother. She was pathetically grateful. "Oh Momma, thank you," she said. "Thank you so very much."

Sophia drew away a little. Not even consciously, it was just that's who she was. "Your eye not good," she said, almost matter-of-factly. "Is going to be dark black in morning."

The girl turned away to the mirror. "I'll have to stay home. I can't go to work." She touched her eyelid and flinched. "It hurts a lot, Momma," she said.

Sophia rummaged in the medicine cabinet. "You take two Advil Gel Cap," he instructed her daughter. "Tomorrow you wear black eyepatch I have. It important you act normal."

Dawn ran water into the sink glass. "I should have taken these before," she said. "I'm so stupid sometimes." She swallowed two.

Sophia Gretsko had been following her own thoughts. "I lie to policeman," she said, suddenly worried and uncertain. "Wijay his name. I say you not been out."

"He saw me outside Joe's."

"You speak with him?"

Dawn shook her head. She could see that her mother was deeply concerned. "It was nearly dark out. He was up on the patio. I was across the street."

"You in enough trouble. No reason get police inwolved." Sophia insisted. "Neighbours find out. Story in Times Dispatch."

They stared at each other, horrified at the thought. Dawn's bottom lip trembled. Her mother was patently unsure of herself. Not at all the Mrs. Gretsko who had stared down Vijay. "I tell bad lie to police," she said, guiltily. Scared even. "You think maybe they find out, they send me back Croatia?" she asked uncertainly.

Dawn instantly understood where Sophia was coming from. "Deport you?" she said, trying to smile. "No, Momma," she reassured her. Sympathetically. "You're a Canadian now." She laid a comforting hand on her mother's arm.

Sophia went rigid. "I make lie for you, Donja," she said stiffly. "I do this again if you need."

Fresh tears sprung into Dawn's eyes. "Oh Momma," she said emotionally and reached out to hug her dearly.

Sophia started to pull away. But there was so little extra space in the bathroom. She caught herself and, almost timidly, started to hug back. Both of them were weeping a little.

"You good girl," Sophia said, unexpectedly clasping the young girl her tightly to her bosom. "You wery good daughter."

It was a long and tearful hug.

Sophia and Donja were mother and daughter at last.

Chapter 5 The Black Wally

Back at the legendary Smuggler's Den, the 23rd Anniversary celebrations of the Walter Black Munch were reaching their climax. The skirl of bagpipes echoed through the conference hall.

"Ladies, gentle folk and Black Wallyburgers," announced the Man-in-Black in his most sonorous tones. "The moment you have been waiting for is finally upon us. I give you the 23rd birthday of the world-renowned Walter Black Munch."

Resplendent in tartan kilt and Scottish warrior costume, Rabbie "Braveheart" Balliol piped in the spectacular three-tiered iced cake. The familiar tune was the Black Watch battle anthem, loosely adapted to the Black Wally. The cake was carried on a crested Hotel Siebert silver salver by Sam Seagram and his perspiring wait-girl, who had most of the weight.

They were followed by two more wait-girls with plastic plates, forks and a gleaming silver knife. Jimmy the bartender and his assistants Calpurnia and Rose came next with trays of long-stemmed, disassembled flutes and magnums of medium grade champagne. Finally came Bertie Stanislav sporting a golden crown and long crimson robe, with his two comely submissives Mindy and Jennie bearing his train and additional magnums of bubbly. Bertie's costume had last been seen at the medieval fair in Blackberry Park. On top of being a tenured professor of computer science at Laurier U. he was also a leading light in Waterloo Region theatre.

More 'Wallyburgers' had crowded in from the adjoining conference halls and private dining rooms. They all clapped enthusiastically and the occasional ribald comment was heard. It was a legitimate moment of celebration. Munches came and went across Ontario, but the Black Wally seemed likely to go on forever.

"Aficionados of this famed international internet group," resumed the Man-in-Black portentously. He rarely used one or two words when a dozen could do. "It is my singular honour to introduce your host and mine, one of the two original founders of our Walter Black rituals, Bertie Stanis, rightful monarch of the seven kingdoms of Westeros." He grinned at the slight error. "Oops, sorry, wrong continent. I give you Bertie 'unthreatening' Stanislavsky."

There were lots of genial quips about Bertie's small stature and amiable manner. But it was common knowledge that not everything about him was small. He was a highly skilled player in more ways than one and kept Mindy and Jennie in a state of constant satisfaction. He was also responsible for introducing innumerable nubile newbies to the lifestyle.

He began his obligatory anniversary speech quietly. "Twenty-three years ago, when Walter Black and I convened the first Black Wally in Waterloo Region, we sure didn't visualise this evening. I only wish Sir Walter was still around to sink his sweet tooth into a double slice of this mouth-watering cake." He spoke softly, but his voice carried through the hall. He was an experienced and eloquent public speaker. "Thank you, Sammy Seagram and the Hotel Siebert catering staff. You've done us proud."

Sam inclined his head and shoo-ed most of his minions safely out of the conference hall. His main intent as the evening progressed was to keep the liquor flowing and the wait-staff buzzing, too busy to register some of the more revealing comments.

"Back then," Bertie continued. "Kitchener-Waterloo was a wasteland when it came to the Scene. Eight people showed up for our first Munch. We were fortunate that Walter was Old Guard and well able to mentor us in the Lifestyle traditions we had barely dreamt about. We were equally fortunate that he left us Madame Claire, his wife and partner, who has become a trusted mentor herself."

Whistles and applause brought Claire to her feet at the red table. She lightly clasped both hands above her head and winked at Leeza, who raised her champagne in a smiling toast. It was clear that Claire was well-liked and respected among her peers.

"Where's your megaphone, Bertie," called out Francis Dickie in his booming, usually jovial tone of voice.

Bertie grinned. "Only need that in your Culotta campground at Long Point, Francis," he said laughingly "Three, four hundred mostly naked lifestylers is a challenge even for Stanislavsky vocal training."

Mindy and Jennie, his girls, anticipated his needs both at the annual camp and at home. They had pitched in and were expertly slicing the cake and passing it around on Sam's birthday plastic plates. "What's the icing, luvies?" demanded Celeste, who had a carrying voice of her own.

"Vanilla, what else?" laughed Claire, who had made the same joke for ten years or more. "With copperplate chocolate lettering."

"Happy 23rd Anniversary," Bertie read off. "Original, ain't it? But believe me, times have sure changed. Mindy counted over 150 of us here tonight."

Loud applause broke out again. Bertie held up his hands for quiet. "By the way, folks, I came up with an interesting statistic at Laurier today. “You may not know it but there are 151 OPP detachments in rural and small-town Ontario. Provincial Police, that is." He ignored the groans from his audience. "Coincidentally, what struck me was this. Across the province there are almost 150 different Munches. Five in Waterloo region alone."

"Jesus, we're becoming mainstream!" exclaimed RubyThursday.

"Ye Gods, I hope not," moaned Missy Alexis at the purple table. Alexis was a 6'3" Aussie cross-dresser who liked the under-the-covers cachet of the present system.

There was a sudden clatter of noise and loud voices from the entrance archway. Sam Seagram was trying to bar a brassy blonde from barging her way in, complete with iPhone camera. "You can't take no pictures in here."

The blonde was short, stocky and totally pushy. “I’m Angele Del Zotto with the K-W Times-Dispatch, “she proclaimed importantly. “I heard there's a celebration underway in the Smuggler's Den."

Bertie Stanislav took over from a fussing, outclassed Sam. "Ms. Del Zotto, good to see you as always" he said urbanely. "I'm so sorry but we don't permit cameras at our meetings."

A number of bodies had miraculously appeared at the archway and banned her entry into the conference hall. Big bodies with their backs to her. Lord Saxton, Dom Perignon, DasUberdomme, even the brawny shoulders of Missy Alexis. Being outed in a newspaper photograph was not high on most lists.

Del Zotto snorted derisively. "But I gather it's a special occasion, a twenty something anniversary. It's just a teeny picture, for Christ's sake."

Bertie stood firm. "You and your iPhone will have to leave, Angele," he said. "We're an internet group. Cameras are strictly verboten."

Angele was showing her frustration. But she didn't give up easily. "Didn't know the internet had been around that long," she protested to Sammy Seagram, who shrugged weakly.

Madame Claire had left the red table and come over to the brick archway. "Why doesn't Ms. Del Zotto take a snap of just the cake," she offered diplomatically. "I have no objection to wielding the knife." Claire figured it was sensible to defuse the situation. She flourished the silver cake-knife. Mindy and Jennie had followed her lead and brought over the cake. Half the bottom layer of the three-tiered cake was still uncut.

"Not much fucking cake left," the reporter sniffed.

Bertie joined Claire. "Grand idea, Madame," he congratulated her. "You and I are pretty okay with pix and publicity." He was gracious with the brassy blonde woman. "You win, Angele."

Angele stared at him hard. "Better than nothing, I guess," she said with poor grace. She took a couple of quick pictures featuring the half cake and Claire brandishing the knife.

Bertie showed why he was a Dom. "Sorry we can't ask you in, Angele," he said unwaveringly as he and Claire politely ushered her back into the passage and away from the conference hall.

Angele sneered her disdain. "What's the name of this piddling organisation anyway?" she demanded, leaving.

"Online Anonymous," said Claire graciously, turning back into the hall. "Thanks, folks," she said to Lord Saxton and the others "You make a great barricade".

Missy Alexis waved a limp wrist. "What a bothersome bitch," she lisped. In her male incarnation Alexis was Alex, a noted Australian quantum physicist at the renowned Perimeter Institute.

*

Over at the red table, Leeza had pushed back her leather chair and was exchanging a farewell hug with Celeste. "Lovely to meet you. I'm just sorry to walk out on all the excitement," she said, as Claire made her way back. "And Celeste, why are most of you so against pictures?" she asked.

Celeste smiled. "We're not truly mainstream quite yet, Leeza. Some employers might get antsy."

RubyThursday gave the girl a rib-crushing goodbye hug. "I was kidding about the mainstream," she said. "There are still suburban soccer moms who would freak out at the idea of a dominatrix teaching little Johnny or Kathy."

"You're a teacher, Ruby?"

"Math," said Ruby. "Desmond Trout at the pink table over yonder teaches biology. We're off to a teacher's convention in Toronto this weekend."

Claire had taken Leeza's arm and now accompanied her to the exit archway. "I have to congratulate you, girl," she said proudly, when they were alone. "Right from your striking entrance you handled your baptism of fire just fine. Didn't put a foot wrong. Which was amazing in itself."

"Leeza sweetie, you're deliciously delectable," lisped Alexis, stepping in for an ardent farewell. "Mwah, mwah," she said, planting wet air kisses on the girl's cheeks. "And Mwah…" Even in her 5 inch heels Leeza was petite beside Missy Alexis.

"You're a total doll, sweetheart," said Claire, moving in for a good night kiss of her own. "Give my love to Matt. Tell him he can be very proud of your adventure tonight. And I'll call you tomorrow. I promise."

*

Across the hall, Sir Robert and Lady Grace had been circulating through the Munch, stopping by the pink table to exchange a friendly greeting with Francis Dickie and Des Trout. There they had been trapped by an earnest GeorgyBoy and his girls, GeorgyGirl and the emollient PuddenandPie. Robert was his customary courteous self.

"So you're dating both of them," he repeated patiently. "That's so cool, George. Wouldn't you say so, Francis?"

The Major grunted. "Takes all kinds, Sir Robb," he said, and turned his attention back to Desmond. "Gonna miss you, Des," he added, sotto voce for him.

GeorgyBoy ignored him and continued to belabour Robert with his pet topic. "We're polyamorous, you see. You know what that is, right?"

Robert was a little strained, but still polite. "Of course. Yes indeed, Grace and I know what Polyamory is."

"It'll be a damned long weekend," growled Francis, his attention totally fixed on Desmond. "Too damned long."

"The crucial thing is it's not just about sex," steamrollered GeorgyBoy to Robert, giving him a beady eye. "It's about three, or more, sincere relationships, you understand."

"Yes, Georgy," said Grace, trying to come to her husband's rescue. "We're familiar with poly."

The Major was off on his own private horse. "And I'm s'posed to twiddle my thumbs," he muttered gloomily. "While you're off cavorting with five hundred sex-crazed teachers." He had been hitting the Scotch quite heavily all evening.

For his part, GeorgyBoy wasn't taking 'familiar' for an answer. Lots of new polyamorous twenty-somethings seemed impelled to educate anyone handy. "Because the thing is, I'm not charging around screwing just anybody. Our relationships are full blown relationships, you understand."

Desmond Trout had feebly protested to Francis that not all of the five hundred teachers were gay. "And, Frankie, I am going with RubyThursday," he emphasised.

It was Robert's turn to come to Grace's defence. "Believe me, my young friend, we do have a clear notion of how polyamory works."

"That's good," agreed GeorgyBoy, who was still warming to his favourite theme. "Too many people don't, you see. They make this false assumption it's all about lust. But you know it's not. Not even a smidgeon."

"More drinks, gentlemen?" asked Sam Seagram respectfully, at GeorgyBoy's elbow.

"Another double Scotch and easy on the rocks," barked Francis Dickie. "Toute suite, as you say."

"More white wine for the girls and me," GeorgyBoy said. Grace said "Oh, yes please." Robert shook his head. His patience was wearing thin. But GeorgyBoy hadn't finished. "Our relationships are every bit as monogamous as ones like yours."

"George, I don't doubt it for a second,' said Robert, turning to flee.

GeorgyBoy grasped Robert's arm. "Our relationships are about so much more than mere sex."

Robert gently but firmly peeled off GeorgyBoy's fingers. "Listen, my young friend, we know what poly is."

His young friend nodded. "Amor is Latin for -" he began.

"I simply have to pee," said Robert, grabbing Grace's hand and hauling her away.

"Goddammit all to hell," snarled Major Dickie, thumping the pink table with a heavy hand. "Is sex all we can fuckin' talk about at this fuckin' Munch?"

GeorgyBoy wasn't thrown off for a second. "That's the point, Major, polyamory isn't all about sex." He glanced around the table, obviously pleased with himself. "Nice old coot, that Sir Robert," he said. "Though he doesn't understand much about poly. I'm running a Polyamory Munch in Cambridge now, you know. Let me explain ...."

What he didn't quite understand, or GeorgyGirl or PuddenandPie come to that, was that poly had long been a big part of the alternate values that ran right through the lifestyle. At least a third of the older folks at the Black Wally were either in or just out of a polyamorous relationship. Or at the very least a triad. Only the comparative newcomers to poly seemed to feel the need to justify themselves. It could be hilarious and a touch underwhelming at times.

*

At the red table down front, Claire and Celeste had a long-term relationship of their own. Not poly, by a long chalk. Just open and available to each other when the spirit moved. Which it did from time to time.

"It's our anniversary as well," said Celeste, idly twisting a long curl of fair hair around her ring finger. "We met at the first Stratford Munch. When Molly and I launched it twelve years ago."

"Dearie, I remember it well," replied Claire, resisting the impulse to burst into song. "You were wearing a full-length white brocade gown from the Festival costume department. You looked very fetching. Still do, as a matter of fact."

"Fetching is good," Celeste said, in a husky undertone. "And I don't know about you, darling Claire, but I'm more than ready to move on from the Black Wally and slip into something more personal."

Claire and Celeste smiled at each other. They had a lovely, affectionate moment. Neither was exclusively lesbian or heterosexual. Both played both sides of the four-poster, though Celeste was tight with SuperMoll in Stratford, home of the Shakespeare Festival and Justin Bieber, a festival in himself.

"Holy Hannah," said Fleur, who had moved over to the red table and now slipped into Leeza's vacated chair. “That Leeza is one hot looking babe."

"Strong, too," observed Celeste, who didn't have a jealous bone in her make-up box. "She steadied me when I nearly tripped over saying goodbye."

"Matt Llewellyn is a jockey," Claire told her. "He's the controlling twin. Fifteen hundred pound racehorses are like silly-putty in his hands." She smiled tenderly at Celeste. "But before we can depart, dear one, I haven't had my regular shot of Shakespeare yet."

"Actors," said Fleur with a strained grin, and quoted romantically. "I could spend my life in this sweet surrender." She smirked. "That's not the Bard of Avon," she said. "That's Aerosmith."

"I dig the sentiment and go you one better…" said Celeste, who was a born submissive. She gently took Claire's hand and said, softly, not declaiming - "'Being your slave, what should I do but tend - Upon the hours and times of your desire? - I have no precious time at all to spend - Nor services to do till you require...' And that is Shakespeare."

Claire squeezed her fingers lovingly. "Never my slave, Celeste darling," she said, her dark eyes round and soft. "My beloved Celeste for sure."

Fleur clapped her hands together. "If I'm reading the runes right, you guys might have plans for later." There was a touch of envy in her voice. She always felt a little left out.

Celeste batted her eyelashes at Claire. "I did tell Molly I'd be home between one and two A.M."

"And you'd need something interesting to tell her. Risqué in fact" said Claire good-naturedly. The three of them were well aware that SuperMoll got off on hearing all the facts of Celeste's late night encounters. "All righty," Claire went on, with a twinkle. "So I guess its violet wand time." She grinned. "I even have a new accessory since the last time we played."

Their amorous idyll was interrupted by the tinkle of spoon on glass. The Man-in-Black had taken the stage again. He had an ancient-looking roll of parchment under his arm. "Friends and Wallyburgers," he pronounced sonorously. "Once again I have a passel of exciting announcements to make." He disregarded the groans and turned to Bertie. "With your permission, Maestro?" Bertie nodded, patient and long-suffering as always.

The Man-in-Black made a great show of unrolling the parchment like a town crier of old. "First and foremost," he said mellifluously. "'Ask Madame Claire.' Your not so anonymous internet podcast."

Fleur rolled her eyes at Claire. "Doesn't miss a chance to pontificate, does he"

"He's our publicist, among other functions."

He publicised. "Madame Claire has three fascinating interviews scheduled in the near future. Next week, Dana Gennifer Van Lith, aka Gennifleur, or simply Fleur."

This time Fleur crossed her eyes at Claire, who smiled back in amusement. The Man-in-Black was in full flight. He swept on resonantly.

"Fleur is universally celebrated as the Canadian emissary of the Washington based Sexual Freedom Coalition. She will be chatting with Madame Claire about the pros and cons of Rape or Ravishment play. I gather the content will be highly expurgatable. I made several pertinent notes but Claire expurgated them."

A half-hearted Boo rang out. Claire held up her hands in mock protest. "I'm totally innocent," she cried.

"That'll be the day," said Celeste, adding in a stage whisper: "So what's the new accessory, darling?"

"Oddly enough, it's called a Leopard," Claire said simply, if a touch coyly. "You'll love it."

The Man-in-Black had moved on. "The week after Fleur, 'Ask Madame Claire' will feature a long-awaited interview with Sir

Robert and Lady Grace Challenger. The subjects will include the ever-popular FatMan play parties and Predicament Bondage."

Celeste applauded and whistled. "I won't want to miss that show," she said to Claire. "You actually lured them out of the manse?"

"I told Robert he could wax lyrical about sub-space. One of his pet themes." She shook her head in some admiration. "He maintains it's a spiritual doorway."

"En passant," said the Man-in-Black, "I might also mention that our future guest list will highlight our Antipodean friend, Missy Alexis." He said this with a flourish, it was another programming coup. "Alexis will be giving an enlightening view of BDSM history around the world, an entertaining spiel on Cross-Dressing and a short talk on quantum physics."

He dramatically unrolled the last few inches of his parchment. "In conclusion," he intoned, "And if this reminds anyone of the Forum crier in TV's Rome, so be it." He cleared his throat. "Finally, I am honoured to announce that Lord Saxton and his submissive Trilliumchic, which only looks like Trilliumchick, will be undergoing a solemn handfasting on the tenth of next month."

The applause was surprised and then ear-splitting. "That's awesome," enthused Fleur. “They’ve been Dom and sub for so long, I was afraid they'd never make it legal."

Celeste was also very happy for them. "One of the lifestyle's leading D/s couples." she said whole-heartedly.

Claire smiled. "Wait for it." she said,

The Man-in-Black's timing was impeccable. "The handfasting ceremony will be held at Madame Claire's Black Walnut retreat in Marybourne. Three o'clock in the afternoon. Mad Angelus will officiate."

A buzz of appreciation went through the conference hall. Celeste and Fleur clapped softly. "You've done it again, Claire," mused

Celeste affectionately. "Pulled off another Claire Faversham miracle."

Fleur was more serious. "You know something, sweetie. You've taken over from Sir Walter as our go-to mentor in the Southwest Ontario Scene."

"And we love you for it," said Celeste fondly, smoothly slipping in another question. "And if you don't mind my asking, what exactly is your new Leopard?"

"An electrified Cat of nine tails..." Claire responded, very matter-of-factly.

Celeste gulped visibly. "Can't wait," she said and rose gracefully to her feet. She retrieved Claire's leopard wrap from the chair. "I'll follow your car."

As they made ready to leave, the Man-in-Black deftly re-rolled his parchment. "That's my stint for tonight, folks" he said, closing with his familiar basso profundo radio wrap. "Wend thy wicked ways homeward and committeth thee every delicious sin thy wayward heart's desire. This is your announcer, the Man-in-Black, wishing you pleasant dreams."

"I think we might manage a sin or two," said Claire, giving Fleur a goodbye hug and leaving arm in arm with Celeste.

The first Black Wally of summer was winding down.

But the melody lingered on

*

Later, at Madame Claire's Walnut Cottage, nestled in the Mennonite farming country east of Kitchener-Waterloo, the Black Wally melody was soon coming back full force.

Claire had taken out one of Celeste's favourite BDSM toys, the celebrated violet wand. "We used to play with this for hours," she said fondly. "Back when we were first getting to know each other."

"You introduced me to electrical play with the Tens unit," remembered Celeste, her bottom lip quivering deliciously as Claire gently passed a mushroom electrode over her breast. "We haven't played in months." She gasped with pleasure as jumping violet sparks skittered over her pebbled aureolae.

"Only any time you make it to the Black Wally and aren't hurtling back to SuperMoll," Claire said, smiling.

Celeste ran her tongue over her lips. Her body was trembling a little. "She's getting much more Open," she breathed softly. "I'll have to remember what we... get up to.... Ooh, that feels so good."

"A jot more warm-up, then the Leopard," said Claire, testing her by holding the mushroom well away from her skin. It worked better than way. A flurry of violet and purple sparks of dancing electricity leapt between the tip of the electrode and Celeste's expectant nipples. There was a faint scent of summer lightning.

They were in Madame Claire's home dungeon. It occupied most of the basement of Walnut Cottage, save for the small enclosed furnace and laundry rooms. The dungeon decor was a typical Claire affair. Wall hangings, cushions and throws of leopard fabric, with two 9 x 12 leopard rugs on the red-tiled floor. In one corner, a black walnut spanking bench; opposite that, a 4 x 4 Gorean whipping post in leopard motif. Both were glossily sanded and finished. Wally Black had been a highly skilled woodworker who liked nothing more than the gleam in Claire's eye when she was thoroughly satisfied, in more ways than one. There were also a couple of his superbly fitted pine chairs, a capacious leopard massage table, two leather wrist cuffs on blood-red hanging chains and an early model exercise bike. Claire was eminently practical in many ways and the bike did have hidden BDSM uses apart from her daily workouts. .

Celeste was quite dreamy by now. "There's nothing like a vi-violet wand to put the s-spark back in one's s-sexlife," she said, finding it difficult to be coherent.

The violent wand they both regarded so affectionately was the size of a standard water bottle. Maybe a bit taller and less wide, but who was measuring. It fit comfortably in the hand like a

Canadian Tire flashlight. It came with an astonishing variety of electrodes for external and internal usage. The electrodes, like the mushroom or the miniature garden rake Claire had started with, were fashioned out of tempered glass, containing a vacuum backfilled by a noble gas like argon or neon.

The high voltage current set up by the wand's built-in transformer excited the gas, which emitted a glowingly colourful display, violet or purple, blue or pink, depending on the gas involved. When switched on to a reasonable level, the wand created incredible spark streamers outside the glass. They leapt and vibrated across open space and produced fabulous sensations that drove the gasping submissive wild. The farther from the tip of the electrode to the skin, the greater the array of sparks and the resulting shocks.

Celeste was lying face up on the leopard massage table. Her hands and feet were not cuffed or tied. Claire wanted the whole body free and mobile, not fastened down. She was naked of course. Violet wands and nudity were de rigueur. Her Stratford Festival barmaid's breasts seemed even larger in the flesh. Her big brown nipples were now hugely erect from the wand's tender ministrations.

"I do so a-adore this gl-glorious tingling," she said lovingly to Claire, cupping her breasts sensuously in her palms. Celeste was comfortably natural in her appreciation for her own vibrant lushness. That was partly why Claire loved to top her. Her unspoiled reactions sometimes set off a primitive sexual response in Claire that often took them by surprise. Both confidently hoped that tonight would turn out exactly that way.

"I think it's way past time we moved on to the Cat," announced Claire, throatily. "My Leopard is primed and ready to play." She took the cat-of-nine-tails out of her toybag. "Sneak a quick look, then you should turn over, butt in air."

At first glance, the Leopard looked like any normal cat-of-nine tails. Claire smiled to herself at the 'normal.' The tails were about eighteen inches long. "Made of expensive, copper-coated gold bullion thread," she told Celeste. "Very tightly woven. Very electrically conductive."

There was a growing sense of mutual anticipation. "The matt black handle is metal, of course. I added the leopard spots myself. So, while you get on your hands and knees, I'll switch to direct current for the flogging." She grinned, not coyly but heading in that direction. "And don't forget, darling, I know how much you like it when I pass the current through my body to yours." She ran her fingernails down Celeste's flanks. "Maybe after a while I'll switch to highly charged leopard claws. Grrrrr!"

She switched off the wand and replaced the mushroom electrode with a flexible body-contact cable. She clipped the other end to her dress, making sure the contact was sitting firmly on her skin. Duct-tape had many uses in BDSM. "The current will shoot right through me to the tips of each tail. Same as with cat's claws, I won't feel a thing. I'm just the conductor."

"And I'm the mildly apprehensive recipient." said Celeste breathlessly, looking forward to the many-tailed, electric Cat. She had assumed the requisite position. Head resting on her hands, curvaceous butt high in the air, at present wriggling provocatively.

"Most fetching," laughed Madame Claire, and turned the wand back on. She gave the Leopard a gentle swish. Sparks erupted from all nine of the copper and gold bullion ends. "This is a genuine, honest-to-god impact toy," she said. "Not one of those silly Christmas Mylar kinds. Hold still now."

She slowly draped the nine tails over Celeste's exposed ass. The tails felt alive, rather like tiny electric bubbles trailing across her skin. They sparked and sizzled deliciously. Celeste was almost literally on pins and needles.

Claire raised her arm and the lashes rained down again, harder this time. Celeste heard and felt the distinctive zap and crackle of charged particles and sensed the foot-long streamers of sparks flowing around her bum.

Next, Claire gave her a sharp strike to her defenseless perineum, the firm flesh between bottom and vulva. 'The chinrest" as Claire always called it, Celeste remembered fondly, before a sudden swarm of numinous bee-stings flooded her mind. It was like liquid fire spreading through her already moist cunt-lips to her clit.

"Oh, my sainted G-goddess," Celeste muttered as the pungent smell of a thunderstorm permeated the dungeon. Ozone and nitrous oxide, she knew.

Again Claire brought the Cat down, this time across her submissive's shoulders. Celeste's entire body started to shake violently. As the tails pulled away, she could feel kinetic violet streamers painting a pattern over her shoulder blades and around to her ribs.

"A little delicate wrap-around," said Claire, with a naughty smile.

Another heart-pounding blow, now across the tender back of the thighs, always a highly sensitive area. Another, back to the perineum. And another to the sweet spot where thighs joined buttocks. And another, to the same succulent crease. They were much heavier now. Celeste couldn't even estimate the myriad accumulating bee-stings as the bullion tails withdrew and left hot burning shocks in their wake. She was increasingly aware of actual pain from the flogging itself. But over and above the pain she could feel the juices starting to drip from her pussy.

Again and again the Cat rose and fell. A hot sizzle and crack assaulted her ears. A heady perfume of forked lightning invaded her nostrils. Sweet, lingering pain stabbed her flesh, then vanished in a timeless rush of molten heat. Then a single, unimaginably intense spark to her clit as Claire reversed the well-shaped handle of the Cat and thrust it into her wet and waiting cunt.

"Holy Mother," she screeched, beside herself in pain and ecstasy. She was panting and wheezing, on the absolute verge of orgasm. It was coiled in her clit, pressuring her womb, ready to explode. "Yes...yes," she cried out.

But, suddenly, unexpectedly, the rise and fall of the Leopard lash came to an abrupt, mind-shattering halt.

"Not yet, Celeste baby," she heard Madame Claire's voice, as if from a great distance. "The Leopard has carried you to the brink.

Every nerve ending is screaming for release. There's just one thing to remember. One fact on which to concentrate your mind." Her voice throbbed with limitless power. "I too am electrified from head to toe!" ALL OF ME!"

As if floating in a cloud-filled sky, Celeste could feel Claire's electric fingers creeping around her ribs and reaching for her swollen nipples. A trail of purple and violet sparks emanated from the scrabbling fingers. A fresh and ever higher wave of riveting shocks zapped into existence.

"Go with the glow," Claire instructed her, a sound like purring coming from deep in her being. "What once were fingernails are now the leopard's claws. Fiery electric talons are kneading your breasts. Squeezing your aching nipples. Tantalising electrodes are sinking deeply into your yearning flesh."

Madame Claire was right in the moment now. Seductively leading Celeste into a more fanciful world. This was the domme in her. A Claire only her true submissives could ever know. Creative, earthy, overpoweringly intimate.

"My leopard body is pressuring you into obedience," she said melodically, the tempo ever rising. "You are weak and vulnerable beneath me. I am your masterful leopard. Ready to flip you on your back again. To eat and devour you. Opening your precious cunt to my touch. Making you mine for the taking."

Celeste could offer no resistance. The thought of resisting was nowhere in her mind. All she wanted was to be utterly, abjectly, innocently submissive. To surrender any last vestige of self.

Without conscious movement, she was spread-eagled supine again. Her legs raised. Her feet splayed. Her knees wide apart. The leopard, her leopard, was crouched on all fours in front of her sex. Its incisors were bared and gleaming. It's tongue flicking in and out. Curling up and down. Emitting a glowing glissade of red-hot sparks.

She couldn't even begin to imagine what it would feel like. The almost inconceivable sensation of being on the receiving end of an electrically charged animal tongue.

"Oh, C-Claire," she breathed. "My lustrous leopardess..."

The melody of the Black Wally built to its pulsating crescendo

"I just love it when you come to our Kitchener Munch," Claire said, her tongue taking over. "Love it!...Love it!..."Love it!..."

Creamed, as Madame Claire thought, luxuriating in mutual orgasm.

And the 23rd Anniversary K-W Munch was well and truly done.

Chapter 6 Sorry Girl

Myra Hessiani, SorryGirl23, had never been to a Munch. Which was a great pity. She was not a socially minded girl and had no real friends. She had joined Kinklife.ca mainly because real names or references were not required, she could hide behind a pseudonym and read up on all the members and their BDSM activities.

Myra was a born, dyed in the wool loner with dull scraggly reddish hair and bottle glasses who lived and went through life always alone. She had never had the Munch experience of talking to anyone who understood her deepest feelings of numbing sadness, of powerlessness, of submissiveness, of guilt. Always guilt.

Until she met Richard, Rickie as he said his Mom always called him.

He had contacted her out of the blue in the early spring. A personal email on her Kinklife.ca PM's - her Private Messages. He was smart and seemed fairly considerate, though he confessed right off that he was a Dom. He seemed to want her as a friend.

At first she had thought him quite interesting, though she barely responded to his approach. '*Thank you for writing me,*' was basically all she said. She couldn't believe he would want to be friends with her.

But the simple fact that she had replied had been more than enough for Richard. He leaned back in his chair, smiling, patting himself mentally on the back, feeling good about opening yet another door. For a moment he considered telling her that he was a Master, in search of a sub, a slave even.

On second thoughts he kept his reply mild and totally unthreatening. "*So nice finally to reach someone I feel I can actually talk to,*" he wrote back, and the smile and a seeming sense of relief came over in his words. She waited a week and then said "*Yes, it was nice.*"

Gradually, a friendly correspondence started. He told her that he was 27 and had been in the army, trying to 'find himself' he said ruefully. In Afghanistan, he said. It was spectacular, he told her, and terrible. Haltingly she started to tell him about her life, her dreams. He probed gently, looking for the special weakness that was always there.

One day she mentioned her deepest interest in life. She wanted to be an artist, a body artist, a tattooist. He sniggered when he read it, pleased that his patient cleverness had paid off one more time. He had no idea at first how he would use it but knew at once that it was the key to getting her to do anything he wanted. "Whatever that might be," he smirked, the dark eyes behind his tinted glasses glittering as his mind turned to his next move.

For Myra, although she didn't really know it, that was when it started, the growing relationship that had led up to the previous evening and the frightening "scene" (if that was the right word), behind the tennis courts at the Sport's Complex in Tilverdale. The scene with Richard, who had told the blond girl his name was Edward, Eddie, and who he called EarlyMorn, Dawn.

Even now, Myra felt sweaty and feverish remembering it. It excited, fascinated and horrified her. It had been the worst thing she had ever seen, even dreamed of. Yet she had done nothing....said nothing. She knew she should have tried to stop it, but no words had come. She had merely watched, gasping, panting almost, with a spreading wet between her thighs.

It all seemed so far removed from their first emails and the eventual meeting that followed, as if by accident. He, Richard, had been so sweet and encouraging about her hopes. He assured her that he admired her ambition. He wrote quite openly that he himself had once wanted to be a graphic artist but had been forced to admit that he didn't possess the artistic talent. She was very lucky to be artistic, he said. Not having that gift was one of his biggest disappointments, he told her, exposing his vulnerability.

Later, she mentioned in passing that she was now working at a small tattoo parlour in the city - *"but only on trial, as a sort of apprentice*," she added wistfully. He again said how fortunate she was in her artistic talent and asked how she got her ideas. "*There are hundreds and thousands of ready-made stencils*," she wrote back informatively, and described happily how rewarding it was to ink or shade in the patterns on a client's tender skin. "*Under Igor's supervision*," she admitted a touch defensively. "*He won't let me do anything free-form*."

"The boss doesn't give her too much leeway," thought Richard, filing the titbit away for future reference.

"*But tell me, Myra*," he asked with a seeming note of apprehension. "*Doesn't being tattooed hurt? I've always thought it must hurt.*"

"*Of course it hurts,*" Myra wrote back, revelling in showing him her knowledge. "*You're piercing the first layer of skin and inking the derma, the second layer. Hundreds of times a minute.*"

"Jesus," he said, reading her words. "She fucking well likes doing it! Stupid tramp."

"So how long does it take," he asked, probing further.

"An hour," she replied. "*Maybe much more. You pay by the hour.*"

"I guess I'm a tad squeamish for a Dom," he said in his next email.

"Most customers make out they're hard-boiled and totally brave," she pointed out.

"But you still get to hurt them?" he commented.

"*It's part of the job,*" she wrote back, letting her satisfaction show. "*I don't care if they hate it. Grin and bear it I say.*"

Richard chuckled to himself. "Jackpot!" he murmured.

Two weeks later he strolled casually into Igor's Tattoo Salon on King Street. He was wearing a sharp, black Reebok track suit and lightly tinted sunglasses. His hair was parted down the middle and he looked, well, average. Nothing memorable. "Pure coincidence," he said blithely when he was introduced as Richard

Smith to a blushing Myra. “Rick," he said, “or Rickie as my Mom calls me." and gave her a friendly smile.

"And you know something," he went on. "I been thinking of getting a tattoo for ages. You helped me make up my mind. Somethin’ smallish on my upper arm,” he told Igor. “A sort of baby dragon, maybe. Oh and the chick can do it.”

He smiled his pleasant, friendly smile at her. “Like it a bit free-form, sweetie. Artistic, you know what I mean.” She blushed again, her whole moon face patchy red and white.

For Myra, after that first unexpected meeting life suddenly moved into high gear. Richard was well-spoken when he felt like it and in the beginning invariably patient and polite. When being tattooed he wasn’t exceptionally squeamish. In fact she found the faint beads of perspiration on his forehead as she worked endearing and rather reassuring.

Of course, he was a Dom and she was not particularly surprised when he soon started to tell her what to do. How to behave in his presence. That, too, was reassuring. She didn’t have to think too much, fret about whether she was pleasing or annoying him.

By the time of their first real date he had started spelling out in more detail exactly what he expected of her. “I don’t want to alarm you, Myra dear,” he said coolly. “But if you’re going to be my girlfriend I have definite standards I need met.”

She had nodded quickly three or four times. “I’ll do whatever you say is best, Rick,” she said, still hearing him say ‘my girlfriend.’ “Anything you tell me, anything you want.”

“First of all, Myra, you will never call me Rick again. From now on, it's Richard, or perhaps, later, Master. Is that clear?”

“Of course. I understand.”

‘Secondly, I expect a fair degree of service. You must learn to anticipate my wants. Coffee. Slippers. Thee...Yourself, I mean. “He smiled that special smile again. “The regular domestic items in a relationship. You savvy what I’m sayin’?”

A relationship, she thought, I'm in a relationship. "Yes, Rick - Richard," she had responded brightly, breathing hard. 'I'm in a relationship" she thought again, almost hugging herself.

"I don't have a very high opinion of girls," he had said, as if explaining himself. "Of women in general," he added. "I've been all over the world, in the army. Too many women are crude or bossy. The only places I'd like to visit again are Thailand or maybe the Philippines. Girls there know who's the Master. Western women are the most obnoxious there are. Know what I mean?"

"I think so, Richard. I'm sure I do."

"Then we'll get along fine. Just so you understand that when I say 'Now' I mean NOW!" He paused, wondering idly to himself how far to go. He wanted someone he could control completely. He wanted to control everything she did, what she ate, when she peed, when and how she had sex - if she ever had, he thought drily.

He wanted someone happy to obey his every whim. Grateful to him for relieving her of the necessity to think. He wanted a slave. A perfect slave. Someone empty enough that he could lead her to places she had never even dreamed of going. Dark, hidden places that only he knew existed.

Like last night, he thought, coming up to date. The scene with EarlyMorn, Dawn baby. He had kept Myra waiting outside Tim Hortons while he met the over-eager girl for coffee and sweet-talked her into leaving with him, her light summer cardigan loosely tied over that white tennis singlet.

It was dusk out by then, and he had Myra wearing a big, floppy hat that virtually hid her face. "Dawn dear," he had introduced them "This is Patty. Patty, this is my new friend Dawn. As I explained inside, Dawn, if it's okay with you Patty will accompany us to the tennis courts. She's a sort of chaperone," he added with his boyish grin. "Just so I don't get carried away"

Dawn was a lively, bouncy blond in her late teens. "Fine with me, Eddie" she laughed "I'm up for just about anything."

For the life of her Myra couldn't understand why Richard had wanted her tagging along. Why he'd manoeuvred the other girl into allowing it. Later, behind the bleachers, she had understood even less. She should have stopped it. Somehow. She knew that. But Richard was so…Masterful.

"Did you have a good time last night, Myra," he asked her now, almost solicitously.

"I…. "

"Yes, Myra? What are you trying to say?"

Myra hesitated, trying to find the right words. It had been so frightening to stand there, dumbly watching. But she didn't want to make him angry at her. Offend him in any way. He was so sure of himself. So much a part of her new happiness.

"You still can't quite make it out, can you?" he asked, in his softest, most understanding tone of voice.

"Dawn was in dreadful pain, Richard," Myra blurted out. "I think she thought you were going to kill her. I thought you were gonna kill her. She was so scared. Terrified."

Richard was quiet when he replied. Very patient. "It's called performance art," he said, looking deep into her eyes. "Like a reality show. Carried to the nth degree, of course," he added with a touch of wry, black humour. "You understand about art, you're the artistic one, right? RIGHT?"

Myra flinched under his penetrating gaze, blinking, wanting to drop her eyes but unable to.

"That's what she wanted, Myra. She virtually asked for it, for Christ's sake!" He took off his glasses and loomed over her face, his eyes boring into hers, black in their intensity. "And I don't mean that fucking idiotic tennis outfit or the cheap, whorish way she went on. Get this through your feeble mixed up cuntish head, Myra girl. These stupid chicks are so fucking crazy they practically beg for it."

Myra still looked at him blankly, uncomprehending.

“On Kinklife.ca," he said, "And it’ll be different next time,” he told her, straightening up, with a faint, crooked smile. “Next time, I’ll bring you more fully into the whole fucking picture. Then you’ll understand, you SorryBitch.” His face coarsened. His voice became curt, cutting. “Now, Myra. Give me your glasses. Take them off and give them to me. NOW!“

She was completely taken aback. Lost. “But - I can’t see without them. You wear glasses. You know I can’t see past my nose with ---“

His face clouded over as he interrupted her. “My eyesight was always fine,” he snarled. “Perfect vision. 20/20. Then that goddamed Afghanistan. All that accursed dust and corrosive, blowing sand.” His voice hardened. “Give me your glasses. Now!”

Trembling, she slid them off and passed them over.

“You can wear them when I say, and not before. Understood?”

She nodded, dumbly.

His voice was cold and steely. “Is that understood, Myra? Answer me!” he snapped. “NOW!”

“Ye-es, Richard,” she said slowly, licking her lower lip

“Yes, Master!” he barked. "I've told you before - You call me Master. Is that clear?"

“Yes, Master,” she replied, trembling.

He smiled thinly and, reaching out, gently patted her left shoulder. “Then don't forget again,” he said with a flicker of better humour. “Remember that and like I said we’ll get along just great.” His voice hardened again. “Correct?”

“Correct… Master, “she said more firmly, trying desperately not to blink. “Whatever you say, Master.“

Chapter 7 Radio Interview

Transcript:

MUSIC: FADE IN "ASK MADAME CLAIRE" THEME - TEDDY BEARS PICNIC

SOUND OVER: SLOWLY CHIMING CHURCH CLOCK

ANNOUNCER: (VERY DEEP VOICE) This is your friendly announcer, the Man in Black, bringing you our weekly internet radio program 'Ask Madame Claire.' The next thirty minutes are dedicated to kinksters already in the scene and folks who have an interest in learning more about BDSM. We are broadcasting from a secret studio in Niagara-On-The-Lake, Ontario, Canada.

SOUND: CLOCK FINISHES STROKE OF TWELVE

MUSIC: FADE TO BACKGROUND, THEN OUT

MADAME CLAIRE: Good evening friends and fellow travellers. My program tonight is about a subject controversial even among some kinksters, Rape or Ravishment Play. I shall be interviewing a young woman deeply involved in Rape Fantasies. Along with her experiences in actually living them out.

ANNCR: Listeners are invited to ask Madame Claire and her guest any relevant questions that come to mind. A brief description of your own fantasies is also welcome. Our telephone number is 1-900-925-0000. That's 925 followed by four zeros.

CLAIRE: There are three key words in the BDSM community, words I emphasise in every show I do. Safe, sane, consensual. Tonight my guest and I will be discussing rape, or ravishment fantasies. We shall not be talking about the abhorrent crime of rape itself. Speaking strictly personally, I believe that the legal penalties for actual rape are far too lenient. I'd lock the bastards up and melt down the key.

MUSIC: COMMERCIAL MUSIC CREEPS IN

ANNCR: First, a word from tonight's opening sponsor. Northland Leather and BDSM Gear.

NORTHLAND REP: Northland Leather is hands down the best and largest fetish and leather goods emporium in Canada. All the leather and latex on display is made in the three-floor Toronto store. We're a third generation family business which designs and handcrafts our own top quality lines of BDSM clothing and accessories.

SALESGIRL: We specialise in Victorian corsetry, skirts and leather accoutrements as well as off the rack and custom made gear for every perverted desire. Our leather whips and floggers are world famous. We also carry PVC, and rubber and provide cutting edge designs for performers in film, TV and music videos. Our highly professional retail consultants are all attired in our very latest designs.

NORTHLAND REP: Some of our premier custom items can be expensive, but we also carry many affordable BDSM costumes and accessories, such as wrist and ankle cuffs. For more information, visit our website or come to the store at Yonge & Wellesley. Bring your unique BDSM ideas to us and we will make them for you. To perfection.

MUSIC: FADES OUT AS MADAME CLAIRE RESUMES

CLAIRE: Northland also hosts the country's biggest fashion show and BDSM Party. An evening with five thousand celebrating kinksters is not an experience you'll readily forget. As for my guests, she'll be well known to many of you by her Kinklife.ca name, Gennifleur. I know her simply, and beautifully, as Fleur. Welcome to 'Ask Madame Claire' my dear.

FLEUR: Thank you for asking me to join you.

CLAIRE: Fleur as in Flower, right?

FLEUR: My maternal grandmother was from Waterloo. Not the Ontario Waterloo. The other one, of Napoleonic fame. Just outside Brussels in Belgium.

CLAIRE: Is French your native language?

FLEUR: Not really. My grandmother was a Flemish immigrant. I was raised in Woodstock.

CLAIRE: With a Toyota plant.

FLEUR: 2,400 workers. 200,000 crossover utility vehicles annually. 40,000 total population. A small but successful community Munch.

CLAIRE: How long have you been involved with BDSM, Fleur?

FLEUR: I came across it online when I was twenty-two. It made me realise that I wasn't alone. My first Munch was an eye-opener.

CLAIRE: Mine, too. Twenty-five years ago now.

FLEUR: I thought I was sick. Or my fantasies were sick. I had been sexually assaulted in my teens. On my sixteenth birthday. Raped. Brutally. It was the most hateful experience of my life.

CLAIRE: Did you have post-traumatic stress disorder? PTSD?

FLEUR: For years I wrestled with problems of intimate relationships and sexuality. I just couldn't understand how I could be struggling with the horrific experience of actual rape and yet, well, having ravishment fantasies.

CLAIRE: That must have been difficult to accept.

FLEUR: Very. I went through exposure therapy, insight and drug therapy. Then, one day, a Kink Aware Counsellor said something very simple. Rape, she said, is something sexual you don't want. Rape- or ravishment-play is something sexual you do want.

CLAIRE: Are most people into ravishment role-play participating because of a real life rape?

FLEUR: Not at all. In your introduction you mentioned that one in three women fantasise about being raped. Statistically, by the way, it's also one in five men. If we're honest with ourselves many of us will remember lying in bed, probably prior to masturbating, clutching the sweaty sheets and feeling helpless and overpowered. Such thoughts enable us to let go. Goodbye anxiety, inhibitions, even residual guilt. Submission, surrender, is a universal turn on.

CLAIRE: I guess we civilised Westerners haven't outgrown our basic primitive sexual urges.

FLEUR: We transmute fear and aggression into socially acceptable hockey or bungee jumping. A person who is in charge in everyday life may fantasise about physical bondage as the freedom to receive without the need to reciprocate.

SOUND: PHONE RINGS BG

CLAIRE: I have always felt that the impulse to be desired is the great motivator. To be irresistible.

FLEUR: It's the rape-top who surrenders to irresistible desire.

CLAIRE: Are you saying you took back your power?

FLEUR: Precisely.

ANNCR: Madame Claire, we have a question for Fleur. It's from Brightstar.

CLAIRE: Ah, one of our regular listeners. Go ahead, Brightstar.

BRIGHTSTAR: Hello, Madame Claire. Hi, Fleur. A very important topic.

FLEUR: I think so, Brightstar. Can I clarify something for you?

BRIGHTSTAR: I wonder if you could tell us about your first experience of consensual ravishment-play.

FLEUR: Consensual, of course, is the watchword. It means respecting the limits outlined by each party. A fantasy becomes rape or ravishment play only after extensive negotiation.

CLAIRE: Fleur, I notice you use ravishment as a synonym for rape.

FLEUR: I tend to think that the verb to ravish better describes the fantasy nature of play-rape. It helps us distinguish between the brutal realities of actual rape and the make-believe erotic fantasies that reflect our primitive urges in a mutually acceptable and consensual way. Phew, quite a mouthful. Sorry.

CLAIRE: Safe, sane and consensual. With the word 'safe' meaning we understand the actions and practices we engage in and, importantly, the degree of risk involved.

FLEUR: And 'sane' indicating we can tell fantasy from reality. One is a self-directed sort of script, negotiated in detail. The other is out-of-control and totally non-consensual.

BRIGHTSTAR: How much negotiation did you use in your first scene?

FLEUR: A great deal. And, believe me, it wasn't easy finding a man capable of role-playing well enough to be my ravisher, my rape-top.

BRIGHTSTAR: So how did you locate him?

FLEUR: Through the rape and ravishment sites on Kinklife.ca. I rooted out three possibilities and started a serious email correspondence with each. My then top had no wish to participate though she encouraged me to go ahead. She felt the experience would be good for me. She knew my sexual hang-ups and the reasons behind them.

CLAIRE: When was this, Fleur? Recently?

FLEUR: About, oh, seven years ago. I'm thirty-seven now, I was just turning thirty back then. I decided it would be a birthday present to myself.

CLAIRE: I'd say that was pretty courageous.

FLEUR: I was good and determined to take my life back. Do you understand that, Brightstar?

BRIGHTSTAR: I do, Fleur. I know that rape itself has little or nothing to do with sex. It's all about power and subjection.

CLAIRE: The typical rapist is profoundly insecure. A coward and a bully.

FLEUR: Two of my three prospects for rape-top, or ravisher, were washouts. They probably wouldn't have turned up anyway. That's one of the biggest problems in settling on a good top. They're full of sound and fury and tend to cop out at the last minute.

CLAIRE: And your third possibility?

FLEUR: Inexperienced, but a natural role-player, with an innate service-top mentality. He got off on negotiating this new - for him - role, and pulled it off most effectively.

BRIGHTSTAR: Where did it take place?

FLEUR: At a large park, down by the lake in his hometown of Hamilton. I particularly wanted it to occur out of doors. It was spring. The trilliums were in bloom. It had been raining. It was very muddy.

BRIGHTSTAR: At night?

FLEUR: Late evening, under a full moon. It seemed appropriate. I still remember walking through the park to the meeting place we had decided on. The trees and bushes were bathed in a pale silver glow. The grass was squelchy. I thought 'this is insane.' A real rapist could come bursting out of the bushes and seize me. I became afraid.

CLAIRE: I take it no one did. Come bursting out, that is. .

FLEUR: No, but Sir Stephen, not his real name, surprised the hell out of me. I'd said that he could, if he thought it would work. He grabbed me thirty yards or more before I reached the meeting place. Hauled me down into the mud, on my front, and dragged me into the bush. He was amazingly strong, quite overpowering.

CLAIRE: I assume you had negotiated limits? Set parameters for the scene.

FLEUR: Oh yes. I hadn't taken up Muay Thai then. That came later, when I got into the rush of resistance and serious struggle. This first time I was virtually defenceless. So I'd firmly established that there were to be no heavy blows, no blood. No bondage or arm-twisting. I didn't want to cramp his style. Not too much.

BRIGHTSTAR: You trusted him?

FLEUR: He had assured me he would observe our safewords. Red for stop, instantly. Yellow for caution. Green for go ahead. As it happened, I never used one of them.

CLAIRE: So how did the scene pan out? Was it what you expected?

BRIGHTSTAR: What do you recall most?

FLEUR: The taste of grass. And that's regular green grass, not marijuana. Sir Stephen didn't merely pull me off my feet. He pushed my face into the wet grass. I didn't have to wonder how it would happen, it just happened. Then he hauled up my dress - we had decided on a loose dress rather than slacks. I was literally crushed into the muddy grass. When he entered me, I felt a sudden rush of vindication. I had asked for this. . I wanted this. It was MY doing.

CLAIRE: Down and dirty for sure. Thank you, Fleur. And thank you, Brightstar for the question.

MUSIC: COMMERCIAL INTRO - PARTY THEME

ANNCR: Thanks also to Madame Claire for leading us into that Hamilton park. When we resume, Fleur will have a few words about After-care and some helpful tips on gang rape. From a Play POV, of course. But first a few words from our second sponsor tonight, Fantastico Home Parties

FANTASTICO SALESGIRL: Are your tired of traditional dinner parties or mundane get togethers with friends? Fantastico is the leading erotic and BDSM house party business in Canada, with over two hundred professional consultants. Book an evening of home fun and light-hearted debauchery through our website and a highly trained representative will bring a full line of popular adult toys and BDSM paraphernalia for your guests to sample and enjoy.

The spicy merchandise includes latex and PVC clothing, handcuffs and collars and top quality floggers and Perspex and wooden paddles, along with lubricants, edible creams and, wait for it, our ever mirth-provoking line of variously sized strap-ons. Every Fantastico party-giver will receive adult gifts based on sales. We guarantee you will also receive valuable sexual and BDSM information, plus a barrel of laughs through the entire presentation. Our business is built on referrals and on giving our valued clients what they most desire. Quality products. Quality entertainment.

MUSIC: PARTY THEME FADES AS ANNCR TAKES OVER

ANNCR: Fantastico is a charter member of the Ottawa Better Business Bureau. There are 372 party reviews on its website, the vast majority overwhelmingly favourable.

CLAIRE: And now some further comments from my guest on Ravishment-Play and After-care.

FLEUR: Virtually every scene in BDSM calls for some tender and understanding After-care. This is especially the case in Rape Play. However, there are differences. If the Ravisher, the Rape-Top, is a stranger, you may not want After-care from that person. It may actually detract from the scene. Better to have someone else on standby. Someone trained to soothe and listen and generally counsel the ravishee as needed.

CLAIRE: Would I be correct to assume that rape-tops would also benefit from decent After-care?

FLEUR: Very much so. Your actual rapist is most frequently a vicious sociopath, with no concern for others and a desire to further only their own sick fantasies. The good top, on the other hand, seeks solely to fulfill the Ravishee's fantasy. The scenes are highly focussed and intensely physical and emotional. It takes time and control to come down from the top high. Being a good ravisher can be an exhausting and angst-ridden journey.

CLAIRE: A few quick pointers to wrap up, Fleur. How about a summary of another scene you were involved in?

FLEUR: They don't always go as planned. I remember one scene where I was supposed to have a roadside breakdown in my Honda Civic. The idea was that my rape-top would stop by and take advantage of me in the back seat. Unfortunately, by the time he arrived three people had already pulled over to help. Three Mennonites in a horse and buggy, with straw hats and blue denim farming overalls.

CLAIRE: Expect unexpected Good Samaritans is what you're saying.

FLEUR: They were marvellously helpful, but I never set up a roadside scene again.

CLAIRE: When you're negotiating, what's the most important fact to get across?

FLEUR: That's easy. You have to convey to the top whatever it is that you, the bottom, wants and indeed needs to FEEL. To be desired, maybe. Other people may like to be humiliated. Perhaps made to cry. The tone you want to achieve is the most crucial part of any negotiation.

CLAIRE: Can someone else negotiate for you?

FLEUR: That's frequently the case. A top who knows you well. A close friend.

CLAIRE: Can a couple get into rape play?

FLEUR: Couples try it all the time. Depending how well they know each other I suggest wearing someone else's clothes, different glasses, change your hairstyle, even your aftershave. Voice too. Maybe silence is golden. And it's a good idea to set up an agreed but inexact time. A surprise is always....surprising.

CLAIRE: How about props?

FLEUR: Unlimited. Knives, blunted. Guns, unloaded. Rope, gags, handcuffs. Anything that enhances the scene and, most important, that the top knows how to use.

SOUND: PHONE RINGS BG

CLAIRE: How about multiple rape-tops. I gather that's an extension of the play-rape scene?

FLEUR: Gang rape is a fairly common fantasy, even among vanillas. Mind you, setting one up can be the very devil. You have to find rape-tops who can perform in front of other men. That's not so common. I tried to organise a group effort some weeks back. I had four remarkably enthusiastic volunteers. When it came right down to it, none of them showed up.

ANNCR: Sorry to interrupt, ladies, but you have another caller. Alphamale69.

CLAIRE: We're getting tight on time. What's your question, Alphamale?

ALPHAMALE: I'm kind of interested in being what you guys call a rape-top. How do I go about it?

CLAIRE: Fleur?

FLEUR: I'm working on creating a sort of Ravishment Club. I have a questionnaire for bottoms and am working on a complementary one for tops. About fifty questions that determine suitability on both sides.

ALPHAMALE: Geez, that sounds like runaway bureaucracy to me.

FLEUR: Not really. It's a case of winnowing the chaff from the wheat. Or whatever that expression is.

ALPHAMALE: If you ask me, being a rape-top would likely turn into a gateway drug. Let the rapist out and the guy would definitely crave more. I think you people are real creepy.

CLAIRE: I'm tuning you out now, Alphamale.

ALPHAMALE: SPLUTTERS OUT

ANNCR: Sorry.

CLAIRE: We're almost out of time anyway. And how about that, Fleur. Are folks into rape-play creepy?

FLEUR: No more than individuals who phone 'Ask Madame Claire' to bitch about guests. In my spare time, by the way, I'm the Ontario representative of the North American organisation NCSF, the National Coalition for Sexual Freedom. We still have a long way to go.

CLAIRE: Don't we just. And thanks for joining me, Fleur. Perhaps a final word of advice as we wrap.

MUSIC: TEDDY BEARS PICNIC MADAME CLAIRE THEME SNEAKS IN

FLEUR: Always establish a clear paper trail. Ravishment-play has to be seen as a consensual activity. A written or audio record of the negotiations, the safewords, may help if for some reason the authorities get involved.

And believe me, folks: rape or ravishment play, is not a gateway drug.

CLAIRE: You have been listening to Fleur and myself, Madame Claire, discussing rape play. In our next show, Sir Robert and Lady Grace Challenger will introduce us to the complexities of Subspace and Predicament Bondage.

MUSIC: THEME UP

SOUND: CHIMING CHURCH CLOCK

ANNCR: (VERY DEEP VOICE) On behalf of Madame Claire and her dedicated research staff this is your nefarious announcer, the Man in Black, wishing you sweet and undeniably pleasant dreams. Next week, the complexities of Subspace & Predicament Bondage.... (AND HE LAUGHS, MENACINGLY)

MUSIC: TEDDY BEARS PICNIC UP AND

FADE OUT

Chapter 8 Richard & myra at home

Richard, and Myra were in the dilapidated bedroom of his Waterloo apartment. His parents in Toronto paid for it monthly, just so long as he never contacted them. The apartment and a small allowance. "A 21st Century Remittance Man, "Richard thought bitterly, the bitterness tempered by an edge of satisfied glee that his mother and father still paid to keep him out of their sight.

He was sprawled back on the king-sized bed with its blood-red comforter, his hands clasped behind his head, a glass of red wine on the night table beside him. He was wearing his black Reebok track pants and a plain white T-shirt. His hair was combed back and parted in the middle. Even in the house, he was still wearing his tinted sunglasses. Myra was sitting cross-legged next to him, without her glasses, bone naked. He liked to keep her naked when she was in his home. It amused him and anyway it was mid-summer. Her face was red and blotchy. She had been weeping.

"Igor said I was too much of a downer," she said, gulping. "He claimed Heather was always sexier with the clients. She gave them what they really wanted, he said."

"Gave 'em a better blowjob more likely," Richard said unsympathetically. "And for Christ's sake, girl, get over it. You're not the first chick to be fired because the boss is sleeping with some other bimbo." He grinned mirthlessly. "I told you to go down on him now I've taught you how to do it right. "

"I dunno what I'm gonna do next," Myra moaned pitifully, tears running down her cheeks.

He was crisp and to the point. "Get another job, that's what," he said bluntly, casually kicking a box of Kleenex at her. "Tattoo salons are sprouting up all over like the pimples on your bloody ass."

"But not for me, Richard," she wailed. "I tried before. For months I tried. Igor's was the only business that'd hire me. He said I'd make the customers feel welcome and wanted. Till that shitty Heather bounced in." She broke down again, sobbing uncontrollably. "I dunno what to do if I can't have my tattooing. It's all I got. My gift, my talent. Nobody ever give me a real chance. Igor didn't, he wouldn't let me do free style. Nobody ever give me a proper chance…."

"I did!" said Richard coldly, rubbing the baby red dragon on his upper arm. "Christ it's hot in here. That wretched air conditioning doesn't work worth a damn." He sat up on the bed and rescued the box of Kleenex from where it lay in her crotch. "Now listen to Daddy, girl," he said, almost gently, pulling out a tissue and dabbing her sopping cheeks. "I'll help you get in some tattooing. " He took her chin in his hand and tilted her face up to his. "As free-form and artistic as you wanna get. Okay?"

She peered at him blankly. Her mouth formed the "How?" but no sound came out. "No one'll ever want to hire me again," she said at last. "Ever again, Richard," she moaned, her eyelids fluttering up and down, up and down. "I'll never get another job. Never again."

Richard slapped her face, hard. "Shut the fuck up with your goddamned whining and listen to me," he snarled savagely. "And stop blinking all the blasted time. Christ, you can be an ugly bitch. For fuck's sake, Myra, I said I'd help you with your tattooing, didn't I?" He jerked her face within an inch or two of his own, his eyes behind the tinted glasses fierce and intent. "All you need is a fucking canvas to work on, right? A human fucking canvas. RIGHT?"

She nodded. Once, twice, three times. Struggling to keep her eyes wide open. Gulping back her sobs.

"Then you can leave it to Master," he said definitely, expansively. "I got me a brainwave while you were crying in buckets. If they won't hire you, if nobody'll give you a damned job, we'll fucking hire them. We'll hire them, just for you. Got it?"

She nodded reflexively, without understanding. But he cared… he really cared. Even in her abject misery the thought reached through the ache to her heart. Richard was truly concerned. For her.

“It’s like this, you silly slut,” he said quietly, wiping her eyes. “Tomorrow night I have another chick all set up. Just as stupidly eager as that crazy MorningGlory, Dawn. Got the new babe off Kinklife. Or Henry did. I was Henry when I contacted Carol. That's her real name, Hank wormed that out of her. She says it’s always been her fantasy to be violently raped. Here, I’ll show you.” He grabbed the laptop off the other side of the bed. It was already set to Kinklife.ca. Richard was always a step or two ahead.

“Forcibly taken, is the way she puts it. She wants to be forcibly taken in the back of a Pet Shop. That’s what she dreams of.” His finger stabbed at the screen. “See, Myra! She’s asking for it, like I said. The stupid sow wants to be raped in a goddamned Pet Shop.”

Myra looked scared, disbelieving. She blinked and peered closer. “Another girl?” she said, not fully registering what she was hearing. “Another girl - like Dawn?”

He laughed. He was patient with her now. “The way I read it,” he told her. “It goes back to when she was thirteen. She was nearly raped in his store by her old man. But he couldn’t get it up, see.” He closed the laptop and picked up his glass of wine. “Kinda left her wanting more.” He raised the glass and toasted Myra with a look of almost exultation on his face. “They sort of advertise on this Rape and Ravishment site, see. Email about what they really want. Tell stories. Come fulfill my desires they say... Which is where I come in. Where WE come in,” he added, tossing back the rich, red wine. "Henry this time, got it?"

Myra was disbelieving, but at the same time beginning to believe. “You want to do it again, Richard?” she asked, automatically shaking her head from side to side. “You mean like Dawn? Another girl?” She was incredulous, frightened. ”You want to beat another young girl? Like last time?” She ran her tongue over her lips. “It’s so cruel, Master. So dangerous.“

He grinned, a sense of success and anticipation on his face. “Isn’t it just,” he said, satisfied with himself. “Cruel and dangerous, like the doctor ordered." His eyes were glittering behind his glasses. "I told you there'd be another. There's always another. This one's nick is Nymphette. A pretty little Nymph, got it? Also like the doctor ordered." He stopped gloating and became practical and businesslike. "Tomorrow night we'll be heading for Stratford. The Tim Hortons right downtown, the corner of Ontario and Waterloo. She wants it, I tell you, Myra." He laughed with pleasure and admiration at his own cleverness. "I got this one just like Dawn - hook, line and pussy."

Myra was still having trouble putting it all together. "Tim Hortons again," she said worriedly, her brows tense.

He dismissed her concern instantly. "Good old Timmie's," he said. "Everybody meets there. Even the cops. It's their favourite hang-out. And mine," he grinned, his mind racing. "Hey, baby, maybe we can take in the Stratford Shakespeare Festival while we're in town. They got Othello at the top of their bill. I took it in school, at Upper Canada College" He laughed as a thought struck him. "I always figured it should've been called Iago. He's the cat who makes it all happen. Some character that Iago is. "

"You know Stratford well," she asked, again showing concern.

"Back of my hand," he replied confidently. "Even went to a Munch there once. Only one I ever been to. Stupid whore running it got all feminist on me and I never went back. Marie-Celeste Baron," he added. "I even remember her goddamn name."

Myra wasn't remotely concerned with the Stratford Munch, or the Shakespeare Festival come to that. "You want me to come with you," she asked hesitantly. "Again? Like last time?"

"You're my girl," he said suavely. "My most valued assistant. I've hired you on." He reached out and took her nipples between his strong fingers. "Myra, honey, I'm gonna give you what you most want. What I think you most need." He increased the pressure on her left nipple. "D'you remember telling me once about how you played with your dollies? The pretty blonde one with the eyes that opened and closed… Remember?" His fingers tightened on both nipples. "You tattooed her all over, as I recall. Back, front, arms, legs……..and then her eyes." He twisted hard with both hands. A gasp escaped her lips. “Finished with her eyes didn’t you? Tattooed them shut, I think you said. Right?”

“Please, Master, not so hard.”

He twisted both nipples again. “Tomorrow night you’ll come with me to Stratford. Justin Bieberland. And Myra,” he went on, twisting and squeezing. “You’ll bring your tattoo kit, won’t you?”

She winced. The pain shot through both breasts like a sudden tongue of flame. “I will, I will, I promise.”

With a smile he relaxed his grip. Momentarily. “Tell me, Myra,” he asked in a silky voice. “Are you a good Christian?”

“Christian?” she repeated, doubting she had heard him right.

His fingers tightened. “A saffron Buddhist, maybe? A ragtop Moslem?” He lowered his voice. “I never asked you. What religion are you, Myra?”

“I have no religion, Richard,” she cried out, as he twisted her nipples again. “I’m not anything.”

“Right first go,” he said bleakly. “You’re nothing. NOTHING! A screaming nothing trapped in a body that bewilders and scares the living daylights out of you. What are you?”

“Nothing….nothing,” she groaned, her whole body on fire.

He let go of her aching nipples and pushed her head down into his lap. “But you’re my nothing,” he said, almost affectionately. “And you like to suck my dick, don’t you, sweetie?” He lifted her head up a few inches.

“Yes, Master,” she said plaintively, the tears drying on her face. “Whatever you want. Anything. You’re my Master. I’m your slave….”

“Humble slave,” he corrected her coldly. “Humble slave,” Myra said, instantly complying.

“And if I say you’re accompanying me to Stratford and obeying Henry in whatever he asks?”

“Immediately, Master.”

"Without question?"

"I'll never question you, Master... Never again… Ever…"

With a satisfied grunt he pushed her head back down on his cock. "Then get to work, you SorryBitch," he said. "Get me good and hard." She knew what was in store. He liked the stimulus of dishing out pain. "And you'll bring your fucking tattoo kit, right bitch?"

"Yesh Master," she gulped, her mouth full and busy.

He threw his head back on the pillow. "Then we'll have a fuckin' ball," he promised, grimacing. "And that stupid Nymphette will never forget it. We'll leave her a pretty little bunch of blue-pink "forget-me-nots" on her forehead." He laughed sadistically and abandoned himself to passion, while tattooed little forget-me-nots danced a rhythmic downbeat in his mind.

Chapter 9 Initiation

It was already late afternoon when Madame Claire picked up Leeza and drove to the Tilverdale Mac's Milk. "Just for cream," she said gaily. "I wouldn't want to run out tonight of all nights."

They had plans for the evening. Claire had promised to introduce the young girl to some of her favourite BDSM gear. "Floggers for your first scene," she said sunnily. Floggers were short impact toys with lots of tails. They were usually used on the back and bottom. Leeza had been building up to this since the Black Wally Munch. She had got off on the people there and wondered why they were into something as far-out as BDSM. "Whatever that really is," she said to Claire. "You all seem so normal to me. Well, most of you."

Claire laughed and turned the car into the convenience store parking lot. "Like I told you, darling," she said. "BDSM is a bit of a catch-all title. We're not all into Bondage or Discipline or extreme Sado-Masochism. If anything, it's a personal journey into ourselves." They got out of the car and she automatically locked the doors. She was careful like that. A small suitcase of whips and floggers had once vanished off her back seat. She could still smile wryly at the look she imagined on the thief's face when he, or she, pried open the case.

"It's a very personal journey," she went on. "Not everyone has the courage to take it. Facing up to who we really are can be a real shock." She gave Leeza a sly grin. "A sort of transformation tends to sneak in." She made no secret of the fact that she hoped Leeza would get involved in the scene. But she tried not to influence her unduly. Not too much anyway. An informed choice was the way she thought of it.

"There isn't a "C" in BDSM," she noted. "If there were it would stand for Consensual."

Leeza had the glint of a smile in her eye. "Know Thyself and Consensuality?" she teased Claire. "Sounds like watchwords for a happy life." They gazed at each other for a moment, straight-faced. Then they both broke out laughing.

"Oh my, did I say that aloud," Claire said ruefully. "I guess my seduction techniques have slipped somewhat."

"Not entirely" grinned Leeza, and held open the door to the convenience store. "Though there's one thing I do know, about myself. Nothing much happens in my life without my consent."

"And I figured you were just an impressionable young girl," Claire said playfully and walked in to the store.

"We all have our little secrets," the girl said, and followed.

"You most of all, I think," Claire said over her shoulder as she paused by the milk fridge.

"I have no secrets from you, dear Madame," Leeza said. "You know me almost as well as I know myself."

They exchanged a fond look and the bell over the door finally stopped jangling. The Mac's Milk was one of a few hundred such stores in small Ontario townships. Liberally stocked with milk and bottled drinks, cookies and chocolate, cigarettes and bread. All the impulse and last minute items.

Dawn was at the cash, keeping her head down. She looked unhappy and careworn. She was wearing a patch over her right eye and the flesh around it was black and purple. She had a largish band-aid on her forehead. She probably shouldn't have been at work, but there was no ready replacement.

"Missed you at the Munch, Dawn dear," said Claire, putting a small cream on the counter. "Just this and a Rothman's, please" She glanced back at Leeza, who had stayed in the cool of the refrigerators. "For the glove compartment. It makes it easier just knowing they're there." She smirked at the girl "I never actually smoke them, my friends help me out there..." She turned back to the cash. "This is my good friend Leeza," she said. "I usually introduce her as Matt's sister. And how about you, Dawn? Did you win the other night?" She took a twenty from her purse. "Get the job?"

Dawn had tried to avoid looking up. "I didn't p-play," she said weakly, a distinct quaver in her voice.

Claire was suddenly genuinely concerned. She had registered the girl's swollen face and overall appearance. "My dear Dawn!" she exclaimed. “What on earth happened to you?"

"N-nothing," stammered Dawn, concentrating on making change.

"That eye isn't nothing, dear," Claire said firmly. She was very sympathetic. "It must really hurt."

Leeza had come over to the cash. "Sore to the touch, I bet."

Dawn thrust a five and some coins into Claire's hand, still not lifting her head. "I tripped," she mumbled. "At the...tennis courts."

"Do you want to talk about it?" asked Claire. "Sometimes that helps us get through things."

"No," Dawn said abruptly. "Nothing happened. I just tripped."

Claire realised the girl was close to breaking down. She decided not to press the issue. "I had a black eye when I was around your age. I said I'd had an argument with the kitchen door. I hadn't, of course. I idiotically stood on a garden rake." She took a business card out of her purse. "Here, keep this handy. ‘Madame Claire, Radio Host and Tarot Readings.' I'm available if you ever want to chat."

Dawn looked as if she might cry. Kindness did that. "Thank you, Madame," she said, biting her bottom lip.

The doorbell jangled. Two men were entering. One of them was a uniformed police officer from Waterloo Region. Vijay Puri.

"You take care, dear," said Claire, laying a friendly hand on Dawn's arm. "And call me any time. Day or night."

Dawn nodded, blinking. "If I need to."

Claire patted her arm. "There's a good girl," she said and moved away to the door. But not all the way. She had registered the newcomers. She stopped at the milk fridge, picking up a quart of 2%. "They're pretty good at Mac's Milk," she commented to

Leeza. "But the convenience store in Marybourne has to be watched." She took out her glasses and peered myopically at the expiry date.

Vijay hung back discreetly as the other man approached the cash desk. He was a few years older, though still in his twenties. Tall and interesting looking. Well-built with short-cropped hair, grey pants and navy blue jacket. Collar and striped tie, with an OPP lapel badge.

"Good morning, Miss," he said pleasantly to Dawn. "You're Dawn Gretsko, am I right?"

Dawn kept her face averted. "What do you want?" she asked stiffly, busying herself stacking cartons of cigarettes on the shelves behind the cash.

"I'm Detective Bellingham, with the Ontario Provincial Police," he said, and indicated his companion, waiting by the door. "I believe you know my colleague, Constable Puri."

With a polite nod, Vijay slipped past Claire and Leeza, but still held back a little. "Good to see you again, Dawn. Sorry we didn't get a chance to talk the other night."

Dawn looked trapped. "I was in a hurry," she explained uncertainly. She busily stacked up more cigarette cartons and a few single packs.

Detective Bellingham wasted no words. He cut straight to the matter at hand. "Tell me, Dawn," he said. "Have you been playing tennis lately?"

Dawn blinked and fumbled with the cigarettes. A pack fell to the floor. "W-what?" she stuttered, stooping to retrieve it.

The detective leaned into the counter. "Officer Puri here found a tennis racket in the lilac bushes behind the Courts. It had what appeared to be blood on it."

"Blood?" mumbled Dawn, rising to her feet with an effort and putting the cigarette pack on the shelf.

"It looked like an assault might have taken place," he said seriously.

"The night before last," Officer Puri chipped in. "Some of the bushes were broken off. The tall grass was flattened."

Detective Bellingham smiled at her back, trying to put her at ease. "We're just making a few enquiries, Miss Gretsko," he said. "Not an official investigation."

"Not yet," said Vijay gloomily.

"Ahem..." Madame Claire had returned to the cash. "Excuse me, guys," she said calmly to the policemen, stepping deliberately between them. "Dawn dear, could you give me a couple of toonies and four quarters for this five?" She smiled sweetly at the plainclothes detective. "Parking at Grand River Hospital, you know."

Dawn had gratefully turned away from the cops and opened the cash. She groped with the change and collected herself as best she could. "Two toonies and four quarters," she repeated. "No problem, Madame Claire."

The OPP man had reacted rather irritably to Claire's blithe interruption. "Pardon me, ma'am..." he had started to say. Then stopped in his tracks, staring hard at Claire.

"So sorry to interrupt," she apologised amiably. "And don't forget, Dawn. You have my card. I'll call right back if I miss you." She nodded at the detective and bustled out of the convenience store with Leeza in tow. "They must learn to say Ma'am in police school," she said jokingly, as the door jangled shut behind them.

Detective Bellingham had kept his eyes on Claire till she left. "I think I've met that lady before," he said to Vijay, frowning as he tried to recall the when and how. Then he dismissed it and returned his attention to Dawn. "As I said, this isn't an official investigation, Miss, because no one has reported an assault. Without someone coming forward our hands are tied. Which reminds me, are those rope burns on your wrists?"

Dawn was wearing long sleeves, unusual in early summer. Most Canadians switched to short sleeves or even sleeveless as soon as the sun had a glimmer of warmth. She pulled her sleeves way down, covering the ugly red marks. "Just playing," she said, flushing nervously. "With my boy-friend," she added.

The detective nodded. "Playing?" he asked skeptically. "Is that how you got the black eye?"

"Leave me alone," Dawn burst out. "I ain't done nothing wrong."

"I didn't say you have, Dawn. I'm more concerned that something wrong was done to you. Were you assaulted?"

"Go away!" she cried. "I have nothing to say."

The doorbell jangled as a new customer made his way in. He was an elderly gentleman with a white cane and a large Seeing Eye dog. As they came toward the cash, the dog sniffed suspiciously at Vijay.

Bellingham gave up. "Miss Gretsko," he said, very firmly. "If something happened to you, and you don't report it.....Well, it can happen to someone else, you understand?"

"We only want to help, Dawn," Vijay said, showing his concern.

"Nothing happened to me," the girl said stubbornly, greeting the new arrival. "Good afternoon, Mr. Ballesteros. What can I do for you?"

The detective started to leave, then paused. "Please think about what I said, Dawn." He was quite sincere. "We really are here to serve and protect. But we can't do either unless you file a complaint."

The two cops walked glumly out to the parking lot and climbed into Detective Bellingham's unmarked car. "I don't understand the girl," Vijay grumbled. "It's clear she's been assaulted. Maybe even raped."

Detective Bellingham was a little older, a little wiser. "I should have brought Olive from London with me. A policewoman," he said, starting the car. "It's difficult for a girl, talking to a male officer. But you were right to call me in. Though I'm afraid it'll be too late now."

"That woman interrupting wasn't any help."

The detective was more charitable. "I guess she thought she was protecting the girl. And did you notice what Dawn called her? Madame Claire." He chuckled to himself and headed the car for Waterloo to drop off the Regional officer. "I knew I'd run into the woman before. You know what the Madame stands for, my friend?"

Vijay shook his head, puzzled. Bellingham was suitably pleased with himself. "Madame Claire, it's a BDSM honorific," he said. "She's a well-known dominant in the Scene. It's a small world, Officer Puri. Our Madame Claire is somebody quite special. A BDSM radio host, among other interesting things."

He drove out of Tilverdale, staying strictly to the speed limit. He was a very conscientious young policeman was Detective Horatio Bellingham. He and Vijay were fine representatives of the new wave in Ontario law enforcement.

*

Claire and Leeza were in the basement dungeon at Black Walnut cottage. Madame Claire Faversham, Top, Dominant and Mentor. Leeza Llewellyn, scene name Leeza LaBelle, Bottom, submissive, Equal. Great friends. Maybe twenty or more years apart in calendar age, who liked and respected each other very much.

It was to be the night of nights. Leeza's initiation into the secrets of BDSM. It was the equality that most surprised the young girl. There was no sense of inferiority in the submissive role. One of the first things Claire had talked about was the power exchange that would happen between them. Bondage, Domination and Submissiveness, she had said. "With a dash of Sado-Masochism thrown into the mix like a hot pepper. Capsein, that particular element was called. It heightened every other flavour.

"Like roast beef and horse-radish," Leeza had suggested. She wasn't a Vegan. She liked to tuck into a good steak. Matt often said it was a well-done steak that enabled him to handle 15-1600 lbs of fractious horseflesh.

Mozart's Night Music was playing on the stereo. The dungeon was lit by nine candles, arranged around the large room in a flickering circle. "Scentless," Madame Claire had pointed out.

"Your sense of smell is important in a good flogging scene." She gave Leeza clear, concise instructions. Overall equality didn't preclude Claire taking the lead. The responsibility was hers. "Strip down to your panties and stand at the Gorean Post," she said simply. "Clothing and BDSM seldom go together."

"More like a skimpy thong," Leeza said, obeying without hesitation. "High on the sides and cut away around the buttocks"

"And very shapely buttocks they are," smiled Claire wholesomely. "You have a heavenly body, my dear. Such lovely shoulders, with a sense of sleek muscles beneath an alabaster skin."

Leeza stood tall and winning at the whipping post, almost naked and innately proud. She glanced quizzically over one sculptured shoulder. "Are you sure you're not too worried about Dawn?" she wanted to know, genuinely concerned for Claire's feelings.

"I'm very concerned, darling," Claire responded. "But I can do nothing about it now. The older I get, the more important it is to live in the moment." She fastened leopard cuffs around Leeza's wrists and effortlessly clipped them to the rings near the top of the Post. "This is your night, dear girl. Yours and mine. Your first BDSM scene."

"I understand," Leeza said simply.

Madame Claire smiled softly and opened the Canadian Tire gun case in which she kept her most treasured floggers and percussion toys. "So tell me, Leeza, what do you understand by the word 'flogging?'"

The girl gulped faintly. She wasn't quite as blasé as she seemed. "Um... Punishment," she replied. "Pain, I guess."

"What gives you that idea?"

"Movies, most likely. Pirates and sailing ships. Mutiny on the Bounty. The handsome seaman tied to the mast...."

".... With a stalwart bosun swinging a cat-of-nine-tails," laughed Claire. "It may surprise you but flogging doesn't have to involve pain. Not pain as you think of it, anyway." She had crossed to the stereo. "Enough of Wolfgang Amadeus for now. I have a special treat set up for your upcoming initiation into BDSM. One of the sexiest CDs in my collection."

"Sounds right up my alley," grinned Leeza.

Claire changed the CD. "I give you Maurice Ravel's classic work, Bolero," she announced. "The name of a traditional Spanish dance."

Leeza nodded. "I've heard it, I think. It keeps repeating the same notes. Getting louder and louder."

"There's a little more to it than that," grinned Claire. "A full orchestra, to which I add my own instruments. Eight or ten different floggers, which also get 'louder and louder.' First, however, I have to blindfold you. So you can see with your mind. BDSM uses all sorts of different senses, even ones you didn't know you have."

The orchestra had started to play. It was barely audible. The dungeon was bathed in the soft, rhythmic beating of a snare drum. Then a single Italian flute came in, high and haunting. Madame Claire had taken a short, many tailed flogger from her gun case. "This little beauty is called a bunny flogger," she said, loosely draping its ten inch tails over Leeza's naked shoulders. "It has eighteen tails, made of the smoothest, softest rabbit fur. We call them Falls. Like the first part of Bolero, they're designed to warm you up." She trailed the soft falls sensuously down to the girl's bare bottom. Then slowly extended her arm and let the bunny flogger rise and fall in perfect time with the snare drum.

Leeza's initiation scene into BDSM-C was underway. It was consensual on every score. After a while, she giggled contentedly. "It's wonderfully soothing," she said dreamily. "I think I like this type of relaxing warm-up."

"But already the music is heading into its first repeat," Claire said, her voice as soft as the bunny flogger. "New instruments are melding in. A viola. An E-flat clarinet. Even a harp". The snare drum raised the volume of its repetitive theme. A 2nd flute joined the swelling sound. Strings and bassoons added their velvety timbre. Claire matched the increase in tempo by switching to a suede and a Deerskin flogger, one in each hand, wielded efficiently in co-ordinated figures of eight.

"Left shoulder, right shoulder," she intoned in harmony with the caressing strokes. "These are the lightest and most sensual of my toys. The two-handed technique is known as Florentining." Her collection included over a dozen different floggers, which she occasionally used in a single scene. Suede and Deerskin, Cowhide and harsh Latigo leather. "All different in form and feeling," she added. "Even down to the smell."

The young girl nodded. She knew she was being seduced by the music and the rhythm of the falls that fell on her reddening skin like gentle droplets of rain from the sky. "Birch woods and damp soil," she conjectured, wriggling her back and nostrils in rare unison. "The deerskin smells earthy," she said lazily. "And the warm-up is, well... hypnotic in a way."

But the music had other ideas. It grew louder, more demanding. An oboe d'amore and a rich cello highlighted the snare drum and flutes. 1st and 2nd violins came in. The pace and intensity of the Florentine escadrille swished through the dungeon. Claire, too, had moved her flogging up a notch.

She knew that the hardest part of the scene was approaching. She loved playing to Bolero and wanted Leeza to be a part of it, not an easy experience for a new submissive who had never scened before. She decided to talk the girl through the changes to come. "So far, the Deerskin has been soft and buttery," she said, her voice low and mesmerising. "But now you can begin to feel, even hear the falls landing on your bare flesh. They're getting more insistent. Another instrument in the Bolero orchestra."

Leeza was already halfway there. She was beginning to sway with the cadence of the drum beat. "...Makes me want to dance," she said happily. "And it doesn't hurt. I still thought it would hurt."

Claire increased the intensity of her swing again. "Ravel composed Bolero for his favourite dancer. And at the Sarajevo Olympics Torville and Dean adapted it to win Ice Dance gold," she told the girl. "Moving to the music is good for you."

Leeza's journey was unfolding as it should. The sensations imparted by the floggers were growing stronger. "Your back and bottom are turning a very attractive pink," Claire said, in her most comforting tone. "It's as if your body is asking for more...."

A trumpet and a soprano saxophone lifted the snare drum to yet another level. 1st and 2nd Horns added their melody. Claire didn't hesitate now. Smoothly she switched to a three-tailed leopard Samurai of woven Bull-hide. It had inch-wide, viper cut tongues on each tail. Designed to sting.

"Ouch!" Leeza exclaimed, as the Samurai tongues bit into her shoulders. She straightened against the Post, breathing in short bursts like a woman in labour. Bolero was a third of the way on its gradual build to ecstasy. Every cell in the girl's straining body was becoming attuned to the ever mounting tempo. She understood, physically now, that every time the music swelled, the floggers grew harder to process.

"I can...really feel it now," she gasped, less confident but still determined to follow through."

Claire, a very experienced Top, could read the young girl's reactions like an open book. Every twitch, every breathy intake, told her when to intensify, when to back off, if only for a moment. She was listening for colours as well. Yellow, or even red if she pushed Leeza too hard or too soon. "You're bearing up just fine, girl," she said encouragingly. "This stingy Samurai has only one real purpose. To get your endorphins flowing free."

"They reduce the...pain, right?" panted Leeza, admitting to herself that the sensations were less pleasant now.

"Give them time, sweetie."

Flogging was not as straightforward as it appeared, particularly in the middle stages of a scene. Good conditioning and absolute accuracy were a must for the Top. The shoulders and upper back were the prime targets, never the spine or kidneys. Controlling painful wrap-around on the curved buttocks was simply good flogging manners. Attaining the longed-for endorphin high required great skill and no little persistence.

And, all the while, the throb of Bolero beat out its constantly escalating commands. Trombones and bassoons amplified the driving theme. Piccolos pirouetted on high. 1st and 2nd French horns blared out their charge. Claire had graduated to two high tempo rotator floggers. Their many Cowhide falls revolved on steel ball bearings and streamed like pelting rain on Leeza's tenderised flesh.

The atmosphere in the dungeon had grown warm and clingy. The candles cast flickering shadows across the leopard rugs and on the walls. For Claire it was steady, circular wrist action. For Leeza, the whirling falls seemed never to stop but went on and on in timeless space.

"Oh god, Claire," she mumbled brokenly. "Yellow... I'm sorry, but....please."

Claire had been half expecting the colour. Twice in the scene the girl had found it difficult to process the stingy floggers. Some submissives preferred them; others had little love for their biting beestings. Without a moment's hesitation, Claire discarded the swivel floggers and brought a pair of thuddy Moosehides into play as a Timpani signalled the next upward movement and 1st and 2nd Trumpets came gloriously in. A contrabassoon and Bavarian tuba carried the quarter/eight note rhythm

Leeza had heaved a long shuddering sigh of relief as the rotating floggers ceased their stingy onslaught. She was light-headed and floaty now, ready to drift away. Claire expertly brought her back to the present with some heavy thuds from the Moosehides. "Almost there, dear one," she said lovingly, boosting her morale as always.

The young girl gave a faint nod of acknowledgement, either unable or unwilling to speak. She bravely drew herself to her full 5' 8" height and resolutely squared her shoulders. She would not give in; she knew that she was close. Though to what she wasn't sure. The endorphins were rushing now. She had touched her innermost core and moved through it into another dimension of Self. From this point on she was indomitable.

Bolero, too, was nearing its thunderous climax. Oboes and clarinets. 1st, 2nd and 3rd horns and violins. Violas, cellos, kettle drums and timpani. All these and more were coursing like rich red blood through Leeza's pulsating body. She was the music and the music was her.

Claire had briefly thrown in a few culminating strokes with her searing Bootlace flogger and its matching Studmaster. There were twenty-four square-cut Bootlaces and the Studmaster's twenty-six inch falls were shiny with metal studs. Even a handful of powerful strokes had Leeza moaning in deep, if surprisingly exhilarating pain. Nothing could defeat her now.

Out of the blue, a high-pitched choir of soprano voices blended seamlessly into the cacophonous Bolero finale and covered Leeza's piercing screams. Cymbals vibrated resonantly and a bass drum thundered its deafening salutation. In unison, Claire gathered her crowning Thudstinger flogger into both hands. Sixty twenty-seven inch falls. Thirty of Latigo leather on the outside, surrounding thirty more of flexible rubber on the inside. Three full-bodied, two handed throws were all most submissives could take.

The music; the female voices; the flogging; all came to a strident, discordant climax. A veritable orgasm of grinding noise and grating ecstasy.

Leeza stayed perfectly motionless for a long moment. Then her head drooped slowly forward on to the Gorean Post. She was having her first experience of subspace. She was still safely in the dungeon in body, but her spirit was roaming the boundless cosmos.

Claire, perspiring freely herself, was more than satisfied with their scene. Bolero had done its job, as it usually did. She was certain that Leeza would find her involvement energising and, possibly, even transformative. That was the wonder of BDSM. BDSM-C, she thought wryly. And the consensuality was far from over...

She tenderly unhooked the girl from the Post and more or less carried her to the massage table. "Now you must rest a while," she murmured in Leeza's ear. "Enjoy the fascinating new space you are in." She covered the girl with a leopard throw. "You're a brave girl, sweetie. A brave, brave girl."

Leeza managed the faintest of faint smiles. There was an expression of utter serenity on her sweat-covered face.

And the After-care began.

*

Time seemed to stand still, but passed as it always did. Claire stroked and caressed. Murmuring sweet nothings as she gently spread lotion on the girl's tingling back. Leeza sipped her way through two full bottles of spring water and slowly returned to the dungeon. "That was...very, very special," she said softly, as the power of speech started to come back.

"Subspace and all," Claire said informatively. "I'm doing a podcast on that in a couple of weeks. With Sir Robert and Lady Grace."

Leeza was still coming to grips with the flogging. "I came so close... in the middle... to actually calling it off." She hugged Claire warmly. "Man, I feel so good. Weak in the knees but...triumphant, I guess."

"Being flogged to Bolero will do that to you," laughed Claire. "Did I mention that back in the Eighties it was the theme music for one of the sexiest movies ever made?"

Leeza's innate playfulness showed through. "I think you might have," she teased Claire, who was undeterred. "It was called Ten," Claire continued. "The star was a beautiful model named Bo Derek. A Ten on anyone's scale." She went over to the DVD/VHS player. "Coincidentally, I have a copy. All cued up and ready to go."

The young girl's laugh was transparently genuine.as the flat TV screen flickered into sex goddess life. The movie was in Technicolor and stereophonic sound. The music was... familiar.

Claire was charmingly helpful. "In those days, making love to Bolero was sort of expected," she said, smiling. "I did it a lot back then, and I still like to do it now." She cupped Leeza's chin in one hand and bent to give her a loving kiss. The girl was still flying from the flogging. Her lips were warm and welcoming. When they finally broke apart, she said: "You do know, dearest Claire, that I have a few minor hang-ups. I mean, I'm probably no more than a 9.5 on the Richter scale.'

"Fortuitously," said Claire. "I'm a very understanding and imaginative woman."

They kissed again. They were both quite high, basking in the afterglow of a splendidly successful scene. Claire got in the last word. "Back in the day," she said, with a lovely smile. "We would have called this a double feature."

Leeza's initiation was nearing its inevitable climax.

Chapter 10 Come to the Stables

Avalon Stables was rural Ontario at its best. It was the peacefully bustling place that Frances Dickie called home. Peaceful and bustling at the same time, like Francis himself.

The Major, as most folk called him, was a short, serious if sometimes blustery ex-military man in his mid-forties, usually clumping around in highly polished riding boots and a hacking jacket. These days his character veered wildly between comparatively tranquil and ferociously apoplectic. Not so long ago he had been a skilful mediator, serving honourably with the United Nations in Egypt, Bosnia and Croatia.

Francis had grown up at Avalon Acres, as his grandfather the Colonel had named it. It was his safe place and also his dream. He had followed his family tradition into the Royal Military College in Kingston, and returned to the Acres after his accident in the Mid-East.

"I missed the camel but upended the goddamned truck," he would say as partial explanation for his medical discharge. "Made me inclined to go off half-cock, not ideal in a mediator. Have to watch my blasted temper." What he didn't say was that it was largely out of his control.

The stable grounds were neat and orderly, again like Francis. They were surrounded by lush green paddocks and pastures and a good mile-and-a-half of freshly painted white 1"x4" fence. There were mares and stallions and frisky foals cavorting around in their own enclosures. Tidily trimmed hedges and bushes flanked the private road snaking in from the Western hills. There were two large red and white painted barns, with stalls for thirty five horses along with a small training track and two circular trotting pens. Avalon Acres was everything a racing stable should be. A picturesque landscape by Stubbs, horses and all.

An imposing, tastefully restored, yellow brick Victorian farmhouse stood to the south of the white-gated entrance. It had an ultra-modern gleaming green metal roof. The Major was practical like that. Opposite, and still under construction, was a low, sprawling building set up with live-in rooms for the grooms and stable workers. Avalon was a business as well as a heaven on earth.

Francis was having none of it right now. "Goddamn it all to hell, girl," he was yelling at his junior groom/hotwalker, Wendy. "I've told you a hundred times never to show Lady Barbara the whip. She don't like it. I don't like it." He stamped his foot, red-faced and on edge. It wasn't a tantrum but it was close.

"She associates it with the Fort Erie race-track," chipped in Matt to the terrified young girl. "Turko used it on her from the get-go."

"Which is why he'll never ride for the Acres again," said the Major darkly. "Like you, my girl, if you don't smarten up!"

"No real harm done, Major," Matt said calmly. He was standing by Lady Barbara's elegant head, gently smoothing her soft neck. Now he turned his back on Francis and talked softly to the trembling mare, whispering almost.

Francis was aware he had overreacted. "Don't mind me, girl. It's the horse I'm thinking of." He moved closer to Matt. "It's summer, for God's sake. We're still foaling."

Matt didn't stop stroking the mare, but he grinned at the Major over his shoulder. "You can blame your precious RogueMeister for that. Jumped the fence in November he did."

"Somebody should have seen him," Francis said petulantly. He started over to the house, then looked back at Matt. "Send Madame Claire on up when she arrives. You know her, right?"

"My next door neighbour," said Matt

The Major grunted. "A smart woman. I need her advice." He strode off.

Matt had a word of consolation for the young hot walker. "Francis has something eating at him," he said to her. "His bark is worse than his bite, kid." He gave her a kindly smile. "Don't even show her the whip. In fact, give it to me. I have an idea."

He held the racing whip a couple of feet in front of Lady Barbara's muzzle. "We won't need this no more," he said, softly. "Never again." Using a fair degree of controlled strength he bent the vinyl braided rod into a tight "O" till the slapper touched the rubber flange. "Watch it, old girl. Keep your eyes on it. You'll never be struck again. This little bugger is going, going, gone." And he lobbed it twenty yards away into the bushes.

Lady Barbara tossed her head and whinnied.

"Think that'll work, boss?" asked Wendy. The eighteen year old was only a few years younger than Matt, but deferred to him willingly. Matt was a natural leader. "Could be expensive if it don't," he grinned. "Ah, here's Lohengrin now."

"Huh?" Wendy quizzed him.

Matt laughed. "Long story," he said. "Take Lady B. into her stall and rub her down. Keep telling her how fast she can run. Makes a hole in the wind, she does."

He strolled over to the parking lot as Madame Claire's vintage BMW drew to stop by the flagpole. The huge Maple Leaf flag stirred lazily in the hot summer sky.

"This place is idyllic," Claire said admiringly.

"Tell that to the Major. He's running on empty."

She was looking suitably idyllic herself in a cool khaki dress with a leopard collar. "What does he want with me, do you know?"

"Something about advice and a job, I gather. Didn't say what."

He stopped in his tracks and pointed to the paddocks. "Thought you might like to know, horses have a definite pecking order. Only the Rogue gets to stand in the shade of that tree if that's what he wants."

Claire had a fair idea what he was driving at. "Dominant and submissive, in my terms," she said, smiling.

"If it's raining RogueMeister would let them all get soaked before he'd allow them in undercover." He grinned. "Utterly hierarchal, too. 1, 2,3,4,5 and so on. Is that the same in your BDSM?" He accompanied her to the dark green front door of the renovated farmhouse. "I got work to do. I'm trying to convince Lady Barbara that she won't get whipped every time she hits the track. Have a good meeting."

He had known her since boyhood. They were good friends.

*

Her meeting with Francis took place in the high, glassed-in sunroom built on the southern facing of the original farmhouse. The Conservatory, as Francis referred to it. He was formal like that.

"You've never been here in the summer," he said, relaxed in her presence. "This is my favourite room. I have a great view over the mare's pasture."

"It's truly lovely," she responded. "And the setting is absolutely stunning. Those stands of silver birch and pine around the perimeter make it a world unto its own." She sat on a white leather sofa near the sliding doors to the front garden. There were two white sofas in the room, very stylish and fashionable. "You're still foaling, I see."

Francis gave her a rueful grin. "Young Matt would tell you it was all RogueMeister's doing. Covered four mares before we caught on. Very potent the Rogue. Should make a fortune at stud."

"What did you want to see me about, Francis?"

He didn't beat around the bush. "I have another case for you. Not as public as the Butazolin scandal. But sleazy enough to have me good and pissed. Pardon my French."

"I take it the steam rising from your ears means you're ready to explode," she observed calmly."

He scowled. "You know my moods too well, Madame Claire," he said. "I'm trying to learn more control." He finished his late afternoon single malt. "Some filly calling herself TallBlondeChick is threatening to Out me. In writing, of course."

"TallBlondeChick?"

"I see you've never run into her either. I checked her out on Kinklife.ca. A real nothing profile." He was looking hot and bothered.

Claire held up a hand and stopped him before he could go on. "What's this all about, Francis?" she asked.

"Blackmail," he said, gloomily.

He hauled himself to his feet and paced the floor. "She threatens me about the Black Wally and the Lifestyle," he informed her angrily. "Not exactly kosher in Jockey Club circles." His expression went a touch sheepish. "She knows about Desmond and me, I'm afraid. Our nefarious sexual pursuits, as she puts it. Des is a teacher if you recall. Dedicated. He's off to a convention this weekend."

There was a discreet tap on the main door from the house. "Come!" said Francis peremptorily. He seemed grateful for the interruption.

A stern-faced, middle-aged woman entered with a silver tray of tea things. Flowered teapot, sugar bowl and tongs, cream and milk. "Earl Grey like you ask, Major," she said in a heavily accented voice.

"Mrs. Gretsko, my housekeeper," Francis said to Claire. "I like to have afternoon tea for my guests. Seems civilised. Madame Claire will be working for me," he added to Mrs. Gretsko.

Claire didn't know the housekeeper but knew of her. "Hello, Mrs. Gretsko," she said civilly. "How's Dawn?"

The woman's face went totally expressionless. "Donja getting better, thank you. She work one day then I keep her home all week. Back at Mac's Milk soon."

"She didn't look too good when I last saw her. Please wish her well from me."

The housekeeper nodded stiffly and left without another word.

"You know her?" asked Francis.

Claire shook her head. "Her daughter Dawn works at my local convenience store. She's been off work for a few days. I believe she was assaulted."

"She never mentioned it," he said.

"In denial, I think." Claire commented.

Francis had sat down again and was pouring the tea. His hand was trembling slightly.

"How's the neuroplasticity coming along?" Claire asked, allowing him to see her concern.

"You were right, Madame Claire," he said with some verve. "The brain isn't a machine, it can fix itself. When I get the exercises down, the tantrums and panic will be a thing of the past." He added two lumps of sugar to his Earl Grey. "And you know what makes it possible? Desmond. He laughs at my antics and says I'm playing the Avalon squire."

"You do dress the part," Claire joked.

Francis gazed at her seriously. "You and I go way back, Claire," he said. "When I was up shit's creek with the Butazolin, you laid your finger right on Crawford Tucker."

He was referring to the time some years earlier when his mare Lady Marybourne had come in by six lengths at the Fort Erie Futurity. Only to be disqualified for too much phenylbutazone, the pharmaceutical name, in her system. An anti-inflammatory, not dope, but sticky enough to have cost him his racing license.

There had only been five possible suspects who could have administered it, with himself at the head. The others were a groom, the stable manager, a trainer and his regular veterinarian. Francis was desperate and Claire had talked him into hiring her. He knew about her detective sideline from an embezzlement case she had solved for the Community.

"With this TallBlonde bitch, I'm more concerned for Desmond than myself. He's not as strong as he could be. I don't know yet if he got the same email I did. He'll be over soon on his way to

Toronto. I'll know even before I see him." He smiled to himself. Des always made a grand entry when he came to Avalon Acres.

He passed her a sheet of paper. "This is a hard copy of the blackmail letter. Sent two days ago. She's a mean bitch, this TallBlonde. Revelling in her own cleverness, I think."

Claire put on her reading glasses and started to read aloud. *"From TallBlondeChick69. Subject: Request for Assistance."*

Francis grunted indignantly. "I'd give her assistance with a horsewhip."

"It doesn't have to be a her," Claire pointed out. "With a nick like TallBlondeChick69, it's just as likely to be a short, bald, dirty-minded man."

"Whoever it is, chose that font deliberately. It's reeks of blackmail."

Madame Claire smiled thinly. "Bastard knows their way around computers. Cuts out maybe forty percent of the population."

She read the email: -

"It has come to our attention that you do not wish to be Outed as an active member of the Black Wally BDSM Munch.

"Not to mention your nefarious extra-curricular pursuits. Of course, whom you sleep with, and in what unhygienic configuration, is entirely your own affair.

"Unfortunately, divergent sex is always of intense interest to others. We are a notoriously curious species."

Francis interrupted again. He was almost blushing. "That hits close to home. Des teaches biology. In the Catholic school system."

Claire continued: -

"We are the BDSM League of Investigatory and Collection Evidence. Our appointed task is to ensure that this information never becomes public knowledge.

"To assist us in this invaluable work we humbly solicit a voluntary Donation of $225, to cover office and legal fees."

"Hah!" snorted Francis.

"Too clever by half," said Claire. "I'm not even sure you could prove it's blackmail."

She finished reading the email.

"Please forward cash or money order made out to cash to Box 147, c/o Siebert Hotel, Kitchener, N2M 1C4.

"Kindly govern yourself intelligently. This is strictly a one-time appeal for donations. Non-compliance could have dire consequences for your lifestyle.

"P.S. No receipts will be issued."

Claire pursed her lips. "I guess that underscores the blackmail, and it could go to anyone at the Munch. TallBlonde69 could have got your nick off the name tags we put on. OddsOnFavourite, right on your breast pocket."

"It would be an idle threat to someone like Bertie or you. You guys have been out as long as I've known you. But many of our friends might think $225 a small price to pay for privacy."

"That's just the opening salvo," Claire said, depressingly. "Blackmail is an attempt to use private information about someone to pry something out of them, usually large sums of money. It's a particularly serious crime. It's called 'murder of the soul.'"

Francis nodded grimly. "Psychological rape," he said. "I know I feel violated. Vulnerable and bloody angry."

"You have to watch that, Francis. Do your neuroplasticity exercises regularly."

He looked lost for a moment. "Des helps me with those," he said. "And I gathered you're hooked, on the blackmail case I mean." His brows furrowed. "So how do you go about solving this?"

Claire smiled. "Very methodically," she said. "I conjure up a banker's box in my head and fill it with blank files. Then I name them. The idea is to break the puzzle down into separate pieces."

He nodded. "File Number One, the blackmailing email..."

"Legitimate starting place. Content, style, syntax, even font and spelling. What does it tell us? File Number Two, TallBlondeChickorChap. Does anyone know her, know of her, or him. Number Three, Box 147, Siebert Hotel. Number Four, any other blackmailees?" She shrugged. "You get the idea."

"Number Five, Further Demands."

"I suspect there are other victims. A lowballing $225 makes it a standard scattergun approach. Anyone who pays up can expect a second request. For a much more serious amount."

He felt he should make one thing quite clear. "I daren't get the cops involved. It would make the Times-Dispatch."

Claire laughed. "That Angele Del Zotto has sources coming out of her ears."

There was a rap at the sunroom screen door and Matt stuck his head in. "Desdemona will be foaling tonight, Francis" he announced. "And your Des fella is driving in." A few bars of Tchaikovsky's 1812 floated in. Desmond had a musical car horn. "Guess I didn't need to tell you that. Sorry." He popped his head out again.

Francis' whole face lit up. "Des isn't fretting about the blackmailer," he said to Claire, beaming. "He sounds that overture whenever he drops by. Half the stable perks up. They know sugar is coming."

"You as well, I see," Claire teased him.

He grinned sheepishly. "He makes my life worth living," he said, anticipation written all over him.

"And fun," she noted, knowing how genuinely close they were. "My filing system gives me the chance to focus on one piece at a time. For instance, going home and getting Leeza started on real-time folders."

He held the door for her. "I'll see you to your car. Des will be working the stables for a while. He's remarkably tactile with horses."

"And not just horses," she said as they reached the parking lot and she completed their business arrangements. "Same terms as for the Butadolin then. But double the fee when we catch her. Or him."

"I'm glad Des hasn't seen the email," he said. "I'll leave it that way. He deserves a good weekend at the convention."

Matt came out of the stables. "Not staying for the big foaling event, Madame Claire?"

"She has things to do, lad," said Francis. He couldn't wait to go into the stables to see Desmond. "And maybe Des would like to stay for a while. Something to tell his students." He nodded to Claire and vanished briskly inside.

"The Major is in danger of being Outed for BDSM," she told Matt. "A nasty business.

"He's been super-irritable for a coupla' days."

"That accident in Egypt makes him highly emotional. Impulsive."

"Fires me regularly. Don't mean anything."

Claire looked at him thoughtfully. "Do me a favour and keep an eye on him, will you. Any sudden swing in mood or behaviour. I'll scope out the source of the extortion but I don't want to lose him in the process."

She got into the BMW. "Keep me posted, Matt" she said earnestly. "He's a decent man, your squire of Avalon Acres."

*

It was much later that night that the foaling really got underway. Desdemona had stopped pacing back and forth in the double stall and found a comfortable place to lie on her side, a thick bed of straw beneath her.

Des had been congenitally unable to pull himself away. He had packed early that morning, with every intention to stop in briefly at the stables on his way to the teacher's convention. Now, he was fascinated by the whole foaling process. "I rap about biology all day," he said. "Here you've given me a front row seat."

Matt had set up folding Maple Leaf canvas chairs across the front of the double foaling stall. Francis and Des were like kids at a school picnic. Desmond's eyes were wide and bright as he clutched Francis' hand from time to time.

"Do we need the vet, Frankie?" he asked anxiously.

"Matt?" prompted Francis.

Matt was washing off Desdemona's swollen udder. "No complications, I can see," he said confidently. "Her waters broke just fine."

Francis was more specific. "The allantodorion ruptured very cleanly," he said to Desmond, knowing that the teacher in him would appreciate the correct terms. "All that fluid looks a lot like urine, which it is primarily. The amniotic sac should show any minute now."

He broke off the technical terms with a slightly bashful smile and patted Desmond's arm. They were a bit of an odd couple at first glance. Francis, older and usually more serious. Des, youthful for his age and filled with boyish enthusiasm.

"If I'd filmed it, I could feature it in class," he said.

Francis was amused. "Probably gross out half the boys. And I have to say, Des, having you in on the birth means this foal will be real special. A Queen's Plate winner for sure."

Desmond laughed, pleased at the comment but a little shy. "I doubt my presence would accomplish that."

"Horses are incredibly intuitive," Matt said to him. "Believe me, Des, they can feel the love."

"Me, too," Francis said, lightly touching Desmond's shoulder. He drew attention to the mare's vagina. "And, look, there's the first tiny hoof now. In that white sac."

Foals lie upside down in their mother's womb, but turn when contractions set in. Now the foal was lying upright, with narrow head and long foreleg extended. The white amniotic membrane was still intact, protruding, enclosing the feet. The first hoof was soon followed by a second.

"This little bugger is right on schedule. They're usually born between 11:00 pm and 5:00 am," Francis said, for Desmond's benefit. He had profound satisfaction in his voice. "Horses are flight animals, of course. In the wild, the foals have three hours or so before dawn, when the predators come out. Their lanky legs give them a chance to keep up with Mom."

"There's the muzzle." said Desmond excitedly.

"The entire head will be next. Long and thin." Francis informed him. "The amniotic sac stays intact as long as possible. It adds gravity to Desdemona's pushes."

"I want to rush in and help her," Des said, a little shaky.

"It's a natural process. If there are no complications even Matt stays out of the way."

"Not a sign of any dystocia," Matt said, winking at Francis. "Malpresentation," he explained to Desmond.

Desdemona gave another great push and the foal's shoulders and chest squeezed out. There was a textbook rupturing of the white membrane. With his little chest free, the lungs could start to fill with air.

"It's breathing," said Des, quite hushed.

"Welcome to our world, little fella," said Francis, who had determined his sex. "You're going to be a champion."

Desdemona had given a powerful final heave and the foal was lying on the flattened straw. It was a little black colt. There was a white blaze running diagonally down his face. It gave him a saucy, almost smart-alecky look.

Matt clamped the umbilical cord and disinfected the colt's navel. He dried him off and gave him a tetanus shot.

He's beautiful, "said Desmond, marvelling.

"Desdemona's Dancer," Francis said happily.

"Is that his name?"

"We have to submit three choices to the Jockey Club Registrar. Des's Dancer will be first on the list." He gripped Desmond's hand. "Lookit, he's trying to get to his feet."

"This is where we find out how determined he is," Matt put in. "Anything close to ten minutes and he'll definitely be the boss's champ."

The colt's spindly legs were already two-thirds their adult length, so that he could gallop beside his mother. He thrust his front legs in front of him, so that he was perched on his haunches.

"They're like stilts," Desmond worried, hanging on to Francis.

The black colt got his rear end halfway up and promptly fell face down in the bed of straw.

"Can we help him?" Desmond wanted to know eagerly.

Matt looked at Francis, who nodded. "One hand only," he cautioned. "Steady him. Don't actually push him."

Desdemona had clambered to her feet and was nuzzling and gently licking the colt. She made no objection as Desmond put a hand under his small rear. He blinked and tried standing again. Only to immediately flop back on the straw. Twice.

"He's a game little beggar," said Matt admiringly.

Francis let his pride show. "A champion to be," he said, his eyes glistening.

The newborn black colt gave a final burst of energy and somehow tottered to his feet. He wobbled a bit and almost fell again. Then, miraculously, he righted himself and took a half step forward. His nose twitched. He threw up his head and let out a first masterful whinny.

Francis and Matt shook hands, beaming with success. Des joined in and Francis enfolded him in a great big hug. "You helped put him on his feet, Des," he said.

Matt grinned at the two of them embracing. He was pleased as Punch about the colt and relieved to see Francis looking so relaxed and happy.

"You get on home, lad," the Major instructed him. "You've had another long day. Des and I will finish up here"

"Desdemona has milk to spare," Matt said, and added a congratulatory word to Desmond. "You have a natural rapport with horses, Des. They respect you."

Desmond flushed with pleasure. You too, man."

Matt cheekily touched his forehead to Francis. "G'night, sir," he said. "Feel free to do anything I wouldn't do."

"Outa here!" Francis said with a playful scowl, and Matt left.

"He's not gay, is he?" asked Desmond.

"Not our Matt," answered Francis.

Des cuddled up to him. "I am," he said lightly, reaching out and fondling Francis' breast. Even through the white shirt he could feel the nipple stiffen.

"Me, too," said Francis, almost in a groan.

"It's the neuroplasticity," Des teased him. "If I touch you down here your body knows how to behave." His long, supple fingers closed around Francis' penis.

There was another triumphant whinny from the double stall. Desdemona's Dancer had followed his instincts and was beginning to nurse. The milk ran down his muzzle.

Des went down on one knee and wet his lips. "I want you so much," he said softly.

It was all perfectly, wonderfully natural.

Chapter 11 The Human Canvas

The Pet Shoppe in eastern Stratford was dark. It was well off the main drag, the street deserted at this time of a Wednesday evening. It was way after hours. Richard's red Mustang was parked a block away. Richard himself had morphed into Henry, or Hank, one of his more violent alter egos... He had jimmied the lock on the stock room door out back. It was a piece of cake for Henry. He had broken into all sorts of businesses in his time. He could have picked the lock, but that wouldn't have been half as satisfying. Besides, it was half hidden behind a jumbled pile of crates and an open, smelly dumpster, reeking of animal waste.

Henry always gave the impression of being stockier than Richard. More solidly built, his muscular arms slightly curving away from his body. He had on gold aviator glasses; his hair in a short pony tail extending just below a clean white BlueJays baseball cap. He was wearing a plain white cotton shirt under an open fawn bomber jacket. The jacket concealed a short, razor-sharp knife in a sheath on his belt. At a guess he was in his late twenties. Polite at first meeting, rather unsophisticated, Not exactly a red neck, but very much a Dom, courteous enough when he wanted to be but automatically expecting to be in charge.

The young woman with him was tall and almost painfully thin. 172 centimetres, 5'11 in Oldspeak, as he put it. 129 lbs, but he couldn't recall the French terms for that. Her nick on Kinklife.ca was Nymphette32. The numeral allowed as many Nymphettes to sign up as used the name as a desirable alias.

Her everyday name was Carol Weber, with one b. Richard, now Henry or Hank, had learned that little factoid over a second coffee at the Tim Hortons. He was good at eliciting information from highly-strung, nervous women. Carol was a naturally suspicious person and he had decided against introducing Myra as his friend and chaperone. With his customary foresight he had earlier made alternative arrangements with his newly co-opted assistant, his resident tattoo artiste, as he called her these days. His "Pet" tattooist for a fun evening at the Stratford Pet Shoppe.

He politely held the door open for Nymphette. She was wearing a knee length black skirt, a light summer blouse and a short, faded-green Pet Shoppe apron under a smart, pinstriped business jacket, fully buttoned up. “This way, please Ms. Weber,” he said quite formally, playing to her professional appearance and shining a flashlight around the small stock room. He had deliberately left the outside door very slightly ajar. “Would you like me to hang up your jacket now?” She hesitated. “I...suppose so. Yes, of course,” she added brusquely. The apron had a cute retail slogan emblazoned on the front in white lettering - “Two Kitties and a Pup, please.” There was a badge on the apron, Assistant Manager.

“I like that, Carol,” he commented with an open, reassuring smile. “Was the apron yours?” “A long time ago,” she acknowledged stiffly. Then, striving for more normal conversation in a most abnormal setting - “It was my stepfather’s idea to put customers in the right mood. It actually worked occasionally”

Inside the Pet Shoppe, kennelled at the back of the store, one of the four dogs, the German shepherd, was growling with a note of controlled menace. Another dog, a pint-sized Shih Tzu, was whimpering quietly.

‘Henry’ took a Shopper’s Drugmart sleep mask out of his pocket. “We should put this on you now,” he said with another helpful smile. “Like I told you in Timmie’s, it will make everything seem more realistic. We need your imagination fully involved.”

Carol looked carefully into his eyes. He seemed perfectly calm and guileless. “I suppose you’re right,” she admitted, crossing another boundary. “Not too tight, Henry. Please.”

“Not tight at all,” he agreed equably, “And my friends call me Hank, remember?” With a well-practiced hand he covered her eyes and slipped the elasticized blindfold over her ears. “Is that comfortable?” At her last glimpse of him he was smiling reassuringly. 'He seems to be such a pleasant and thoughtful man for a Dom,' she told herself encouragingly. Maybe too pleasant for what they had in mind, for the evening she had imagined for years. He had been so attentive in the coffee shop when her taut nerves had caused too big a sip to go down the wrong way. Seemingly, genuinely concerned, handing her a napkin, lightly patting her back.

Carol was an account executive in training at the TD Bank in Waterloo. Neat, precise, a fine example of a young woman determined to rise in the business world. Henry, she couldn't really call him Hank but she could understand that his mother would, had understood right away. "If anyone can crack the glass ceiling, you will," he had nodded, with just the right degree of support and admiration. "We've made such fantastic progress in women's rights," he enthused.

He had been much more blatant when filling in Myra before they even left the house. "Sounds like your typical feminist pig," he said, irately closing his private messages on the laptop. He loathed women who wound up in a position with power over him. "There was this shitty first lieutenant in Kandahar," he had told her. "Had me on a charge for trying to straighten her out about Moslem beliefs. I coulda killed her if some Taliban suicide bomber hadn't gotten there first."

Naturally Carol had picked up no signs of his true feelings for her and her "bitchy type." Her experience was with columns of figures and spread-sheets, not people, and certainly not men. Her sexual experience was even more limited. The men she knew were mainly on the same business path that she was, heads down and dedicated. She had another side, of course, she sometimes admitted to herself, always fighting off a feeling of guilt and shame. She had discovered in her teens that pain, and even a degree of humiliation, actually turned her on. She blamed her stepfather and found an outlet in BDSM. There was even a handy Munch in Stratford which she attended secretly once in a while. Besides, the Nymphette trait was only a small part of her. It didn't come out all that often, but was a needed escape from time to time. As Nymphette, she visualized herself as girlish and innocent, with long wavy hair and longer, amazingly sexy legs.

As she stood in the store stockroom, tense, more than a little nervous but excited as well, the blindfold accentuating her sense of sound, Carol could hear the soft hum and all too familiar rustle of the Pet Shoppe itself. The German shepherd, still growling his intimidating greeting. The hamsters run-run-running on their squeaking treadmill. A parrot, left uncovered by a lazy clerk, squawking 'Welcome, Welcome' over and over. A sleek ocelot stretching and preening. Two Capuchin monkeys, one grooming the other. Memories of a childhood past but never forgotten.

Behind her, outside in the looming dark, Myra dutifully finished counting to two hundred and stepped silently out of the narrow alley between the Stratford Pet Shoppe and its closed, boarded-up neighbour the Acme Discount Shoe Emporium. The shoe store had gone out of business five months before, a victim of the slow Recovery from the recent Recession. Calmly, without hesitation she quietly pushed the stockroom exterior door partly open and entered, carefully closing the door behind her, silent as the grave. She had a small flashlight in one hand and an Osprey daypack over her left shoulder. In it, a length of yellow rope and her tattoo kit with an extra electrical extension. Just in case, her Master had said.

It was all arranged.

And the German shepherd's growl grew to a bark....

*

Suddenly, unexpectedly, Carol felt his hands grab her hair. Not too hard. She sensed that he had slipped off his jacket and rolled up his sleeves. But he still seemed reasonably civilised. "Lie down on this pallet of dog food," he ordered her, his voice deeper, sterner. "Give me your wrists."

He seized hold of her wrists and jerked her arms roughly above her head. "Around this iron post. Do it now. NOW!"

Carol tried to pull her arms free. "What are you going to do?" She had half expected something forceful like this, it went with the territory. She felt nervous, but not yet seriously frightened.

Without being asked, Myra had silently taken the length of cord-like poly propylene rope from her Osprey. With a nod he snatched it from her and swiftly whipped it once, twice, around Carol's wrists and tied them to the cold iron.

"NO!" she said angrily. "I specifically said no rope. We negotiated no rope!"

His voice was much coarser now. "You negotiated, bitch! I just went along for the ride." He pulled the polypropylene right around her elbows and back across her shoulders and down over her breasts.

"This isn't right," she cried out, beginning to panic. "Henry, I don't consent to any of this. No tying up I said."

"I don't give a fuck what you consent to. I'm gonna give you what you really want."

"Not like this!" she yelled, filled with foreboding and growing dread.

In the store the dogs whimpered. The Alsatian's bark deepened. The Capuchin chattered volubly to its female companion.

"You're disturbing the animals," he snapped, tightening his slip knots viciously. "Can't have that." He reached into his pocket and thrust a large, hard green apple into her mouth, pinching her nostrils and forcing her teeth wide apart. 'This is what you asked for, right?" He sounded way less civilised now. Henry was not a nice man. "Taken forcibly in the back of a pet store, isn't that what you want? So lie back and fucking enjoy it."

The young woman struggled to talk, to breathe, to break the tightening bonds. “Did I ask why?" he demanded. "I did not! I arranged it, without any argument” Roughly he pulled her legs apart and fastened her ankles to the pallet, ignoring her desperate attempt to kick out at him. “Just like the doctor ordered!” It was a favourite expression of his. It went all the way back to his last days in Afghanistan and the ball-busting 2nd looey who had inflamed his deep-seated hatred of bossy women.

Carol tossed her head violently from side to side, trying frantically to form words. “And another thing,” he went on, his voice dripping scorn and outright hatred. “I’m not Hank no more. Not that you hardly ever got your tongue around it. So from here on in you can always think of me as Henry. More of a Dom’s name, doncha know. A Master’s name.”

He leaned right into her face, spitting out his words. "Henry, Ms. High and Mighty banker bitch. Ms. Nymphette! Little Nymph, eh? The hell you are. You're one great gangling bony spinster is what you are. So Henry it is, lady. Get Hank right outa your head and we can get this motherfucking show on the road."

Myra's mouth was half open, her eyes wide and staring in growing shock. The dogs too appeared to know something was wrong. The shepherd's fur was up. The Shih Tzu was yapping aggressively. "Goddam those animals," he bellowed, before looming back over Carol and draping a noose of yellow rope around her neck. "Your old man ran the pet shop, did he? Laid into you right here in the stock room I bet. You shoulda been grateful."

He slid his knife from the sheath at his waist and slowly, deliberately, sliced the apron strings, chuckling at the irony of the action. "And you don't need this no more. Or this." He cut the skirt from around her and pulled it free. Then grabbed the light summer blouse and ripped at it fiercely, disdaining the knife.

The young woman wriggled and squirmed trying to get free, trying to scrape the blindfold off against the bags of dog food. "Lie still, you skinny broad," he grunted. "There!" The blouse ripped and fell to her sides. Tears welled from under the blindfold and ran down her cheeks into the ¼ inch yellow rope around her neck. Saliva slobbered from under the apple in her mouth, tinged with the red of her blood.

"Christ, you're a filthy bitch, ain't you," he snorted churlishly, "And look at these stupid panties, long black fingers crawling on them." Carol had bought them at the Stag Shop especially for tonight's very special scene. She had thought they summed up what she was expecting. Was still expecting, though with great growing fear now, all guilty relish and anticipation long gone. He stabbed a finger under the elastic waistband and jerked hard. "Time to get down to business."

He tore the panties down, cutting them and leaving them around one knee. "You could have shaved closer," he sneered, "Or were you waiting for me to do it." He flicked her short dark pubic hair with the tip of his knife. “And are you scared yet, Carol baby?” he asked in an almost friendly tone of voice. “Most women would be pissing theirselves by now. Thinking about what’s to come.”

He laughed, stroking her between the legs with his knife. “You didn’t have to leave Tim Hortons with me,” he crowed “You could have said no thanks and gone safely home. But you didn’t, did you? You stupid hussy. You wanted it then. So how’s about now? Are you ready for the real action? The piece de resistance?”

At his back, Myra gave a short, sharp intake of breath and mechanically took a step closer... Her eyes were bulging behind the glasses he had allowed her to wear. She was having a hot flash, sweating all over. Wet… The dogs in the store could feel her excitement. Smell it.

“Shut the fuck up out there,” he shouted furiously. “Goddamned Pet Shoppe is like a fucking zoo!” He stopped, panting, pulling himself together, and remembering the task at hand. “And lookee here,” he said directly to Myra, using his knife as a pointer. “A real life human canvas.” He ran the knife sensuously down Carol's flanks, over her pert breasts, still covered by her bra. “It’s like the old song ain’t it?” As a convulsive shudder ran through Carol’s straining body he launched unexpectedly into a sudden, deep baritone. “Who could ask for anything mo-ore....? Who could ask for anything MORE?”

He grinned at Myra, his lips bared over his teeth. “Carol could, that’s who.” In a quick motion he cut the bra from her breasts. “And look at those titties, will you? Are your nipples always this hard?” He glanced momentarily back at Myra. “Look great with big pink forget-me-nots tattooed all around them, wouldn’t they?” Then he traced a knifepoint circle round a nipple, leaving a thin red line on deathly white skin “You like my knife on your flesh, Nymphette sweetie?” he demanded savagely. Or maybe a quick bite on this left tittie" He bit down hard, leaving teethmarks. “Or my favourite tool.” He opened his zip fastener and pulled out his hardening cock. “This one…!” He slapped her face with it, lifting it up and letting it fall, slap, slap, across her nose and upper lip.

Myra gave a sudden nervous laugh. She was almost enjoying herself, this time. It didn't seem real somehow. And this time she had a part to play. She slipped the daypack from her shoulder and took out the small green tackle box. It had pictures of tattoos stencilled all over it the lid. "Now?" she mouthed, licking her lips.

He shook his head. "Me first," he said and positioned himself between Carol's outstretched legs.

A horrible groan escaped from the young woman. "Nah," she shrieked, biting down harder than she had ever bitten in her whole life, chomping her teeth right through the apple core and spitting the pieces from her aching mouth. "No! No!" she screamed, spraying pieces of apple and gobs of spittle and blood all over his face "NO!"

Her terror was palpable. It permeated the whole store. The dogs could feel it. All the animals could sense it. Something was terribly wrong. They barked. They howled. All hell broke loose.

"Goddamn you, you cocksucker!" yelled Henry, punching her chin hard and grabbing her throat in a fit of absolute rage. "You fucking cunt!"

The uproar in the store grew. Carol passed out, rendered unconscious by his fierce blows...

Myra grabbed his arm with all her strength. "No, Master, you'll kill her!" she hissed. "YOU'LL KILL HER!"

He stared wildly at her without seeing. "Stop," she said brokenly. "Please stop."

His grip slackened. He looked down at the bloodied woman beneath him. Some sense and identity returned to his eyes.

"Get your things," he said slowly. "We've got to get outa here. NOW!"

"GET OUTA HERE" screeched the parrot "NOW, NOW. NOW!"

The German Shepherd's harsh bark turned to a whine. It moaned, like a human in pain.

*

It was, Richard said later, on the otherwise silent drive home, as close to a disaster as anything he had seen since Afghanistan. He had tossed the white ball cap in a dumpster behind the Pet Shoppe and discarded the jacket in the back of his Mustang. He wanted no reminders.

Myra was terribly worried. About Carol and about Richard and his alternate identity, Henry. He seemed to be lacking in any real empathy. He had no sense of core values. He was too sure of his own cleverness to seek out advice. The watchwords safe, sane and consensual meant nothing to him. They were just words other people used. The bureaucracy of BDSM as she recalled him saying. He was too sure of his own instinctive knowledge. And he had one major flaw.....Henry had never learned how to play

"It was that filthy rotten Stratford," he said later, much later. "I'll never go to that goddamned town again."

He never did. Not as Richard. Not as Henry. Not as any other of his many roles.

Henry never came out again

Chapter 12 Rapist on the Loose

Kitchener-Waterloo Times Dispatch

BRUTAL RAPIST ON THE LOOSE

New Hamburg Resident Cruelly Raped and Beaten

by Angele Del Zotto, roving reporter

A savage sexual assault took place after hours in the rear stockroom of the Weber Pet Shoppe in Stratford Friday night. Police have not officially released the name of the unfortunate victim, but this reporter learned from a Memorial Hospital admitting nurse that her name is Carol Weber, 27, a bank clerk, resident of New Hamburg.

Ms. Weber's jaw was broken in three places. She had been agonizingly restrained by a 25 foot length of polypropylene rope, recovered at the scene. It is understood from medical authorities that a skinning knife was wielded in the cowardly attack.

According to Ontario Provincial Police detective Horatio "Stuff" Bellingham, the victim was admitted to hospital late Friday evening. Emergency ward sources say she is suffering from acute traumatic shock and extensive and painful cuts and bruises. "It is clear my daughter was in mortal fear of her life," said her mother, Agnes Weber of Perth Street, Shakespeare.

ONTARIO PART OF ALARMING RAPE CULTURE

Waterloo University sociologist Natalie Grumbach says that North America has fostered a rape culture that is every bit as dangerous to young women as the patriarchal societies of the Middle and Far East.

Grumbach maintains that the widespread marketing of blatantly pornographic mainstream movies and music lyrics, and of sexist TV programs, internet jokes, twerking and virtually nude fashionistas, have combined to objectify women and reduce the female body to a dollar-store commodity.

According to radical feminists like Andrea Dworkin or Catherine McKinnon all males are potential rapists and all women are victimised. Dworkin is famed for her statement that any young woman who does not see the penis as a "symbol of terror" must have been brainwashed by misogynist culture. She has long opined that men are sexual predators separated from women by their commitment to do violence rather than be victimised by it.

THE TORONTO SLUTWALK PHENOMENON

The Waterloo Adjunct Professor says that Slut-Shaming, or victim-shaming, is an inescapable corollary of a ghastly sexual assault like that at the Weber Pet Shoppe. The availability of 'attack media' Facebook and Twitter provide the anonymity of source, she says. Youthful suicides result. She mentions Rehtaeh Parsons, Andrie Pott, Amanda Todd, and others.

Dr. Grumbach pointed to the SlutWalk protest rallies, which began in Toronto in 2011 and quickly went global. The trigger was a Toronto police officer, Mike Sanguinetti, telling York University students that to remain safe 'women should avoid dressing like sluts.' A week later over 3,000 dedicated young women, many of them in 'reclaimed slut clothing,' picketed police headquarters on Jarvis Street.

'Students and young working women stuck the crude misogynistic put-down back in his face," she said. It was the most successful feminists protest since 'Take Back The Night' two decades earlier.

"LEGIMATE RAPE VICTIMS" DECRIED

Rape culture posits that most women want to be pushed around and driven slavishly into forced sex. It is seen as part of their ancestral heritage. At the same time, male sexual impulses and behaviours are considered to be uncontrollable and must be satisfied at any cost.

These rationalisations of evolutionary psychology are exemplified by former U.S. Republican Congressman Todd Akin. He is on record as arguing that "Most women are running around hoping some Neanderthaler will force his will on them. The very few who don't really want it are the 'legitimate rape victims,' he says.

Akin also professed to believe that 'If it's a legitimate rape, women don't become pregnant because the female body has ways to shut the whole thing down.'

'The whole idea of 'legitimate rape,' is puerile twaddle," says Waterloo University's Grumbach caustically.

WHO ARE THE RAPISTS?

According to sociological research, almost half of males under seventy admit that they would rape under the 'right' circumstances. Many more confess to coercive sexual fantasies. They believe that rape is a reproductive male strategy that may be used by any man.

Specific motivations for rape include: - Anger; A Desire For Power; Psychopathic Sadism; Sexual Opportunism; Sperm Competition; Evolutionary Proclivities.

“Rape," says the professor 'Is seen as a natural biological product of our human inheritance. The mutation from natural to unnatural has been a long time coming.

RAPE LEAST REPORTED, SAYS POLICE SPOKES-PERSON

Detective "Stuff" Bellingham, in charge of the East Stratford rape investigation says categorically that rape is the most under-reported violent crime in Canadian jurisprudence. It is estimated almost 90% of victims never report their rapes to the police.

Feminist literature confirms that one in four Canadian women will be sexually assaulted over their lifetimes.

Police statistics verify that 91% of Canadian rape victims are female while 99% of perpetrators are male. The 9% of male victims largely reside in jail, where rape is often viewed as collateral punishment.

RAPE IN WAR AND THE BIBLE

It is now officially a war crime, but throughout history abduction and rape of the losers is something all States and their armies have enjoyed. It is said that over one million Berliners were raped after the city fell to the Red Army in 1945. A year earlier, thousands of Frenchwomen in Normandy complained bitterly of rapes by supposedly allied American G.I.'s. 800,000 Rwandans, 30,000 Bosnians, 200,000 Congolese, annually, were among the millions of recent state sanctioned rapes.

In the Old Testament (Judges, Numbers, etc.) abduction and rape, which come from the same root word, are blessed by God. Regarding the defeated Midianites the prophet Moses said 'Kill all the boys and all the women who have slept with a man. Only the young girls who are virgins may live: you may keep them for yourselves.'

Clearly, Moses and God approved of the rape of virgins. 'You may enjoy the spoils of your enemies which the LORD thy God has given you.'

CHRISTIANITY AND MARITAL RAPE

Rape, according to Detective Bellingham, is now regarded as one of the most heinous of crimes. Yet the revered Thomas Aquinas, a leading Catholic theologian in the Middle Ages, argued that rape, though a sin, was far less sinful that masturbation or coitus interruptus since they violated the purpose of sex, procreation.

In Corinthians, the New Testament underscores that sex in marriage is a husband's 'right' that could be taken by force if 'denied.' Spousal rape is now largely illegal in the West, but its discordant melody lingers on in media rape culture.

In Andrea Dworkin's powerful words 'Marriage is an institution developed from rape as a practice. Rape, originally defined as abduction, became marriage by capture. Marriage meant the taking was to extend in time, to be not only use of but possession of, or ownership.'

CRIME AND PUNISHMENT

Under questioning, Detective Horatio Bellingham, lead investigator, stated that the unfortunate Stratford victim - identified by this reporter as New Hamburg's Carol Weber, 27 - will need to have her broken jaw wired together for six weeks or more. Her severe trauma will likely take years to resolve, if ever.

In antiquity, rape along with treason and murder, was a capital offence. In medieval England a rape victim might be accorded the privilege of gouging out the perpetrator's eyes and/or cutting off his testicles herself.

Police would, or could not confirm that a sadistic rapist is loose on our suburban streets. They do advise women to take special precautions until the monster at large is arrested. They still advised women not to dress 'provocatively.'

Professor Grumbach warned 'You can't tell a rapist by his eye colour. Any male, good-looking or ugly, friendly or rude, is a possible dangerous suspect. The important thing,' she emphasised, 'is to catch this bastard before he escalates his foul crimes to murder.'

Detective Bellingham appealed for public assistance, promising that any and all leads will be swiftly followed up. Contact OPP or Crimestoppers.

K-W Times Dispatch Angele Del Zotto, roving reporter (AngeleDZ.ca).

Chapter 13 Ask Mme Claire II

Transcript:

MUSIC: 'Ask Madame Claire' Theme - Teddy Bears Picnic

SOUND OVER: SLOWLY CHIMING CHURCH CLOCK

ANNCR: (DEEP VOICE) This is your friendly announcer, the Man in Black, bringing you our weekly internet radio program 'Ask Madame Claire.' The next 30 minutes are dedicated to kinksters already in the scene and interested parties who wish to learn more about BDSM. We are broadcasting from a secret studio in Niagara-On-The-Lake, Ontario, Canada.

SOUND: CLOCK FINISHES STROKE OF TWELVE.

MUSIC: FADE TO BG, THEN OUT

CLAIRE: Good evening friends and fellow travellers. I'm your host, Madame Claire. Tonight, we shall be interviewing two senior members of the Southwest Ontario BDSM community, Sir Robert and Lady Grace Challenger. For the past several years they have run twice monthly FatMan house parties for 40 or 45 guests at their Victorian home, Challenger Manse.

ANNCR: Listeners are welcome to ask Madame Claire and her guests any relevant questions. They will be discussing the transformative aspects of Predicament Bondage, transcendent as they call them. Our telephone number is 1-900-925-0000. 925, followed by four zeros.

CLAIRE: So, guys, it's taken me 3 years to persuade you to come on 'Ask Madame Claire.' Welcome at last.

SIR ROBERT: We've never actually promoted FatMan -

LADY GRACE: - Just said we're having an Open House. Drop by.

CLAIRE: Friday at the Manse, FatMan. Was it really a manse?

ROBERT: For the Unitarian church on the opposite side of the parking lot at the back of our property.

CLAIRE: Do the churchgoers know what you're into?

GRACE: Probably not. As Robert said, we don't advertise.

ROBERT: Shortly after we got involved in the Lifestyle we realised how difficult it is to find rentable play space. A Gorean Post or a St Andrew's Cross tend to make our vanilla friends rather skittish...

GRACE: With a little ingenuity we turned the manse into a drop-in and play-venue for friends. Free of charge, of course. Though we do accept donations. Candles and toilet paper mount up.

CLAIRE: I mentioned in my introduction that you qualify as senior members of the Community.

GRACE: Only in age, Claire. Robert is probably the oldest active BDSMer in Ontario. Mid-eighties if he's a day.

ROBERT: You've packed a lot of living into <u>your</u> sixty odd years, sweetheart. We just came to the Scene late. We're still learning.

CLAIRE: I understand you used to run a chain of toystores in Toronto.

ROBERT: Ottawa, London, Stratford, K-W, and so on... We covered Ontario almost as thoroughly as BDSM does now.

GRACE: Robert spent nearly 20 years as Mr. Gameways. Another name, another world...

CLAIRE: Then you retired and moved out of the big city to Waterloo Region.

ROBERT: More accurately the business went tits up and we left T.O. with a lot of questions and few answers.

CLAIRE: Which is when you finally clued in to BDSM.

ROBERT: First I had a bout of prostate cancer and the radiation therapy made me impotent.

GRACE: E.D. these days, darling.

ROBERT: No business. No hard-ons. It was about the lowest point of my life.

CLAIRE: And that's when you went to the Sex Show at the CNE grounds in Toronto and wound up in the Community Dungeon.

ROBERT: I don't know whether we discovered BDSM or BDSM discovered us. But I'll tell you one thing... It's been ten years and -

GRACE & ROBERT WHO HAVE DONE THIS BEFORE -- We haven't looked back since! No, sirree, Bob....

MUSIC: DRUM ROLL AS SPONSOR MUSIC FLOODS IN

ANNCR: At which dramatic point, we segue into a travelling message from tonight's first sponsor.

SOUND: VEHICLE BRAKES, WITH SEGUE TO SWISH OF CANE AND BODY CONTACT.

OPERATOR/DOMINATRIX; "Good evening, class. I am Mistress Khristina, owner and pedagogue of the Great Canadian Travelling Book, DVD and Cane Mobile."

SOUND: IMPACT OF CANE ON FLESH AND MOANS OF PAIN

DOMINATRIX; "We drop in at all major exhibitions in Ontario, as well as public and house parties from Knano to FatMan. Our stock includes over 500 'How-To' titles on BDSM sub-categories and the top 250 BDSM DVDs. I also personally offer a wide selection of Victorian and Tattoo drumming canes, along with school desks and regular instruction and caning workshops.

"My top 100 'How-To' Books feature works by Dossie Easton, Janet Hardy, Desmond Ravenstone, Midori and Lady Green. Titles include the ever popular Ethical Slut, The Complete Shibari, The Mistress Manual, How to be Kinky, Radical Ecstasy, The Better Built Bondage Book, New Topping and Bottoming, and Ravishment, the Dark Side of Erotic Fantasy."

SOUND: VERY FAST RAT-A-TAT-TAT OF TATTOO DRUMING AND GASPS OF SATISFACTION

DOMINATRIX: "We also carry a full range of BDSM fiction from The Story of O to Fifty Shades of Grey. Our DVDs go from Maggie Gyllenhaal's Secretary to the latest James Franco or Emma Marx opus. Come visit my travelling lair. If you dare."

MUSIC: MISTRESS KHRISTINA LAUGHS MENACINGLY AS COMMERCIAL THEME FADES OUT

CLAIRE: (RESUMES NARRATION) I can vouch for Mistress Khristina's encyclopedic knowledge of BDSM Books and DVDs. Also the quality of her rattan canes and incredible selection of drumsticks. I have a good number in my toy bag. Which is actually a gun case from Canadian Tire.

GRACE: In addition Mistress Khristina has some ornately carved Black Walnut paddles. Which Madame Claire has used on me. Most effectively.

CLAIRE: And on Robert. It surprised me at first that you two were switches.

ROBERT: (DRILY) Not as much as it surprised me.

GRACE: Robert was always the boss in business. The Dominant in BDSM terms. He actually made some of our first toys. They weren't very professional. A flogger out of leather bootlaces. Ping pong bats as paddles. A small rubber ball wrapped in silk as a ballgag. Heck, he even turned an unused coffee table into a bench to play on.

ROBERT: Naturally I tried them on Grace. Equally naturally, she came up with her feminist card and persuaded me to give the submissive route a try. Imagine our surprise when my rough, hand-crafted toys seemed to work. It was an eye-opener. Before I knew it, we had discovered subspace.

GRACE: Transcendence as we prefer to call it these days. The bottom in a BDSM scene experiences a natural increase in hormones and brain chemistry. This results in a kind of trance, a state of deep recession and incoherence. It can be dangerous if the dominant doesn't keep a close watch.

CLAIRE: What you're saying is that there's more to BDSM than flogging someone, or tying them up, or piercing their skin with needles.

ROBERT: The things we do, Madame Claire, are just the rituals that lead us to an altered state of consciousness. Bliss is another word. Ecstasy. Without wanting to sound too flakey, I think a good BDSM top is a sort of shaman. A spirit guide who helps the bottom, the submissive, get in touch with the energy of the universe.

GRACE: Play, as we so lightly dub it, is simply an intense way to change our state of consciousness. Most types of BDSM play create powerful physical and psychological responses. Bottoms tend to separate themselves from their environment as they process the experience.

ROBERT: During a scene the extremes of pain and pleasure trigger a sympathetic nervous system response that causes a release of epinephrine from the suprarenal glands, along with a mass of endorphins and enkepalins. Part of the fight or flight response. It works somewhat like morphine. Pain tolerance shoots up and the submissive falls into a trance we call Deep Subspace.

GRACE: Which is best described as an out of body experience, totally detached from reality. Flying, or floating, are other terms. It's quite exhausting, which is why the top needs to provide quality aftercare. Robert gets incoherent for an hour or more afterwards. Can't walk or stand.

ROBERT: Grace gets freezing cold. We keep an electric blanket handy.

CLAIRE: (LAUGHING) This is pretty New Age stuff, guys. How long have you two been together? You practically complete each other's thoughts.

ROBERT: Ahhah, this is where I break into song. (SINGS) "We've been together now for forty years, and it don't seem a day too much. Oh there ain't a lady living in the land as I'd swop for my dear old Dutch." Grace's maternal ancestors were from Friesland, in Holland. (HE LAUGHS) Oops, sorry.

CLAIRE: Does BDSM always work this way for you?

ROBERT: Not always, he says ruefully. Everyday life has a habit of getting in the way. But it cured my ED, and does answer some of the questions a person of my age, or our ages, asks from time to time.

GRACE: Who am I? Where do I come from? Where am I going?

CLAIRE: You have answers?

SOUND: PHONE RINGING BG

ROBERT: It's a work in progress. At Fatman we ride the myth of personal demons and transform it into altered consciousness. We encourage our guests to journey safely through self-created darkness in search of the light.

GRACE: It isn't for everyone. It works for Robert and me, but someone else may succumb to the demons. It depends a lot on the guide. And it doesn't just happen, it takes self-awareness and considerable training. Without that it's easy to go astray in the darkness.

ANNCR: Sorry to interrupt this fascinating dissertation but there's a phone call from a James for you, Madame Claire.

He passed her a New Client Card, reading KayJames16. "Line 2"

CLAIRE: Ah, a new fan. And when we come back, guys, I'd like to discuss your feelings about Predicament Bondage.

ROBERT: We'll try to be less esoteric.

GRACE: Less high-faluting, honey.

CLAIRE: (ON SPEAKER PHONE) Hello, caller. Welcome to 'Ask Madame Claire.'

KAYJAMES16: I consider your program most informative, Madame.

CLAIRE: Thank you for your comment. So, KayJamesSixteen, you have a question for Sir Robert and Lady Grace.

JAMES: Not Sixteen, Madame, my correct Kinklife appellation is KayJamesOneSix, all spelled out. And my question concerns last week's program.

CLAIRE: The one on Rape-Play?

JAMES: Indeed, yes. I would like to contact your guest, Fleur.

CLAIRE: Sorry, I can't give out her email on air. But I'll pass yours along to her. Pronounced JamesOneSix, right ?

JAMES: Kindly tell her I am considering becoming a rape top. I would appreciate further information about the questionnaire she mentioned.

CLAIRE: I'm sure she'll be in touch. Thank you for calling.

JAMES: Thank you, Madame Claire.

SOUND: PHONE HANGING UP

CLAIRE: (NON-COMMITTEDLY) A very polite caller. And now, Sir Robert, Predicament Bondage.

ROBERT: Grace and I attended a PB seminar in Toronto, given by Midori. You interviewed her I believe.

CLAIRE: One of the Scene's most spellbinding women. An American author and performance artist, originally from Kyoto, Japan.

GRACE: We have her coffee table book on Japanese Bondage. Breathtaking action photographs.

CLAIRE: So how would you describe PB, Predicament Bondage...?

GRACE: It's the art of restraining a submissive in a way that gives them a limited range of positions they can adopt, each of which has some penalty attached. Uncomfortable. tiring, painful, embarrassing, humiliating. The top has a variety of options.

ROBERT: The submissive's challenge is to find the lesser of two or more evils using their skill, intelligence, physical strength or sheer endurance. It differs from most bondage in that the sub has to have some freedom of movement, but none of their options are penalty free.

CLAIRE: I seem to remember Midori saying that every minute of Predicament Bondage is a mind fuck and every movement an act of willpower.

ROBERT: She kicked off her workshop with a simple example. She had the demo sub hold his arms straight out at shoulder height. Then she placed a full glass of water in each hand. She encouraged him to hold it as long as he could, without spilling any of course. She was most sympathetic in fact. She knew all too well that not failing the dominant is a motivation powerful enough to counteract extended arm pain.

GRACE: At one Fatman Robert came up with something a little different. He had me standing at a post with my nipples fastened above my head with Japanese clover clamps. If I stood on tiptoe, the upward pulling was relieved. But I'm no ballet dancer and he knew I'd have to go flat-footed fairly soon.... Which is when he put an egg under each heel. I could cheerfully have throttled him.

ROBERT: PB can be frustrating or even darkly funny. All parts of the body can be used. Arms, legs, hair, nipples, genitals.

GRACE: Asymmetry can be a powerful predicament. One leg tied up behind the sub, with the opposite arm crooked over the head and tied wrist to ankle. Like a figure-skating move. Without a single happy muscle group.

CLAIRE: Why do we do these things? What's the motivation?

GRACE: We mentioned pleasing the Dom, rising to the challenge they've set. Sometimes there is a dilemma to be solved. Pain or punishment to be avoided. Achieving a personal goal. Going the time limit. Facing reality and surrendering.

ROBERT: That's the hardest and the most rewarding. Accepting that some predicaments are unbeatable. Like a good old-fashioned hogtie. Either you lie perfectly still, or you slowly strangle. The muscles and joints may protest but, by submitting, your mind will transport you elsewhere.

GRACE: We all know that the brain is the most important sex and transformative organ. In PB, if the body can find no answer, escape happens in the mind. Effective Predicament Bondage enables the mind to take over.

ROBERT: Like so much in BDSM it's a tool that is both simpler and more complicated than it appears. It enables the top, the spirit guide, to show that losing the battle can actually mean winning the war.

MUSIC: DRUMMING MUSIC FROM 'IN A GARDA DA VIDA' SNEAKS IN

ANNCR: --- And so this week's 'Ask Madame Claire' moves sonorously into final commercial time. This one was put together by our research staff strictly for tonight's guests. They may never advertise their private house party themselves, but we thought, just this once, we would do it for them.

CLAIRE: Hope you like it, guys. Run the spot and do the wrap up, will you, Man in Black. I have a special visitor due in the board room. Thanks everyone. Enjoy our view of FatMan. Friday at the Manse---

MUSIC: DRUMMING MUSIC SWELLS

STUDIO SECRETARY: "FatMan is a Private Play Party hosted by Sir Robert and Lady Grace Challenger. It is held twice monthly at their home, Challenger Manse, in Kitchener-Waterloo, Ontario. Attendance is limited to 40 to 45 kinksters and must be booked well in advance via the FatMan Group on Kinklife. Guests have to sign a waiver stating they are over 18 years of age and are aware that they may be witnessing nudity, sundry fetishes and are enthusiastic observers or participants therein. They further agree to abide by the following House Requests:

ANNCR: "1) I will exercise discretion when arriving or leaving by the Church parking lot. 2) Doors to play-rooms are to remain open unless hosts decree otherwise. 3) You do not have to play unless you wish to. Watching is okay. Interrupting a scene is not. 4) No inappropriate touching of guests or toys. If it doesn't belong to you, ask first. 5) House Safe words are to be respected. Red, stop immediately. Yellow, slow down/ease up. Green, go for it. 6) Authority to stop scenes or modify behaviour is vested in Moderators (D.M's) and hosts. A request to leave the party is to be respected immediately. 7) Anyone infringing the house requests will never darken the manse doors again. Accredited Moderators will be on hand to apply gentle persuasion."

SECRETARY: "8) Sexual activities must be consensual and may only take place in the 3rd floor bedrooms or in the basement dungeon. Approved Drop cloths must be used. 9) No bodily waste scenes, hard drugs, excessive drinking or illegal activities are allowed. Excessive defined by Moderator or Host. 10) The hosts reserve the right to refuse entry, eject, and/or arbitrarily concoct new rules of conduct that in their judgement benefit FatMan. 11) Be aware of the dog. Her name is Ubu. She stands on guard for thee. Her knowledge of backswing is limited. 12) The basic request for all guests is that you exercise common sense and common courtesy while visiting Challenger Manse."

MUSIC: MADAME CLAIRE TEDDY BEARS THEME MUSIC SNEAKS IN

ANNCR: The preceding has been less a commercial than a partial code of conduct for FatMan guests. Which brings another episode of 'Ask Madame Claire' to an end. This is your friendly announcer speaking on behalf of Madame Claire and the mysterious research wallah she is now meeting in our secret studio boardroom here in Niagara-On-The-Lake. Next week, Mummification. The ultimate in saran wrap and body bag technology. This is me, the Man in Black, wishing you all sweet and undeniably pleasant dreams. Farewell, until our nefarious paths cross again....

MUSIC: TEDDY BEARS PICNIC UP AND

FADE OUT

*

When Madame Claire came into the studio board room, Detective Horatio Bellingham was waiting just inside the polished oak door. At other times it served as the Man-in-Black's ranch house dining room. Detective Bellingham was in plain clothes. He was a tall, well-built young man with close-cropped hair and a serious mien. The catchy notes of the Teddy Bears Picnic were still sounding out over the board room speakers.

"I didn't mean to drag you away from your program, Madame Claire" he said politely. "This is a totally unofficial visit."

Claire smiled her greeting and they shook hands. "I've been on tenterhooks since I received your call. Have I gone through a red light? One of those new ones with cameras?"

Bellingham smiled back at her and put her at ease. "It's not easy to avoid them these days. But no, I'm not with the traffic division any more. I'm with the OPP Criminal Investigation Branch. Horatio Bellingham. We have met before."

"What can I do for you, Inspector?" she asked.

He laughed easily. "Thanks for the instant promotion. I'm a Detective Constable is all. Second class."

Claire recalled their previous, glancing encounter. "I thought you looked familiar when I nearly ran into you at the Tilverdale Mac's Milk. So when did we actually meet?”

He refreshed her memory. "Outside Guelph. Two Christmases ago. About 2.00 A.M. I was still with the traffic division."

"Sit down, Detective." Claire took the armchair at the head of the table. "I do remember now. You pulled me over at a RIDE stop. Fortunately I don't drink when I'm driving - or playing."

Detective Bellingham smiled. It was a nice smile, Claire thought. He had a pleasant manner about him. "I was in uniform then," he said. "You too, in a way. You had a very young fellow with you and a guncase perched prominently on the back seat."

Claire returned his smile. It had been one of those brief encounters that stayed in the mind. "You asked me what I had in it. My toys, I said, and probably batted my eyelashes I was no doubt still high from the party. Er... high, as in Up."

He wasn't at all thrown off by her comment. "Rather officiously," he said, "I asked you to 'Open it up, please, ma'am"

"It's usually in the trunk nowadays," she said sweetly.

"Best place for it, Madame Claire," he replied gravely. "To be honest it was my first encounter with a guncase filled to the brim with whips and floggers and all those other.....toys, as you call them. I was younger then, less blasé anyway. I have a sneaking suspicion I blushed."

Claire remembered that she had felt sort of awkward herself. She was doing nothing wrong, but at 2.00 A.M. it was maybe a little out of the ordinary. "You were very polite."

"Rigorous Ontario Provincial Police training," he said, recalling his confusion. "Er...yes, ma'am. Thank you, ma'am. You're dismissed. I mean, er... you can go. I mean, we're done here. Goodnight. Don't drive and drink...." He turned serious. "When I saw you at the Mac's Milk it all came flooding back."

Claire smiled and became more businesslike. "What's this visit in aid of, detective?" she asked.

He sat up straight in his chair. "Rape," he said bluntly. "One, maybe two or more."

There was a discreet tap on the boardroom door and the studio secretary, more usually referred to as Dolly, the Man In Black's lady, came in. She had a couple of Tim Hortons coffees with milk and cream on the side.

"Your producer thought you might like a coffee," she said, maintaining the studio ambiance. "There's Sweet & Low on the side board."

“Thank you," said Bellingham. "Sweet and Low is fine with me."

"Tell the Man In Black we appreciate his largess, Dolly," said Claire, as the 'secretary' withdrew. "He's the producer, announcer, technician, advertising department, and home owner, all rolled into one."

"He has a great radio voice."

"Sometimes I think that's why he does it. He gets off on wishing our listeners 'sweet and undeniably pleasant dreams' in his deepest basso profoundo." She rose and brought back a couple of sweetener packets from the sideboard. "Two or more cases of rape, you say. Are you talking about the girl in Stratford? There was a brief mention on CBC news."

Detective Bellingham nodded. "She was pretty badly beaten up. He broke her jaw."

“Yes, that was terrible. And the second one? The other victim"

"That's what brought me to your studio today. I thought you might be able to help. The other possibility was Dawn Gretsko, at the Tilverdale Mac's Milk. We have two witnesses who saw her running down the road to her home, her clothing torn, her hair every which way. About two weeks ago now. Trouble is she's clammed up. I can't get any real information out of her."

Madame Claire nodded thoughtfully. "The day of our Black Wally Munch. I gave her a lift to Timmie’s at the Arena. She had a date at the tennis courts out back."

"How was she?”

"Filled with life. Happy. Expectant. Looking forward to a game and a possible job."

"Did she say who she was meeting?”

"I don't recall. No, wait... Eddie. A Sir Edward, I remember. I made a joke about Johnny Depp."

"I don't see the connection."

"Edward Scissorhands. Good Johnny Depp movie, weak joke."

The detective made a note on his Blackberry. "Thank you, that could help. I'll check out any Sir Edwards. Though I doubt he'll still be traceable." He added a sweet and low to his coffee and stirred slowly. "The impression I got at Mac's Milk, at the convenience store, was that young Dawn regarded you as a friend. I hoped she might have given you some details as to exactly what happened to her? She was assaulted for sure, quite possibly raped. Though I could be totally wrong, you understand."

"You could also be correct. Did you notice the rope burns on her wrists?"

"She tried to cover them up. Said she'd been playing."

"Did you believe her?"

"That's another reason I came to your 'Ask Madame Claire' studio. Do you know who she might have been playing with?"

"Not off the top. Though I doubt it was one of our people. Those rope burns were pretty amateurish."

"She's said nothing more to you?"

"Not so far, anyway. Her mother is a pretty domineering woman"

Detective Bellingham sighed, "Tell me about it," he said ruefully. "I tried to interview Ms. Gretsko at her home. Big mistake." He looked at Claire appraisingly. Claire thought he seemed to be wondering how much he should divulge.

"The more I know," she said simply. "The better chance there is that I might be of some help."

He stared at her a moment without speaking. Horatio Bellingham was relatively new at his job but considered himself a good judge of character. He usually went by the book but recognised that outside sources could help an investigation no end. He made up his mind quickly. "Both Dawn Gretsko and Carol Weber, the girl in Stratford, seem to be somewhat involved in your Community," he said, in explanation. "There was a length of yellow rope left at the Stratford Pet Shoppe. The rapist, or would be rapist, apparently bound Carol's hands and feet quickly and reasonably efficiently. The original contact was also made through Kinklife.ca, the same social site."

"Sir Edward?"

He shook his head. "Carol knew her attacker as Henry. Strictly on line. Profile deleted by the time I got there. Which makes me think your Sir Edward will have gone the same way. Same polypropylene rope as well."

"Not mine, detective. Anyway, Henry and Edward are fairly common names. There must be a goodly number, even locally."

He nodded. "Only three featuring Henry as a matter of fact. I checked them out. None of them fit Carol's description. Or the cap size." He hesitated, then went on. "We think we have his plain white baseball cap. It was in the dumpster outside the store"

"DNA?"

"It might help convict him one day, assuming it's really his. She was gagged, incidentally. With an apple.

Claire frowned. "An apple?"

"There were bloodstained pieces where she was tied up. It wasn't pretty." He changed the subject. He clearly thought her knowledge of the Community might be an asset. "I checked you out as well, Madame Claire. Apparently you helped the police on an embezzlement case some time back."

"The embezzler was in the lifestyle."

"Exactly. You helped out on a doping case with Avalon Stables as well"

Claire stood up. "Not really doping." She surmised that he had told her all he was going to. "Thank you, Detective Bellingham. I'll keep my eyes and ears open." She paused, then added. "May I see the rope?"

To give him his due, Bellingham didn't hesitate. "Come to our Western Region HQ, 6355 Westminster Drive, Lambeth Station in London. In case I'm out I'll leave instructions with Officer Chow. Olive Chow." He gazed at her earnestly. "By the way, I caught up on some of your most recent shows. It seemed to me your last guest, Fleur, was asking for trouble."

"All our experienced players are well informed of any risks involved. In the Community we go by the watchword RACK"

Horatio Bellingham finished his coffee. "I checked that out too. Risk Aware Consensual Kink. Classified as a type of alternative sexuality. To me, it seemed that this Fleur was sky-diving. Without a parachute. "

"Consensual is the important word"

"I know the theory. My concern is the application in practice." He moved to the door, then turned back like a TV detective. "Incidentally, I gather from the embezzlement case that anything I tell or show you will be strictly on the Q.T."

"I appreciate your confidence. And your visit...I'll be looking in at the Mac's Milk again shortly. I think rapists are one of the lowest forms of life."

"There I agree with you totally. Frankly, Madame Claire, BDSM isn't my cup of tea, but part of my job is keeping in touch with different groups. Whatever else you people are, you're comparatively legal."

"Comparatively?"

"One bad apple, as they say, can spoil a barrel for everyone." He took a billfold out of his pocket. "Here's my card. My private cell number is on the back. Please let me know at once if Ms. Gretsko opens up to you. Or, in fact, if anything else comes to mind. I'll keep you informed as well. At least insofar as I can."

They shook hands and Claire walked him out to the front hall, where Sir Robert and Lady Challenger were chatting with Dolly, the 'secretary.' Claire introduced them briefly. "Horatio Bellingham. Robert and Grace Challenger." She dropped the honorific and didn't mention his profession."

"I heard most of your interview on my tablet driving down," he said pleasantly. "I learn something new every time I catch 'Ask Madame Claire.'"

"What did you learn today, my friend?" asked Sir Robert, with a twinkle in his eye.

Detective Bellingham paused for a second. "How about 'There are more things in heaven and earth, Horatio, than are dreamt of in your philosophy." he said urbanely.

"Hamlet, Act II, scene something or other," Lady Grace smiled. "Watch it, Mr. Bellingham. Give my husband half a chance and he'll serve up another lecture on subspace."

"Not today he won't" said Claire firmly. "And you're dismissed, Horatio," she went on smoothly. "I mean, er....you can go. We're... done here. Good night.... Don't drive and drink."

"Touché," grinned the detective. "And may I just say I never looked at gun cases quite the same way again. Have a good night, folks." And he left for his unmarked car.

"What a nice young man," said Grace.

"One of your next interviews, Claire?" asked Robert, drily. He had registered Bellingham's short haircut and semi-military manner.

Claire smiled. "I've known him off and on for a couple of years now. More off than on. And to be honest, Robert, I think he was interviewing me."

"Oh... What for?"

"A sort of job, I think." she mused thoughtfully. "Could be rather interesting. And right up my alley."

Chapter 14 The Plot Thickens

Richard was in one of his down moods. Feeling very negative and ill at ease. What had taken place in back of the Stratford Pet Shoppe preyed over and over in his mind. It had even made the newspapers, for Christ's sake. The Times Dispatch, anyway. That cow Angele Del Zotto. Her article made him want to punch her out. Lies, all lies.

On the surface he was pretty much his old self. Wearing his usual Reebok track pants and greasy T-shirt. His hair combed well back on his forehead and the customary prescription sunglasses low on his nose like Victorian pince-nez.

"Jesus, I hate dogs. You know I hate dogs, Myra. Always snuffling around, licking each other's asses, growling, snarling. Don't trust them anywhere near me. Filthy creatures." He was bitter at Henry for not being more prepared. "Should have had some doped meat with him. Knock the bastards out."

Myra found herself getting worried. She remembered the dogs at the Pet Shoppe all too well, barking their fool heads off. And the mindless look he had given her then, the Henry look as she thought of it. She didn't think she would ever forget the stark expression on his face as his sinewy hands tightened around Carol's throat.

His mind was flitting from one subject to another. "What if he hadn't stopped when he did?" he demanded feverishly. "If you hadn't interfered. I'd be a murderer now. Or Henry would. Except he don't exist no more. I hadda kill him off. Delete him." A sudden sense of power swept threw him. Life or death was in his hands. Henry or Carol; he was in control. He'd know what he was doing next time.

And there would be a next time, He knew that now. The feeling of absolute power was too gratifying. It was way past time to set the rape instincts in motion again. Time to bring Myra more fully into the picture. His picture. James's picture, William's picture,

Billie's.... Some other of the diverse sock puppets he had set up. His rush of ultimate power.

He wanted that faculty of feeling now. That was why Myra was here, tied naked to the bedroom side chair. She had become a regular fixture. Someone he could torment when the pressure was too great. Sex when he wanted it. The way he wanted it. Pain at his fingertips.

They were in the steaming bedroom of his 3rd floor apartment in Uptown Waterloo. After the abortive scene in the nearby town-he-never-mentioned-any-more, he had insisted that she do a midnight flit from her uncle's Cambridge bungalow and move in with him, lock, stock and no panties as he put it.

"Your whole sense of discipline is falling off," he had told her unkindly. "If I don't grab ahold of it you'll no longer fit the role as my girl-friend." Regaining his sense of infallibility, of total mastery over her every action, was crucial to his well-being. He wouldn't even let her pee without his long withheld permission.

Myra, of course, recognised this, his deep motivation for treating her as he did. She was at once appalled and strangely fascinated by the events at the Stratford Pet Shoppe. Like him, she could still hear the animals yowling. Still see the look of terror on poor Carol's contorted face as she realised what horrors she had let herself in for. She vividly recalled Richard's incoherent rage and him totally losing control. No, not Richard. That had been one of his alter egos, the catfish Henry. Who wasn't around anymore. Deleted for safety's sake the moment they got home.

She had not hesitated a second when Richard demanded she move in. Her uncle barely tolerated her presence and it was getting harder and harder to fend him off, always brushing up against her in the hallway. She was all too aware of where that was heading. A sleazy, grasping man. Besides, being Richard's girl-friend was by far the most important thing in her life. What was a little pain compared to that? She would do anything to satisfy him. And she deserved the pain. She even revelled in it at times.

She had no qualms prancing around the apartment in a satiny French maid costume or wearing the frilly apron if that was what he wanted. Or nothing at all if it made him happy. Anyhow it was summer and she had always been self-conscious about sweating too much in even the lightest clothes. He had been so thoughtful about that, stocking her up with big bottles of Too Much perfume from Dollarama. Could be tricky in winter, though. She'd have to come up with outfits that would appeal to him. Leather skirts and tight corsets, she thought dreamily. Something to keep him in a good mood.

Like now. He had her sitting on the cushionless chair, her ankles tied with acetate scarves to the clean Scandinavian legs and her wrists tight bound behind the chair back. It made her breasts jut out, her nipples erect and almost begging for attention. She felt mildly apprehensive but sexy as all hell.

He had already introduced her to his Gypsy clothes pins. He had put one on each ear lobe and on the straining flesh of her upper arms. They were painful snapping on; worse, she knew, coming off. But she could take the pain. She was a bad girl, she knew she had earned it. He had told her he was a sadist. Inflicting pain was like a drug for him. She presumed that made her a masochist, except she wasn't fully aware what a masochist really was. And there was a reward too, a warm feeling of self-worth and Being. It took her to places she had never been before.

"I'm glad the Carol girl is recovering all right," she said sympathetically. She had learned a good deal about massaging Richard since moving in. Being around him 24/7 was helping her put her own feelings into words. So long as she was careful. "That reporter Angele you dislike so much said in the Times Dispatch that her jaw will have to be wired shut for four to six weeks. Can you imagine?"

Richard didn't want to talk about Carol or the Pet Shoppe. He wanted to move on and set up another rape session. Maybe bring that woman Fleur into the act, the older bitch from the interview show 'Ask Madame Claire.' Gennifleur, as he had now discovered by listening to it again. Thirties at least, but obviously available for rape-play. 'Play', he thought, wetting his lips. "He'd show her what he meant by rape-play...

He squeezed Myra's right nipple between his thumb and forefinger. Hard. "We'll start with a plastic clothes peg," he said, smiling thinly. "A small black one, it looks so sharp against your pinkish flesh."

She emitted a sharp intake of breath as he ruthlessly clipped the inch-long clothes pin in place around the nipple. The short ones nipped harder. "They're not really very strong, these little plastic ones. The big wooden ones have more bite. Don't you agree?"

"Yes, Master," she said between compressed lips, saying what he wanted to hear. She could almost ignore the red-hot pain in her nipple. She knew it would fade away gradually and would disappear unless he started toying with it teasingly. Then waves of hurt would echo through her.

"I'm gonna run a zip fastener from the other nipple and down to your cunt," he said, almost conversationally. A zip fastener she recalled, a touch nervously, was almost a dozen miniature clothes pins strung together by red twine and ripped off in one agonising motion. It was like a screaming line of fire cutting the body open.

"I was real pissed about losing Henry," he said, threading ten pegs together. "He was one of my first independent sock puppets. Rough around the edges. Kind of a redneck, I guess." His eyes clouded and his concentration wavered. "Now Henry and Edward have both had to be done away with." He finished tying the clothes pegs together and started on her left nipple.

"It ain't at all fair. But too risky to keep them hanging around with Kinklife profiles. It’s bad enough they're still on the bitches' sites - Nymphette and Morning Glory. But it's a cruel world where you have to kill off valuable parts of yourself." My Sock Puppets are me, Myra and I am them."

Myra was gasping with pain as he fastened the clothes pins deep into her skin. Past her belly button and into the coarse reddish pubic hair. She tried hard not to scream too loudly. Just enough to let him get off on her suffering.

He tweaked and played with her clit for a moment. Then suddenly followed up on his earlier thoughts. "Gennifleur," he said harshly. "The old skag on that radio show. The 'Questionnaire' bitch." Focussing on applying the clothes pegs had cleared his mind. He knew the route he wanted to take. "I couldn't locate any Fleur on line. But I solved that yesterday. Her avatar handle is Gennifleur"

He ignored Myra and sat on the bed with his laptop. "Kinklife, Gennifleur.... I'm gonna email her direct. She'll get all hot and sticky over the extra attention." He flexed his fingers and brought up Kinklife.ca. For Kinksters on the Darker Side, it said. "Christ, I love this site. It and Fetlife are the best social media on the Net."

He started typing, using two fingers. Not his forefingers, Myra noticed. The two middle fingers. His personality started to modify. Richard went away and he eased into James, KayJames16, the sock puppet he planned to become with Fleur. The change was almost instantaneous. He became his own sock puppet, free to follow James' thoughts.

"Goodday, Ms. Gennifleur," he said crisply as he picked out the letters, as James' fingers slowed down to his words. "*Subject: Your Questionnaire*." His voice became clipped and professional. His language more fluent. "*I was greatly impressed by your ravishment podcast with Madame Claire. I subsequently asked her to forward you my request for a copy of your Questionnaire."* He paused, frustrated. "Fucking fingers," he snorted to Myra, stretching and working them back and forth. "They've never been the same since that goddamned Pet Shoppe"

Myra could see that he was getting frustrated and confused. The dangling pegs were little more than a quiet hum by now. She thought to divert him. "Why do you use your middle fingers for typing, Master?" she asked him. "Don't most two-fingered typists use their forefingers?"

He coloured slightly, a bit abashed. "Er - sex," he said, almost awkwardly. He had momentarily slipped back to being Richard.

"Sex?" Myra queried softly, wide-eyed and innocent. She was learning how to engage his more susceptible side.

"When I was a kid," he replied, still a tad hesitant, "I was told the middle finger needed more exercise." He made a small series of crooking motions with his middle finger. He could be vulnerable when he wasn't performing. "I was much younger then," he said, almost self-deprecating. "Eleven, twelve maybe."

"I wish I'd known you then, Master," she said, reflecting how nice these little moments were. Talking like boy-friend and girl-friend. Then his lips tightened and he became James again. He exchanged eyeglasses. James was more prissy. He was thinking about addressing Gennifleur on the Rapeplay Questionnaire. Ravishment play, he corrected himself. Stupid name.

"Master, how's about I keyboard for a while?" she asked, knowing he would jump at the chance. Maybe he'd even release the clothes peg that was still throbbing grievously on her clit. "I'm pretty fast," she added, "I took it at St. Mary's."

He didn't hesitate. He freed her hands and thrust the laptop at her. Then he smiled and slowly, painfully, removed the clothes peg from her clitoris. He even took away some of the sudden rush of pain by pressing down on it firmly. "No spelling mistakes or I'll put it back on," he warned. The interlude was over. James was back on track. Even his lips were seemingly thinner. He became crisper, more businesslike.

"Commencing new paragraph," he dictated smoothly. "*Last night,"* he said, *"I tuned into your programme again and realised you were actually introduced as Gennifleur. Entered you on Kinklife and here we are*."

He paused thoughtfully. James was a civil engineer. He calculated the odds of any word or action. "*Obviously, I needn't have gone through Madame Claire. I could have contacted you earlier about the Ravishment Questionnaire. Fascinating concept, by the way."*

He had adapted his speed of dictation to Myra's typing. She was correct. She was fast and good. "Final paragraph," he said, pursing his lips. "*I figured it would be polite to ask for the Questionnaire in person, so to speak. It also provides me with the opportunity to say again what a first-rate interview you gave. I learned a lot."*

He gave Myra a thin-lipped James smile. "Conclude it with *'Yours truly, James.'* An old world touch. Just enough to make contact. Maybe I'll line up a date with her later. Our resident rape or ravishment expert. Then, *SEND.* I'm done for now."

Indeed James had done his share. He had confirmed that he was responsible for the Fleur contacts. He had kept his time down to a minimum. Richard could take back control.

"You can handle all our typing chores from now on, Myra," he said expansively. "Mine, James' and Billie's. You haven't met Billie the Kid yet. He's my most recent sock puppet."

It was weird, Myra thought, how Richard assumed his different catfish characters as if they were perfectly real and independent of him. Not just online either. He would become Henry, Hank, with Carol. Edward, Eddie, with Dawn. In reality, too. Face to face. So much more than merely emailing them.

Now it was James with Gennifleur. And Billie, who would Billie the Kid pair with? Were there other girly victims like Dawn and Carol out there on Kinklife.ca, just waiting to be contacted, set up and ravished?

Richard casually picked up the clothes peg still hanging off the nipple and jiggled the ones running down to her pussy. "Thought you'd got away with this," he said with an evil leer and fastened the bottom one to her clit again. "And it's a zip fastener, remember? It all comes off together. Real soon."

He tweaked the dozen or so clothes pins and the pain spread like wildfire throughout her body.

"There's something I want to show you on Kinklife," he said, ignoring her gasps. He opened the Bound, Gagged and Ravished site. "Chicks write hundreds of silly rape stories. Chat about rape. Some of them even advertise. Take a gander at this." He thrust the laptop in her face.

Myra gazed through tear-filled eyes at the screen.

"Aloud," he commanded tersely.

"Tall brunette twenties legal secretary in SW Ontario seeks... experienced young man for preliminary... non-violent rape," she read off haltingly.

"Preliminary non-violent rape," he sniggered. "What's that when it's home? Finish it, girl."

"Have sacrificial fantasy scene in mind.... Guaranteed mutual satisfaction."

He was caustic. "You see who that was from? Carol 'the Nymphette' Weber, the dog-lover. Christ I hate dogs. Shoulda poisoned the bastards like the guys do in lumberyard rip-offs. They want it, Myra. Dozens and dozens of them." He read off a handful of other posts. "Hi, I'm Kelly from Toronto. Looking for the artist in my ravishment fantasy." Or, more bluntly. "Hoping to be kidnapped and raped." He was shaking his head in phoney amazement. "There are new wannabees available every day."

He was good and pleased with himself. He got off on showing Myra how clever he was, how good his research skills were. But he also knew how long it took to establish viable profiles for Edward and Henry, James and William. William was Billie's avatar, he recalled. It was tricky to keep all his sock puppets apart sometimes.

"I think I'll undo the zipper on a count of three," he said casually, toying with the peg on her nipple. "One. Two Three... Four.... Five.....Just a little mind fuck, darlin'. Ready, steady, GO!" And he tugged hard.

The pain on her nipple, her flesh, her clit was excruciating. Myra shrieked out loud, unable to damp it down.

"And this is just the aperitif," he went on, gloating. "We've done nearly everything I'd figured to do. Brought you up to date on Kinklife. Started to test your limits. Hooked Gennifleur. Now all we have left is to move the game up a notch or two. Or three."

He had taken a faded purple Crown Royal bag out of her Osprey and tipped a fearsome collection of brown metal Bulldog clips on to the bed near her nude body. "Powerful little buggers, aren't they?" he said, his eyes glittering. "They'll snatch your nipple right off if I'm not careful."

Horrified, Myra noted that they were all different sizes, from half an inch to almost three inches. She could well imagine how the serrated Bulldog teeth would clamp on to her aching flesh. She could almost feel her nipple ripped and torn.

"Please, Master," she gasped, dealing with the certainty of pain beyond reason. "Please be kind." He looked into her eyes, grinning all over his face. "You wanna call red?" he asked tenderly.

"Yes, yes, yes," she shrieked silently in her mind. Then steeled herself to take whatever he wanted to give her. She was aware that a red call would put him into a bad mood for the rest of the night. Besides, she knew she could live through it if it pleased him. She couldn't give in now. She might pass out, but she couldn't give in.

"Don't get all uptight," he grinned mirthlessly. "I won't go for a zipper. It would be too messy pulling it off. Great gouts of bloody flesh." He laughed sadistically as he stroked her nipple with the largest Bulldog clip and she shuddered uncontrollably. "Now let's see, where shall we start? They should work fine on, what shall we call them? Your most sensitive parts."

He turned conversational. "You must remind me to take them off regularly. I forgot once, in this bordello in Kandahar. Poor Shakira's labia turned deep purple and she couldn't fuck for a week. Tried to get the lost income outa me."

He waved the large bulldog clip in front of her cunt, then playfully brought it up to her already distended nipple. "I have an even better idea," he said pleasantly. "I'll put this one on your tongue. It'll cut down on the screams."

It did.

And, then again, it didn't.

*

Fleur, Gennifleur on line, was the self-appointed BDSM Community activist for SouthWestern Ontario. She lived in

Shakespeare, a tourist township only a few kilometres from Stratford. She was perhaps best known as the forceful woman who organised and promoted rape-play. 'Ravishment' play, as she preferred to call it.

She was always picketing some recalcitrant business or other or dashing off virulent letters to the regional newspapers, her favourite mark being the K-W tabloid the lamentable Times Dispatch. A glib put down on any of the local radio stations was grist to her voluminous mill. She was also the Canadian representative of the Washington-based coalition of BDSM organisations dedicated to making the Lifestyle and its alternate sexuality an accepted branch of the LGBT umbrella.

Fleur was a short, stocky woman in her late thirties whose unceasing efforts to educate the Ontario media, and by extension the general public, didn't necessarily endear her to the Community at large. Many, if not most of its members would rather have remained in the shadows. She tended to flaunt strikingly outlandish clothes and proudly possessed a goodly number of differently coloured wigs and hairpieces that she wore as fancy took her.

She had an apparently inexhaustible reserve of nervous energy and was usually engaged on some life or death crusade. Most of her acquaintances, and they were acquaintances rather than valued friends, appreciated her good intentions and the way she was constantly trying to improve the Lifestyle's acceptability, but would have been relieved if she had left them off her target list of folks to inveigle and involve. She could be wearying to say the least.

By her own description, she was also 'super-efficient' and when she opened the Questionnaire email from James, KayJames16 she noted, she had already checked out his profile on Kinklife.ca, courtesy Madame Claire's earlier submission. It was a relatively new entry, well written and with a standard listing of common fetishes. Spanking, role-play, topping, flogging, fire-play, masturbation, mutually enjoyable consensual sex and all things rope.

There was no actual avatar photograph but a visually satisfying series of well-shot BDSM images and mercifully no penis porn. He was evidently a well-educated, probably professional man in his late twenties who was leery of exposing too many identifying features. He had signed off formally as James, not Jim or the more infantile Jimmie.

So he was asking for a copy of her ravishment Questionnaire. Probably thinking it would be a cushy way to worm his way into line for some gratis sex as a rape-top or role-play ravisher. Or maybe this one was genuine. Though even long-term males in the Scene had little or no idea how difficult being a good and compassionate ravisher could be. It was role-playing at its most specialised. Many eager young bucks might think the ready sex involved made it an easy choice, but when it came right down to it few had the right temperament.

Men were all so single-minded Fleur thought. Give them a sniff of raunchy sex and they were there with their cocks hanging out. They simply didn't realise that the whole area of rape-play was a major if secret female fantasy and called for intelligent and magnanimous tops. 'Service tops,' she said to herself, not scoundrels with a rapist inclination. Oh, this James was likely harmless enough, well-mannered anyway. Locating the right ravishers, educating them, was another of her time-consuming pursuits.

Her apartment was nothing much to write home about. She called it her condo but it was really nothing more than a pokey, slope-roofed attic over what had once been a general store and was now an ill-fated real estate office. She had lived there for nearly nine years and the walls were still only half-painted in fading turquoise. Turquoise was easily her favourite colour. But then she rarely had visitors and there were still unopened cardboard boxes scattered around on the unstained gray wooden floor. She was finicky and brightly colourful in person, but haphazardly organised in daily life. She had moved in after losing her only son Diego, and her surroundings held no affinity for her. The 'condo' was little more than a place to work and sleep.

She owned a 17" TV she rarely watched, a single metal bed and an old but comfortable armchair. Her desk computer was bang up to date and well used, with piles of files and papers stacked around it. She kept herself frantically busy and was constantly on the go.

Right now, she was suddenly good and mad, boiling over with deep-rooted anger. It wasn't James with his puerile request for a copy of her Questionnaire. He was just another contact on her ever expanding list of Community 'volunteers-to-be.' It was the vicious assault at the Stratford Pet Shoppe that had stirred her feral core.

She knew the signs and had deliberately changed into her bright turquoise athletic shorts and a skimpy red singlet. She had Dumbshell, a five foot smooth-muscled clown punching bag balancing ready on the gray floor in front of her. Pinned to the wall behind it, Angele Del Zotto's graphic article from the Times-Dispatch.

Fleur loathed actual rapists with a visceral hatred that went right back to her own girlhood rape. The thought that a girl from her neighbourhood had suffered such a terrible assault had all of her nerves jangling. In the back of the Weber family Pet Shoppe of all unlikely places.

She pulled up her hard leather Muay Thai gloves and lashed out a fierce double chop at the lugubrious clown's glum-looking head. "Bastard!" she yelled ferociously, throwing in a flurry of fast, accurate punches to Dumbshell's nose and eyes. "Bastard! Bastard!"

Fleur had been mastering Muay Thai for four heavy-duty years. She was strong and powerfully built, with well-developed musculature and trained wind. Give her half a chance and she'd relish the thought of going up against the cowardly rapist. They were all wimpy cowards as far as she was concerned. And to her way of thinking, her fists and feet were the equivalent of lethal weapons. She had even studied with a wizened dojo in Thailand itself. No snivelling rapist held any fears for her. She was super-confident she could demolish him.

What made it worse was that she knew Carol Weber slightly. Not well, or as a friend, but by sight from the occasional Stratford Munch or early evening of High Tea. She knew the parents better, aging John and the tall, gaunt Greta. They lived close by in Shakespeare, a few doors down on Perth Street. Greta had personally converted their wood frame home into an antiques emporium like at least half of the touristy township. Carol, the poor girl with the broken jaw, had often come home for the holidays from her banking stint in Uptown Waterloo.

She aimed another shower of robust blows to Dumbshell's pudgy body. She moved like greased lightning, twirling swiftly and always perfectly balanced on the ball of her foot. Hard, open-handed slaps, tight gloved fists, stabbing feet and a violent double elbow to the squishy, sticking-out ears. Dumbshell rocked insecurely back and forth, but stayed upright. He had been one of her most rewarding investments.

"I'll make you pay!" she panted, giving it her all. "You'd never rape anybody again after I'm done with you."

She was hot and sweaty following her explosive exertion, but well satisfied with her efforts. It took some of the grinding tension out of her system. She towelled off vigorously and went back to the desktop, still showing the email from KayJames16. KayJamesSixteen, as she read it.

"Says he learned a lot from the Madame Claire interview," she mused aloud, still breathing hard. Listened to it twice. Polite enough. I guess he isn't the one. No such luck there. Most probably a pretty harmless type."

She made up her mind to email him right back. Finding understanding rape-tops was definitely one of her trickiest self-appointed tasks. Qualified fantasy Ravishers didn't grow on trees. There were many more girls and women in the fantasy rape category than there were service tops capable of satisfying them. Of course at this juncture James was merely an interested prospect, but at least he seemed genuinely ready to learn.

Her stubby fingers flashed over the keys. "*Thank you for your gentlemanly follow up email concerning my ravishment interview and your request for a copy of my Questionnaire. This, btw, is specifically aimed at the ravishee, or victim, though I must confess I truly dislike that word."*

She decided that a few brief sentences about the whole concept of rape fantasies would be appropriate. *"As I'm sure you know, Sir James, a young girl's rape, or rather ravishment desire, is a sexual fantasy in which she simply imagines herself being coerced, raped or otherwise forced into a demeaning sex act.*

"Some women," she went on, "*enjoy the thrilling sensation of being sexually submissive, while others get off on imagining themselves so irresistible that their attacker must let loose their most animalistic urges. Naturally, you should also be aware that those of us who have forced sex fantasies seldom wish actually to be forced into hurtful violent sex."*

She took a paragraph to emphasise the difference between a fantasy and the horrible real life rape that had so nearly taken place in the Stratford Pet Shoppe. *"It's vital for you to accept that in the fantasy the 'victim' maintains her power. It has been termed a position of supreme domination from the bottom as well as, paradoxically, an act of absolute submission."*

Fleur read through her carefully crafted explanation. It said exactly what should be said. This James character could hardly mistake her meaning. Being a successful rape top was learning how to fulfill the female's deepest fantasy. Or the male's, come to that.

She dashed off a wrap-up to her email. "*So, James, I will forward my Ravishee's Short Form Questionnaire to you under separate cover. I am also compiling an independent Questionnaire aimed directly at you, a possible would-be Ravisher. I shall forward this to you shortly.*

"If, as I suspect, you are contemplating assuming that role, I trust my upcoming listing of specific requirements will be beneficial to your endeavours. Though I should warn you that though many are superficially interested, very few ever make the grade.

"Thank you again for your comments on the podcast. If I can be of further assistance, please do not hesitate to ask.

"Good luck in all your undertakings.

"Gennifleur."

Without re-reading it, she immediately sent the email to KayJames16, then automatically hit the next key on her evening schedule of things to keep busy at. The NCSF homepage. She was attending Celeste and Big Molly's Stratford High Tea later in the week and had pre-booked some time to hold forth on the National Coalition for Sexual Freedom. She was hoping to drum up scads of support for a Canadian chapter. With herself running it, of course. Great goddess, she was a busy woman.

She wondered idly how many people would turn out for the NCSF High Tea. Celeste and Big Molly obviously. They ran the monthly High Teas as well as the Stratford Munch. She would be envious of their activities if they were not such thoroughly nice people. Orphan Annie would be there, the mousey bookseller/masochist who rarely went anywhere without Sir Galahad. Such a sadist he was, she thought. No one except Nan could possibly put up with him. No accounting for where the kinks could lead.

And Madame Claire of course. She had promised to make a few pro-NCSF remarks. She would probably have her new young submissive in tow. What was her name...? LEEZA. Beautiful body, sexy as all get out. Lustrous raven hair, petite and completely alluring. Claire sure had a seductive way with her. Goddess in heaven, she would have to make some time for a little lubricious personal sex somehow. Maybe there would be a stray young thing available after the NCSF High Tea. She could but hope.

There was a partly cracked mirror hanging on the wall near the computer. She found herself staring into it intently, beginning to obsess about the strawberry birthmark over her right ear. The mirror had a pocket-sized school snapshot of Diego scotch-taped to the bottom. As always he was looking preternaturally young and vulnerable, his dark brown hair falling in a quiff over his boyish brow. Very Honduran, she thought, as she must have thought a thousand times over the long, dark years.

She realised two huge tears were rolling down her cheeks. "Oh holy goddess," she breathed to herself. "I'm so alone. So utterly, utterly alone."

Blinking away the tears, and the inexpressible feeling of bottomless guilt, she threw a sudden desultory blow toward Dumbshell the clown. It didn't flinch or move, just stood there like the stupid dummy it was. "I must be losing it," she said faintly, finding herself wishing it was Claire's Leeza standing there, her lips slightly parted, her lilac eyes warm and inviting.

Fleur instantly, artlessly, dismissed the thought from her mind. She knew she really should start putting some facts and figures together for the NCSF High Tea. But it was so hot and humid in the apartment, the Condo she corrected herself mechanically. Maybe she should clean up and go out for a stroll. Stop by Carol's parent's place, see how she was coming along. No, she could do that tomorrow or the next day. Maybe Carol would like to venture out to the NCSF meeting...

Which made her imagine Leeza again, looking so deliciously pure and innocent, yet so oddly knowing. Unattainable, of course. Dear Madame Claire had so clearly staked out her amorous claim at the Black Wally. But the young girl was so warm and glowing, so brimming with tempting promise. Why did she, Fleur, always fall for lovely young innocents so far out of her reach.

Or maybe not. Maybe Madame Claire, sweet Claire, wouldn't mind, she was always so generous and even sharing. Maybe the delightful, beauteous Leeza felt as she did herself, eager for a trip to the stars. Anything was within the gossamer realm of possibility if the mutual vibes were right. It wasn't exactly real anyway. A tantalising fantasy, neither more nor less. Enticing, though, a web of imaginary enticement,

She languorously closed her drowsy green eyes and let the fantasy grow. She could feel her eyelashes caressing the upturned curve of her cheek.

Tentatively, timorously, she stretched out her aching hand and seemed to sense Leeza's fancied touch as the girl swayed imperceptibly toward her. Her loving fingers reached up and lightly brushed the girl's now meltingly receptive lips.

"I need you so much," she murmured, her voice deep and husky. It was all in her mind she knew, but her want was so beautifully real, so tangible and achingly true. Her parting nostrils were filled with the aromatic scent of Leeza's flawless perfume... Chanel #5, she fondly recalled from the Black Wally Munch.

As in a filmy dream, she envisaged her palms radiantly encircling the girl's slender waist and slowly, gradually, turning her around while serendipitously unloosing the back of her flowing white and gold gown. Without missing a single heartbeat she could feel Leeza stepping gracefully out of it. If this is fantasy, she thought lovingly, give me excess of it, for this is who I truly am.

Expertly her thumb and forefinger unclipped the lacy cream bra and Leeza's youthful breasts were suddenly and gloriously there, awaiting the touch of Fleur's lips and tongue.

"You're so wondrously beautiful," she murmured, aware of the satiny wetness welling like heavenly nectar from her tender sex. "Your breasts are so perfect and delicate with their pink and virginal tips. I want to embrace and caress them, love them and make them mine."

Her limpid soft green eyes were part open now. She could almost see as well as sense Leeza's serenely real presence before her. It was so much more than a fantasy, she told herself dreamily. It was on another plane, somewhere magically out of space and time, a fairy land of long ago and far, far away.

Fleur needed this. Sweet goddess above, how she needed this.

She settled tranquilly back in the stuffed damask armchair, abandoning her cares and worries to sheer sensation. The milky gown had long since vanished, only the filigreed cream panties remained.

Tactfully, considerately, she held the narrow elastic waist well away from Leeza's rising and falling tummy and let her face and lips slip within. There were fragrant waves of body juice and the scent of musk flowing in the lambent air.

Without aid or help, the panties slipped effortlessly away and she brushed her soft lips to the very essence of Leeza's femininity. Gently she trilled the quivering tip of her pink tongue against the wet and trembling nub, the sweetly innocent clit now standing bold to Fleur's loving caress.

Way back she leaned in the red-patterned armchair, her hand slipping into her gold and turquoise gym shorts, rubbing, tweaking, moving sinuously in delectable little circles.

She had no thoughts of the NCSF or of KayJames16 or Carol or the ruthless rapist. Even Diego was gone fleetingly from her absented mind.

"If this be fantasy, give me fantasy," she breathed again. "For I am sorely tried by reality."

She knew what her spirit strained for. "What I want, what I need, is so far beyond the confines of matter," she said in dream-speak. "Give me the fantasy of all things bright and beautiful. Give me eternal love."

It was only in ineffable moments like this that Fleur could be honest and true to her innermost Self.

Perfection was all.

Chapter 15 Appearances Can Be Deceptive

Dawn had been utterly uncommunicative with everyone in the days after her terrifying experience at the tennis courts. Claire had twice dropped by the Mac's Milk but each time Mrs. Warren, the elderly franchise holder, was filling in. Dawn's mother, she said, had kept the girl home.

"She much sick," Mrs. Gretsko had said, when Claire telephoned and tried to make an appointment. "She back at work Monday." It was Wednesday that she returned. Her black eye was almost healed and the worst of the physical pain had gone. But she was still stubbornly not talking about what had happened that night. "My Mom says I shouldn't speak about it," she insisted. "I just want to forget."

It was Angele Del Zotto's article in the Times-Dispatch that finally made her realise how wrong she had been. The tabloid had a display stand in the convenience store. Carol's suffering made Dawn feel horribly guilty. It made Claire righteously angry. "The chances are it was the same man," she told Dawn. "You ought to have come forward from the beginning."

"I know I should have," Dawn said abjectly. "I feel awful."

"So you should," Claire was less than sympathetic. "There's a dangerous criminal out there. He must be stopped before he kills someone.".

"It's because of my Mom," Dawn said unhappily. "She worries she lied to the police. She's a refugee from Croatia, in the former Yugoslavia. She's scared of being deported."

That was when two customers came in and Madame Claire decided to curtail the conversation in the store. She would set up a meeting at the Gretsko house. A double interview. "What time do you get home from work?" she asked.

"Twenty past five," answered Dawn.

Claire had no qualms about taking charge. "I'll be there at six o'clock sharp," she said assumptively. "And Dawn, don't waste those forty minutes. Talk to your mother about Carol. He broke her jaw."

She started to leave, then turned back, looking at the young girl appraisingly "You were beaten and raped. Correct?"

Dawn barely hesitated. "Yes." she said. She took a deep breath. A great weight had been lifted from her shoulders. It was out in the open.

"Thank you," Claire said sincerely and went out to her car.

She sat motionless in the driver's seat for a moment, thinking about what she had just done. It was almost a complete commitment. She had arranged a double interview on what was essentially a police matter. "Interviewing is a big part of who I am," she told herself. "I like learning about people. Solving puzzles." Her thoughts turned to what Detective Horatio Bellingham had seemed to offer her. A chance to do some sleuthing on her own. Another part of her makeup was admitting that she was a detective story junkie. She loved a good mystery.

*

It was precisely six pm when Madame Claire pulled into the driveway of the Gretsko bungalow at 2775 Main North. It was small and neat, with dark green wooden siding and small, old-fashioned windows. The postage-stamp front lawn was short and immaculately cut. There were flower beds around the front door, mainly geraniums.

"Did you discuss the Stratford case with Mrs. Gretsko?" she asked Dawn, as the girl let her in.

Dawn nodded. "The Times-Dispatch was delivered this afternoon"

Claire had decided this session was to be different from her regular interviews. More impersonal. She knew of Mrs. Gretsko's austere reputation. She had phoned a couple of her Tilverdale acquaintances.

Dawn introduced them. "Momma, this is the Madame Claire I mentioned. This is my Mom, Sophia Gretsko."

Sophia was wheeling a tea trolley into the small living room. It was set for late tea. Small china cups and saucers in rose patterns. She was wearing her yellow apron. The living room was spotless. The furnishings were from Ikea. Inexpensive and efficient.

"You are French, Madame Claire...?" Sophia asked politely.

Claire shook her head. "It's a courtesy title," she said, taking the comfortable chair opposite the sofa. Both pieces had slipcovers in autumnal colours. Golds and greens.

"Donja say you would prefer tea," Sophia said quietly, sitting on the sofa beside her daughter. "Is Earl Grey"

"Black, no sugar, please," said Claire. Though I must tell you, Mrs. Gretsko, this isn't a social call." She was establishing parameters from the outset." She took out her iPhone. "This has a Voice Recorder app. I will have lots of questions." She placed the phone on the coffee table between them. "I gather you're up to date on the Carol Weber matter?"

"From newspaper. And Donja and I talk."

"Carol had no idea your daughter had been attacked. You should have reported it right away."

The woman was taken aback by Claire's directness. Guilt was written all over her broad Slavic face. "When she come home, I give bad advice. I not thinking clearly."

"I'm so ashamed, Madame Claire," said Dawn shakily.

Sophia was quick to come to her daughter's defence. "I was one who lie to policeman," she said. "Donja in bathroom."

"Please tell her she won't be deported," broke in the girl. "She was trying to protect me. She's my Mom."

"It was very wrong," Claire said shortly. Then her face relaxed somewhat. "But it isn't a deportation offence, Sophia. This is Canada."

"In old country, lying to police much bad"

"Here, too," agreed Claire. "Now I have a few questions specifically for Dawn. I'd like short, truthful answers."

"She good girl," said Sophia.

"Try not to interrupt," Claire told her. She switched on the recorder and headlined the recording. "Dawn Gretsko interview regarding alleged rape at Tilverdale tennis courts," she said clearly.

"Not alleged," Dawn corrected her. “And it was behind the tennis courts."

"Did you know the man?"

"Only on line. On Kinklife.ca."

On Kinklife. How did that start?"

"He emailed me."

"He knew your nick?"

Dawn flushed and cast a sidelong glance at her mother. "There's a rape site I visit occasionally. Rape-Play, it's called "Mrs. Gretsko almost interrupted, but caught herself in time. Dawn continued. "I had emailed that I thought this girl was very brave to share her fantasies. I had them but couldn't possibly write about them. He sent me a private message saying he agreed."

"What name did he use?"

"Sir Edward, Eddie. He's not on Kinklife anymore."

Claire nodded. "Probably a short-term trolling account." She turned to Sophia. "He would have set up a false identity and 'trolled' for victims." She returned her attention to Dawn. "I'll need copies of any correspondence between you."

"I'll forward whatever I have."

How about his profile? Anything relevant?"

"Some pictures of kittens. A list of standard fetishes. He said he was a tennis coach at the Racquet Club in Guelph. He said his mother called him Eddie."

"How old?"

"Twenty-four. He said."

"What did he look like?"

"On his profile he held a tennis racquet in front of his face. Job worries, he said."

"How about when you met him?"

Dawn shuddered. Her mother squeezed her hand in silent support. "Good looking, I guess. Dark brown eyes, almost black. About 5.11. Lots of dark hair, brushed back. Sunglasses."

"At night?"

"He explained his eyes were damaged. Service in Afghanistan, he said."

Claire changed her approach. "There were marks on your wrists. Did he tie you down?"

"To a big lilac bush"

"Did he know what he was doing? With rope, I mean."

Dawn didn't hesitate. "He was no rigger. He punched me first. I was dazed."

Claire switched again. "Where did the blood come from? On your racquet?"

"I hit him with it. It was lying on the grass when he cut me free."

"His DNA, then?"

The girl nodded. "I hit him with it, then threw it at him. Then I ran like hell. He had a switchblade."

Madame Claire could visualise the horror of the girl's experience. But there were elements of the story she still needed to pursue. "Did Edward arrange that first date?"

"Yes. He knew I was into tennis from my profile."

"He suggested a game?"

"We'd chatted some on Kinklife. He thought we might play after he finished work at the Racquet Club. He said maybe I could become an assistant tennis pro."

"Did he ask you to dress the part?"

"I was swept away by the idea. After the... Afterwards, he said he'd cut me if I told anyone. I hurt everywhere. I was scared to death. I didn't think they would let me go."

Sophia could hold back no longer. "This gone on long enough," she burst in. "Must stop now. Please."

Claire was forceful. "Sophia, it's obvious this was a premeditated seduction and rape. Edward, as he called himself with your daughter, is probably a confirmed serial rapist. He's the one who must be stopped." She turned back to the young girl. "You said they wouldn't let you go?"

Dawn turned red. "He had a girl with him."

Madame Claire was taken by surprise. "Really...! What sort of girl?"

"He introduced her as his current assistant. Early twenties. Plump. Long, scraggly reddish hair. She was wearing a huge floppy hat. She was nervous, on edge."

"Did she participate at all? Talk?"

Dawn shook her head. "She didn't say anything. Except once she called him Master."

Claire registered what the girl had divulged. She switched off the iPhone app. "That will do for a first interview," she said. "Forward his correspondence and email me anything else you can think of." She paused and looked seriously at the girl. "And Dawn, don't let this bastard screw up your life. You have to be strong."

Sophia Gretsko spoke up again. "Madame Claire, please. I must talk about past. Is important Donja know." The expression on her face was set and determined. "This concern where we come from."

"Croatia...?" said Dawn, puzzled.

Sophia took a deep breath. "I never tell you of wars in homeland." She gazed across the coffee table at Claire. "You being here, make this better evening for talk." She turned back to Dawn. "You must know past, Donja. It help understand."

Mrs. Gretsko said nothing for a moment. She was gathering all her strength. She had never told her daughter about the Dark Days. She had never told anyone. But she was committed now.

"Old provinces of Yugoslavia were warring each other," she said. "Croats, Serbs, Bozniaks. Family live small town in mountains. When Arkan soldiers come in camouflaged trucks they shoot men and boys. Women and girls they take to camps. Girls as young as...twelve." Grim memories crossed her face. Claire realised that Sophia was telling her own story.

"You understand I am talking about military policy," she said, quoting. "They kill father and brothers. At camps they want all women get pregnant. Have Srbska babies."

"Oh, Momma," breathed Dawn, not trusting herself to speak.

Sophie was clutching a tightly rolled paper napkin between her fingers. It was like a Rosary, Croats were Catholic. "Madame Claire, I think you know why I must tell Donja what happen."

"It was another time, Mrs. Gretsko."

"Yesterday," Sophia said, very quietly. She resumed her history. "The rapes would begin when they play Blue Danube on camp loudspeakers. It play many times. There many soldiers. Many beatings."

Claire was contrite. "I was too quick to judge," she told Sophia.

"This Canada," the woman responded, with a sad affecting little smile. "You catch this bad man, yes?"

"The police will put him away. I promise."

"Sorry I tell lie."

Madame Claire put her cup and saucer on the trolley and stood up. "I think it's time to leave you two alone," she said, extending a hand to Sophia. "Thank you for the Earl Grey. And for letting me sit in on your story. You are a strong woman, Mrs. Gretsko." She hugged the girl goodbye. "Dawn, I'll see you at Mac's Milk. Your mother will help you through this." She smiled and added - "You must help her as well." She left without another word.

Dawn closed the front door very slowly. She had gone deathly quiet. The interview with Claire and the weight of her mother's story had affected her deeply. She followed Sophia into the kitchen. They washed cups and saucers in silence.

"Momma," she said, after a while. "I was four when we came to Canada." She was having difficulty framing the words in her mind. "Was I.....Am I.....?"

Sophia took Dawn's wet hand in hers. "You are my daughter," she said simply. "My own sweet Donja." Very softly she kissed the girl's cheek. Just under the still slightly swollen eye.

"You are my life," Sophia said. "We beat this Edward. Together." She gave Dawn a brave little smile. "And you know something? I think I go Stratford, to hospital. Visit with this other girl, Carol Weber."

"I love you, Momma," said Dawn, hugging her.

They had both learned a lot in a short time.

Now, it would have to sink in.

*

It was only a short drive back to Black Walnut Cottage from the Gretsko house. Tilverdale and Marybourne were less than six kilometres apart, mainly uphill from the Tilver valley.

As she started for home, Claire couldn't help thinking how lucky she had been to be born in peaceful Canada rather than the tumultuous Balkans. The break-up of Yugoslavia after Marshal Tito's death had been long and bitter. The Wars of Secession had pitted Croatia, Bosnia and Kosovo against Serbia and had lasted well into the 2ist Century. Independence had been hard won and very bloody.

Canadian troops had been in the middle of the fierce conflict as U.N. Peacekeepers. Unlike in the later Afghanistan where they had been actively fighting the Taliban under the NATO banner, along with the Americans, the British and many other NATO forces.

Canada itself had been much more fortunate when it came to its own secessionist problems with the province of Quebec. There had been some violence in the Sixties with the FLQ, the Front de Liberation du Quebec, a separatist splinter group in La Belle Province, but French and English Canadians had been similarly appalled and both rejected any form of terrorism. Canada truly was the Peaceable Kingdom: one of the most civilised nations on Earth, naturally law-abiding and tolerant of dissent and difference.

By the time she reached Walnut Cottage Claire knew that she would do her part to defend and even expand the Canadian way of life. She firmly believed in Fleur's Coalition of Sexual Freedom as it applied to folks in the Scene. Helping to catch the occasional bad apple was part of that. Ruefully she admitted to herself that she was most probably signing on for another bout of what she called 'sleuthing.' It was a typically Canadian decision.

Because Canada wasn't all sweetness and light. The country also had its own lawbreakers. The man who had so brutally assaulted Dawn Gretsko and Carol Weber would have to be tracked down and incarcerated. Then there was Francis Dickie's blackmailer, going by the assumed name of TallBlondeChick. Even the best of human societies had its criminals and psychopaths.

Claire also realised that if she became fully involved she would have her hands full. It never rains but it pours, she thought wryly. She wasn't much concerned about being Outed herself. She had never hidden her activities. But she could completely understand how the Major must feel. And the boy-friend, Desmond Trout, a schoolteacher. Exposure could seriously affect both their careers.

Nor would it stop with them. Blackmailers were notoriously greedy people. There were most likely other members of the Black Wally under threat. The low-balling scattergun approach almost certainly meant that there would be a number of potential victims. Locating them would be a first step.

As for the rapist, at least she had Dawn's narrative to go on. He was young, good-looking, carried a knife and threatened to use it. Edward, but no longer online. Not as Edward, anyway. She felt it likely that he had simply come up with another name, another sock puppet.

She would have to make an appointment to see that O.P.P Detective. Bellingham, Horatio Bellingham. She would relay Dawn's story and hope for more details about the Carol Weber case. There was obviously much more than Angele Del Zotto had been able to convey in a short tabloid article. From experience Claire knew that if the detective was seeking her input from a Community viewpoint, she would need a more rounded and accurate picture herself. And he had indicated that he would keep her as up to date as possible.

Already, with two cases to think about, she could see the work piling up. Information, information, information. If there was one thing she had learned from her earlier investigating, it was that good sleuthing was largely about assembling and absorbing reams of information.

"I'll need an assistant," she said aloud. "Someone bright enough to research, collate and even bounce ideas off."

A smile wreathed her lips.

"Leeza Llewellyn!" she said brightly, with an instantly accepted wave of confidence. "Who better? I'll call her right after I talk to Horatio Bellingham."

She felt relieved and happy. "Claire and Leeza," she said. "We'll make a perfect team."

The universe was unfolding as it should.

***

Chapter 16 Questionnaire I

QUESTIONNAIRE #1 - RAVISHEE

(To be answered honestly and shared with Ravisher)

Key to graduated answers - a) By importance: Absolutely important. Very important. Less important. Unimportant - b) By frequency: Always. Often. Rarely. Never - c) Subject to mutual negotiation (STMA).

YOU - THE RAVISHEE

1. Do you understand the difference between rape in real life and rape/ravishment role-play?
2. How do you most identify yourself? Straight? Gay/Lesbian? Other?
3. Have you ever had a fantasy about being raped/ravished?
4. Do you find this common fantasy arousing? Remember, be honest.
5. Have you ever masturbated to a rape/ravishment fantasy?
6. Do you sometimes feel guilty about having such fantasies?
7. Have you any idea what first triggered them - (ie, movie, story, real life)?
8. How old were you?
9. Were you molested or sexually abused as a child?
10. Have you ever been raped in real life, or come close to it?
11. Do you understand that by its very nature a rape/ravishment role-play scene calls for consensual non-consent, whereby partners agree to make believe they are not actually consenting though of course they are?

KINDS OF FANTASY RAPE-TOPS (RAVISHERS)

12. Do you fantasise about being raped/ravished by someone you know, or by a stranger?
13. Do you have a preferred type of fantasy ravisher - (i.e., soldier, biker, pirate, coloured, white, etc.)?

14. Are your fantasy scenes usually one-on-one, or do they extend to gang rape?

15. Are your fantasy scenes "soft" - (i.e., taken against your will, but easily overpowered)?

    - Or "hard", as in slapped, punched, brutalised (if only for effect)?

16. Is it important to you that your fantasy scene includes convincing struggle and resistance?

17. Do you expect your fantasy ravisher to degrade you verbally with words like bitch, slut, whore?

18. Threatens you, or is more or less silent?

19. Do kidnapping, captivity, repeated rapes, play a part in your sexual fantasies?

20. What is more important to you, the sex or the humiliation and degradation?

LOCALES AND BEHAVIOURS

21. What are the most common settings for your fantasies - (ie, outdoors, dungeon, bedroom, prison, hotel room, camp)?

22. Would you prefer your rape-top to be partially or fully undressed?

23. Masked or unmasked?

24. - Threatening you with a weapon, such as knife or gun?

25. Do you accept that some physical force will likely be involved, albeit for effect?

26. In your fantasy ravishment scene would you prefer to be naked from the waist down or totally nude?

27. Would you prefer to be forced to undress or have your clothes pulled off in a struggle?

28. Or torn or cut off?

29. Is a blindfold or gag acceptable to you?
30. Does your role-playing scene extend to the possibility of handcuffs or rope?
31. Will being tied up add to your sense of utter helplessness - (ie, to a bed, furniture, or in the woods a tree)?
32. Does your fantasy include the rapist/ravisher's ejaculate, and if yes where will it end up?
33. Will safe sex practices apply throughout?
34. How important is the size of your ravisher's cock (or strap-on) in your fantasies?

SEX ACTS

35. Does your fantasy ravishment include the use of a vibrator on nipples, clitoris or exterior of vagina or anus?
36. - Interior of vagina or anus?
37. Do your fantasy rape scenes include fondling and or licking and sucking of breasts and nipples?
38. Do these fantasies allow for forced masturbation by rape-top?
39. Do they extend to forced oral sex on rape-top?
40. Oral sex on balls?
41. Forced rimming?
42. Licking or sucking of clitoris
43. Vaginal fingering?
44. Is anal fingering acceptable, with penetration by two or more fingers?
45. Anal rape, with copious lube?
46. Vaginal rape, with or without lube?
47. In real life, have you ever experienced, or thought about, rape role-play?.
48. By reading this Questionnaire, you have now. Correct?

AFTER-CARE

49. To be given by rape-top?

50. Given by Third Party (available on request)

END.

"Jesus God Almighty!" Richard burst out derisively. "You know what I'd call this, Myra? A fucking Questionnaire on How To Take the Rape out of Rape-play. Rape for well brought up young ladies. Fifty-one goddamed questions for moronic virgins!"

He was genuinely affronted. "I didn't think this Gennifleur made much sense in that stupid interview with Madame Claire, whoever she fucking is. After reading all this bullshit I think Fleur baby is teaching Sunday school. How to be raped without mussing your hair, for Christ's sake."

He scornfully tapped his hard copy of the Questionnaire. "Listen to this malarkey. *'Is it important to you that your fantasy rape scene includes struggle and resistance?'* It's a fucking rape. Of course there's gonna be violence. It's what makes the scene work." He snorted his contempt. "Or this... *'Do you understand that a rape fantasy calls for consensual non-consent, whereby the partners agree to pretend they're not actually consenting, though of course they are.'* Fucking gobbledygook, that's what that is."

He scowled his contempt for Fleur's efforts. "A bunch of meaningless garbage designed to reassure the stupid chick who wants to be raped like there's no tomorrow. Mind you, I can see using some of it as a follow up to my aw shucks personal style. Harmless old me and this Fleur's reassurances should double the market. Christ, it's hot in here."

He passed her the laptop. "Time for James to make nice, I think. I mean I'd like to tell the silly cow what a putz I think she is, but that would be missing a god-given opportunity. I'm James with Gennifleur baby, right? A professional man, always calculating the logical next step."

He straightened his shoulders and removed his Richard tinted sunglasses. He blinked a few times, Became his more serious alter ego. James Renfrew, civil engineer.

"Dear Ms. Gennifleur," he dictated, picking up his horn-rimmed glasses from the dresser. He was very terse and businesslike. "*I am in receipt of your excellent Questionnaire #1, for the Ravishee. I must congratulate you on a superb platform for the victim's clandestine requirements."*

He smiled thinly at Myra, now typing away with due diligence. "What Gennifleur really needs is a good old-fashioned forcible fuck, if you'll forgive the crudity."

Myra finished typing the first two sentences. "It still amazes me, Master. You even sound different when you're James.'"

"Of course I do," he said coolly, completely in character. "I am James." He smoothly resumed his dictation. *"Incidentally, Gennifleur, I must admit that like you I have never been comfortable with the word 'victim.' I am convinced your usage of ravisher and ravishee are more relevant. I might add that your use of the term ravishment makes it considerably simpler for me to contemplate this form of play as a serious option for myself.*

"Surveying prospective answers to the Questionnaire makes me confident that indeed I have the right experience and temperament to be... to be a successful and empathic rape-top. Or, as I am now beginning to think of myself, a conscientious and solicitous ravisher-to-be. A dollop of business orientated soft soap," he said in an aside to Myra. "Don't include that."

"Of course not, Sir," she said meekly.

"Sir James," he replied brusquely.

"Yes, Sir James," she responded immediately. She was definitely learning.

He struck his dictating pose, fingers steepled in front of him, blinking owlishly behind his horn-rimmed glasses.

"Allow me to state that I believe you are performing a valuable service to the Community by adding body and structure to this momentous and somewhat neglected element of fantasy role-play.

"Further, that I await your Questionnaire #2, covering the prerequisite conditions of the ravisher's role, with profound

interest." He unsteepled his hands. "Close off with my standard salutation - *Thank you for your courtesy, James* but add below *Civil Engineer*. Read through for spelling and format and SEND."

The horn-rimmed glasses went back in their Hakim Optical case on the dresser and James slipped silently away. He was nothing if not discreet.

Richard shook his head a couple of times and replaced his prescription sunglasses. "James is spot on, you know," he told Myra with a satisfied air. "All those juvenile questions are a perfect way to make the nervous prospect feel safeguarded and mollycoddled. Jeez, it pisses me off that the cunt is right even when she's wrong."

"Gennifleur?"

"Who else are we fucking talking about? Genni-fucking-Fleur-baby. If she weren't so long in the tooth I'd suggest James do what he said. Rape the bitch till her goddamed fillings drop out. How did he put it ? A good, old-fashioned..."

"Forcible fuck," she finished for him, raising an eyebrow. "Could you ? I mean, could he? Sir James?"

"If he could stand the flab and deep wrinkles. Personally, I'd rather fuck you."

Myra batted her eyelids at him. "I'm at your service, Master."

"That's the trouble," he said, with a scowl. "You always want it too much. Takes some of the excitement out of it."

"I could struggle and resist," she offered helpfully. smiling. "Try to fight you off."

"Wouldn't be the same," he said. "None of this consensual non-consent for me. Anyway, you get real wet and slippery at the slightest poke and --." He stopped abruptly in mid-sentence as a new and intriguing idea struck him. Fucking A, he thought, a tad sick even for his sadistically bent mind. New for them, anyhow. She had always been against it.

His face lit up. "I know what I'll do," he announced in an intimidating tone. I'll do what you've always run scared of before. Bumballing. I'll rape your fucking ass."

Myra flinched. She was suddenly very apprehensive. "Master," she said in a scared little voice. "I never been fucked there."

"All the better," he responded mirthlessly. "Besides, it'll open up another avenue for the future." He grinned. "That was a joke, bitch. Another passage to poopsville, get it?"

She tried to be firm. "Master, I'd rather not."

He looked at her coldly, his black eyes glittering with power, frightening in their intensity. The Henry look, she thought fearfully. It took her back to that last terrible moment at the Nymphette girl's Pet Shoppe.

"Your virgin ass is what I need, bitch. A shot of brown. Now, climb on the fucking bed. Kneel on the edge. Knees way apart"

"Richard," she said pleadingly..

"Get on the fucking bed!" he growled fiercely, growing impatient. "I'm gonna rape your cocksucking asshole, bitch, and there's damn all you can do to stop me."

She hesitated. It only added to his intensity. He roughly pushed her into a kneeling position, her face half buried in the wrinkled, soiled sheets.

"Stick your fucking ass out!" he commanded her forcefully. "Right fucking out! Pucker up your asshole. Now make like you're gonna shit. Open the fuck up. Don't be a goddamned wuss. You know you want it."

He thrust a lumpy pillow under her sweaty hips. Her ass stuck up high in the air, defenceless. Her asshole was tightly clenched.

"This is the way James'll take that Fleur cow. The cunt first, then the asshole."

He crudely parted the butt cheeks with his hands. Then spat on his fingers and pushed his middle finger into her ass.

"I tell you, that Fleur baby won't know what's happening to her! Christ, I love bumballing. Always so good and tight."

"Careful, Master! Take it slow, ple-ease."

He ignored her and rammed another finger into her asshole. She moaned desperately in panicky anticipation of his next move. She could hear him hastily pulling his Reebok pants down. He didn't kick them off but left them hanging around his ankles. He was in a hurry now. He pushed his hard cock against her anus and rubbed his precum against her nether lips.

"Easy, Master!" she cried out.

"Fuck easy!" he snarled, then stopped. "I got a better idea! Flip over on your back Instead of doggie-style I'll rape your bum from the fucking front. I wanna see your Christly face when I shove it in."

He forced her on to her back, her ass raised high on the crumpled pillow.

"Push yourself wide open," he said mercilessly. "Here comes fucking Richard!"

He pushed and shoved and thrust his rigid cock into her. She squealed despairingly like a pig in pain. It felt like she was being torn apart.

"Christ!" he yelled, as he tried to force his way in. "Jesus fucking Christ!"

The pain was a horrible agonised burning. Her asshole was on fire.

"In!" he cried out triumphantly, as he pushed through the first sphincter. "In and out!." He pushed through the first barrier again and started to pump back and forth as his eyes slammed shut and his mind picked up the primeval rhythm. "In and out! In and out"

His whole face contorted spastically. For a pounding moment he was James, and Myra, shrieking in bitter pain, was Gennifleur. "God Almighty," he yelled. "Fleur baby will love this."

Myra screamed. "It's too big! Too fucking big!

"Shut up, cunt" he snarled, blood flecking on his cock. "The pain'll let up if you fucking relax."

Myra was taking short, fast breaths, like a woman in labour.

"Oh God," she cried. "God help me!"

"You want it," he said cruelly, prodding his bloody cock past the second sphincter.

Pungent juices ran from her cunt and down to her ravaged backside. Warm and slippery.

You want it," he said savagely. "Tell me you fucking want it. Fucking tell me!"

"I w-want it!" she got out brokenly "Oh Mary, Mother of God, I FUCKING WANT IT!"

The pain diminished. Her clit was pounding against Richard's clenched abdomen. Her pussy juices were flowing down her perineum and into her ass.

"I want it," she mumbled again, tears still streaming from her eyes. "It fucking hurts, but Jesus I want it. Hard. Hard!"

Richard's iron control slipped and vanished from his control. He came in wild, explosive spurts. One, two, three, four molten jisms of thick cum erupted into the depths of her ass.

They collapsed together.

The rape was over.

At least for now.

Chapter 17 the Tethered Goat

It was the morning after Madame Claire's meeting at the Gretsko home with Dawn and her mother. The previous evening she had already taken two definite steps toward becoming fully involved. Three, if she included looking up Francis Dickie's TallBlondeChick on Kinklife.ca. That had been less than rewarding. The blackmailer's profile had been kept to an absolute minimum.

Her first real commitment had been a short phone call to Detective Bellingham at Ontario Provincial Police Western Headquarters in London, ON.

She had informed Horatio, she already thought of him as Horatio, that Dawn had been assaulted and raped behind the tennis courts in Tilverdale some two weeks earlier and that she would now cooperate totally with the police. "Poor girl," he had said, showing genuine concern. "Too terrified and ashamed to report it, I guess. Such a pity, the information might have spared Carol Weber her ordeal in Stratford."

Claire had filled him in on most of Dawn's statement and now had an appointment to see him at Lambeth Station on Westminster Street, London, at 9.00 A.M. Friday morning, when she would make a full report. She had also asked that he brief her on some of the details about the Stratford assault, since all she knew at this point was the Angele Del Zotto article in the Times Dispatch.

"That's a typical tabloid story," he said dismissively. "A few facts and lots of exaggeration. I'll set you straight on Friday. What I will tell you here and now is that it's even more likely that the rapist is one of your people. Contact was established through the BDSM social media site Kinklife.ca"

"His profile deleted, I presume. The same as Dawn's Edward."

He nodded. "Carol's attacker called himself Henry and, yes, deleted by the time I looked him up." He brought the conversation to an end. "So, I'll see you Friday morning," he concluded, adding:. "And, believe me, Madame Claire, I'd appreciate whatever you can come up with about any of your members. This effing bastard is becoming increasingly dangerous."

When they had finished speaking, Claire thought long and hard about the Kinklife connection. It didn't necessarily mean that Henry or Edward were active kinksters, though she could certainly understand the police suspicions. She could foresee lots of arduous digging in the near future. Research. That was when she made her second planned telephone call of the evening, to her young friend Leeza. In the strictest confidence she had brought her up to speed on Dawn's testimony.

"It's horrible," Leeza had responded, very upset. "Heartbreaking. And it's happened again. I was just reading about it in the Times-Dispatch. A girl in Stratford."

"Carol Weber," Claire had said. "And Leeza, the police have asked for my help, from the Lifestyle perspective. I have some experience as a private detective of sorts. They think the criminal is into BDSM."

"One of our members?"

"I'm not so sure. Sex is readily available in the Community. I can't see any of our Doms turning to rape.' She paused a moment, and had then launched into the reason for her call. "Anyway, Leeza dear, I've pretty much decided to give it a go. Investigating the situation, I mean. I wondered if you'd like to pitch in as chief sounding board and general research assistant. A sort of Dr. Watson to my bush league Sherlock Holmes," she added drolly.

The charming young girl's reaction had been everything Claire could have wished for. "I'd absolutely adore to help," she said enthusiastically. "In fact there's nothing I'd like more than having a hand in jailing this Edward guy."

Claire was very pleased. "It'll be a lot of hard work," she said, in a half-hearted warning..

"I need a new challenge in my life," said Leeza, her eyes bright.

"I'm being a little selfish," Claire admitted. "I enjoy your company. Your natural joie de vive" She also had a high regard for Leeza's innate intelligence and thought they would work well together.

Leeza grinned. "That's decided, then. You have an assistant private eye."

Claire had suggested they meet up at Walnut Cottage around noon Thursday. Leeza said that would work out fine with Matt's long Thursday lunch hour.

"Oh, and by the way,' Claire added with deliberate and practiced casualness. "We'll also be looking into a creepy blackmailer who has turned up in the Community." She could almost feel Leeza's eyes popping from her head in the Llewellyn house down the hill.

"Blackmailer?" the girl squeaked.

"I'll fill you in when you arrive," Claire had said wickedly. "And, Leeza, we'll have our work cut out for us."

*

That was pretty much where Claire was at right now, at nine thirty on Thursday morning. Before going to bed she had decided that the simplest way to bring Leeza into the whole picture would be to show her the unusual blackmail-cum-donation email and introduce her to TallBlondeChick's rudimentary Kinklife profile. A profile that seemed to be nothing more than a vehicle to send out dunning messages to Francis and, in Claire's considered opinion, other vulnerable Black Wally members.

She was ensconced in the cottage sitting room, comfortably rocking to and fro in her favourite pine rocker. It had been the last thing Wally made for her before his death. It had a leopard motive, of course. And as usual, when she needed a clear head, she had her sewing basket on the rolltop desk beside her and was making crackers for her whip collection, starting with Khaleesi, her bullhide eight-footer.

Crackers were what they sounded like. They cra-acked when the whip was thrown. Three to six inches long, fashioned out of thin string, they were changed every time a whip was in play. It was a cleanliness factor, in case of blood or bodily fluids. Making them kept her hands physically active and left her mind free to concentrate on other thoughts.

This morning those thoughts took in the overall situation. She was appalled at the prospect of a monster stalking innocent girls in the Community. Her Community. She found it difficult to believe that any of her peers could be involved. Certainly some of them, Sir Galahad for example, might seem a bit odd by vanilla standards, but most all were her dear friends, just slightly different from the norm. She understood and accepted their alternate values. She knew, and knew that they knew, that the one cardinal rule in the Lifestyle was that everything had to be consensual. Rape or Ravishment Play, in particular, had to be negotiated between both parties, all parties. By its very nature it was fantasy, not horribly real.

Rape Play was the name of the group on Kinklife.ca through which 'Sir Edward' had contacted Dawn. Eddie, as his mother supposedly called him. He had to have been a Kinklife.ca and Rape Play member to have made the connection. Or had formerly been a member, now deleted according to Dawn and her own research last evening. And deletions were dead, gone forever. No records. No way to track them down.

Even so, the Kinklife Rape Play group was a valid starting point. He, Edward, was most likely still trolling the group for Southwest Ontario victims, just under a different scene name. Sometimes she thought half the members were sock puppets. Okay, she was exaggerating, the Kinklife caretakers deleted any they could find. Maybe 5% was a legitimate estimate, tops. Now, she and Leeza would have to find a way to reach him. He would be local, too. Ontario for sure. Nothing was impossible, if you could think outside the box.

Her fingers on the cracker continued to move automatically. She had a foot-long length of embroidery cotton stretched between her outstretched hands. The string was twisted not braided and her nimble fingers were twisting it more. Embroidery cotton for sensuous whipping, the style she would use if introducing Leeza to the esoteric and surprisingly caring art of whip play. Harsh synthetics for the stingy, biting crackers she normally kept on

Khaleesi. Even dental floss at times. Without conscious thought she took the middle of the twisted cotton between her teeth and brought the ends together so that the doubled string twisted around itself.

Dexterously she tied a reef-knot an inch or so in from the ends and stashed the finished cracker in her leopard embossed sewing box. The box had been a typical spontaneous present from Bertie and Mickey. Friends were always giving her neat gifts with leopards on them. "Just couldn't resist buying this for you," they would say happily. It was invariably a pleasant surprise and much appreciated prezzie.

Oops, where had that thought come from? It wasn't about Sir Edward or TallBlondeChick, that was for sure. Her mind was straying off topic. She was supposed to be thinking about a sensible plan of action in the rape and blackmail cases. A way to bring Leeza into the picture quickly and proceed from there into actual investigation.

Let's see, she had been grasping at something, visualizing Edward, not Edward any more, but still trolling the Kinklife.ca Rape Play group. Using another made-up name. Another sock puppet. Still hunting out his next local victim. His next Dawn or Carol.

The idea hit her like a ton of bricks. Another Dawn. That's what was needed to get this show on the road. Another Dawn.

Leeza would have to become another Dawn.

It would all start on Kinklife.ca.

*

"Actually, It's quite a simple plan, Leeza," Claire said, some fifteen minutes after the girl breezed excitedly into Walnut Cottage "There's very little chance we can track down Sir Edward's new identity. There are at least twenty-five thousand Southwest Ontario profiles. So I've come up with an utterly different approach."

They were seated at the rolltop desk in the sitting room, with Claire's computer open in front of them. She had made Keurig coffee in Tim Hortons mugs. Rainforest Espresso for herself and Summer in Paradise for Leeza.

"You're convinced he'll have set up a new profile?" asked Leeza, who was looking very summery in a sleeveless purple sundress and pink flip-flops encrusted with rhinestones. "Another sock puppet, as you call it."

Claire was quite confident. "I'd bet the farm on it," she said. "Dawn posted a single comment on the Kinklife Rape Play group. Edward, or the person behind him, picked up on it and contacted her. I think Horatio, Detective Bellingham, will confirm that he, or possibly another sock puppet, also made the initial contact with Carol Weber. I'd say the use of sock puppets are part of his M.O."

"His Modus Operandi?" smiled Leeza, who had entered wholeheartedly into the spirit of the investigation. It helped that she had seen a mystery movie or three .

"How he finds his victims," Claire agreed. "Sock puppets are simply phoney online identities. Easy to delete when necessary. I expect to find out what else they have in common when I drop in at Lambeth OPP station in London."

Leeza nodded thoughtfully. "Edward wasn't just on line. He met Dawn in real life. Then there's the guy who broke Carol's jaw. I guess he and Sir Edward are our prime targets." She indicated the hard copy of Francis' blackmail email. "Rather than TallBlondeChick."

Claire spoke very seriously. "I regard them as ticking timebombs. A serial rapist is entirely different to a sleazy would-be blackmailer who thinks he or she is awfully clever. From everything I've researched, serial rapists tend to escalate. Their violence, I mean."

"You did say he threatened her verbally with his knife before he let her go. Carol was even more brutally treated."

"That's escalation," said Claire. "I'm afraid he could wind up killing someone."

Leeza impulsively reached out and put a hand on the older woman's arm. "Claire, I can't tell you how exciting this is for me. It's thrilling and potentially very worthwhile."

Claire smiled fondly and took Leeza's hand in her own. "You're not just a pretty face, my dear," she said sincerely. "There's a keen mind beneath all that raven-black hair. A lot of courage, too. We may need that if my plan of action comes to fruition."

"Here's hoping it does, whatever it may be." Leeza said simply. "And, by the way, dear lady, it was your business card that set me up for all this. 'Radio Host, Massage Therapist, Tarot Reader and Private Detective'."

"If it weren't for my vanilla clients, I would have added BDSM Domme"

Leeza gave her a wicked smile. "You could have tried Bolero Interpreter," she said.

Claire laughed. "That's what I mean by a keen mind" she said, and returned to the task at hand. "Anyway, sweetie, we have two main things to accomplish today. Starting with a few more facts about TallBlondeChick. A nick, incidentally, that makes me think our blackmailer is probably a short, bald, dirty-minded man."

"Who you checked out on Kinklife.ca."

Claire already had a tab pre-set. She went to it. "A question mark instead of an avatar picture. No friends or photos like most profiles. Not even a list of fetishes."

"Just a way to send a blackmail message to Mr. Dickie."

"I doubt if he's the only recipient."

"Who else?"

Claire shrugged. "Anyone at the Black Wally who values privacy. Someone like Georgyboy, the TNG host."

"TNG?"

"A Munch for The Next Generation of Kinksters. Your generation, eighteen to thirty. Merely a hunch."

Leeza tried a different tack. "Could TallBlonde be Dawn's Eddie in a different incarnation?"

"I thought about that. Like Edward, she - or he - has scene names down pat. Knows about Black Wally guests, off the name tags, I guess. Even has general details about sex lives." She shook her head. "But it just doesn't compute . They're totally different crimes. One sneaky, the other violent. I'd say the timing is purely coincidental."

"In Edward we have Dawn's face-to-face description. Early to mid-twenties, fairly good-looking. With TallBlonde all we have is a Box Number at thc Siebert Hotel. Can we stake that out?"

"That's what the police might do. But Francis is adamant he can't have them involved. He's a charter member of the Ontario Jockey Club. Desmond is a biology teacher In the Catholic school system ."

Leeza nodded her understanding. "So what's our second mission for this afternoon?"

"Straightforward research. I intend to take you deeper into the actual workings of the Rape Play group on Kinklife.ca. That will lead us into the approach to Edward that I've come up with. I think, to use your word, you'll find it quite exciting."

"Dangerous?"

Claire smiled. "Perhaps a little more so than looking for a sock puppet in a haystack. And the idea is simplicity itself. If we can't go to the mountain, we must bring the mountain to us."

"Huh?" said Leeza, frowning.

"Specifically," Claire said, taking the time to explain carefully. "I believe there's a way to use the Rape Play group to get him to contact us. Or, to be even more specific, contact you."

*

Kinklife.ca was one of the biggest social media websites aimed at the BDSM marketplace. Other major English language sites were Bondage.com, Fetishworld.com, BDSM Guild.com, Fetlife.com, a couple of dozen more. Kinklife had nearly four million members worldwide, 85% in Canada and the U.S. It was still growing exponentially.

"As you probably know," Madame Claire said to Leeza with a touch of pride. "Both Kinklife.ca and Fetlife.com started business in Canada. Most of their early members were right here in Ontario. For example, my membership number is 1628."

"I had no idea they were from Canada," said Leeza, suitably impressed. "I guess Kinkife.ca is a Canadian success story."

"Come to that, so is John Baku's Fetlife. It even cuts threads short by saying 'Sorry, this discussion has been fermée. That's French for toast'. We are multi-lingual like that.'"

"You know John Baku?"

Claire smiled. "He's a friend," she said simply.

She brought the Kinklife Rape Play group up on the computer screen. "This is only one of the groups on Kinklife.ca that deals with rape fantasies," she said. "Bound, Gagged and Ravished" is another one I'm familiar with. But we'll concentrate on Rape Play because we know Edward trolled here."

She indicated some Stickies at the top of the page. "There are 34,978 members of this particular group. Five introductory Stickies. Number One, the inevitable FAQ, frequently asked questions. Followed by Number Two, Group Rules, and so on. We'll be taking a brief look at each.

"First, though, I want to give you an impression of the breadth and type of discussions involved. They're posted in date order. Beginning an hour ago, two hours, one day ago, two days and so on. Each discussion triggers a number of comments and whoever makes a comment is listed by their Kinklife identity. Dawn made one comment. Two brief sentences. That was enough for Edward to pick her out as a local member and send her a private message."

"That was all he needed? One comment."

"Yes, although individual comments can get missed in all the activity." Claire observed. "If I scroll down you'll see that there are 4,295 discussions underway. In this group alone."

Leeza was amazed at the numbers involved. "And over 46,560 ongoing comments," she said, awestruck.

"Lots of them from folks trying to understand their rape fantasies," Claire said. "Especially women who were actually raped at some time in their lives."

"Not my cup of tea at all," said the young girl, wrinkling her nose.

"Nor mine. but to each their own kink," Claire responded. "I interviewed Fleur on the subject. There are endless discussions about all kinds of fantasy rape scenarios. Whether one fantasizes Date rape or Stranger rape. Or maybe a Home Invasion. Or perhaps Sleep or Drugged rape. Personally, I think the whole genre is genetic, harking back to the caves or tribal slavery."

She guided the cursor back to the first Sticky. "Rape Play FAQs. 'Am I normal?' 'Can you realistically rape play with a spouse?' 'What can go wrong when you select a rape play partner?' 'Where are personal advertisements posted?' Yes, Leeza, there's a place to advertise, headed with another bunch of Stickies. 'Rape play by State, Province or Town.' 'Women looking for men to rape.' 'Men looking to be raped.' It's a significant sexual fantasy."

"But for Dawn and Carol the fantasy became all too real."

"That's why we're researching this. Edward, or anyone like him, is preying on young girls trying to come to grips with their most baffling urges. He makes me very mad." She took a moment to collect herself and went next to the Group Rules Sticky. "These are guidelines you should familiarise yourself with if you're going to get really and truly involved. Which I very much hope you are."

She paused, then resumed in a very matter of fact tone. "Neither Kinklife nor Fetlife allow any discussion, comment or stories concerning children. Group leaders and caretakers delete any reference to minors under eighteen. Discussing real-life rape that occurred before age eighteen is permitted only providing it isn't eroticised."

"That sounds eminently sensible."

"Similarly, bullying or name-calling. Raping someone who is drunk is also liable to be deleted. Rape Play is one of the tightest controlled groups on Kinklife.ca. Fetlife.com as well."

Leeza had been putting two and two together. She had a glimmering of what Claire might be leading up to. "I can see I have some reading ahead," she said with a half-smile.

"You can skip the Rape Porn Sticky. It deals with favourite scenes that members want to share. Movies, books, erotica. Not at all relevant to our plans to draw in Edward."

"That just leaves the Rape Stories Sticky."

Claire nodded. "That's where you'll focus most of your attention. There are literally hundreds of stories, listed initially by title. They're in date sequence and have loads of comments. The quality of the writing varies enormously. Many are just plain sexy. Others are attempts to understand where rape fantasies come from."

She gave a sigh of relief. The detailed introduction to Kinklife was over. She exited the website and closed the computer. "Which is the end of my tutorial for this afternoon. The rest is up to you. I need another Keurig espresso."

Leeza stretched her arms and joined her in the kitchen. "Same for me, please. Good and strong."

"This type of research can be unexpectedly stressful," Claire noted. "I visualise Edward poring balefully through every discussion."

"Patting himself gleefully on the back when he finds another Dawn."

"Which is where you come in."

*

They took their foam-flecked espressos out onto the sunlit patio behind the cottage. Claire had a green thumb and the summer flowers were a welcome change from huddling over the computer. There were pansies and petunias and Gerber daisies. Impatiens and pink verbena ground cover. Honeysuckles and English ivy festooning the white pergola. Geraniums in hanging baskets.

"Tell me, darling girl," asked Claire. "Have you figured out my master plan yet?"

Leeza smiled and bent down to smell a delicate pink flower. "These are alyssums, right? Such a lovely fragrance." She straightened up. "Your mistress plan I'd call it. And if I'm correct, you want me to write a story." She looked quizzically at her mentor.

"But not as Leeza Labelle," Claire said softly. "There's no point asking for trouble."

"Change my name?"

Claire had thought it all out. The crackers had done their job. "You have a fairly new and uncomplicated profile. You modify it enough to become Dawn Two. Bethany, say. Or Miley or Tiffany. Something sweet and girly."

"What about my avatar photo?"

"Temporarily retired. You own a cute blonde wig I believe. Maybe different contacts. Baby blue, to go with the wig." She perched comfortably in a hanging wicker chair. She was drawing a picture for Leeza. "You list Waterloo Region as your domicile. You, or Tiffany, post a sprinkling of innocent comments on the Rape Play group."

"To be followed by a story."

"I thought maybe one about a rape that didn't quite happen. You rather regret this. Or Tiffany does."

Leeza was thoughtful. She was quite caught up in Claire's narrative. "All aimed at a good-looking young man who was once named Edward and might have been in Afghanistan."

"It may not work."

"He got in touch with Dawn off a single posting. Do I - I mean, does Tiffany get to meet him?"

"That shouldn't be necessary. We'd monitor any responses closely of course. Edward's emails to Dawn enticed her to the tennis-courts on the pretext of a game. I think he'd use a similar

M.O. here, depending on the story. He'd appeal to Tiffany's fantasy as written."

"But if we aren't sure it's him. Surely a casual meeting would be called for?" She took a long drink from her Tim Hortons mug. "Coffee, perhaps?"

"I'd watch over you like a Mother Hen."

Leeza put down her mug. "Dear Madame Claire," she said, her eyes gleaming with anticipation. "As I told you earlier, this whole affair is positively thrilling. "A soupcon of danger only makes the heart beat faster." She grinned impishly. ""Matt would love it."

Claire looked at the girl admiringly and finished her Rainforest Espresso. She was secretly very pleased that she had read Leeza's reactions correctly.

"Where did the Tiffany idea come from?" the young girl asked curiously.

"From Wally's favourite writer, Rudyard Kipling," Claire responded without hesitation. "It's how they used to catch tigers in India." She smiled at Leeza's look of bemusement. "The tiger-hunters would tie a bleating goat to a tree in the jungle to lure him into range."

"Oh my sainted aunt," said Leeza, her eyes dancing. "Claire dearest, you've surpassed my wildest expectations. There's even a name for it."

"A tethered goat," Claire said with a straight face. "But only, darling, if you volunteer."

They burst out laughing.

It seemed quite funny.

At the time.

Chapter 18 Legwork

The word that came to Madame Claire's mind was legwork. By car, of course. A circular drive to look up most of the Munch hosts within fifty or sixty kilometres of Kitchener-Waterloo before her upcoming meeting with detective Horatio Bellingham at the Ontario Provincial Police Western Regional Headquarters in London, Ontario.

It was the day after her productive afternoon session with young Leeza. She was immensely pleased to have found a capable and enthusiastic assistant, although maybe 'co-opted" was a more accurate description. She admitted ruefully to herself that she had a tendency to co-opt her friends into helping her with her projects. Rather like dear Fleur, but perhaps with greater success.

Besides, Leeza was already more than a mere sounding board. The girl was perceptive and seemed to be quite adventurous. They would make a good team, with Leeza already volunteering to interview some of the Munch organisers herself, starting with GeorgyBoy and the TNG, the Next Generation of under thirties kinksters based in Waterloo. Then there was the Triple S Munch, run by Janey and Harold who played a mean djembe at Claire's regular body drumming evenings. Switches, Submissives and Slaves, not exactly an ideal source for a rapist or blackmailer but worth a cursory investigation.

Then again, maybe Leeza wasn't as submissive as she professed to be. Natural enough, thought Claire, knowing Matt and the complicated family background. Indeed, she remembered her long personal struggle to find her own true identity. It had been Wally who had first seen that she wasn't a genuine submissive but more likely an unresolved dominant. From the moment she had moved into Black Walnut Cottage he had encouraged her to explore her independence. She recalled fondly how warmly he had approved when she started to wear more leopard accessories and clothing. He had even presented her with a three foot leopard whip to play with.

"Try it, I think you'll like it," he had told her, with that ever-present twinkle in his eye. Maybe Leeza would go the same way. She herself had certainly found the power and accuracy of the little leopard whip highly addictive. Which was when she had taken the next big step and painted the front door of their home - Leopard, of course. Wally was already very sick by then, but he had loved her initiative. "I bet this is the only leopard front entrance in Ontario," he had laughed, weak but totally supportive. Then, two days later, he had had the leopard seat-covers installed in his prized vintage BMW. "You're doing most of the driving nowadays," he had said. "And Lohengrin was overdue for a lift."

She blinked away a solitary tear and turned into the driveway of the first stop on her planned tour for the day, Bertie Stanislav's backsplit in the Waterloo suburb of Old Westmount. There was a highly developed social scene in the BDSM Community and Bertie had been lucky enough to land a double lot with a good-sized backyard masked by a thick and very prickly hawthorn hedge. There was usually something private and interesting going on at Bertie's.

Today it was a small pony play class run by Mindy, one of his polyamorous partners. There was even a well-stamped-down earth training track running around the lawn out back and one of the pony girls in attendance, Huguette, was high-stepping between the shafts of a pink and purple compact sulky. Another girl in her twenties, along with a pony-boy, Paulette and Pauli, were being put through their paces by Mindy, reins in hand.

When Madame Claire came expectantly round the gated side of the backsplit, Bertie himself was sprawled in a lounge chair on the deck, alternately watching the prancing and luscious pony play and working on his Microsoft Surface tablet. Actually he was trying to concentrate on his third book, tentatively entitled A Beginner's Guide to Living Kinky. His previous works included a History of Dinner Theatre in Southwest Ontario and a university textbook on early esoteric computer languages. Bertie was a polymath as well as a polyamorist.

Down on the track, Mindy was exercising her charges. She was wearing a smart summer riding outfit. Black cap, fetching jodhpurs and a crisp white shirt. She had a red crop in her silver belt and a Viennese carriage whip in one hand, along with the two sets of reins. Mindy was also a multi-tasker.

"Whoa!" she instructed her three ponies. "Sir has a visitor. Say hello."

The ponies obediently stopped what they were doing and whinnied in unison. Pauli, the pony-boy, pawed the ground enthusiastically, almost overbalancing in his high hoof boots. He was way less experienced that Paulette or Huguette when it came to walking on his toes without heels to lean back on. Knee-high hoof boots took a deal of dedicated practice.

"Hey guys," Claire greeted them. "You look absolutely spectacular. And you know what they say, looks make the pony. You're simply beautiful."

And they were, a long way from the harsh and painful visuals usually associated with BDSM. All three were resplendent in eye-catching pony gear, artistically designed to make them look and feel more equine than human. Good pony girls and boys were a very rare breed. They loved posing and performing. Even the arduous, diligent practicing set free a deep-seated animal instinct of grace and beauty. Like puppy play, Claire knew, but with more elaborate equipage to feed the fantasy.

Apart from the hoof boots and gloves they were clad in studded leather head and bridle sets with high posture collars, pointy pony ears and rich, wavy plumes, the girls in jet black and Pauli in crimson. They were stark naked except for a criss-cross body harness that did nothing to cover breasts or sex. Their arms were strapped behind them at the elbows which, combined with the harness, thrust out their breasts into straining prominence. Pauli's cock was strapped up to his navel and they were all showing long, flexible horse-hair tails mounted on stainless steel butt plugs. Claire thought they were magnificent.

Mindy cracked her Viennese whip. "We're doing a retrospective on actual horse gaits," she noted and returned her attention to her ponies. "Huguette, don't let the sulky drag your knees down. And you guys, high-step walking is next. Knees ninety degrees from the ground." She was very much in charge. "Right, WALK!"

Claire and Bertie had exchanged fluid, warm hugs. Meaningful hugs were invariably a part of Scene greetings between both sexes, all sexes come to that. "Mindy is getting them ready for the August camp at Long Point," Bertie informed her in his easy-going way. "So, Claire, what's up? You have that 'mission from God' look."

"It's the recent cases of rape in the Community," Claire responded, a frown crossing her face. "The police think the rapist is most probably in the Scene. Initial contact seems to have been made through Kinklife.ca. The O.P.P. has asked for my input. And, as I'm sure you've heard, there's a blackmailer on the loose too. Threatening to Out people."

"And you're investigating that as well?" He glanced at her in all seriousness. "I've always wondered why you don't take out a license and set up a business as a legitimate private detective."

"Too many petty regulations," she said, "I'd rather keep my feminine amateur status." Her attention was drawn back to the track, where Mindy was moving ahead to the trot, which she called a two-beat gait.

"For the bio-equine," she proclaimed definitively. "This means two feet are in the air while two remain on the ground, moving as diagonal pairs. For ponies this translates into an energetic jog. Right, ponies, TROT! Knees still up, Pauli. But fifteen degrees lower than the walk."

"I can't imagine how you can focus on work with all this lovely nubility on display," Claire said, admiring the view.

"Astounding willpower," he grinned. "It is kind of exquisite, isn't it?"

"Stamina is what I'll need today," she said smilingly. "I'm doing the grand tour of local Munch hosts. You, Roseanne in Guelph, Nicholas in Brantford, Cambridge, Woodstock, and finishing up with Celeste in Stratford. It's High Tea day, with Fleur making a

NCSF speech. Potentially exhausting, but I want to see if any of our Munch guests stood out. In a bad way, I mean."

"Like someone who came to a Munch or two and didn't stick around, or whom we politely asked not to come back."

Claire nodded laughingly. "Yes, one of those. Possibly a guy with a smattering of online knowledge. But in no way a people person."

"In other words, not one of our regulars."

"In his twenties according to the first of his known victims. Good-looking, she said. Familiar with rope, but of the yellow polypropylene variety."

"Definitely not a rigger, then," Bertie agreed. "Sorry, but I haven't had any real objectionable newbies lately."

There was a sudden clatter and muffled curse from the track as Pauli fell sprawling. "Bad pony." Mindy admonished him and flicked his naked ass with the carriage whip. "You can do this," she added encouragingly, helping him to his feet. "And you're so graceful to look at. The strut will come."

"Not easy in hoof boots" Claire commented sympathetically, getting ready to leave as Mindy moved on to the hardest gait, the canter.

"The canter is a three-beat gait," she was saying, giving her ponies a mental picture. "When the horse canters, one of his rear legs propel him onwards, say right rear. During this beat the remaining three legs are stretching forward. Then on the next beat, he catches himself on the left front leg while the diagonal pair are still briefly touching the ground. The lengthened foreleg is matched by an extended hind leg on the same side, referred to as the lead."

As she took Highway 7 to Guelph, Claire knew that Mindy was explaining to her ponies that the closest humans could come to the canter was a sort of skipping motion. Skilfully performed it was a highly attractive feature of the pony's repertoire. She recalled the Beauty books by Ann Rice and her heart went out to the young pony-girls and boys who took so much time and effort to become the very best ponies they could be. It was a wonderfully different and captivating part of the diverse BDSM Scene. Not at all the way the general public tended to imagine it.

*

It was a good five hours later by the time Madame Claire made her way into the Queen's Inn parking lot in Stratford. She had spent a fun and fascinating day socialising with the various Munch hosts on her circular itinerary and was looking forward to relaxing at Celeste's traditional High Tea, a banner event on the BDSM social calendar.

Like the Munches it was held in an everyday hotel-cum-pub, with guests in regular street clothes engaging in warm and affectionate conversation. Very Stratford, as everyone said. There were often special parties dropping by on their way to the Shakespeare Festival, the biggest celebration of the Bard's works outside of England itself. Out-of-town visitors from Toronto or the States. Stratford was a popular tourist Destination Point.

She had really enjoyed her time spent socialising with Roseanne, the Munch host in Guelph, commonly known as the Royal city after the Hanoverian electoral family. It was the bustling centre of Wellington county and Roseanne always had a fund of earthy anecdotes from the local Guelph agricultural university. The city had a burgeoning population of around 132,000 and was barely twenty-seven kilometres east of Kitchener-Waterloo. It was noted for its vibrant BDSM community and had two well-attended Munches and its own frequent parties.

Cambridge, and its tall, very funny Dom Sir Christian, was even closer. Fifteen minutes from K-W, with 128,000 Cambridgians and three regular Munches. Sir Christian was well known as a bit of a card and kept Claire chuckling for an hour or more. Though unfortunately neither he nor Roseanne had any news on the rape or blackmail fronts.

Then there was Brantford, thirty or so klicks to the south. It had another 90,000 people and Lord Nicholas hosted two packed Munches. Brantford was named after Joseph Brant, a valued British Mohawk ally during the American Revolution, though nowdays it was probably better known as the city where Walter Gretsky had built a backyard hockey rink for his smooth-skating son Wayne.

Finally, to the west of Kitchener, there were the smaller cities of Woodstock and Stratford, the first with 40,000 people and a small Munch and the latter boasting Celeste's regular Munch and the theatrically inclined monthly High Tea. The more conservative London, On., was also to the west of Kitchener-Waterloo and considerably bigger, with some 400,000 ardent Londoners in its sprawling environs. It was the headquarters for the Western division of the O.P.P., which Claire would be visiting in two days time when she met with Horatio Bellingham.

The whole of Southwest Ontario, she thought, from Barrie to Niagara and Kingston to Windsor, was alive with the sound of BDSM activities and social happenings. It was constantly amazing to her how many hundreds of folks were intimately involved. Many thousands if you added in Toronto and the rest of the GTA.

By the time she stepped down into the Rosalind Room at the Queen's Inn, the hotel wait staff was already bringing in the ornately labelled teapots for High Tea. Along with gleaming cannisters of reserve hot water and silvered three-tiered plates of crustless cucumber and watercress sandwiches, delicious nibblies and an assortment of miniature sausage rolls and sundry other treats. There was usually a speaker for each Tea, with Gennifleur on tap for tonight. Or sometimes Celeste would set up what she loosely called 'dramatic readings.' She and her partner Big Molly played up the social side of their BDSM Teas for all they were worth..

"We have chosen four unique teas for this evening's festivities," Celeste announced in her plummiest High Tea tones. "The gold teapot is Lapsang Souchong. It's a black tea cured in the smoke of Chinese pinewoods. The name actually means 'smokey variety.' The flavour is in a class by itself and laced with oriental pine smoke."

Big Molly took up the formal recitation of the teas. They had been lovers for so long they could finish each other's sentences, and frequently did. "The rose patterned teapot contains Jasmine Special Grade, Chinese Green tea leaves scented with fresh jasmine flowers. It originated over 700 years ago, is traditionally served with meals and is reputed to be a remedy for coughs and sore throats. Darjeeling, in the silver teapot, is from West Bengal in the Indian sub-continent. It has a musky spiciness referred to by connoisseurs as 'muscatel.'"

"I love the notion of musky spiciness," piped up Sir Galahad wickedly. He was one of only five males present at this month's High Tea. "And I hope there's some standard Earl Grey for non-afficionados like me."

"In the copper teapot as usual, Sir," said Celeste sweetly. "By the way, our speaker for tonight will be Gennifleur from Shakespeare." Galahad groaned audibly and Celeste smoothly cut him off at the pass. "She'll be telling us about recent European psychiatric studies that show BDSMers are actually better balanced mentally than most so called normal folks."

"Together with some news on the U.S. National Coalition for Sexual Freedom that she's been researching," said Molly informatively. "But Fleur's running a bit late so first I'm going to ask Madame Claire for a few words."

Claire made short work of a bite-sized fish paste sandwich. "My word, they set a tasty table in the Rosalind Room," she said. "And as some of you will already have heard, I'm working with the O.P.P. to coordinate the Community efforts to track down dear Carol Weber's assailant. That and a little blackmail case on the side."

"Poor Carol," said Ann, Sir Galahad's submissive. "I don't think she's been out of her parent's house in Shakespeare since her release from hospital."

Claire nodded sympathetically. "The police believe that the rapist is one of our members. If so, I have reason to think it may be a short-term Munch guest who dropped out before really learning anything."

"Had one of those characters a few months ago," Celeste offered. "A real pill. Twenty five or so. Thought he knew everything, but actually knew nothing and wasn't remotely ready to learn. Certainly not from a woman. Thoroughly undesirable type. Never turned up again, and good riddance."

There was a sudden flurry of activity from the entrance steps to the Rosalind Room as Fleur bustled in with two other people in tow. "Hello, everybody," she said, her face flushed and excited. "I have a super-stupendous surprise for you all."

With a great deal of pride she shepherded Carol Weber from the Pet Shoppe down the three broad steps leading from the main inn premises. She was accompanied by a thin middle-aged woman who was obviously Carol's Mom. "Our High Tea is Carol's first day out in public," Fleur crowed, with a distinct note of triumph in her voice. "The Webers live only a couple of doors down from my condo. Carol's promised to help me with my work on the Coalition for Sexual Freedom. When she's fully recovered, of course."

There was a welcoming chorus of applause and heartfelt greetings as Celeste showed Carol and her Mom to comfortable chairs. "Marvellous to see you out and about, dear," she said warmly. "And you must be Mrs. Weber, right? Good of you to come."

"These monthly Teas are a long-standing tradition with us Stratford kinksters," explained Big Molly.. "We're quite civilised in our way."

"That's nice," said Mrs. Weber faintly.

Carole had blushed at all the attention and scribbled a hasty note on the stenographer's pad she was carrying. "Thanks, guys," she wrote. "Fleur insisted it would do me good."

"Difficult to resist, our Fleur," said Madame Claire with a friendly grin.

"Gave me something different to think about," wrote Carol, trying to smile back. She was still sorely battered and bruised, her jaw still wired shut, but obviously on the mend. Seemingly tougher than she looked.

"I was just telling Carol's Mom about some of the new Finnish studies that show those of us into BDSM aren't mentally ill," Fleur said with her usual zeal and total lack of tact. She was wearing a short black Scarlet Johansson wig and a turquoise jump suit. A bit of a bull in a china shop but always with the best of intentions.

"This major Helsinki study recruited 902 Lifestyle practitioners and 434 vanillas," Fleur went on, almost bursting with enthusiasm. "They found that kinky folks were less neurotic, better adjusted, considerably more secure in their relationships and have much deeper mental well-being."

"According to a British research project it's because we communicate more readily about our secret sexual desires than people in the mainstream," added Big Molly, who rarely missed an opportunity to educate a member of the public.

"That's nice," said Mrs. Weber again. She looked mildly bemused but was also kind of relieved that Carol's friends seemed to be regular down-to-earth folks. Carol herself was evidently a little concerned at her mother's exposure to things BDSM but grateful to Fleur and the others for trying to make her Mom feel at home.

Fleur had rushed to thrust a rose-patterned cup and saucer into Carol's hands, creating some inevitable confusion with the pad and pen. "You can sip on this, dearest girl," she said helpfully. "It's Earl Grey, one of Celeste and Molly's absolute High Tea staples. "It's a Chinese-Indian blend with an aroma derived from the oil squeezed from the bergamot orange."

"It was first brewed for Earl Grey, a British P.M. in the 1830s," added Celeste. "From fermented black Indian, Ceylon and Chinese teas."

"That's Sri Lanka these days," Molly chipped in helpfully.

Fleur took over again. " Carol and I have been chatting about the NCSF, the American National Coalition for Sexual Freedom. Well, I've been rambling on and she's been writing. We're forming a Canadian chapter."

"It's very prominent in the States," said Madame Claire. "Over fifty leading coalition partners, from the ACLU to the National Gay and Lesbian Task Force."

"Our ultimate aim is to win the kinky community the same human rights as the now well established LGBT members," Fleur informed Mrs. Weber. "It's the most crucial new front in Sexual liberation."

"LGBT-FORWARD-SLASH-K," said Celeste, her eyes lighting up.

"Mein Gott and little fishes!" chimed in Sir Galahad dolefully. "I'm so damned normal it hurts!"

"Just so long as it hurts me," said Ann, his longterm masochist, batting her eyelashes.

Claire adroitly brought the free-flowing High Tea socialising back to her own purpose. "When you came in," she said, "I was telling the group that I'm now working on your case, Carol. With detective Horatio Bellingham of the O.P.P. I'm seeing him in London the day after tomorrow and I've been wondering if you've remembered anything new since you made your statement. Something you haven't told him yet."

Carol coloured and nodded. "There was one thing," she spelled out rapidly. "I told him I was sure there was a girl present. I could smell her cheap perfume."

Fleur jumped in again. She couldn't keep quiet for long. "I took Carol to Shopper's Drugmart and Dollarama earlier this afternoon. She identified it."

"The perfume?" asked Claire. "That might be really significant."

"Too Much, at Dollarama," said Fleur proudly. "It's a Tony Burch knock-off. Their 'impression' of the Burch original."

I recognised the smell at once," wrote Carol. "Very citrusy. Grapefruit and lemons."

"Well done," Claire congratulated her. "That could help I.D. her."

There was another smattering of applause. "There's nothing wrong with Carol's nose," said Fleur, patronising but proud of their achievement.

Celeste picked up on another part of their earlier conversation. "That possible suspect I mentioned before," she said thoughtfully. "The young pill as I described him. He announced himself as Lord Mordred, King Arthur's illegitimate offspring and nemesis. I remember because we had just completed a boffo production of Camelot at the Festival. He said he was an ex-Canadian army officer."

"Boasted about killing lots of ragtops in Afghanistan," put in Big Molly. "Nasty piece of work."

Celeste nodded. "I looked him up on line afterwards," she said. "But there was no Lord Mordred on Kinklife.ca, FetLife.com or any of our BDSM social media."

"I'll mention that and the perfume to Horatio," Claire said pensively. "Not one of our regulars, as Bertie would say. And if anyone has any further ideas about the rapist or the blackmailer you can contact me or the Man-In-Black at 'Ask Madame Claire.' Any time."

She smiled as she rose to her feet and hugged her goodbyes. "By the way, our next guest is Missy Alexis. She'll answer everything you've ever wanted to know about cross-dressing. With a dash of astrophysics from her day job at the Perimeter Institute." She had a special hug for Carol. "You're a very brave girl, Carol" she said compassionately. "I'm glad Fleur got you to venture out."

Claire had greatly enjoyed her day of legwork and socialising, especially at the companiable Stratford High Tea. She deeply appreciated the dedication of the six Munch hosts she had visited with and gave them high marks for their sterling efforts to give the BDSM community a highly successful social side. She was also intrigued by Celeste's memory of the former military man. Right age, too. Then there was the Too Much perfume. Another possible clue.

As she left, he heard Fleur launching into yet another new topic, something about a would-be ravisher named James and a lengthy

Ravisher's Questionnaire she had concocted for him. Fleur was well-intentioned, she knew. But she could be exhausting with her ceaseless flow of ideas and crusades.

The woman seemed to recognise it as well. She had actually asked Madame Claire for a cathartic drumming scene some time in the near future. Said she wanted to take a new stab at reorganising her life. Apparently she felt with some justification that she wasn't fully in control. Claire had been less than enthusiastic at the time. A catharsis scene could be difficult and time-consuming. On the other hand, a re-evaluation of Fleur's seemingly constant activity might not be such a bad idea after all. It would have to be carefully researched, of course.

She drove back to Marybourne with Fleur's problems, fruity perfume and Afghanistan on her mind. Killing ragtops was such a demeaning phrase. Not at all what the Canadian forces were about.

It had been a busy day of legwork. Six social stops and over 250 klicks in the BMW. Surprisingly exhausting in a way. But so much more rewarding than a slew of emails.

"Legwork," she said to herself, remembering the three beautiful, high-stepping ponies of that morning..

She smiled at the coincidence of the day's events and concentrated on her driving. It was all a matter of legwork after all.

Chapter 19 Of Boxes and Cups

Madame Claire and Leeza were taking the winding back roads from Marybourne to Kitchener, a few kilometres to the west. Wally's vintage BMW was purring along very nicely. These days, of course, it featured Claire's custom-made leopard seat covers, but she could still feel her husband's much loved presence in the car. Lohengrin had been his pride and joy.

Claire was dressed for a downtown business lunch. She was wearing a smart black dress with a gold leopard brooch high on her right breast. She had added her regular fascinator and high-heeled leopard shoes. She was a picture of the elegant woman around town.

They were heading for lunch at the Smuggler's Den, downstairs in the renovating Siebert Hotel. Claire intended to check out the postal boxes in the lobby. Specifically Box 147 that TallBlondeChick had designated as a drop-off point for her nefarious donations.

"I just want to inspect the layout and see how they're serviced," she told Leeza. "Only a look-see for now."

"I wish I had more time," Leeza said. "But Matt has to work this afternoon. They have a sick foal."

"He puts in crazy hours." Claire commented.

"Too many summer births. Registering a racehorse is all out of whack this year."

They were on King Street by now and Claire had to slow down for the Ion light rail cars than ran smack down the middle of the main drag. The spanking new transit system had only recently come into service. It ran eighteen kilometres from Fairview Park Shopping Centre in the south to Conestoga Mall in the north. Both Downtown Kitchener and Uptown Waterloo were benefitting enormously from the billion dollar system, but traffic and parking were still sorting themselves out.

"There are five construction cranes between us and the Siebert Hotel," Claire pointed out with a sigh. "Though it's great to see the downtown core bustling again."

"I guess we'll know to park farther out and take the Ion in future," said Leeza, idly flicking the tiny leopard floggers hanging from the rear-view mirror. "And here's something else I've learned recently." She smiled mischievously at Claire. "These miniature falls of yours are made of deer-skin."

Claire laughed. "I'm in awe of your attention to detail," she said. "Especially since you had other things on your mind when I told you that."

Leeza smiled impishly. "It does illustrate how different my life is these days. Having you for a mentor, I mean."

"I love you, too, girl," said Claire, appreciating the lifestyle by-play. "Lunch should be fun," she added, as she manoeuvred the BMW through the stop-and-start traffic and into the Siebert Hotel parking lot.

"Box 147," said Leeza. "Since it's the Siebert, I'll bet they're brass and highly polished."

They were.

*

"Are these P.O. Boxes still active," Claire asked the wizened clerk at the imposing front desk.

"Not as busy as they used to be in the 19th Century," replied the elderly man in the gold Siebert vest. "It's mainly iPhones these days."

Claire nodded pleasantly. "Only a short while ago it would have been all Blackberries." She peered around the construction scaffolding cluttering up the spacious front lobby. "Who on earth uses P.O. Boxes now?"

The clerk fastidiously dusted a speck of dust off his carved Victorian counter. "Clients still have private liaisons," he told her, straight-faced. "And, with the Ion we're getting lots of new job-hires in the core. Two weeks or a month before they get settled into a new condo or apartment. All the bankrupt factories are getting gentrified."

'Manulife is expanding again," put in Leeza, who kept up on the flourishing job market.

"And Google," he said. The old Lang Tannery and the Breithaupt are filled with start-ups."

"Must be hard keeping all this ancient brass gleaming so brightly," Claire said. "With the ongoing renovation, I mean."

He nodded sagaciously. "The boxes go back to when Berlin was the main stagecoach stop between Toronto and London. Kitchener was Berlin till the First World War. Brilliant shiny brass is a Siebert tradition." He turned to greet a man approaching with a wheeled suitcase. "Excuse me, ladies."

"147 is right at the top of the stairs down to the restaurant," Claire observed to Leeza, starting down.

"Visible from the armchairs in the lobby," the girl said.

"The carpenters and plasterers probably work all night," Claire noted. "Stake-outs R Us isn't in the cards."

They were greeted at the foot of the stairs by Sammy Seagram, manager of the Smuggler's Den. "Madame Claire, how nice to see you again. You too, Miss. Discreet table for two, or are you expecting a crowd?"

"Just us, Sam," Claire told him. "This renovation must be driving you crazy."

"It will all be worth it someday," he assured her. "The Siebert is going to be real grand again. A four million dollar face lift."

He led them through the small six-to-eight person dining rooms to an unobtrusive table for two near the arched entrance to the convention hall where the Black Wally was held. "No one will even know you're here," he said obsequiously, signalling for a waitress. "We cater for private assignations at the Smuggler's Den."

Claire put her leopard shoulder bag over the chair and glanced briefly at the menu. Leeza took more time, she was less familiar with the Smuggler's Den fare. After they had ordered, Claire beckoned Sam over again.

"Sammy, I'm thinking of booking a room for a daytime Tarotherapy seminar," she said, using a cover story she had come up with in the car. No more than forty, forty-five participants."

"The Wallenstein Room would be ideal, Madame Claire," he said smoothly. "Four hundred dollars from ten AM to four-thirty. Seeing as it's you, I could give you a special 15% discount. 20% if the renovation is still in progress.

"A Friday in August," she informed him. It all sounded legitimate enough that maybe she would go ahead anyway. She did use the tarot in counselling sessions.

"20% then," he said. "I'll be honoured to arrange the catering."

"What you do for Sir Robert's FatMan parties would be excellent."

The wait-girl brought their lunch. Quiche for Leeza. French Onion Soup for Claire, who continued chatting to Sam Seagram.

"I plan to bring in a guest lecturer from the States," she improvised. "Here for a week or more. I wondered about the Post Office boxes upstairs?"

He puffed up his chest. "A traditional service for Siebert guests," he said importantly. "I supervise them, as a matter of fact. At least in terms of any incoming mail or messages."

"How are they operated?"

"Any guest signing up for a box is given their own key."

Claire nodded wisely. "Is there much of a charge?"

"Like I say, Madame Claire, it's primarily a hotel service. $5 a day. Our clients seem to appreciate the traditional aspect and the guaranteed privacy. Enjoy your lunch." He smiled politely and left them to eat it.

Leeza raised her eyebrows. "You're very adroit at eliciting information," she congratulated Claire. "Pity we can't just ask him who has the key to 147."

"We'd need a good reason."

"A nasty blackmailer isn't dramatic enough?"

Claire smiled. "Maybe we could enlist his help. I'll have to think about it." She toyed with a long strand of cheese, expertly twirling it around her soup spoon. "He was perceptive enough to give us this secluded table."

"I guess he could tell I'm smitten," Leeza said softly. "One of my favourite expressions right now."

"Smitten?" repeated Claire, savouring the word. "It makes me feel deliciously sexy."

They looked into each other's eyes. There was something almost tangible between them. Pheromones flickered between the French Onion soup and the Quiche.

"I wish I were free this afternoon," Leeza said longingly. "But I can't let Matt down."

Claire was very understanding. "He's everything a...sibling should be."

"I think of him as a brother, but I sometimes think he regards me as a shameless nuisance."

"He should know," Claire said with a half-smile. Then her tone dropped an octave and became almost husky. "You're unbelievably lovely today, dear girl. I adore the jacket."

Leeza was dressed largely in white, with a purple Bolero jacket and matching shoes. With her long raven hair and lilac eyes she was quite stunning. "I don't often get out for a business lunch" she said softly. "And the Bolero seemed most appropriate."

They picked at their lunch in companionable silence for a while. Claire finished first.

"I've been thinking you'd probably get off on Japanese bondage," she said, feeling her way. "You're so tactile."

Leeza's eyebrows raised. "Tied up?" she asked, a touch surprised.

"The sensation of rope drawing silkily across your flesh is one of the most sensual feelings there is."

Leeza was intrigued. "Mind you, I've seen Japanese rope-play on Kinklife.ca," she said thoughtfully. "Very neat and precise. The knots are so fantastically intricate."

"You'd have to abandon yourself to yet another fabulous new experience. No worries about Matt, or even Leeza come to that." As usual, Claire knew what she was talking about. She had been into bondage for years. "Being bound and helpless means you are free to be your true self. You just leave everything to me"

Leeza smiled. "That's one of the things I most like about BDSM. As a submissive, I don't have to Do anything. Simply be."

"With luck we can fit some play in over the weekend," Claire more or less promised.

They chatted easily for some time about bondage and the secret pleasures of total Suspension. "I have a beam and pulleys set up for it in the dungeon," Claire said.

"I'm sure I'll love it," said the young girl, fascinated by the world opening before her. "Now we really must go." Leeza might be submissive, but she wasn't a doormat. She had a mind of her own.

Claire took her arm and steered her through the dining rooms and back to the cash desk, where Sammy Seagram was keeping an eye on things. "You ladies look very contented," he smiled. "A tribute to our cuisine, I hope."

"And the company," said Leeza, as Claire handed her Visa to the cashier.

Sam was at his most sycophantic. "Have a nice afternoon, Madame Claire. You too, Miss..er..?"

Leeza shot a sidelong glance at Claire. "Tiffany," she said with unexpected firmness. "Tiffany Purejoy."

Claire coughed in surprise. She was still covering up a chuckle as they made their way up the stairs and out to the car. It turned over a couple of times, then caught. "Nice to meet you, Ms. Purejoy," she said, with a satisfied smile. "You're a writer, I believe."

"Short stories," the girl said, looking very pleased with herself. "And do call me Tiffany. It's my given name."

*

After dropping Tiffany/Leeza off at the foot of the hill, Claire decided to spend the afternoon doing necessary domestic jobs. She thought it would be a good idea to bake a pie or two in the evening, so she added the ingredients to her bi-weekly grocery list and spent nearly an hour at the Marybourne Loblaws. Feeling energetic, she also deadheaded the geraniums on the patio and polished Lohengrin for her early morning trip down to London to visit Detective Horatio Bellingham. She liked a day catching up on her chores.

It was gone eight o'clock by the time she took out her baking trays and lined up the requisite ingredients. She had two pies in mind, a Mermaid Marshmallow and a special Falling In Love pie. That had been one of Wally's favourites. As she mixed and stirred she remembered how it had come about, five years ago now.

They were tootling back from a Christmas spent in Florida and had stopped off at a pie bake-off In Jonesboro, Virginia. A Falling In Love pie had taken first place and Wally had coaxed the recipe out of a perky gray-haired woman with a glorious Southern accent.

"Best pie I ever tasted," he had said, when they reached home and she made one for him. "Falling In Love pie. You'd kinda figure someone was trying to tell us something." Something really special, Claire recalled fondly. They had gotten married five days later.

She whipped the whipping cream the way the recipe called for. Very stiffly. Heavens, she missed that man. He had been a continual joy to have around. The love of her life, that was for sure. Sometimes, even with all her friends and steady busy-ness, she felt very alone.

"Tut, tut," she said to herself, dismissing her nostalgic thoughts and popping the pies in the oven. She would have to give a slice to Leeza the next time she came over. Tiffany-to-be. Another person who was good to have around.

Which is when there was an unexpectedly loud knocking at the leopard-painted outside door. "Perfect timing," she said and headed for the front hall, thinking it must be Leeza. "Though she usually knocks and enters" she thought idly. The main door was rarely locked and as she approached it opened.

"Claire! Madame Claire! It's me, Matt."

Claire was surprised. She hardly ever saw Matt in the evening. "You're always welcome, Matt dear," she said, with no little pleasure. She liked Matt very much, even though he was skeptical about BDSM. He was very genuine in his own fashion.

"Sorry to barge in on you," he apologised perfunctorily. "I have to see you. I didn't have time to change." He was in working clothes. Corduroy pants, Wellington boots and a denim windbreaker. He was tense. Not at all his usual dryly upbeat self.

"We had a rotten blow at the stables," he explained, kicking off his boots. "We lost a foal. Too weak to survive." He was talking in short, urgent sentences, almost staccato. "I got home late. I was real tired. Sat at my desk, I had a report to write. I took a slug of McClelland's to wind down."

They had gone into the kitchen. "Coffee for you, m'lad, Claire said and loaded the Keurig. "Have you eaten?"

"I'm not hungry. I been putting in long hours," he said, looking exhausted. "Six AM for exercising. We have thirty-five race horses to stretch out. Lunch, and then I'm back at two o'clock for my whispering stint. We're grooming RogueMeister and Lady Barbara for the Prince o' Wales Stakes in Fort Erie."

Claire smiled. "You still talking to them, the horses?" she asked.

"Tell 'em we can leave the rest of the field behind," he said with a tired grin. "Then, with all this late foaling, it's often an evening break and an all-nighter."

He stopped in the doorway of the sitting room and took a sheet of copy paper out of his jacket pocket. "Claire, did you check your emails today?" She shook her head. He spoke sharply. "Check it now," he said tersely.

He took a large gulp of coffee. The Keurig always came out at a drinkable temperature. "Leeza uses my tablet," he explained. "This email came in for her late yesterday." He opened the sheet of paper but kept it in his hand.

Claire's laptop was on the coffee table. She went to Microsoft Outlook. "You seem upset, Matt..."

He leaned over her shoulder, pointing to her screen. "You've got one as well. Third one down. From TallBlondeChick. Go to it on Kinklife...... Same as Leeza's. Sent last night."

Claire wasn't surprised. "To be expected, I guess," she said, glancing at the familiar email and matching it to the hard copy Matt held out. . "Request for assistance....Outed as an active member.... Divergent sex - Ah, this is new - Leeza and I are 'dyke and dolly.' Poetic, isn't it? Wrong, too." She skimmed the rest of the email. "Basically the same as the one Francis got. I'm looking into it."

"Some creep out there thinks she's real witty," he said angrily. Unlike Leeza, Matt was naturally dominant. "I can't afford to have Leeza Outed, Claire. The whole fucking mess could jeopardise my jockey licence."

Claire knew where he was coming from. "What's the purse for the Prince of Wales?" she asked him quietly.

"$300,000" he replied, his face darkening. "The winning rider gets 10%." He punched the coffee table with his fist. "There comes a time, Claire, when a man just has to assert himself."

The oven buzzer rang out. Claire put on her kitchen gloves and took out the pies. "Leeza would never take advantage of you," she said. "All through lunch she was concerned about getting home. She knew you had to go back to work."

Matt frowned. "She's so damned busy being Leeza. I'm supposed to just go along."

Claire cut into the Falling In Love pie. "She's changing. Growing up, I guess." She put a slice of pie on a dessert plate. "Here, it's my special Falling In Love pie. Careful, it'll be hot."

He sighed deeply. He was looking despondent. "She loves being Leeza. The thing is I get treated differently since she came out. Even by you, Madame Claire. You want her as an assistant. Your Doctor Watson."

Claire could see that he was hurting. Feeling hard done by. "Matt dear," she said. "You were the first one I asked to help."

"Huh?"

"I asked you to watch over Francis. To stop him going off half-cocked."

He had never looked at it that way. "I guess you did. Yes, you did. Sorry."

"Leave this blackmail business to me, Matt. I'm good at what I do."

He threw up his hands, apologetically. "What else can I do? I don't want to ruin things for Leeza. Or for me, come to that." He forked up a piece of pie. "Hey, this crust is close to perfect."

"Light and flaky, just like me. That's what Wally used to say."

He grinned, a touch sheepishly. "Christ, I'm beat." He took another mouthful. He was making amends for his ill humour. "It's great. What's in it?"

She stood behind him and massaged his shoulders. "Condensed milk. Chocolate pudding mix. Unsweetened chocolate and whipped cream. Take off your jacket," she added. "Your neck muscles are all knotted up. You say you lost a foal?"

He was under a lot of strain. "Cute little fella. Didn't have the strength to get up on those splindly legs. Couldn't nurse either."

Her thumb dug into his shoulder muscles. "Like slabs of iron," she said. "This one is the size of a goose-egg."

"I feel like shit," he sighed. "Some TallBlondeChick bugging Leeza was the last thing I needed."

"What you need is something really therapeutic," she said, and had a sudden brainwave. "Chinese cups, that's it. They would loosen you up." .

"Chinese cups?" he asked, relaxing a little under her ministrations.

"An esoteric branch of Chinese medicine. Very deep massage. Maybe a bit New Age for you."

He was interested. He knew how uptight and petty he had been about Leeza. "You forget I'm basically a horse whisperer, Claire. Chinese remedies aren't exactly New Age in my book. I've had acupuncture and used it on horses."

"I have a full set of cups downstairs," Claire said buoyantly and headed down to the basement dungeon... "Slip your shirt off and we'll have a show and tell."

He partly unbuttoned his shirt but didn't take it off. "I'm not fully sold yet," he said, stretching out.

"I bought these in Toronto's Chinatown," she told him, bringing up a bamboo carrying case. "They're thick glass globes called cups. The bottoms are flared and open so they can sit on the skin. I have four different sizes."

The largest Chinese cup was roughly the size of a big breakfast cup. The smallest, not quite as big as a tennis ball. She lit a candle and held the opening of a medium sized cup over the flame. "I heat it to create a vacuum," she said. "Then, place the cup over the tense spots." She demonstrated on her own arm. "Once it seals itself, you can move it around."

Matt was mildly suspicious. "Is this part of your BDSM gear?" he asked.

"The Chinese certainly don't think so." She was right as far as she went. She didn't think it necessary to tell him that she had learned about Chinese cups at a BDSM workshop. Submissives loved the deep muscle sensations and really got off on the florid circular marks the cups left. She often used them successfully in her straight massage sessions.

"Take your damned shirt off and lie on your belly. It won't hurt, I promise."

He stripped to the waist and lay back down "I guess if it doesn't hurt, it's not BDSM," he said, gently kidding her. "And Claire, I'm sorry if I barked at you when I came in."

"Close your eyes," she said simply. "This is a half-hour process. You'll sleep like a baby tonight."

She heated a succession of cups over the flame and affixed them to his back and shoulders. The smallest ones went on his neck.

"I don't usually talk much when I'm cupping," she informed him quietly. "The action has a mesmerising effect on me. How are you feeling?"

"My back...? Just f-fine," he replied, not opening his eyes. "Very... relaxed."

She heated and positioned more cups. Soon there were well over a dozen on his back and shoulders. Some were touching. Some spaced a little apart. She picked up the candle and very gently blew the heat of the flame over his skin between the cups. To Matt, his eyes tightly closed, it was as if he had a cityscape of globular highrises on his back, with a warm breeze blowing through. He recognised the physical impossibility even as he appreciated the oddly visual sensation

"S-Sky-scrapers," he murmured, with an intake of breath as Claire drizzled a small amount of coconut oil onto the naked flesh around the base of each cup.

"This makes them slide easily over the skin. Oh, and keep your shirt on at work for a few days," she instructed him softly. "The Chinese leave you with a timely bodily reminder. If you start to feel at all tense, peer at your back in a mirror. Muscle memory will have you relaxing in no time."

His flesh was bunched up in the cups for about an inch. The vacuum was causing the upswell. Because he was lying on his stomach, he couldn't see it, of course, and there was absolutely no pain.

"How's the BMW holding up?" he asked idly, totally off topic. "Lohengrin."

"Still a bit slow starting at times," she said, smiling as she understood how good and high he was getting.

For a while she continued adding cups and walking them across his back and down his shoulders. She blew more flame and he shivered with tactile enjoyment. For the most part, he had stopped moving or speaking. You didn't talk to horses the way he did without understanding that there were more things on heaven and earth than philosophy could account for. "Horatio." he mumbled. One disembodied word. It was his first speech in almost ten minutes.

"Yes, I'm seeing him in the morning," Claire said, pretty high herself. Focussing on placing and moving the cups worked on her mind rather like making crackers. "And I think you'll sleep very soundly tonight," she added, starting to remove the glass cups from his back.

"Like a...baby," he agreed blissfully.

"But not here, Matt. Not tonight. I have things to do." She continued prying up the Chinese cups with the tip of her finger and depositing them in their bamboo case. Later, she would wash and polish them.

"Plans to make," he said at length. "B-blackmailers to catch."

She moistened his back. "Before you go to bed run some of Leeza's body lotion over your shoulders. Your skin will be a bit dry."

Matt was delightfully mellow now. Stuff that had freaked him out before, no longer bothered him. It felt stupid to be jealous of Leeza's success. "You have such a w-wealth of folks in your life, Madame Claire. A jockey who's gonna win the Prince o' Wales stakes and a silly young filly who says she's a natural s-submissive. An' a b-blonde blackmailer an' a r-rabid rapist. You'll figure it all out I'm s-sure. You and my crazy, mixed up L-leeza...."

Claire smiled. "Who just may be Tiffany Purejoy before you know it," she said. "And I don't have a clue who's who yet. But my subconscious is working on it."

"I gotta admit one thing," Matt said, owlishly. "They're real clever."

"Who's clever?" she asked.

He nodded his head wisely. "These Chinese," he said, very seriously.

She grinned and threw a cushion at him.

Leopard, of course.

Chapter 20 OPP

In which Detective Constable Horatio Bellingham evidences his mettle and Madame Claire goads a ShortBaldingPrick

Claire couldn't help smiling to herself as she drove into the Western Region Headquarters of the Ontario Provincial Police. Lambeth Station, the sign said, 6355 Westminster Drive, London, ON.

It was an imposing building with elaborate brickwork that would not have been out of place in Whitehall of London, England. The one feature that could have made it even more traditionally British was if the traffic had been right-hand drive, barrelling along on the wrong side of the road.

"Tradition gives us pride of birth, just hearts and flawless manners," said Detective Constable Horatio Bellingham as he led her through the large foyer and into the inner offices of the C.I.B., the Criminal Investigation Branch. He was in uniform today, looking very smart and professional in his dark blue tunic and matching pants with a lighter blue stripe down the leg.

"A quick tour before we hit the evidence room and meet my colleague Olive Chow."

"You still get to show off your uniform, I see."

"It's who I am," he said good-naturedly. "The O.P.P. polices well over a million square kilometres of Ontario, together with 174,000 kilometres of water. We have 6,100 uniformed officers and 850 auxiliaries. Based at the Western headquarters here, we have 1,175 officers."

"Not a lot for the territory you cover."

"Hence the uniform. We need to make our presence visible, though I'll switch to civvies this afternoon when I come to Tilverdale to interview Dawn Gretsko."

Madame Claire gave him an innocent look. "With a woman along, I trust."

He grinned and dropped five years. "Olive will be with me. She's a sketch artist as well as a Detective Constable."

"That could be very useful. Dawn's a bright kid. A few instant sketches could trigger some additional memories."

He turned serious. "You didn't do too poorly yourself. Can't tell you how much I appreciate it. Most succinct telephone briefing I've ever had. Even the mother seemed more cooperative."

"Sophia's had a hard life. Be kind to her."

There was a twinkle in his eye. "Yes, ma'am" he said.

"Just Claire is fine. Though I guess an occasional Madame is all right."

They had entered a small office. A wooden desk, three chairs, an ultra-modern computer, a whiteboard headed "Stratford," a tidy collection of files and papers. He picked up a few typed pages.

"Anyway, Claire, I was impressed enough to give you a rundown of the Carol Weber case." He passed her the stapled sheets. "Put these notes in your bag for later. The man who assaulted her so brutally was named Henry. Olive did a sketch. He's roughly the same age and build as Dawn's Edward."

Claire surprised him. "What did his mother call him?"

He raised an eyebrow. "Hank. Is it relevant?"

"Edward was Eddie. Their profiles were both deleted, I take it."

He nodded. "I've included Henry's emails from Ms. Weber's computer. One-sided of course."

"I'll be interested in any similarities."

"Why?"

'I thought he might be made up. A sock puppet."

"Your Edward?"

"Not my Edward, please. I also wondered about Carol's Henry.'

"Actually, the chances are they're both your people," he said seriously. "They each used the social website Kinklife.ca to make contact. "

"It doesn't follow that they have to be in the Lifestyle."

"It's only one point in a growing chain of evidence. I said we'd meet Olive down there at 9:30, the evidence room, that is. She should have everything laid out for your perusal."

"It was the yellow rope you mentioned that made me skeptical. If I'm right it doesn't sound like a rope anyone really into BDSM would work with. Doms are very particular about what they use."

He ushered her to the elevator. "There are two pieces of the rope now, one from each crime scene. And, Claire, tell me exactly what you see. Though to be fair, we're leaning quite strongly to a BDSM perpetrator."

*

Detective Constable (3rd class) Olive Chow was a dark-haired young woman who didn't look much older than Leeza Llewellyn. Probably, like Horatio, in her mid to late twenties, thought Madame Claire. Born in Hong Kong, she learned later. She had long, slender fingers and greeted Claire with a firm grip.

"I've been looking forward to meeting you," she said pleasantly. "Detective Bellingham says you're old friends."

Detective Bellingham coloured slightly. "Acquaintances I said. Honest."

The young woman grinned. "Anyway, Claire, you come highly recommended. I have a dozen pieces of evidence set out for your inspection."

They were in clear plastic bags, each sealed with a stamped and numbered tag.

"That sounds awfully official," smiled Claire. "And if we were playing Kim's game in Brownies I'd say there were only ten."

"You're right," said Olive, smiling back. "Two are out for DNA testing."

"Most of these are from the Stratford case," Detective Bellingham said. "I'm hoping Dawn will have some clothing or photos this afternoon."

"I think Mrs. Gretsko burned the clothes, and I very much doubt they were into pictures."

"The rope you picked up on. This short piece in Bag 1 was untangled from a lilac bush in Tilverdale by Dawn's friend Officer Puri. It was knotted very tightly to the bush according to Vijay."

"Cut off rather than untied," Claire observed. "Dawn said he threatened her with a sheath knife."

"Carol called it a skinning knife," said Olive. "He used it on her. The photographs in this plastic bag show a circle around her right nipple."

"Not deep," Horatio Bellingham pointed out. "More of a scratch. Beginning knife play we assumed."

"He was interrupted you say?"

"Ms. Weber was blindfolded early on, but she could still hear. Apparently the animals in the Pet Shoppe were kicking up quite a fuss."

"There are also pix of the left breast in this other bag," Olive said. "Bite marks."

Claire was thoughtful. "This long length of yellow polypropylene rope, 25 feet or so. Why did he leave it?"

Bellingham answered her crisply. " 25 feet exactly. He had her tied down with it. To a pallet of dog biscuits."

"Are the two pieces from the same coil?"

"We think so, but we haven't been able to get a scientific ruling on that yet."

Claire picked up another bag. "These pieces of apple. Lots of blood and signs of chomping. Was this what Henry used as a gag?"

Olive looked a little disgusted. "Somehow she bit through it and spat it up into his face. That's when he got incensed and punched her. Broke her jaw. Then he nearly throttled her. Bag 6 is photos of her throat. She was lucky to survive."

"Going back a bit. That big bag. The skirt she was wearing? And Number 8, her panties?"

"Cut off," Olive said grimly. "The blouse in Number 9 is covered with bloodstains. Hers."

"Am I to take it the blood on Dawn's tennis racket is still out being tested?"

Detective Bellingham took over. "That and a Blue Jays baseball cap we fished out of a dumpster out back at the Pet Shoppe. Carol Weber said Henry was wearing one. Wrote, actually. Speech was virtually impossible."

"The blood on the racket was definitely Edward's. She hit him with it during her escape. Her flight, actually..."

Bellingham nodded. "I think we'll soon have conclusive proof Edward & Henry are one and the same." He changed the subject abruptly. "Tell me about the girl who accompanied your... this Edward."

"Early twenties. Barely spoke. Plump, long scraggly reddish hair under a big floppy hat that covered most of her face." She glanced at Olive. "Maybe a rough sketch will jog Dawn's memory."

Horatio was following his own thoughts. "Carol thought there might have been a woman present. But she was blindfolded almost from the time she got there."

Madame Claire slapped her forehead with an open palm. "Dammit," she said explosively. "Sometimes I think my mind is going! I meant to tell you something important right away when I got here. Sorry." She collected herself. "There was a girl at the Pet Shoppe. Carol and Fleur proved it."

"Fleur?" he asked, frowning.

"When I saw Carol at the Stratford High Tea she said that she had remembered the smell of cheap perfume on the night of the assault. Citrus, she wrote. Fleur took her shopping. You recall Gennifleur, Horatio. My guest on the Ravishment show."

"Shopping? " queried Olive blankly..

"Shopper's Drugmart and Dollarama. Fleur can be very persuasive. Quite pushy in fact. She hauled Carol off to smell all kinds of scents. She recognised it immediately. Grapefruit and lemons. It was called Too Much at Dollarama. Citrussy and cheap. She's convinced it was what she smelled in the stockroom."

Detective Bellingham was very businesslike. "Olive, get a statement from Carol and Fleur, Claire will tell you how to contact the latter. Dawn may remember the citrus smell as well. We'll drop into a Dollarama on the way to Tilverdale." He smiled at Claire. "I wouldn't be too concerned about your mental state, Claire. I've been firing facts and questions at you since you arrived."

Claire smiled weakly. "I guess nobody's perfect."

He grinned and promptly took another tack. "You say Dawn's girl spoke. What did she say?"

She hesitated for a moment before replying. "Dawn figured the girl in the floppy hat had addressed Edward. Very briefly."

"In what way?"

"Dawn wasn't 100% sure. She thought the girl said 'Yes, Master.'"

Horatio's eyes lit up. "Which is a BDSM term, right? It ties in with Kinklife.ca as a conduit."

Claire nodded slowly. "It would appear so. Yes."

He saw this as the lead to something that had been nagging at him. "Which I gather from your earlier attitude, the yellow rope doesn't. Not to your satisfaction, anyhow. Why not?"

She attempted to explain. "I've been bothered by it since you first mentioned it at the studio. Yellow polypropylene rope and BDSM just doesn't compute. No one with any experience in the Scene would touch the crappy stuff."

"What would they touch? Use?"

Claire shrugged. "Hemp as first choice. At the very least jute, cotton, linen, even silk or nylon. Never Poly propylene."

The detective constable wasn't buying it. "Maybe he left it behind deliberately. Trying to confuse the issue."

"Vijay Puri said the knot on the lilac was a bugger to undo," Olive put in quietly.

"There's also the skill level involved," Claire pointed out.

"What did Dawn say?"

"Not a rigger," Madame Claire pointed out determinedly. "A rank amateur who had to stun her first. Bondage Doms have great skills."

Horatio pushed her hard. "Okay, so he's not a bondage expert. He's a damned rapist, right? A rapist who can tie Dawn and Carol up so they can't move. Who's a member of Kinklife.ca."

"Anyone can join," protested Claire. "References aren't needed."

"He contacted the two girls off a very specialised site. A rape site, for crying out loud."

"Any remotely interested party could locate that. Kinklife.ca is easy to move around in."

"How's about 'Yes, Master?'"

"I agree that points to BDSM"

"And you agree you don't want him to be one of your people?"

"I don't, for sure. But I've done a lot of research. Talked to dozens of LIfestylers."

He was interrogating her now. "Such as?"

"Every Munch host within a sixty kilometre radius of K-W. Kitchener, Guelph, Cambridge, Brantford, Woodstock, Stratford, all face to face. Many others by phone. Milton, Hamilton, Stoney Creek, London. Even Mississauga and Toronto."

"What are you looking for specifically?"

Claire was blunt. "First, anyone of our regular crowd we think might be capable of such a horrible act. Between us we know everyone in the Scene. Really know them, I mean."

He was skeptical. "Rapists are notoriously good at concealing their urges. Secondly?"

"I've also been enquiring about short-term guests. Someone who came to one Munch, maybe two. A person who obviously didn't fit in. A pill, as Celeste, our Stratford host, described one possibility.."

Horatio relaxed and gave her an approving smile. "You've evidently covered a lot of ground. And thank you for bearing with me. I'm like a dog with a bone sometimes."

"He's good at his job," Olive said reassuringly. "Drove me straight up the wall when he interviewed me to be his assistant. He'll go far, will our Horatio."

Detective Bellingham gave them one of his mildly sheepish grins. "Women," he said ruefully, and snapped right back into his questioning. "What would you do, Claire, if you or one of your hosts came up with a promising lead?"

"Three possibilities. Tell you, tell Olive, or try to get the lead to contact me."

He stopped her. "Whoa!" he said sternly. "What makes you think he'll contact you?"

"Edward got in touch with Dawn off one brief comment on a Kinklife.ca rape-play site."

He stared at her hard, without speaking for a moment. "He's violent, you know. And getting worse"

"I'm not proposing to meet the man. At most a description. Age, manner, maybe appearance. A winnowing process."

He nodded slowly. He was satisfied. "It's been an interesting meeting. Thanks for coming in. You've given us something different to think about. You have any questions, Olive?"

She laughed. "You've got to be kidding, boss."

"Claire?"

"There is one more piece of evidence, Olive. I think you accidentally covered the bag with the skirt."

The young woman grinned. "You don't miss much, do you?"

"I can be forgetful sometimes."

Olive moved the skirt bag and took up Bag Number 12.

"Ah yes," said Horatio. "The blindfold. The one Henry used on Ms. Weber."

Claire took the plastic bag in her hand and examined the blue blindfold carefully. "You're not going to like this, detective," she said slowly. "It's another inconsistency." She was firm. "Like the polypropylene rope."

"Meaning?"

"Meaning it's got dirty smears all over it and it's held together by a little gold safety pin. It is tacky and even possibly dangerous. No experienced Dom would use it."

"That's a pretty sweeping statement," Detective Bellingham said doubtfully.

"We take care of our toys. Canes for example are sanded against splinters all the time. I cannot reconcile the title of Master with a blindfold that's pinned together."

"What do you think, Olive?"

Polypropylene rope, tacky blindfold, even an apple as a gag..." Olive ticked off Claire's inconsistencies. "Looks like you might have been right when you said he was trying to mislead us. A Master, as the mystery girl called him, deliberately covering his tracks."

"Maybe a slip of the tongue," he ruminated. "According to Dawn Gretsko that was all she said, right?"

"And not a word at the Pet Shoppe," Olive pointed out.

Claire was thoughtful. "She could be his weak link. Another lead, for sure."

Detective Bellingham nodded. "When Carol spat the bloodied pieces of apple in his face he lost control utterly. His breed of rapist hate women so much they truly want to see them dead. Maybe Ms. Too Much intervened."

He turned to Claire and extended his hand. "Madame Claire, I think we're done for now. You have opened the box we were falling into. A Master, covering his tracks. Or possibly an untrained amateur. Follow up with the pill as you suggested. Give him a titbit on Kinklife.ca. It worked with Dawn and Carol. Just remember, he's dangerous."

"There's a fine line between violent rape and murder," Olive said.

"A description is all we need. Youthful twenties. The victims can identify him. Between them and his DNA we'll separate him from the other three."

"You'll follow up on the mystery girl?" Claire asked.

"You could be right about his weak link." His manner turned very earnest. "We really do try to serve and protect, you know." He gave her a faint, almost vulnerable half-smile. "And we really do have to catch him. Before he goes right off the rails and kills his next victim."

He walked her out of the headquarters building and across the parking lot to Lohengrin.

"Nice car," he said admiringly.

"Restoring it was Wally's project. My late husband."

"The seat covers are very You."

"I don't know where he found them. It was one of his last gifts to me."

He smiled. Such a warm smile, she thought.

"No silly risks, remember."

"Not my style.'

He raised his hand in a half salute and went back into the building.

The car started right away.

*

As she took the cloverleaf off Highbury Avenue on to Highway 401 Claire couldn't get Horatio Bellingham's dire warnings out of her mind. She had always known that with some blackhearted rapists the crime of rape itself was not enough. Either by mischance, by getting carried away, or by sheer malicious intent, rape could become murder.

Or, looked at another way, the desire to kill was the underlying factor that led to certain rape. How terrible, she thought, if that was the lurking motivation here. Not yet quite out in the open, but heading inexorably in that direction. Perhaps the wretched rapist didn't know how far his hidden impulses wanted to push him.

By and large, she was pleased with her visit to Horatio Bellingham's London HQ. He had listened attentively to her skepticism regarding the accumulated evidence like the Polypropylene rope and the flimsy sleep mask. She didn't think it had changed his opinion that someone from the Community was involved, but at least he was now aware that some things didn't quite add up. Not that the use of 'Master' was something that she could readily dismiss. It was used extensively in the Scene, she reflected, as she drove down the highway, the 'four-oh-one' as it was generally known.

In effect, the 401 was Ontario's Main Street, running 827 kilometres from the Windsor/Detroit River to the Quebec border. The part that ran through North Toronto was the busiest freeway in the world and with twelve to eighteen lanes, one of the widest, handling well over half a million vehicles a day. It skirted several important cities, like Kingston, Oshawa, Guelph Kitchener/Waterloo/Cambridge and London, and even the one Waterloo Regional exit had to cope with 130,000 vehicles daily. It's official name was the MacDonald-Cartier highway, after two early Canadian premiers, one English and one French. It was spectacularly laid out in long sweeping curves between timbered hills and rich agricultural land. It was by far the biggest truck route on the planet and due driver attention had to be paid, but it was still a perfect drive for deep thinking.

And Madame Claire had plenty to think about. Not simply the merciless rapist, Edward, Henry, whoever, but her good friend Francis Dickie the medically retired Major, and his problem with the blackmailer. Her problem, Matt and Leeza's problem, even Tiffany's, was the central point where the two such different cases converged.

She had a late afternoon date arranged with Leeza/Tiffany to go over the O.P.P. meeting, set up so Tiffany could work on her Kinklife.ca 'story' that evening. But Claire was in excellent time and the Smuggler's Inn at the Hotel Siebert was on her way home. She decided to drop in to see if Sammy Seagram had any news on Box 147.

"I done my level best, Madame Claire," he protested volubly. "But I can't watch it all the time."

"How about incoming mail," she asked him patiently. "Is our TallBlondeBlackmailer receiving scads of responses?"

"Not that many," Sam said. "There were two the day before yesterday and I haven't spied anyone come to collect."

"Maybe you could open it up and see if they've gone." she suggested.

"Yeah, I guess I could do that for you," he said grumpily. "I'm down in the basement Den most of the time, you know."

He rummaged through his pockets and came up with the skeleton key. "They musta been picked up," he said, a bit sulky. "Though I didn't see no one."

Claire nodded gloomily. "I understand, Sammy. You can't exactly do a stake-out, can you."

"I'm sorry, Madame Claire, truly I am." he said obsequiously. "I wanna catch this TallBlonde female as much as you do. She shouldn't be sullying the Siebert post office boxes for her blackmailing tomfoolery."

"We'll catch her in the act, Sam. Or him. The "chick" could be a cover. Criminals always make silly mistakes when they think they're safe." She smiled at him. "Just keep me posted, that's all I can ask."

"That's a good one, Madame Claire," he said with a leer, and sidled back down to the Smuggler's Den.

She watched him go with a thoughtful frown on her face. then collected her thoughts and went out to Lohengrin. "More activity around the P.O. Box, that's what we need," she said to herself as she headed for Walnut cottage. "It's time we gave our miserable blackmailer more work to do."

*

Later that afternoon, after bringing Leeza up to speed on the information about Carol, Madame Claire was ready to tackle her idea of giving TallBlondeChick a crash course in Blackmailing 201.

"We'll flood Box 147 with new mail," she told the beautiful young girl. "Letters from you, me, Francis and so on. The more we can come up with, the better chance there is that TallBlondeDipshit will make a mistake."

"Letters she or he has to answer, you mean. What, for example?"

"You'll have a busy evening writing out your Tiffany story for Kinklife. So let's say we have an hour before you leave. We need something that will annoy Dipshit no end. I'll draft out an approach from Francis this evening. Maybe an offer to pay up, providing certain guarantees are met. Impossible guarantees."

"I have to remember I'm still Leeza with the blackmailer. I've been thinking Tiffany all day."

"Complicated, isn't it. Tell you what, use my laptop to edit your Leeza Labelle profile. Delete lots of information. Minimal information, the blackmail made you thin it out. What could you use that will spark anger?"

Leeza grinned. "That I lost my waitressing job and don't have any money, let alone $225.00."

"Good start, but let's make the bastard good and mad. I know, instead of the money order TBC asked for send in a counter check with a fictitious account number. Though I very much doubt there's a bank account set up in TallBlonde's name."

"How much?"

"Pick an odd figure, say $79. All you've got after being canned, remember."

Leeza bent over the laptop. "What are you thinking of from yourself?"

"I came up with it on the way home from the Siebert. My intention is to goad the bastard into doing something stupid. I thought I'd start with "Hello, you TallBlondeDrinkOfPiss... "

Leeza gulped. "That does grab the attention."

Claire smiled beatifically. "So will the email, I think. It will go something like this... *"I'm responding to your unbelievably retarded piece of blackmailing shit of recent date. Sorry, you dumb cluck, did I say retarded? I meant bloody fucking moronic. $225? You figure I'll pay you $225 not to Out me as a Black Wally BDSM bigwig?" She winked at Leeza. "Good God, you cocksucker, pay me $225 and I'll gladly Out myself to the Times-Dispatch, for Christ's sake. They'd love to flash my face on the front page and expose me as a raging dominatrix and sexual pervert. " She grinned. It was a refreshing change of pace. "So grow up, you worthless piece of smelly shit. Fuck you, Madame Claire."*

Leeza looked both amused and appalled. "I didn't think you even knew some of those words. Though I must say mentioning the tabloid is a bit risky.

Madame Claire smiled. "Not if I want the response to wind up on Angele Del Zotto's desk."

"You're kidding me?"

"She has more sources and cowering slaves than you can shake a stick at. If anyone can track down our TallBlondeDrinkOfPiss, she can.".

"But - "

"She has a past, too. Something that could put her squarely on our side. If I read Angele's motivations right, TallBlondeDrinkOfStale Piss will soon be toast."

"Stale is good."

"So's the fact that I'm joining you on the front line. Now, dear Leeza/Tiffany, we're both becoming tethered goats. Though I guess you're still the goat. I'm just a humble goad. "

She laughed. It had been an interesting day. She was enjoying herself.

Chapter 21 The Tiffany story

Leeza knew exactly what she had to do if she was going to be Madame Claire's tethered goat. Quite simply, she had to become the best tethered goat in tiger-hunting history.

It was late on a warm, humid summer's evening. She was sitting comfortably on the cedar bench in the lush rose arbour at the bottom of her mother's well-tendered English garden. Her Mom was on vacation in Tuscany. There was a gleaming white full moon over the arbour. She was wearing a light cotton summer dress. She had Matt's new Tablet with her.

The first thing Madame Claire had suggested was that she should change her name. Goodbye, Leeza LaBelle. Hello, Tiffany Purejoy. She thanked Kinklife.ca for recognising that name and profile transformations were common in the Scene. BDSM was a constant learning and re-evaluation process

Then came the photographs, starting with the avatar picture at the head of the profile. She had selected a particularly cute ancient photo to replace the raven-haired beauty and her lilac contacts. It was an old black and white snapshot of Matt sprawled on a fluffy blanket, all androgynous blond curls and totally naked. Of course he was only six months old. He had a perky bottom and an open-mouthed expression of incredulity on his oh so pretty face. Claire would love it, she thought deliciously. The blanket was leopard.

For the general pictures she had staged a camera session in the shower, showing her peeping out from behind the semi-opaque plastic shower curtain with the pink and green seashells. The outline of her shapely body was plain to see, but her face was half hidden by the seashells and topped by the blonde curls of a short wig. Her eye contacts were baby blue. Very attractive and artistic, she thought with satisfaction. Upload.

For good measure she had added a head and shoulders of her kissing and cuddling Leyuka, the Llewellyn tabby. Much of her face was covered by the kitten, but again the blonde hair and blue eyes stood out. A sweet and innocent girl who would attract the attention of the cruel stalking tiger. Upload.

Next on the revised profile was the list of fetishes. Not too many. Just enough to tell a story that Edward or Henry, or whatever name he was now going by, could relate to. "Mild masochism....Barehanded spanking.... Being restrained so you can have your way with me.....Exposing my secret desires..... Being the opposite of Barbie......Being overpowered.....Tattoo drumming......A well-hung mind....... Being dominated in French...... Consensual non-consent..... . Being told what to do..... Writing sexy stories...."

It was something she had always excelled at, making up and telling stories. Tales of throbbing romance, recorded in red under the bedcovers. Now she needed a story that would whet the tiger's appetite and have him view her as a potential rape victim. A Come Hither story that would inspire him to contact her on Kinklife.ca. Lead him to stalk her in her tethered cage.

Perhaps she could try a romantic tale of an attempted seduction from her, Tiffany's, perspective. That would be a little different. A failed attempt at girlish enticement that somehow morphed into a need for ravishment play. Tiffany "LaBelle" Purejoy, left unsatisfied in the sexual stakes, straining for release.

She wondered in passing what Matt would think of her new and more lurid activities. Would he feel that what she was doing with Madame Claire was foolish? But then she remembered that in his own way he was at least as creative as she was. She could always feel what he would be thinking. Yes indeed, Matt would most likely approve. He was a born risk-taker. He rode fifteen hundred pound racehorses thundering around dirt tracks at forty, forty-five kilometres an hour.

Leeza, in her new role as Tiffany, thought and thought about her story. Then the plot flashed in her head. "School days," she said out loud. "I'll write about my school days. Such as they might have been."

An owl hooted in the sycamore tree. A wisp of cloud drifted over the moon.

"And, of course, there'll be a handsome young teacher at the centre of it. A French teacher. Monsieur Desjardin.

Tiffany had her muse. She laughed delightedly and started to write.

*

"TEACHER PETTING," she spelled out in caps, all too aware that she had to grab the tiger's attention right off. "*A RAPE THAT DIDN'T QUITE HAPPEN," by Tiffany Purejoy, all rights reserved.*

She began. "*My scene name is Tiffany Purejoy, but sometimes I call myself Tiffany LaBelle because I have always felt I'm a French Canadian girl at heart. I adore Francoise Sagan and desperately want to be Julie Delphy when I grow up. She is my absolute idol as an actress.*

"I am twenty-one now. I was sweet sixteen when I plotted to seduce our French teacher. He was 'tres charmante.' Henri Desjardin. When the rape that didn't quite happen took place I was very hurt and then super mad. I say that because what I really truly wanted, I just didn't get. Didn't quite get, I add thoughtfully, with a cute smile on my amazingly youthful Julie Delphy face.

"My parents had recently enrolled me at the Sainte Agathe Academy for Smart Girls. The girls were all dressed in navy-blue blazers and berets, crisp white shirts, striped ties and plaid skirts, with knee-high socks and 'sensible' black leather shoes. The teachers were black-habited nuns, except for Monsieur Desjardin. He wore a tweed jacket with patches on his elbows and rumpled hair. He was dreamy and seemingly very shy, and only seven years older than me. But as the Mother Superior was wont to say, I was mature for my age. To her, that was a bad thing.

"The Sainte Agathe Academy for Smart Girls is in the model Kanata suburb of Meditation Meadows, just outside Ottawa, our Canadian capital city. The main school building is impressive and picturesque. It has a high-pillared white porch running majestically across the front, with scads of perfectly proportioned mullioned windows. Or so the guidebook says. It also has a cute tower with a 'crenellated battlement' and a Maple Leaf flag on

top. Everything is ivy-clad and in a stiff breeze the rustling leaves make the redbrick school seem to shimmer and dance.

"Meditation Meadows itself was a developer's dream. He, the builder that is, grew up in Goderich on Lake Huron, a noted Ontario market and legal centre. Goderich is famous for its large centrepiece, the circular Courthouse Drive. Same at his pet project. At Meditation Meadows all the roads were laid out like spokes from an open grassy hub. There's a huge ornate bandstand and a twelve metre flowered clock in the manicured grass circle. Le Circ'le, as we natives called it.

"You see there were an equal number of English and French Canadian shops and cafes and boutiques spread out around Le Circ'le. The whole subdivision is half English and half French and totally Canadian. No cockeyed provincial turf wars in Meditation Meadows. We are civilised and -- " She broke off.

"Non, non, non, I can hear Monsieur Desjardin saying in his mellifluous Parisienne French."N'est pas un circ'le. C'est la round point." As in 'Pwoint' of course."

"Non, non, non, Non, " I said, going him one emphatic Non better. In the Meadows it's Le Circ'le. Le Circ'le, Monsieur Henri."

"That was the nub of the standing argument I had with my esteemed and so yummy-looking teacher. He flourished his stuffy old Catholic Curriculum and wielded a Parisienne French textbook. When I signed up for his nightschool class in Conversational French, I had actually prayed to Sainte Agathe that he would switch to our familiar Canadian vernacular. "La Round Point, indeed! Dozens and hundreds or words were completely different. But Henri was born stubborn. So was I.

"I want to speak colloquial French to my boyfriend," I told him, pleadingly. Class was over by then and he had politely offered me a drive home. Through Le Circ'le naturally. I had been counting on his simple Gallic gallantry.

"You have a boy-friend, Mademoiselle Tiffany?" he teased me gently. "Ahem, but certainly you do. You are an uncommonly

attractive girl, dear child. Une fille uncommonly attractive --- in French.

"Deux boy-friends - in French" I sniffed coyly. "Jean-Guy Lesvesque and his twin brother Rene."

"He refused to see reason."Parisienne French is what the Church and Education Ministry call for," he said pedantically. Maybe a shade defensively I thought.

"I drove home my point. "And in Paris they can say and pronounce it as they like," I said, long-suffering. I both meant it and, I have to admit, I was teasing him back. Our teacher-pupil relationship allowed for that. Plus I knew that he was turned on by the intellectual byplay. I liked feeling I was turning him on.

"Henri Desjardin was a tall slim man with a trim figure and slightly rounded shoulders. I thought he was lovely. As usual he smiled uneasily and maybe even blushed a little. Did I mention that he sported a modern well-trimmed black beard and that I found it funny when his cheeks and forehead went beet red all around it? Funny endearing.

"I thought he looked like Justin Bieber if Justin had a neat black beard. We were sitting in his car, a roomy 2010 Buick. We were parked on the Rue De La Paix, just past the lights of Le Circ'le. The engine was running, but we were not yet going anywhere. I figured it was time to bring my wicked little plan into motion. Without saying a word, I reached out and gently touched the back of his hand.

"He flinched perceptibly, but didn't pull away, "I want to talk openly to Jean-Guy," I said softly, knowing all the time that he knew it was him, Henri, that I was really talking to. I was truly sweet and innocent at sixteen, but I had my feminine wiles. "I'm dying to touch him, to stroke his hand," I said, gently stroking away. "I want to tell him I love him. I love you, my dearest mentor."

"Oh I was daring in those not-so-distant days. Deliciously naughty. I stroked his hand sensuously, as I conceived it, and gazed deep into his eyes. His glistening brown eyes, behind glasses with green in the stems. The green was there because he

was forever absent-mindedly dropping or misplacing them and the green showed up on the tweed carpet. He truly was the cutest and most endearing young Mr. Chips. Only five years older than me if you gave me credit for being two years older than I was by the silly calendar.

"I decided it was now or never. I had to cross the river Rubicon, take the bull by the horns. I had my next line on the tip of my tongue. "I want to tell him to kiss me," I said in hushed tones, so cute and pure of heart. "Ask him to put his lips on mine and savour the sweet honey of our kiss." I was recalling the words from the bodice-ripping romances I concocted under the sheets.

But, horrors, perhaps I had gone too far. He straightened up, shook his unruly hair and gripped the steering wheel tightly with both hands. "We're at le round point," he said, slightly mixed up. " You can...Vous pouvez acheter un sac de bonbons..at the Bouchard & Femme Confiserie."

"Un sac de Candy," I corrected him demeurely, in Quebec French. I leaned toward him, my face no more than a few centimetres from his. I had determined to throw caution to the wind and make him desire me. Find me irresistible, wildly sexy. It was daring and it was so fun. I wanted to arouse him.

"I took his right hand off the wheel, unprotesting. I gently lowered our two hands into his lap. Now I could feel him through his grey flannels. He was quivering.

"I want to be absolutely open with him," I said, my eyes wide and sincere. "I need to say that I desire him desperately. That I am his for the taking. His humble slave-girl Son jeune esclave..."

"Vous etes une jeune escalve," he repeated hoarsely, in halting Parisienne speak. "This is too much, Tiffany," he said, breathing hard. "Absurd."

"I curled my hand in his lap. He drew in a sharp breath, but didn't move to stop me. "Agite," he mumbled. "Fou......." His penis was standing to attention now. I could imagine the glistening drop of pre-cum on the purple tip. I was sure I knew a lot more about sexual activities than any of the naive girls in my class. I had devoured oodles of Harlequin and Spice romances.

"Tiffany... dear one," he said brokenly, and kissed me full on the mouth. His lips were so soft and so satisfyingly, dreamily wet. His tongue delicately parted my lips. "Tu est une wondrous cocette," he breathed. "Je t'adore...."

"Suddenly I pulled my hand back a little. Something didn't feel right..... What was I doing ? I was a good girl. I couldn't be acting this way. If he really wanted me he would have to be a strong man and take me....wilfully, manfully. I was a good girl."

"Take me, Henri.......," I said in my huskiest voice, a voice I didn't recognise as my own. "I want to feel you inside me. Take me - please."

"Time seemed to be standing still. I was barely conscious of my words. "Ravish me, dearest, I whispered in his ear. "You'll have to force me. Rape me. I can't resist."

"He raised his head, staring into my eyes. His pupils were like dark saucers. " Te violer?" he muttered, his words strained and hardly audible.

"I'm a good girl," I murmured. "Make it all right, dearest. I need to be ravished.... PLEASE!"

"The perspiration stood out in droplets on his forehead. His face was red and strained. He plunged his lips down on mine. His probing tongue entered my mouth and tasted mine. I was overpowered, helpless....

"Which was when the wretched man abruptly jerked back, a scared look on his flushed, sweaty face. "I mustn't do this," he cried. "Je ne dois par le faire! Il est terriblement mal!"

"With trembling fingers he pulled up his pants zipper, which had somehow become unzipped. "Sortir de la voiture!" he said fiercely. "Get out of the car....Aller maintenant tu est dans Le Circ'le."

"Even in all the confusion I knew that I had won. He had called it Le Circ'le. But though I had won that I had lost so much more. My beloved French teacher had copped out of our lovemaking at the critical moment. It was incredibly frustrating. I was deeply hurt. And getting seriously angry.

"I recall stubbing my toe when I kicked one of the black traffic stanchions grouped around the circle. I was mad, mad, mad. The stupid man had backed away from ravishing me when I wanted it so much. In Harlequin terms he was an utter cad. I hated him.

Later, when I had calmed down a bit, I stomped around Le Circ'le to Meubles Levesque Furniture to see my darling Jean-Guy. Before I went in I promised myself that one day, when I was older and maybe wiser, I would meet Henri Desjardin again. I told myself that next time he would take me the way I wanted. Ravish me, so that I had no choice but to go along.

"Rape me, Mr Desjardin," I would say coldly. "Violer moi come je desire d'etre voiler! Rape me the way I long to be raped!"

Then I met up with Jean-Guy and his twin brother Rene and lost my cherry on a kingsize bed in the showroom on the second floor of the furniture store. Twice.

*

Leeza slowly lifted her raven head from the tablet and gave a deep sigh of satisfaction. "Jimminy Cricket," she said to herself. "That was kind of hot, for a beginner...."

She gazed up at the silvery moon, now high in the sky. A dark cloud drifted across it like an eclipse. "You'll have your tethered goat, Madame Claire,' she said firmly. It had been a good night's work, she thought.

She set Matt's tablet beside her on the cedar bench. The familiar smell of honeysuckle and roses wafted through her nostrils. As her fingers crept beneath her summer dress, she leaned back on the bench, her lips parting.

Leeza was a very contented girl. And becoming more so.

Chapter 22 Questionnaire II

QUESTIONNAIRE #2 – RAVISHER

(To be answered honestly and shared with Ravisher)

Key to graduated answers - a) By importance: Absolutely important. Very important. Less important. Unimportant - b) By frequency: Always. Often. Rarely. Never - c) Subject to mutual negotiation (STMA).

YOU - THE RAVISHER

1. Is it absolutely clear to you that the first person a good rape-top has to learn to control is himself/herself?
2. Can you, as Ravisher, confidently assure the Ravishee that you are fully aware of the distinction between real rape and Fantasy rape <u>and will honour this profound difference?</u>
3. Do you completely understand that as Ravisher you are essentially a service top enacting the Ravishee's fantasy?
4. Are you cognisant that all aspects of a ravishment scene <u>must</u> be negotiated with the Ravishee?
5. Do you honestly believe that every ravishment scene must be entirely consensual?
6. Is it crystal clear to you that every fantasy rape scene requires a paradoxical form of consensual non-consent, under which the parties agree to <u>pretend</u> that no one is actually consenting?
7. In such a fantasy scene do you accept full responsibility for 'safety', 'sanity' and 'safe sex?"
8. Will you always negotiate and abide by safewords and be willing to stop or modify a scene should the ravishee so desire?
9. Are <u>you</u> capable of gaining personal pleasure and satisfaction solely from fulfilling <u>the Ravishee's</u> needs?
10. Do you realise that the ravisher is duty bound to provide such necessary items as safety scissors, lotion and a first aid kit?

11. Further, that the rape top will provide any negotiated BDSM gear and guarantee their expertise in its usage?

RAVISHER'S RAPE FANTASIES

12. Have you ever raped someone in real life?
13. Have you sublimated or controlled any such criminal desires?
14. Do you currently fantasise about being a rapist?
15. Has the socially acceptable fantasy completely replaced the former cravings?
16. Do you masturbate when you fantasise being a rape top?
17. When you read rape stories or watch rape movies?
18. Do your fantasies more often involve one-on-one scenes?

- Or multiple rape-tops?

19. What is your favourite type of victim - (ie, virgin, tease, schoolgirl, housewife, business woman, nun, prisoner?)
20. Do your fantasy scenes typically include your cum and if yes, where does it end up?

BEHAVIOURS

21. Do you accept that only such toys as have been covered in scene negotiation will be introduced?
22. Is it clear to you that for both ravisher and Ravishee the scene as negotiated can still be intensely emotional?
23. Do your fantasies include convincing resistance by the Ravishee?
24. Are you confident of your ability to overcome such struggles with force used <u>only for dramatic effect?</u>
25. Are your fantasy scenes 'soft' - (i.e. readily overpowering?)

- Or 'hard' - (i.e. requiring face slapping or punching, but always only for dramatic purposes.)

26. Is it important to you that your fantasy victim is pleading with you, begging you to stop, etc.?
27. Do you wish to degrade your Ravishee with words like bitch, cunt and so on?
28. Do you imagine your victim tied up or in handcuffs?"
    - Gagged or blindfolded?
29. Is the possible pregnancy of your victim part of your fantasies?
30. Are you willing to provide the Ravishee with a written personal description prior to negotiating your scene, including age and any distinguishing marks or tattoos?
31. Will you guarantee to hold a preliminary meeting with the Ravishee in a public place such as a mall or restaurant?
32. How important is rough sex in your fantasies?
33. Is the suffering of your victim relevant to your fantasies?
34. Are you convinced you can sublimate any and all of your fantasies into a dramatically acceptable context for the Ravishee?

SEXUAL

35. Does your fantasy sexual ravishment scene include the use of a vibrator on nipples, clitoris or exterior of anus?
    - Interior of anus or vagina?
36. Do your fantasy scenes include fondling and/or licking/sucking of breasts and nipples?
37. Is nipple or breast torture important to you?
38. Does your projected scene allow for forced masturbation?
39. Does it include forced oral sex by Ravishee?
    - Oral sex by Ravishee on testes?
40. Licking, sucking, or painful clitoral torture?
41. How important is anal stroking and fingering to you?

- Anal penetration by 2 or 3 fingers?
- Vaginal penetration by 2 or 3 fingers?

42. Anal rape?
43. Vaginal rape?
44. What is more important to you, the sex or the humiliation and degradation?
45. Do kidnapping, captivity, repeated rape, play an important part in your sexual fantasies?
46. Have you ever enacted a rape role-play scene in real life?
47. If yes, rate it on a scale of 1 - 5, with 5 as highly satisfying.

AFTER-CARE

48. Do you recognise that a ravishment scene may require considerable after-care and possible follow-up?
    - To be given by ravisher or by mutually acceptable third party.
49. Are you fully aware that the strain of the scene on the ravisher can be as great as that on the victim?
50. Do you accept that even an experienced rape-top is likely to need a sympathetic winding down period. Pre-arranged after-care by and for the ravisher is vital to any first rate rape-play scene.

With sincere wishes for your success.

GENNIFLEUR.

END

*

Richard had gone strangely quiet. It was apparent from the distracted expression on his face that he was thinking deeply. He didn't dismiss Fleur's Questionnaire #2 as quickly and caustically as he had reviled Questionnaire #1.

Myra observed him closely. She half expected him to launch into another scornful tirade about Fleur and her palpable ignorance. Who did she think she was? Telling him how to behave?

Instead, his unblinking countenance seemed set in stone. He stared fixedly off into space, one finger beating muted time on the print-out Myra had run off for him.

"This is even more juvenile than the Ravishee's Questionnaire," he said at last, in a supercilious but surprisingly reasonable tone. He had a thin, calculating smile on his face. "I figured the pointers she dreamed up for the victim were pretty pathetic. But these, supposedly for the Ravisher, for ME for Christ's sake, are closer to pure garbage."

He held up his hard copy contemptuously between thumb and forefinger. "All these sorry bitches begging for it, and dear Gennifleur wants to turn it into a women's social club. On the other hand, it could be perfectly usable garbage." He was coldly weighing the possibilities. "The questions she asks, the obvious answers she's angling for, might actually work to my advantage. Yes, very usable."

"I think she's striving to protect her girls," Myra said solicitously. She was trying to gauge where he was heading.

He was brusque. "They don't want protection," he said bluntly. "They want to be raped good and proper, with bells on"

He abandoned his seat on the bed and paced the bedroom like a caged animal. He seemed quite rational, but a pulse was beating rapidly on his temple. "Gennifleur's got no idea what a real rape is all about, " he said disdainfully. Give her half a chance and she'd castrate every last man on earth. She's no more than a meddlesome busybody, making like she's the patron saint of rape victims."

He had made up his mind what action to take. He was abruptly filled with purpose, his voice snappy and staccato. "James," he said curtly, a sudden peremptory summons. "<u>You</u> respond to her. Toute suite. Tell her she's brilliant and that a completed Questionnaire #2 will follow later. Make sure it says exactly what she wants to hear."

His chin lifted and his slightly stooped Richard shoulder straightened. Within a second or two Richard had become James. He took the horn-rimmed eyeglasses from the dresser. He was prompt and immediately efficient. James with Gennifleur.

"Take a letter, Myra, he said briskly, without wasting a word. "*Dear Ms. Gennifleur,"* he dictated. *"I have this moment finished reading your extraordinary Questionnaire #2. Precisely what I need to become an accomplished Ravisher."*

It was uncanny, though Myra, how quickly and totally Richard had become James. It was as if the two of them were present in the bedroom together.

James had continued dictating. "*The instant you mentioned service top I realised that is exactly what I am. A dominant without being domineering. Simply stated, turning a woman on, turns me on. I have always found myself bending over backwards to please women. A natural ravisher, I believe."*

As James paused for breath, Richard's voice cut in. He was at once decisive and a little sarcastic. "Set up a date with her, why don't you? Strike while her indebted juices are all wet and flowing."

James took his meaning instantly. He steepled his fingers and smoothly resumed the task at hand. *"Now, Ms. Fleur, I have a special request. I would greatly appreciate the benefit of your experience to cement my ravishment training. A brief, educational scene, perhaps? I'll return the filled in Questionnaire shortly. Sign off, Circumspectfully, James, Civil Engineer, BSc, B.Com.* Done," he said, directed to Richard.

"Excellent," commented Richard, taking off the horned-rimmed glasses and becoming himself again. "We'll soon see if she's all talk or is ready to be seriously ravaged. I suspect some tiresome negotiating will transpire. Your bag."

James accepted his dismissal without a hint of protest. Efficiency in all things was his watchword. Richard, meantime, had moved on to other matters. "Mind you, this Fleur creature would have no idea how much work I do, setting up all these different profiles, letting loose all the characters. Henry and

Edward, James, William and Billie." His dark eyes narrowed as he peered myopically at Myra. "To tell the truth, I'm none too sure about Billie. He's William's younger self, but he troubles me. Always seems to want to go his own sweet way."

His eyes had begun darting back and forth. "The fact is, Myra, these moronic Questionnaires are making me think I've been selling myself short. With Fleur baby's questions I could sweet talk many more victims into role-playing . I think they'd lap up the answers we'd give them."

Myra watched him with increasing concern. She could see that he was getting excited, beginning to ramble. "Though she really don't have a clue what it feels like to literally have to rape some young chick. It's all about my need, MY pleasure. They're just there to take it in the cunt. Painfully. To prove how much better and stronger I am that they can ever be. Nobody like the Fleur woman or my fucking mother on my case. Telling me what I can or can't do."

He suddenly stopped his growing rant and launched unexpectedly into a completely different mode. "Makes me think of L. Ron Hubbard," he said cryptically. "He'd been a science fiction writer in the Thirties and Forties." He looked at Myra earnestly. Out of the blue he had unpredictably slipped into his familiar, frequently used lecturing mode.

"L Ron Who?" she asked dutifully, thinking that this was better for his mental state than going on incessantly about rape. Since the Stratford Pet Shoppe she had learned how to take advantage of his mood swings, divert him a little. Not exactly manipulate him, but encourage him along less stressful lines.

"Hubbard," he said, patient with her. "With his S/F plots he lived constantly in the future. He particularly hated idiots telling him what to do. Editors and bitchy proof readers. Then came the Fifties and he put together this massive tome. Dianetics, he called it. Started his own religion with it. Scientology was the fabulous name he came up with. He hated all women. I'm a lot like him."

He switched back abruptly to his previous rant. "The dozen or more I-wanna-be-raped sites on line," he said, marvelling. "When

I first discovered them on Kinklife I figured for sure I had hit the mother lode. All these demented chicks, even older women, quite plainly asking to be raped. I thought I'd died and gone to heaven."

He was getting keyed up again. His mind was racing. "And it's as if this Gennifleur has given me all the answers these stupid girls want to hear. It's what I say in my emails to them. It's wide open for all the new contacts I could ever wanna make. I'm a compassionate, caring ravisher. Who can possibly refuse me? I'm everything they dream of. Until I'm not. Then it's too late."

The vein in his temple was pounding furiously. "I could handle many more than I've been doing. Not just Dawn and Carol and the aging Fleur. Dozens of them. One every week if I plan it right. Fifty-two a year."

She went to slow him down, but he didn't wait for her. "L. Ron Hubbard," he said, again totally out of the blue. "He was a real Master."

Myra held her peace. She felt safe with the pedantic, bookish Richard. He talked and talked about nothing and everything. He had a broad smattering of general knowledge, filtered through his rapacious consciousness.

"After Scientology nobody ever told him what to say or do again," he announced, almost triumphantly. "No mother-fucking Fleurs, no maternal monsters, nobody ever again." He grinned wolfishly at her. "He was still wed to a woman named Polly when he married his second wife. Bigamy they said it was. Early Poly, I'd say. It was the Fifties," he explained. "Back in the day, everyone had to get hitched if they wanted to fuck. What I --"

He stopped talking in mid-sentence, looking oddly puzzled by what he found himself saying. She could feel his frustration growing. Then it cleared and he spoke excitedly again, the adrenalin flowing.

"All I need to take on loads of extra chicks is more willing helpers," he said, now bursting with energy. "More supporters, like James, and William, and, yes, even Billie the Kid. Sock puppets and catfish. A growing army of dedicated followers. A system of beliefs like Scientology. A cosmic struggle between

God and the devil, except this time Satan is in the right. My own mythology. Valhalla."

She could see Edward staring out of his eyes. Hear Henry in his voice. It was frightening.

"Richard," she said warningly. "You're getting carried away."

He ignored her. "And I know what I have to do," he said feverishly. "And how to go about doing it." He stared at her fixedly, his black eyes glittering. He was no longer the Richard she thought she knew so well. "I must go forth and multiply," he proclaimed, in a stern voice like a clamorous portent of doom.

"I d-don't understand you, Myra stammered out weakly, fearing the worst.

"They're all within me, Myra girl," he said jubilantly. "Not just good old James and the others. Adam John and the cute Cockney kid Stevie King. They were all around long before James or Henry and company turned up."

"Who's Adam John? Stevie? I don't follow you at all."

He was elated, exultant. "But they will!" he said euphorically. They'll follow me anywhere." His voice took on a simpler sound. He was like to a small boy.

"When I was a kid, in pre-kindergarten, I told everyone I was curly-haired young Adam John from Columbus, Ohio. The pupils, my teachers, my black-hearted mother, I had them all more than half believing I was really Adam John from the U.S.of A. It was the gospel truth, Myra. He'd be my age now."

He sprawled back on the bed and gave her a faint, almost boyish grin. "I was sweet little Stevie King in Primary school. He was from the foggy banks of darkest London town. Later, I was precocious Jean-Paul Marois from Trois Rivieres and at Upper Canada College I was the smartest of them all, Jimmie Moriaty, the son of Sherlock Holmes' wiliest rival.".

He was deadly serious, she realised. The Questionnaires had opened his febrile mind to forgotten permutations of character.

"I've always been other people" he said, very simply. "I can be whoever I want to be."

Trustingly, he laid his head in her lap and closed his eyes. He looked young and innocent and fell instantly asleep.

She stroked his hair and thought of fetching a cold compress for his forehead.

But then he reared up abruptly, his cheeks hot and feverish. He was soaking wet. His eyes were like huge black saucers.

"Who am I?" he asked uncertainly, an expression of terror on his face. "I don't know who I am anymore."

His grip on reality, never strong, was fading fast.

Chapter 23 An Email to Tiffany

Richard, clad in his usual Reebok black track pants and shirt, was standing in front of an easel and blackboard in the dining room of his Waterloo apartment. The blackboard was already marked out with an organisational chart of familiar names. Edward, James and so on, some crossed out. He had more or less recovered his composure after the unsettling Questionnaire affair and was functioning adequately in what he thought of as 'planning mode.'

He had a vintage First World War British officer's swagger stick under his arm. He used it to indicate boxes on the blackboard organisational chart as needed. At times such as this he saw himself as a highly professional senior staff general, in charge of complex military operations for his devoted troops.

"Operation TiffanyPurejoy21," he said in clipped tones to Myra, sitting straight-backed at the Swedish modern dining room table. "Our newest potential Ravishment Target. She has just published a rape story on Kinklife.ca, under the 'Bound, Gagged and Ravished' heading. You can glance through it later. The question for this staff conference is basic. Who amongst us is best qualified to take her on. Understood?"

"Yes, Sir," Myra replied, quite seriously. She was perched rather uncomfortably on an Ikea dining room chair. She was wearing a very short, high-necked camouflage singlet and nothing else. Richard did not allow staff work to interfere with his visual pleasures. His laptop was open on the teak table in front of her.

"Earlier in the campaign, it would have been Edward or possibly Henry," Richard went on, using the brown leather swagger stick to point out their designated boxes. "But both Henry and Eddie are no longer on active service. James, on the other hand," he went on, tapping the James box, "Is fully engaged with Gennifleur, aka Fleur. Ms. Purejoy, incidentally, has yet to officially sign on."

He rapped his 1914 swagger stick on three boxes composed largely of dotted lines and others only faintly delineated. "John and my old friend George of Hanover are still in development stage with their profiles, while young Alfred is taken up with kitchen detail." He allowed himself a wintry smile at his bon mot. "As for the boys, it will be a while before they'll have serviceably adult profiles.

The swagger stick came to rest on another box, one with a big chalk question mark over it. "That leaves William, one of our oldest and least successful archetypes. William-the-Conqueror, as he classified himself in a vain attempt to disguise his birthright insecurities; William-the-Vacillator, as I dubbed him. Not, I freely admit, at all in accord with the historical record."

He paused briefly, suddenly irresolute. "That brings the choice down to the point of this meeting," he said tentatively. "William's younger self. 'Billie' as their Viking grandmother called him. 'Billie the Kid.'"

Myra frowned. "Sir, you always seem hesitant when you mention this Billie. So unlike you."

It was obvious that Richard was unsure how to proceed. Slowly he tapped out the name written under William's box. Something about Billie didn't sit at all well with him. "Billie the Kid," he repeated, still visibly balking. "I don't know him as well as James or even William. He's very young and has all the over-confidence of youth. Recklessly sadistic. Boyishly dominant."

Myra was curious. "Do you see him with what's-her-name - Tiffany? Can you trust him?"

Richard looked gloomy. "Not as far as I could throw him. He's an independent young cuss. Has no time for William, or even me come to that. Though I guess his bright-eyed enthusiasm might go down well with Ms. Purejoy. They're of an age."

"It's your decision, Master," Myra said. "You must do what you think best."

He stalled one more time. Don't see as I have much choice," he complained. "But maybe shouldering all the responsibility will make him grow up... " He took a deep breath and finally accepted that he simply had to commit himself. It was to be Billie with Tiffany. The die was cast.

With a sigh Richard took off his prescription sunglasses and left them with the swagger stick among the Melmac crockery on top of the Ikea sideboard. He peered myopically in the frameless dining room mirror for a moment and then deliberately mussed up his hair. It fluffed down loosely over his forehead. His Richard shoulder drooped into a more regular pattern and his whole body took on an almost gangly demeanour.

"He's naturally untidy, too," Richard said disapprovingly, partly rolling up his sleeves. "Always grinning like a Cheshire cat and acting like he's barely out of his teens. Wears these big round glasses." He took Billie's eyeglasses from a case idly stuffed in a black Melmac serving dish on the sideboard and put them on. He stared at his changed reflection in the mirror and grinned cheerfully at his new self, all teeth and youthfulness. Richard had vanished. Billie the Kid had taken his place.

He wheeled around and almost shambled over to Myra's chair, all stiffness gone. "Gee whiz!" he proclaimed in an exuberant tone of voice, much less deep and serious than his predecessor's. “It's so great finally to be here. I been kicking my heels for donkey's years" After Richard's strained military manner, Billie was like a breath of fresh air.

He grabbed her hand and shook it vigorously. He was warm and friendly. "You're Myra, of course. I've watched you from the Inside. Seen you growing up, as our Dickie would say. And now, if he has his way, you'll get to see me, Billie the Kid, turn into a shining example of adult judgement and seasoned maturity"

He clapped a dramatic hand to his forehead. "That'll be the day! All this sudden responsibility, I dunno if I can handle it." He flung out his arms, the sleeves rolled at different lengths. "Holy Batman, that Richard can be such a drag." He gave a raucous peal of laughter and picking up the swagger stick rapped his name on the blackboard. "Which brings us to Billie," he continued boisterously." An incorrigibly independent S.O.B! Charm the pants of any young filly. But you never know what he's gonna do next. Don't think he knows himself."

He flourished the swagger stick like a 17th Century rapier and deposited it back on the Scandinavian sideboard. "Okay, Myra sweetheart, time for you to earn your keep. Don't worry about spelling or grammar, just take it down like I say it. A Private Message to TiffanyPurejoy, 21 years young and as sweet and naive as I am myself. NOT!" he added with a wink. "But for starters, to get me in the right head-space, a soup-spoon of visual inspiration."

"Huh?" Myra said blankly.

He indicated her extremely short camo shirt. "Okay, sexy inspiration. Gotta give Dickie-Boy his due. At least I don't hafta charm your panties off."

Myra coloured slightly, but decided Billie was much friendlier and nicer than anyone gave him credit for. Harmless, really, and Richard had sort of set her up. She rose slowly to her feet. She was much less self-conscious about semi-nudity than before Richard had taken her in hand. And Billie was part of the family in a way.

Billie whistled and applauded her with unrestrained glee. "Yay, I got high hopes for you, girl," he crowed delightedly. "Now bring that luscious ass over here and stick it in my face." She hesitated momentarily and he was quick to follow up. There was a note of command in his voice. "It's what Richard would want you to do, girl. Don't you grasp he's made you my submissive for the night. Anything Billie wants, is what he'd tell you."

Myra realised he was probably on the money. Richard was constantly encouraging her to show herself off. "You got it, flaunt it," was the way he put it. Besides, it was all in a good cause. And only 'visual inspiration' after all. Plus, Richard was right on another score, Billie was boyishly dominant for sure.

She gathered her courage and sashayed around the dining room toward Billie, now sprawled in the captain's chair at the head of the table. She could almost hear Richard encouraging her, giving her instructions. "Make like a lap dancer, Myra. Give him his twenty bucks worth."

Billie applauded some more as she bent over in front of his eyes, twitching her naked butt lasciviously. "That's my girl," he said happily and playfully slapped her behind. It was stingy, but a good stingy. Billie was in a fine mood. Billie usually was, until he wasn't. Myra knew she had done well, both by Billie and Richard. She felt well satisfied and appreciated.

"Later, sweet cheeks," Billie said, running his hand between her parted buttocks and taking a contented whiff of his fingers. "I gotta get this Tiffany bimbo hooked first." He affectionately patted her bum again as she made her way back to the laptop. "Visual inspiration was A-Okay."

So what if the inspiration hadn't been strictly visual. Billie was just doing what came natural to him. That was the secret of his charm, she thought. Didn't appear to have any meanness or pettiness anywhere in his makeup.

Or so she thought.

*

When it came right down to it, his method of dictation was also much more casual and off the cuff than James or Richard had relied on. Way less formal and seemingly intended to make Myra an integral part of the email. It was very satisfying for her.

"Start with *'Hey there. Tiffany Purejoy'*," he said expansively, and grinned at Myra. "First, we make her feel good." He moved on to dictating. "*I'm writing to tell you what pure joy it was to read your beguiling story on Kinklife.ca, the Bound Gagged and Raped threads. You sure have an awesome way with words. I was blown away. No exaggeration, I was HOT all over.*"

He broke off again to bring Myra into his thinking. "I'm just gonna tell her what I really, really liked... Okay?"

"Great opening," she responded, smiling back at him. He was wonderfully considerate, she told herself. Actually making her an ally in his seductive wooing of Tiffany Purejoy.

He stretched lazily like a big cat, not a tense muscle in his easygoing body, and unhurriedly resumed his dictation. "*I especially like the kind of nostalgic sentences about your school days, all of two, three years back as I read it. Oh and Tiffany, I absolutely loved the description of your schoolgirl outfit. I thought how fabulous it would be if we could do a scene together and you came dressed in that. I bet you look real cute in it these days. Give it some thought anyhow."*

He leaned back in the captain's chair, gazing enraptured toward the ceiling. *"Come to think of it, the whole scene could be set at the school, with that French master, Monsieur Desjardin. I know you describe the 'rape that didn't happen' as taking place in his car, but maybe that's why it didn't... happen I mean. Maybe locating it at the school would be just as real, and way less cramped than my sport's car, that's for sure, LOL. Hey, maybe I could find an empty school to rent.*

"I got to tell you that I have that lovely image of your ivy-covered alma mater in my mind's eye right now. That, and you in a school blazer and beret with your loosely knotted tie and knee sox. Take a few moments if you can to visualise the whole sexy event taking place in the school with you dressed as the ultimate schoolgirl. Maybe then, this silly M. Desjardin would do what you want and follow through. I know I would. Will, if you give me half a chance."

He gave Myra a pleased-with-himself grin. "Bingo!" he said. "First real contact. Make her feel like she's God's gift to English Lit, Kinklife genus. Warm and sunnily enthusiastic, with a smidgeon of bait and switch. Plus, an empty school would be so much more atmospheric than Richard's Mustang... And I'll lay odds she loves the idea of the schoolgirl costume."

"It is kind of cute," agreed Myra.

"So, now she can see herself in a school setting. Next, we gotta draw her a picture of being there with me. Good-looking and mushy young Billie. Time to sell her on me."

He resumed dictating in a soft and friendly cadence. "*To keep everything above board I should tell you that my given name is actually William, from that old Norman king of England, William the Conqueror. Not exactly me at all, to be honest. My Mom always calls me Billie. She says things like 'Be polite, Billie,' 'Don't stay out too late, Billie.' She thinks I'm still about nine years old. I'm not, I'm twenty-four. Well, nearly twenty-four, next month. I work for the City, in the Planning Department on King. I know how to be discreet. I like my job."*

He winked at Myra. "A last little bit of soft soap. Massaging her ego again. *'And, btw, Tiff, I got to say you must be a real courageous person. I mean to write so openly in a public forum about the fantasies you have. Myself, I'm stuck with Private Messages and even here I'm, well, a bit shy."*

Myra laughed "Sir Billie, you're the least shy person I know."

He scowled comically. "Ms. Purejoy don't know that. So, finally, a touch of poetic romance..." He picked up his dictation again. "*Talking about names, I truly get off on yours. Tiffany reminds me of lovely coloured lamps or one of my mother's favourite old movies, Breakfast at Tiffany's it's called, starring Audrey Hepburn I think it is, looking like that exquisite photo on your profile, blonde hair covering half your beautiful face. Quite honestly, dear Tiffany, I don't mind admitting I'd really enjoy knowing you."*

He threw Myra another cheeky grin. "We've used that before," he told her cheerfully. "Or James did. Yeah, he said that to Fleur, the older woman on 'Ask Madame Claire.' He'd really enjoy <u>knowing</u> her."

Myra was fascinated by the way he had thought everything through. And so simple and totally unthreatening. Though, after all she remembered, Tiffany had initiated the Bound, Gagged and Ravished contact herself, with her M. Desjardin story. The not-quite-so-naive girl obviously knew what in essence she was asking for.

Billie was perfectly happy to reveal his email techniques. "Gets a bit long, but about now I'll give Mom a parting word. How I relate to her increases my trustworthiness." He dictated: *"Another thing my mother always wants to know is when I'll make her a grandma. Mom, I say, I have to get married first. And, hey, Tiffany, I hope you don't figure me for a Momma's boy. I just go along, she's not getting any younger after all. Another thing, Tiff, I'm not a hardcore Dom. Too squeamish to be truthful. Can't stand the sight of blood."*

He rubbed his hands together, satisfied with his efforts. "Time to bring this first Tiffany email to an end," he said. "Gee whiz, Ms. Purejoy, didn't mean to ramble on like this. Fact is, I have a confession to make. I've never actually done a full ravishment scene. I'm virile enough and I did come close once at a party, but it was just too darned public." He smiled a tad sheepishly at Myra. "I never been to a real life play party as a matter of fact."

"Me, neither," she said reassuringly. "Richard thinks they're a waste of time."

"We both know what Dickie-Boy would rather be up to." He sniggered and rapped two fingers on the table. "Closing paragraph," he said. *"Tiffany, I'm real keen to do a ravishment scene with you and I've done my research. I found this Questionnaire for the Ravishee on line. A series of simple questions outlining what you want and, more importantly, what you* <u>*don't*</u> *want. I'm sending you a personal link. It will be deleted after I absorb your responses.*

"End with *'Thank you for reading my email. I hope we can get it together. This is a firm offer'.*

Your new friend,

Billie."

He waited for her to catch up. "Set up a separate link for the Ravishee's Questionnaire, and add this postscript to the current email. *P.S. Tiffany, if you decide to take me up on my offer, I would suggest a first meeting on neutral ground. One with lots of folks around for your comfort, like a handy Tim Hortons for coffee. I'll email possible times and locations when I get my next work schedule. P.P.S Please do consider a school setting for the scene. Along with your awesome schoolgirl outfit. "* He stretched both arms in the air and questioned Myra: "Think she'll buy it?"

"Can't see why not. You give good email."

He ran his fingers through the tuft of hair hanging loosely over his forehead. "So you think she'll come, then?"

"To Timmie's? For sure. What has she got to lose? Nothing"

"Which makes two of you," Billie said with a sly grin. "The workday is over. It's time for a change of pace."

There was a glitter in his eyes. "You've done real well so far," he said. "Now we'll get to see how you handle playtime."

*

Billie seemed to have changed somehow. Physically he was still the same overgrown teenager. But now there was a much stronger sense of purpose about him. A suggestion of danger.

"Besides, we have some unfinished 'inspirational' matters to complete," he said, with a distinctly crooked smile. "From now on you will call me Sir and jump to it when I tell you to do something. Is that clear?

"But, Sir..."she began to say.

"There are no buts" he said coldly. "I decided to take you in hand somewhere between my mother's wishes to be a grandma and my supposedly not being a hardcore Dom. Those comments were strictly for Tiffany's benefit. I am hardcore, Myra. More so than you can possibly imagine."

She tried to protest. "Richard will want to take over again."

He gave a short, unamused Billie laugh. "Don't be stupid, girl," he said. "He expects us to get to know each other. We're to be Tiffany's 'handlers,' like in a spy movie. Understand, he has 'gifted' you to me, at least for the night. Dominants do that with their submissives. It teaches obedience."

Abruptly he changed the subject. "Ever been seriously raped, Myra."

Myra sat up straight in her chair. In her mind she could hear Richard warning her. "Billie is a danger to everyone," he was saying. "A total sadist, mentally and physically. Even more than me, he has no conscience, no brakes."

"Not that I'm gonna rape you," Billie continued, like a very young man with a marvellous new toy. "I'm more original than that. With me, it'll be something you've never tried before." He grinned. "Even thought of, I bet."

In one swift motion he moved the chairs away from the table and put the laptop on the sideboard. "Dickie-Boy raped your ass, right? He's always been an ass-man. Took your keester cherry, right?"

Myra was taken aback. "How do you know?"

He was sarcastic. There was some obvious friction in his attitude toward Richard. "Multiple characters spend a lot of time together, doncha know." He turned masterful again and fetched a cushion from the living room.. "Here, get up on the table. Put your bum on this cushion." He took his time placing it. "Knees bent, feet on the edge of the table."

She tried to resist, but Billie was very strong and demanding. "Like I said, sweet cheeks, none of the same-old-same-old for this initiation." A dimple formed near the corner of his mouth. "What I'm gonna do is fist you."

"Fist me?" she blanched.

"He seemed very young and earnest as he held up his hand. "See, my fist ain't that monstrous." He was almost hugging himself at the thought. A fourteen year old's dream, his eyes bright and shining. "See my finger? See my thumb? See my fist? And here it come!"

He jabbed his fist forward against her cunt lips. Not hard, just menacingly. "And so another cherry falls from the Myra tree. Don't you love it? I sure do."

"I thought you liked me," she wailed, scared to death.

He had turned playful again. The changes of mood somehow made it worse. "Cheer up, sweetheart," he said lightheartedly. "It don't come in as a fist. Another word for it is handballing." He gave her a boyish grin. "You can even do it on yourself. Lots of lube and it'll easily slip in right to the wrist."

He was holding her down on the table with a heavy elbow across her breasts. Part of her wanted to kick and scream but he was so much stronger than she and another part of her said he was only doing what Richard had set up. Dominants gifted their subs, Billie had said. It could be part of the sub's contract, she knew.

He waved his free hand in front of her face. He had taken a small tube of Purrfect Gel from his pocket and now dexterously smeared it over his hand. His eyes were glistening with anticipation. "Be a good girl, lie still, and I'll give you a little demonstration. Duck-billing, it's called"

He shaped his fingers into a pointy cone, with the thumb tucked out of the way. "I make a kind of duck's beak out of my fingers, see. They're sort of scrunched together for a nice, slow entry into your vagina. No pain. No sweat. Like so."

His curved fingers, smothered in lube, gradually pushed and twisted their way into her cunt. "Quack, quack," he said blithely, maintaining his narrative. Billie knew what he wanted and how to go about getting it. Relaxing her was crucial. "Two, three, four fingers," he said, talking her through it. "Done right, handballing will give you the most awesome orgasm you've ever had."

Myra was surprised at the care he was taking, the patient way he was coaxing her along. She hadn't expected this technique from the new Billie. "Later, you may want to try punch-fisting," he said softly. "But for now all those sensation-filled vaginal muscles just grip and relax, grip and relax. No other sex act comes close to reaching this same sweet mixture of pleasure, pain and endorphins...."

He gazed deep into her eyes. For a while he was the old, considerate Billie and she could feel herself drifting with his words, starting to co-operate without pain or fear. "I'm right in to the knuckles now," he told her, an expression of youthful elation on his face. "Your cunt will expand to take them in, no great effort just a natural expansion. Once the knuckles slip in I can keep the fingers straight or gently clench them into a fist. You'll have a tremendous sense of fullness. Like nothing you've ever felt before."

Sir Billie was actually quite solicitous, she thought dreamily. His voice as he explained his actions was low and mesmerising. He knew exactly what he was doing and was totally in command. Surprisingly, she felt she was in the safest of hands. Or fists, she smiled to herself.

"Just remember, Myra girl, if you think something is gonna hurt, it almost certainly will. Instead, look at it as yoga for the cunt, your pelvic floor muscles relaxing and your vagina expanding like the flexible canal it truly is. For straight folks it's usually taboo. Only kinksters and lesbians know it's more than just another sex act, it's the ultimate in sex acts. Feel how wet and slippery you are," he added, and the triumph in his voice was almost palpable. "And it ain't all lube, believe me."

She was breathing hard now, feeling her inner muscles contract and relax, each time looser and more widely open. Waves of deep pleasure were roiling through her body. "I thought you were going to tear me apart," she said, as if from a great distance. "But I want it now. The whole fucking fist."

"Purely consensual fist-fucking," he said, breathing deeply himself. "Feel it slide all the way in, girl," he said, matching her intensity, moving his fingers back and forth, in and out.

"Aieee!" she cried out, as the pressure increased and then seemed to dissolve. His whole hand was in.

"Now my fingers are forming a fist," Billie told her, his eyes glittering like pools of oily black. "From now on it will just get better and better. Fuller and fuller."

She was in her seventh heaven. "Billie, Sir Billie," she managed to gasp. “It’s mind-bogglingly wonderful. It's so different to just a regular cock. More, I want more."

He wiggled his fist inside her and she felt the sheer ecstasy mounting beyond imagination. "Oh god," she mouthed, saliva slipping down her chin. "It feels so incredible. So filling. So impossibly good...."

That was when he stopped. Stopped dead. Stopped moving his fist inside her. Stopped and reared up on one elbow. "And it's over," he said unexpectedly. He was the same young Billie, but there was a sudden hardness in his eyes. "You forget, young lady. This is only a demonstration."

She stared up at him, not understanding. Sweat was beading on her forehead. She was primed and ready to explode in massive orgasm. On the very verge.

Billie threw back his head and laughed till the tears ran down his cheek. "You should see the expression on your face," he said cruelly. "Like I've stolen away your favourite new toy." He was asserting his Domness. Staking out the future. Showing her who was in charge. Here. Now. Always.

Her head tossed wildly from side to side. "Don't stop, Sir," she pleaded desperately. "For God's sake, please don't stop now."

He laughingly ignored her plea. Without the slightest hesitation or compunction, he withdrew his hand from her cunt and stood to his feet. "You've got a lot to learn, girl," he said sadistically. "You don't get to climax unless I say you do. Until your dominant gives you permission. And right now, I'm not so inclined. No orgasm, sweetie. The demo is over."

He was well satisfied with her despairing confusion. "But I've taken your fisting cherry," he boasted. "This is a fuck you'll never forget. Not as long as you fucking well live."

Coolly he took off his round glasses and put them in their case on the dresser. Straightened his hair. Located Richard's prescription sunglasses. "I have my own way of running things," he said calmly to Myra. "And right now I've had more than enough of you. In future you'll always know who's your real boss. And it ain't Dickie-Boy. For now, he's welcome to you."

Billie had made his mark.

With a sly grin, he tossed the brown 1914 swagger stick up in the air.

When it came down, Richard caught it.

"And I run things *my* way," he said tautly. He was very Richard as he regained control. Still the general, disposing his fractious troops.

"The fact is, Myra," he said. "I told you young Billie could be cruel."

He smiled thinly.

"Now I suppose you'll expect me to do something about your unslaked libido. Except I'm not in the mood for, what shall I call it - sloppy seconds."

Myra was still discombobulated. "It's not fucking fair," she said bitterly. "Nobody wants me. I might as well be dead."

"That," said Richard snarkily, bitter for his own reasons. "Can always be arranged."

Chapter 24 Drums along the Mohawk

Madame Claire was on the hunt. She had driven in from Marybourne to Kitchener but, remembering the construction downtown, she had parked on King Street at the Grand River hospital Ion station. The Ion LRT itself was bright, airy and efficient.

She had a dinner appointment with Fleur, Gennifleur, partly about the NCSF and more to discuss the BDSM scene she had arranged at Black Walnut cottage for the evening. A Tattoo Drumming scene, with half a dozen drummers and a human drum. More important, it was to be a very special occasion, a cathartic scene entirely for Fleur.

First, however, she planned to bring Sammy Seagram, the manager of the Smuggler's Inn at the Siebert Hotel, fully into the blackmail picture. She had been thinking a lot about the blackmailer on the pleasant drive through the Ontario countryside.

It had to be someone, more likely male than female in her opinion, who was familiar with the scene names of his victims and could contact them on Kinklife.ca. It bothered her no end that this indicated that the blackmailer had to be a member of the Lifestyle, probably involved in the Black Wally Munch.

Even more troubling to Claire was the possible Scene connection of the contemptible rapist - Edward, Henry or whatever name he went by now. She also wondered if these were actual names of real life people, or whether he was using sock puppets all round. If so, she concluded, there must be a real person at the centre of thing. A prime mover.

At least his M.O. - and in her mind his ignorant choice of polypropylene rope and the amateurish apple gag - seemed to suggest he wasn't an experienced BDSMer. Nor could she believe that anyone really knowledgeable would come up with elaborate scenarios luring his victims to a tennis court or a pet store. It just didn't compute.

On the other hand, the blackmailer knew lots about personal lives as well. Sex lives and proclivities, as with Francis and Desmond. Such details came double-barrelled with the threatened Lifestyle Outing. Not necessarily 100% accurate, but close enough to cause additional grief.

Hoping for a breakthrough, she had laid out a tarot reading for him, or her, the previous evening. He had come up as the Knave of Pentacles, the only pentacle in the ten card reading. The Jack, she had noted drolly, not the Jill. Not that there was a Jill, of course, and Jacks could be of any gender..

Afterwards, Claire had spent a couple of hours analysing the possible knaves in the Scene. There were a few candidates she was unsure about, but none of them seemed bad enough, or petty enough, to go in for blackmailing friends. Nonetheless, her character analysis had given her the glimmerings of an idea.

Well after midnight she had finally decided that, after all, she would try to enlist the aid of Sammy Seagram, the Smuggler's Den manager at the Siebert. For at least a partial stake-out of Box 147.

They had met up in the hotel lobby. "Blackmail!" exclaimed Sam, visibly taken aback. "At the Siebert? That don't seem possible."

"Many of your Black Wally regulars could be seriously inconvenienced if they were Outed. Jobs. Family, The Media. Our choice of activity is still largely undercover. Secret, even."

"You mean they'll pay up?"

"Some will. It makes no nevermind to people like Bertie or myself. I've been pretty much Out since I moved in with Mr. Black five years ago."

"He was a fine man that Walter," commiserated Sammy.

"Salt of the earth," Claire agreed, then returned to the task at hand. "The fact is, Sammy, this miserable blackmailer is using your Siebert Hotel postal boxes as a mail drop."

Sam blinked a number of times. "You...you're kidding me."

"On the contrary, I'm dead serious. We're being asked to mail money orders specifically to Box 147."

He looked a little sick. "That's dreadful, Madame Claire. The private boxes are a traditional Siebert service."

Claire nodded. "You look after them, you say."

"Y-yes."

"Put the mail in?"

"Part of my duties."

"Would you see anyone who came to collect it?"

"If I was around. I'm downstairs most of the time, in the Den."

She frowned and pursed her lips. "Do you remember who rented the box? 147?"

"Not really."

"Was it a man or a woman?"

He shook his head. "I don't recall. A woman, I think."

"Could you keep an eye on that box?"

"I sure will." He sounded indignant. "Them boxes are private"

"There'll be a reward if you can find out who's emptying 147, Sam."

Sam perked up. "How much?"

Claire looked thoughtful. "I'll have to talk to some of the folks being blackmailed. I'm sure they'd rather pay you if we can stop this bastard. Say $25 - $35 a head. A fair chunk of change."

Sammy did some quick mental calculating. "Eight or ten people would be, what - $250 - $300," he said, whistling. "Mind you, I'd do it without the reward. The boxes are supposed to be a special service."

"Not so popular as in the past, I gather."

He grimaced. "Everybody has their own i-phone these days." A slight leer flitted across his face. "The boxes used to be handy for making private appointments. Assignations, they called them. Not no more."

He stabbed his finger on the reception desk. "Could be a teenager doing the pick ups," he said. "Folks used to send in a flunkey to get their mail. I'll watch 147, Madame Claire. Like a hawk I'll watch it."

A woman's voice rang through the ongoing renovation hubbub in the hotel lobby. "Hey there, Claire. Sorry if I'm late."

Fleur had arrived, red wig and all. She looked hot and sweaty. "Sheesh, it's like an oven downtown. The traffic was super-horrendous."

Claire smiled a hello. "I should have warned you. The Light Rail has turned central Kitchener into a budding metropolis." She nodded to Sam. "Thank you for your help, Sammy. We'll make our own way to that small table downstairs."

"Ah yes, Madame Claire," he said, winking slyly. "Very discreet. Ideal for a quiet tete-a-tete. And I'll look after the Postal Box matter for you, don't you worry your head none."

Fleur casually linked her arm with Claire's and steered her downstairs into the Smuggler's Den. "I don't much like that little man," she said, as soon as they were almost out of earshot. "A bit creepy, if you ask me."

Claire was less judgemental. "Sammy's all right I guess. He's usually ready to pitch in and do whatever needs doing."

"For a tip," snorted Fleur. "Makes me think of a weasel."

"And when was the last time you saw a weasel?" smiled Claire.

"Wind In The Willows," said Fleur. "There was a weasel in that I think."

*

Fleur, aka Gennifleur on line, had come up Highway 7 from Shakespeare, her home base near Stratford, for a very special occasion. To start, an early dinner with Madame Claire at the

Smuggler's Den, and then a tattoo drumming evening in the Black Walnut dungeon.

Body drumming, a Claire speciality. Five or six drummers, with an in-house djembe-player and a nude body stretched out languidly on the leopard-blanketed massage table. And not just any old body drumming. It was Fleur's time to be the drum and she had virtually begged Claire to organise a special cathartic scene.

"I've watched so called cathartic scenes at BDSM parties," she had said to her. "They seem always to involve heavy caning or whipping. Not at all my Red Rose cup of chai. I'm a bottom in most things, but I'm just not into pain."

"Some folks would call that a contradiction in terms," Claire had smiled.

"Fantasy ravishment is definitely bottoming," Fleur had countered. "But it doesn't have to be painful. That's why it's called fantasy." She had suddenly become very earnest. "I can't see why catharsis has to be excruciating. And that's what I most want. A complete change of perspective." She had looked deep into Madame Claire's eyes. "I don't like who I've become, Claire. I'm too driven. Too prickly. I tend to put people off."

Claire took a sip of her white wine. "There's not supposed to be any pain at all in tattoo drumming, Fleur. The drumsticks and drumcanes constantly striking your body are simply rhythmic and resonant. Transporting even."

Fleur giggled uncertainly. "You sound like Sir Robert and his version of subspace," she said, still a touch apprehensive about what she was asking for.

"Tonight, Robert will be your Speaker for the Drums," Claire emphasised. "He and Grace have turned your sparse notes into a sort of musical script that the drumming will get you to follow. That script is the only real difference between our regular drumming nights and your desired cathartic scene."

Claire knew how cranky and highly strung Fleur could be. She had set up the dinner meeting at the Smuggler's Den so that they could chat casually about tattoo drumming and Sir Robert's contribution to the upcoming scene as Speaker. She hoped to quiet any fears or hang-ups Fleur might have and put her into a receptive space. Besides, the food at the Siebert was usually very good and she didn't want to get into pre-party cooking.

Feeling hungry after her talk with Sam, she had ordered Smokey Elora Chicken, a Den specialty that featured juicy breast and thigh of range-bred Chicken, Coleslaw, Blackened yams and spicy Pecan butter. She knew that an hour or two of concentrated drumming burned up a lot of calories.

"I didn't think we'd ever get around to a cathartic drumming on me," Fleur said, tucking into a Pingue Niagara Pork chop. "I don't get that much play you know."

"Too many of our service doms are leery of you," Claire told her, factually but in a kindly way. "You're always bustling around on some crusade or other. It can scare folks off. Anyway, no one quite knows who's going to turn up. What colour your hair will be."

When it came to fashion, Fleur was a firm believer in colour and texture. She had seven favourite wigs. Her choice for dinner with Claire, and the unique scene to follow, was short-haired and a bright metallic red. She was wearing a long tartan skirt with a purple bustier.

"I want people to remember me," she said. "There's so much more available than black leather skirts and corsets."

Claire smiled. "You'll probably need to be more conservative if you start appearing in Court as an expert NCSF witness."

"I'll wear my pinstripe suit and a close-cropped brunette wig. Fact is, Claire, there are so many miscarriages of justice where BDSM is concerned. People charged with assault and battery when it was purely consensual."

She pushed aside her half-finished first course and started in on the dessert. Raspberry Sorbet with Maple Brandy. "The psychiatric powers-that-be may have decided we're normal, but the justice system and the general public are lagging way behind.

Getting our particular type of sexuality on the LGBT list isn't going to be a picnic. We're back where gays were before Stonewall and the Barracks in T.O." She made a swift Fleur transition. "So will you be on my Board, Madame Claire?"

For the National Coalition?"

"International soon, "Fleur announced proudly. "The International Coalition for Sexual Freedom."

Claire was hesitant. "I have a lot on my plate, Fleur dear," she said.

Fleur grinned. "Not any more. That was your last mouthful." She was pleading now. "You won't have to do much. Honorary Chairperson. I'll do all the running around."

Claire could see how important her participation was to Fleur. "I'll think about it," she said at last.

"The Community Seal of Approval," Fleur said eagerly. "You're such a mentor to us all."

"My husband Wally was the mentor," Claire corrected her, with a faint smile. "He taught me everything I know about people and motivations." She returned to the Robert and Grace script for the upcoming cathartic drum scene. "Were you ever married, Fleur? It wasn't in your notes."

Fleur shook her head. "I cohabited with a Honduran refugee for a few months," she said dourly. "I had a son, Diego."

"You never talk about him."

"It's difficult," she mumbled awkwardly. "Maybe that's part of the reason I'm interested in a cathartic drumming. I have to get a better grip on my life."

Fleur was suddenly brutally honest. "People don't like me very much," she said. "They think I'm a fanatical busybody. A militant do-gooder." She spoke very sincerely. "I want to be more like you, Madame Claire. Everyone likes you. Respects you."

Claire smiled in encouragement. "We'll hope that the drums, and Sir Robert as their Speaker, will show you the path. And don't forget that there'll be up to six drummers playing on you tonight, five of them very experienced. The other, Leeza, will be topping for the first time. That's the great thing about drumming, virtually anyone can do it. Four year olds can bang a saucepan with a spoon. We all have heartbeats just naturally beating time."

"Body drumming is a special art, you know. An exercise in communication between drummers and drum. Mental as well as physical. In a good session like this will be, we blend into one cohesive rhythmic unit. Oh, and Fleur, the drummers get very high and dance a lot."

"I'm looking so forward to it. I just pray it works."

Madame Claire let her enthusiasm show. "It will work, darling, believe me." She wanted her confidence in the outcome to fill Fleur's mind. "And, as Robert will tell you, the drum high, your high, is quite different to our regular BDSM Subspace. More somnolent. The constant repetition of drumsticks and drumcanes beating the naked flesh induces a state halfway between sleeping and waking. Not hard, but more and more intense. Thousands of light repeated hits all across the body. Over an hour as many as twenty, thirty thousand. There's an almost dreamlike quality to it."

Fleur's accustomed cynicism had evaporated in the face of Claire's fervent description of drumming affects. "This is shaping up as a fantabulous day ," she said, eyes glowing. "Having dinner with you at the Smuggler's Inn. The NCSF coming together. And tonight....catharsis. I can't remember when I went into something feeling so positive."

Claire allowed herself a small satisfied smile. Like Fleur she was looking forward to the evening to come. It was even extra-curricular in a way. No lurking rapist or sleazy blackmailer. Just a straightforward drumming scene designed to help a friend in need.

BDSM, she assured herself wryly, truly could be a force for good.

*

It was nine-fifteen that evening. In the dungeon at Black Walnut Cottage, Fleur's cathartic drumming scene was well underway.

In his role as Speaker of the Drums, a sort of Master of Ceremonies for the longed for catharsis, Sir Robert had opened proceedings by calmly asking Fleur to strip down and assume the position on the massage table, face down.

She had obeyed at once. It didn't matter that she was the only person undressed in the candle-lit dungeon. There was no false modesty in the Scene, nudity was a natural part of play. In fact, Fleur had gone farther. With a touch of bravado she had removed her crimson wig. With a dramatic flourish, it must be said.

"I guess I won't need this for a while," she said. Underneath it was pure Fleur. Her head was largely clean shaven, except for a black and purple Mohawk that matched the much smaller, landing strip of her pubic hair.

Robert had smiled knowingly at his wife Lady Grace. He had woven Fleur's scribbled notes into a low-key recital of her life. By now he knew her well. So did Grace, who had prepared the drumming playlist, starting with a selection from DrumSex featuring the sonorous and driving drumming of Brian Lewis.

Some thirty drumsticks and drumcanes were laid out next to the massage table. Claire had seen to it that there were five experienced body drummers on hand - Robert and Grace, Celeste and Janey and herself. Along with the newbie to topping, Leeza. Claire had her reasons for that.

Janey was married to Harold the regular djembe player at Madame Claire's drumming evenings. He brought the MP3 drumbeats and melodies right into the dungeon. Janey's job was to carry the djembe and adjust the MP3 volume so that Harold could riff away as the fancy took him.

"This first solo from Drumsex is called Temple of Love," said Grace informally, using regular drumsticks on Fleur's shoulder. "It will segue into Needy, Needy, Needy."

Robert was beating steadily on Fleur's other shoulder with a pair of tympani mallets, soft but thuddy. Her flesh was already turning a healthy shade of pink as the blood circulated. Claire was tapping away on Fleur's bottom with her favourite leopard drumsticks. She was pleased to see that Leeza had followed her lead and was wielding short dowelling drumcanes on Fleur's free buttock. Celeste and Janey were lightly caning her feet.

"Normally, there isn't much conversation in a drumming scene," said Robert. "But this is a little different tonight, Fleur. Let my dulcet tones guide you on your way to catharsis. Relax with the drumming. You are the drum. Become it. The constant beat all over your body will carry you into drowsy, almost hypnotic state."

They were all drumming on her now. Not hard, never hard, but enough to make her very aware of the rise and fall of the Lewis drums and Harold's choing accompaniment right by her head. Needy, Needy, Needy.

"See yourself as a child, Gennifleur." Robert said softly. "Jennifer Van Lith, you were called then. What were you like as a five year old? Needy? Or carefree?"

Fleur had snuggled down into the leopard blanket on the massage table, her head resting on one side, following the DrumSex beat. "Happy but needy too, "she said, her voice slightly slurred. "I believed the birthmark on my face was a gift from the goddess. Like my Mom always said."

Janey lowered the MP3 volume and Harold went to town with a mounting barrage of slap strokes to underscore the background melody. His fingers were held close together and the tone of the djembe was crisp and tight.

The drummers circled the table, each moving sideways to a different part of Fleur's exposed body. Now Robert was drumming up a storm on her shapely, muscular buttocks. He had switched to two-foot rattan canesticks, flexible, with a little bite. He was well into his Eighties but had been a drummer with a Beatnik house band in his youth. Drumming reinvigorated him.

"Can you recall your school days, Gennifleur?" he asked, increasing the pace of his strokes. "High School, College?"

"Bullying!" she exclaimed bitterly. "Right through primary school, high school and my ghastly year of college."

She opened her eyes and stared up owlishly at the drummers circling around her. "Ronnie Lonergan said I was marked by the devil." Tears filled her eyes as she heard the children's voices behind the music, taunting and jeering her. "You're not one of us," Patty Forbes simpered cruelly. "You're short and fat with an ugly stain on your face."

The drumming went on and on as Robert took her back to girlhood, making her experience what she had gone through on her sad journey to becoming the Fleur she was now.

As if in a dream she heard Grace say that the Brian Lewis DrumSex had long since morphed into Dragon Ritual Drummers and their powerful Masters of Chaos. She felt rather than heard Sir Robert suggesting that she revisit her twenties and early adulthood. All her thoughts were woven into the incessant, pounding drumming. For a moment she tried to count the beats. It was impossible. Literally thousands of light, rhythmic strikes were falling like pelting rain all over her body. The reverberating sound of the drums filled her mind. She lost all sense of time and proportion.

"It's like our Bolero scene," Leeza whispered to Madame Claire. "Only with a wider range of music. Drums, drums and more drums."

"Most BDSM scenes use music to heighten the play," Claire said sotto voce. "We nearly always start softly and then build up as the body responds."

Claire was impressed at how readily the young girl had adjusted to topping. It confirmed what she had seen developing, a growing need for more independence. Like Matt, who would certainly have been a Dominant if he had been into the Lifestyle.

And then again Harold's ljembe signalled another major change in the drum music. Fleur had been drifting through her lonely and misspent twenties when suddenly it switched to original rock and roll.

"In-A-Garda-Da-Vida is the longest, most atmospheric piece Grace and I chose for your cathartic scene," Robert told her warmly. "Seventeen minutes of classic rock by Iron Butterfly, circa 1968. Ideal for free association into adulthood and through current entanglements. What have you become, dear abrasive Dana Gennifleur?"

It was nearing the midpoint of Fleur's journey. The drumcanes were longer and thicker now. Almost, but not quite painful. Just close enough that she started to fret..

Claire noticed this and offered some techniques to keep the pain at bay. "If the drumming gets too hard on one part of your body, Fleur, focus your attention someplace else."

Grace clarified what Claire had said "It's called localising your pain receptors. If your bottom starts to hurt, concentrate on your shoulders. Any bottom pain will fade completely away."

"Try it," said Claire. "I guarantee it works."

Fleur tried it and relaxed again. "My parents used to listen to Garda-Da-Vida," she said calmly to Robert, who was carefully patting her Mohawk with shimmering metal whisks.

"They're gone now, I understand," he said.

"In a car crash when I was ten."

"Grace knew that Garda Da Vida had deep meaning for you," he said sympathetically. "And there's an amazing drum solo coming up."

Fleur closed her eyes again and drifted off into the music as Robert led her into her recent life. He asked why she had become the acknowledged scene authority on rape-play. He wanted to know why she ran so many workshops, why she was constantly posting comments to Kinklife, why she maintained her voluminous blog. He was curious about what drove her to study Muay Thai at its Bangkok source. Would she ever use it? Was she training herself to combat a rapist?

Not likely, she thought, as a fleeting consideration of KayJames16 passed through her mind. Though why had she spent so many hours writing out his Ravisher's Questionnaire? Why was it so important to her that she try to educate would be scene ravishers? Come to that, why was she working so hard on setting up the Canadian chapter of the American National Coalition for Sexual Freedom. Why was she always trying to organise and control? Was her constant activity a mute cry for attention? Like her Mohawk, her change of wigs, her Muay Thai? Was she trying to protect the girls who wanted to be ravished? Or Diego, the son she had born and lost.

Many minutes had passed. More drumbeats had reverberated through her body and soul. She was a human drum and her skin from top to toe was the tautly vibrating skin of that drum. She was a living vibration, an echo of the tiny strings that some said made up a universe.

Crash! went In-A-Garda-Da-Vida. Boom,boom,boom! went Harold's djembe, with all the strength of his arms behind it. Rat-a-tat-tat! went the twelve canesticks as Iron Butterfly came to its resounding crescendo...........Only to fade into the sound of waves breaking tranquilly on a sandy, rock-strewn beach.

And again Sir Robert set the scene. "The waves of the ocean, Gennifleur, are transporting you to what was once known as the Dark Continent. It is nine years ago. We are going back to the most critical time of your life."

As the African drums came in, Grace completed the transition. "These are the tribal sounds of Ubaka Hill's Shapeshifter album. The opening chant is called Mother Beat. You are in your early thirties. You have taken your young son to the Serengeti."

Fleur had gone very pale. "No, no," she breathed, barely able to speak, her voice trembling.

'YES, Gennifleur," Robert said, in his deepest, most mellifluous tones. Then he softened, coaxing her. "Tell us about the Serengeti."

Fleur shook her head feverishly from side to side. She opened and closed her mouth helplessly. She was looking desolate. The drumming intensified.

"Talk to us, Gennifleur," said Robert. "You never have. Not about Africa."

There were tears in her eyes. She struggled to speak. But no words came.

"You took your son to the Serengeti," Robert prompted her. "Diego, your lovely boy."

"I told him it was for his birthday," she said, her whole body remembering. The unremitting drum beats had quickened every cell, awakened her very soul. "But really it wasn't for him. I had always wanted to see the veldt. It was my dream." She spoke in an almost mechanical tone. "It was for me, not Diego."

"How old was he?"

Her voice was very flat. "He was seven that April. Only seven."

The Great Plains of Africa were written in the drums. A woman-centred tribal beat. Wild animals in headlong flight. Predators stalking.

"I loved him so much," Fleur said, still expressionless. "He was all I had."

"Tell me, Fleur," Robert said gently. "What happened in the Serengeti?"

She hesitated. The drumming was relentless. "He was afraid," she said. "The roar of the lions terrified him."

"And you?"

"I loved it. I felt I had come home." Her voice broke. She was crying silently. "I wanted Diego to feel as I did." The tones of Mother Beat faded andHarold'sslapping melody led the segue to a heavier, more masculine beat. Now Celeste and Leeza were clapping their hands to the African music. The other drummers had taken up longer, much thicker canesticks.

"This new piece is from the Dead Can Dance," Grace said. "It penetrates to the absolute depth of Being."

"The Dead Can Dance, Gennifleur," Robert repeated strongly. "And this is their most powerful tone-poem - The Snake and the Moon"

Fleur shuddered and moaned. Her body went rigid. The heavy, four-foot drumcanes pounded on her shoulders and buttocks. Two each from Robert and Claire. The clapping grew.

"The Snake and the Moon," Robert said forcefully. What happened in the Serengeti, Gennifleur?"

"Guilt!" she burst out at the top of her voice. "Guilt," she repeated brokenly.

"Tell me," he said quietly.

It was a first for her. She had carried the burden for nine years. Never speaking of it. Hiding the anguish in constant activity.

"He was such a sweet boy, my Diego," she said. "I forced him to come with me. He was just a frightened little kid. Don't leave the camp, I said. But a lioness roared behind us. He ran out into the bush." Her voice faltered.

"What happened?" Robert asked.

"He tripped over a snake. A green mamba. It struck his calf. Just below the knee."

Harold had taken the djembe right down to a damp filler tone using only his weak hand. Janey had brought the Dead Can Dance down to low background. The clapping had become stroking ana the large drumcanes barely touched Fleur's flesh.

She wept. "I should never have taken him to Africa. He wasn't ready. I should have stopped him running out into the bush. I failed him in every way."

Madame Claire draped a comforting arm around Fleur's shoulder. "And you've been over-compensating ever since." She was infinitely gentle. "You poor, poor woman."

Grace stroked the black and purple Mohawk with deep compassion. Celeste tenderly rubbed Fleur's legs and feet, while Leeza....Leeza kissed her forehead.

Sir Robert was still in character. Still the Speaker of the Drums. "Time to forgive yourself, dearest Fleur. Your cathartic scene nears its end."

Janey slowly raised the volume as Brian Lewis launched into a different cut from Drum Sex. Much mellower.

'It's called Reflections," said Grace, who had chosen the closing music with great care. "Turn over on your back, Fleur. It's time to look to the future."

Fleur barely felt Madame Claire's hand reaching under her shoulder, turning her. "The rest of your life is ahead of you," she said. "A good life, a happy life."

Fleur was lying on her back now, one leg slightly crooked. She felt exhausted but strangely relieved, free. She started to drift with the reflective music, aware that the drumming had stopped and only soft hands were caressing her gently.

Claire had laid her drumsticks and drumcanes back on their table and instead had brought out her gleaming Chinese cups. The dungeon was quiet and loving.

Sir Robert held a candle for her as she warmed the cups and started to position them on Fleur's pulsing skin. Four high on the shoulders and two more leading down to her breasts.

Fleur breathed a sigh of growing relaxation as the cups settled and her nipples swelled into them, taut and erect.

Down Fleur's tummy Claire took them, past the navel and through the black and purple pubes. "Oh my!" moaned Fleur as the last one settled over her straining clit.

"Go with the feeling, Fleur darling," Claire whispered softly. "You are nothing but feeling...."

Celeste and Leeza drizzled some coconut oil and slid the cups over her shoulders and breasts, breathing warm air between them.

"You are much loved, sweet girl," Grace said in her ear as Claire moved the last cup in small concentric circles.

"And I probably shouldn't say this," said Robert, who was a sly old dog at times. "But it seems to me that just maybe your catharsis is coming to a climax"

"You wretch," laughed Grace, and threw a cushion at him. A leopard cushion, of course.

Somehow, at Claire's, Cups and cushions went together.

It was a happy ending.

And for Fleur, a new beginning.

Chapter 25 Back to Avalon Acres

The mid-July sun was beating down on the modest but effective training oval at Avalon Acres. There was a mock-up starting gate and enough initial straightaway for a horse to work up a fair clip.

Matt and Wendy, the young groom/hotwalker, were taking Lady Barbara through her paces. She was noted for an explosive take-off, but Matt's training emphasis was still on getting her used to the presence of the racing whip. "Hold it in your right hand," he instructed Wendy. "Let it rest on her shoulder or rump. Don't move it around, just let it lie there."

He closed the automatic gate and stood out front and off to one side. He had a compilation of crowd noises on an MP3 player. "Sense her intensity building," he called to Wendy. "Let her 'feel' your voice. Visualise her bursting out of the gate."

The young groom was no longer overly apprehensive of Lady Barbara's skittish reactions. She knew her mount was ready. She could sense the powerful muscles tensing. The racing whip was forgotten. The mare wanted nothing more than to run. To make a hole in the wind, as Matt called it.

He brought his hand down and tripped the gate. The bell clanged. Wendy uttered an encouraging yell and Lady Barbara took off like an exploding bullet. "Yes!" cried Matt, excited and not a little triumphant.

"I seen worse," said Sam Seagram of the Siebert Hotel, who was perched on the low white fence around the training track. He had his ever-present old Leica slung around his neck and had taken a shot of Lady Barbara's take off. "Though I still don't see the Major entering her in the Prince o' Wales stakes," he said to Matt, negatively. "She threw her jockey last time out."

"I told Turco she didn't fancy the whip," Matt said gruffly. “And you shouldn't be here, Mr. Seagram. Francis don't like punters hanging around"

Sam looked comically hurt. "Where is his highness anyway?"

"He's sick"

Wendy brought Lady Barbara around the last bend as a familiar BMW pulled into the parking lot. Matt had asked Madame Claire to drop by. He was worried about the Major.

Sam snapped off another flash and Lady Barbara almost bucked Wendy to the turf. She clung on for grim death.

"That does it," Matt said impatiently. "Sam, you're outta here."

"Got what I come for, man," snickered Sam. He was accustomed to be moved along at stables he frequented on his days off. "She's fast, but unreliable."

Wendy on the other hand was now beaming with enthusiasm. "She was running real smooth, Matt," she told him. "You wanna try the gate again?"

He grinned and shook his head. "Once around in an easy breeze, kid. Keep telling her how fast she could be if she opened up." He looked across at the parking lot, where Claire was already getting out of Lohengrin. He smiled, feeling a clear sense of relief.

"Afternoon, Madame Claire," Sam was saying, in his usual obsequious tone. "Didn't know you followed the horseys."

"I don't really, Sammy," she said, in her friendly way. "I'm here on business. I only place bets when Matt says it's a sure thing."

The Smuggler's Den manager snorted. “Watch out for that Lady Barbara," he said derisively. "She spooks real easy." He kick-started his noisy motor-cycle and drove off. Claire shook her head at the clatter and continued across the neatly trimmed grass to Matt.

"Sam Seagram is one of a kind," she said.

"He's gotta bad eye for horseflesh," Matt responded. "Can't wonder the bookies love him."

Claire smiled and came to the reason for her visit. "How's Francis bearing up?"

"Terrible. He came home from the hospital after Desmond's accident and hasn't been out of the house since."

They watched Wendy slowing Lady Barbara to a canter. Neither of them spoke for a moment.

"It all seems so unfair," Claire said at length.

"Accidents always are," Matt said judiciously. "Even Mrs. Gretsko is at her wit's end. I was hoping you could reach him."

"A little tough love, I think. Though I do have some news for him."

Matt looked at her keenly.

"Nothing spectacular," she said. "But things are coming together."

She smiled at him sadly and went on up to the house. Despite all the blue sky and warm sun there seemed to be a pall of gloom hanging over Avalon Acres.

Even the horses in the paddocks seemed aware that something was very wrong.

*

Francis was slumped in the white leather sofa by the sunroom sliding doors. He was still wearing his striped pyjamas and a blue military dressing gown. He was unshaven. There was an untouched roast beef sandwich on the coffee table in front of him.

Mrs. Gretsko was hovering nearby. She was not a hovering type of person, but Francis had worn her down. "You got to eat, Major sir," she was saying. "Mister Desmond would want you to eat."

"I'm not hungry," mumbled Francis.

"If you not eat, you get sick like him."

Francis glared at her. "Desmond isn't sick, woman," he said irritably. "He's in a coma. He's dying, for Christ's sake." He pushed the sandwich away roughly. It fell on the floor. "I'm not fucking hungry."

Sophia knelt and cleaned it up without complaint. She had kept the sunroom neat and tidy. Only Francis himself and three partially open Fed Ex boxes seemed out of place.

"Swearing to me not help Mister Desmond," she said calmly. "You not being sensible."

"Sensible!" he exclaimed sharply. "There's nothing sensible about murder."

He buried his face in his hands and barely looked up as Madame Claire rapped on the open screen door and entered. "So what the hell do you want?" he demanded.

"Francis, you look like shit!" she said, without a trace of softness or empathy. "Mrs. Gretsko, good to see you again."

"He not eat for two day," Sophia said. "No supper last night. No breakfast, no lunch. He terrible stubborn."

"Chicken soup," Claire said firmly. "And tea for me, please."

Sophia Gretsko was clearly relieved to see Claire taking over. "Homemade, Madame Claire. I have yesterday chicken in Frigidaire." She turned back before leaving. "He good man," she added, making sure Claire knew. "He was with United Nations in Kradjina. I make rich soup right quick."

"Take your time, Sophia," Claire told her. She turned to the Major, her voice filled with authority. "Now, Francis. Tell me what happened with Desmond. I overheard you say 'murder' to Mrs. Gretsko."

"Deliberate, wilful murder," he said bitterly. "Attempted, for now." He made a half-hearted apology. "I'm sorry if I snarled at you." He completed what he had been saying. "Des hadn't checked his computer before leaving for Toronto. It was mainly bills, he used to say. The blackmail email was waiting for him when he got home Monday."

He looked sad and beaten, guilty even. "I should have warned him, Claire. I let him go off to the damned convention without knowing anything was wrong. It was my fault."

Claire decided to cut those thoughts off before they got worse. "As I recall, you wanted him to have a trouble-free weekend." It didn't work. Francis was too busy blaming himself.

"That's what I told myself," he said gloomily. "It could have been I just didn't want to upset the applecart."

She frowned, but went on. "How did he take it?"

"He opened the email Monday evening. Phoned me right away. He was absolutely convinced he'd lose his job. BDSM and sex. I told him to come straight over. We're investigating, I said."

"Which is when the accident happened?"

"If it was an accident," Francis said darkly. "I thought he sounded suicidal. I actually thought that."

"He struck the railway bridge on Highway 7?"

"Head on." His eyes were wide and staring. “It angles across the road. He'd driven under it a thousand times. Smashed right into the brickwork." His voice took on a desperate tone. "The doctors say he may never come out of the coma. Even if he does, he'll likely never walk again."

"TallBlondeChick has a lot to answer for."

Francis stared morosely out of the window. "I hate her, Claire. Or him, I understand it could be a him." Bitterness filled his words. "Murder of the soul," you called it. I want her to suffer."

Sophia Gretsko tapped on the door from the house. "Chicken soup," she announced. "Real chicken. No from can."

Francis looked rebellious. But Claire would brook no nonsense. "I have some progress to report," she said. "You eat. I'll talk."

"You need strength, Major Francis," Sophia added.

He glanced from one to the other. They were both strong women. Unbending. He gave them a wan half-smile and sat at the pinewood games table.

"Thank you for the Earl Grey, Sophia," Claire said. "I meant to ask, how's Dawn coping?"

Mrs. Gretsko's careworn face looked suddenly younger. "You make good advice, Madame Claire," she said. "The bruises all gone. She smile again." The expression on her face was almost shy. "We very close now."

"She's lucky to have you for a mother," Claire said, meaning it whole-heartedly.

"And you as a - how you say - a mentor," Sophia said earnestly. "That her word." She smiled, and for the first time Claire realised that Mrs. Gretsko was probably much younger than she was.

It seemed as if Sophia wished to say something else. "Donja still cry sometime," she started. "Much tears in bed. Then throw up before go to work. But she strong girl now. Cope with life good...." She paused, and the moment passed. She smiled politely at Claire and left without saying another word.

Madame Claire stared after her, puzzled. Something important had not actually been said. She wondered what she had missed. Then she knew. Or thought she knew. "I was so very wrong about Mrs. Gretsko," she said to Francis. "You can depend on her, no matter what." She gave him a small, almost secret smile. "So, how's the chicken soup?"

Francis sighed. "I couldn't fight the two of you," he said weakly. "It'll probably do me good," he added, albeit grudgingly.

Claire decided to hold on to his attention while he was more or less compliant. She could be very dominant when she wanted to be. "I looked up Blackmail in Wikipedia," she said forthrightly. It has nothing to do with letters or emails. It comes from the Northumberland-Scottish border back in the 16th Century."

"It does?" he grunted non-commitedly, now tucking into his soup.

"Maille was an old Norse word meaning Rent or Tribute. Regular tax was paid by white maille, pieces of silver. Black maille was paid under the counter by the Scots in goods and cattle. Mainly Black Angus. It graduated to a vicious protection racket, hence blackmail. By the way, the OPP haven't cottoned on to it yet." .

"No doubt they will," he said gloomily, pushing aside his empty plate.

She opened her leopard briefcase. "And we were right, Francis. The $225 is a scattergun approach. I've located half a dozen other recipients to date. Including Leeza and myself."

"You seem to be implying that's good?"

Claire nodded. "It gives us a chance to muddy TallBlonde's waters. Leeza and I have already sent responses back, in her case enclosing a counter cheque for $79. Almost certainly uncashable. Said she got fired and that's all she has. For my part I've been utterly rude. Told ShortDarkHo to get stuffed"

Francis finally showed some interest. "Looking for a reaction, I suppose? The cat among the pigeons."

"Thereby increasing the chances of a TallBlonde misstep. I'm setting up emails from the other victims as well. I shall want one from you and one as Desmond's executor." She passed him hard copies from her briefcase. "These are the drafts."

"Snow the bastard under, right?"

"I also checked out Box 147 at the Siebert Hotel. We can't actually stake it out, but I'm sweetening up Sam Seagram. He supervises the P.O. Boxes."

"Gets under my skin, that pesky little man. Always snapping photos of the horses."

"In my own email, by the way, I went so far as to suggest sarcastically our 'amateur' blackmailer forward the information to the Times-Dispatch. I didn't mention Angele Del Zotto by name, but I figure that's pretty obvious."

"Why Del Zotto of all people?"

Claire smiled at her own subtlety. "She knows me and has sources coming out of the whazoo. Tracking down a blackmailer should be right up her alley. Especially when the information she's getting is bogus."

"How in God's name did you arrange that?"

"There are personal titbits in each blackmailing letter. Leeza and I are called dyke and dolly. Minor mistake, but a dyke I'm not."

She smiled sweetly at Francis. "Which means our TallBlondeBlackmailer doesn't know our finer points at all. Not a big gaffe, but revealing, I think."

She put the papers away. "Now, you tell me something. It's been bothering me since I came in. You have three Fed Ex boxes in here. One has been opened, one partially, and one still sealed. What's that about?"

He had finished the chicken soup. He stood up. "You don't miss much, Claire."

"Are they relevant?"

His face had completely clouded over again. "They were. Now..." He broke off. "I haven't had the heart to open them."

"Tell me, Francis."

He still hesitated. "The last time you were here, Des stayed for hours. For the foaling. Des's Dancer." He blinked uncertainly. His voice was shaky. "I ordered them the next day."

He went to the partly opened box. "This is very hard, Claire," he said, his face strained. "Desmond loved horses you know. I always teased him he must have been one in a past life."

He ripped down the Fed Ex wrapping and fished out a large shoe box. "A present," he said, voice cracking. "He has a birthday coming up." He peeled back the tissue paper and took out two knee-high black leather boots. Hoof boots. High raised heels. Shiny aluminium horseshoes. Studded with angular nails.

"I keep a sulky at camp. At Long Point. I figured he would get off on being a Pony Boy."

He cleared his throat and tore open the second box. "This is a complete bridle mask. Only the finest leather." He held it up so she could see. "Harness, blinders, muzzle and pointy ears. Top of the line."

His voice was becoming thick and emotional. "The third box is straps and a set of reins. Lots of studs and horse brasses." He stared at Claire blindly. "I was into Pony Play in my youth. Des would have loved it."

There were tears in his eyes. "I don't think all this will be much use for him now."

He sank slowly back into the white sofa, his shoulders shaking. "Oh God, Madame Claire," he said, like a small and vulnerable boy. "I don't know what to do."

Claire dropped to the sofa beside him. The tough love was all gone now. She put a tender arm around his shoulders. "Let it out, Frankie," she said softly. "Tears are good. "Let it all out."

His lip trembled. "He calls me Frankie," he said. "Des calls me Frankie." The tears ran down his cheeks and he broke down completely. "I love him so much, Claire," he wept. "He's my whole life."

She held him to her, his face buried in her chest. He was crying without restraint. Deep, inarticulate sobs.

Claire clasped him tightly. "You shouldn't be home," she said. "Not at Avalon Acres. You should be at the hospital with Des."

"I can't be there," he moaned brokenly. "I yelled at the doctors. Cursed them. They had security drag me out."

"You poor, dear man," Claire said, all sympathy. "You've had a horrible time."

He was desperate. "The administrator said I couldn't stay. I wasn't a relative."

Claire's lips compressed tightly. She was suddenly righteously angry. "You belong with Desmond," she said, determination spreading over her face. "To hell with sorry-arsed bureaucrats and blackmailers!" she burst out. "Getting you and Des together is the first thing we'll fix."

She rose to her feet with total resolve. She knew exactly what she must do. "Wash your face, Francis. Put on something comfortable. We're going to the Grand River Hospital."

He stared at her blankly, but with dawning hope.

"Move it, man," she barked. "I don't have all day. Goddamn it all to hell, Francis, we have some doctors to straighten out. Not a fucking relative indeed!"

He moved it.

*

Less than an hour and fifteen minutes later they were standing in Desmond Trout's private room at Grand River Hospital. Madame Claire had threatened everything from sexual discrimination charges to the human rights charter. She was a difficult woman to refuse when her dander was up.

She was examining Desmond's chart. "There's no change in the coma," she said. "It isn't medically induced. "It's his own brain, fighting back."

"I'll try talking to him," Francis said. "A familiar voice can help."

"Just allow the doctors to do their jobs. No more tantrums, Francis."

He was much more in control now. "You've been a tower of strength, Madame Claire. I won't fall apart again. God, he looks so frail."

Desmond was stretched out on the hospital bed, swathed in bandages. His right leg and right arm were heavily wrapped and in traction. His whole torso, ribcage and head was largely covered. There were faint bloodstains on the bandage around his forehead. What could be seen of his flesh was ashen. One eye, the left one, was exposed, although closed and badly swollen. He was surrounded by expensive medical equipment, constantly monitored from the nurses' station down the hall

"It's so blasted unjust, Claire," Francis blurted out. "Des was always so gentle. I kidded him when he took a ladybug out of the stables into the sunshine. Now look at him." .

"He should have been the Francis," Claire said, with a slight smile. "He was a true Catholic. I'm sure it was an accident." She picked up her briefcase from the chair. She was preparing to leave them alone.

"Caused by TallBlondeBastard," he responded harshly. "She's responsible. Or he is."

"I know that," she agreed. "When I find out who it is, they'll go to jail for a long time." She opened the door. She thought Francis could cope now. "Talk to him about the foaling. Des's Dancer, right? Your lives together. The birthday present. And remember your exercises, my friend."

He managed a tight smile as he watched her go. But the vein in his neck was swelling dangerously. He walked around the bed and stood by Desmond's bloodstained head. The neuroplasticity exercises were far from his mind. "A few years in a cushy Canadian prison won't even come close, Des," he growled, his hurt and anger taking over.

His eyes narrowed and his face grew set and unutterably menacing. He could feel the pressure in his head again. With a terrible finality he made the sign of the cross over his lover's bandaged body. "I have never been a vengeful man," he said, his nostrils flaring. "But you have my heartfelt oath on this, Desmond my boy. TallBlondeChick will be paid back in kind."

A single tear seemed to come from under Desmond's lone exposed eye. It escaped the closed eyelid and slid slowly down into the bloody bandage around his head.

Francis didn't see it. He was lost in a dangerous world of his own volition.

"This I do attest before God," he said, the veins in his neck bulging like livid ridges. "One day you will be avenged. So I do solemnly swear. So shall it be!"

* * *

Chapter 26 A Double Recci

Richard was in one of his military modes. Reconnoitering the lie of the land, in his terminology. Scouting out potential locales for two upcoming scenes. Billie the Kid with the new Tiffany chick and James with Gennifleur.

He was at the wheel of his red Mustang. He got off on driving, fast if he thought the roads were clear of police speed traps. He was a relatively good driver, with a natural aptitude for things mechanical. He liked gearing down and up and could throw in a great 180 if he felt like showing off.

Myra was in the passenger seat, firmly belted in, with the laptop in front of her. She had also brought along the WiFi stick in case. She never knew when Richard, or James, or Billie might launch into dictation. She was accustomed to his driving by now, but still sat up straight and even rigid when he took a sharp country corner at twenty klicks over the posted speed. Not that she felt unsafe, it was what he termed the roller-coaster effect. She was looking much cuter these days, with a hot pink cap and a multi-coloured pashmina over her shoulders. Even her complexion had cleared up. Regular sex, said Richard.

They were engaged in 'location research,' which was another term he used a lot. Coffee shops and possible meeting places. Locations that added dramatic spice to the scenes his 'prospects' had hinted at or, like Tiffany and her ivy-clad school description, covered in some detail. He usually tried to match the girl and the location. It was a relevant part of his tried and true modus operandi.

"It's not all that easy to get girls to come out and meet a stranger," he had told Myra. "It goes against everything they've been taught by parents and teachers. I look for a location that fits their fantasies and is unthreatening. Make them think it's their idea, that's my secret."

He was wearing his familiar Reebok track suit, with a short black leather jacket. He like to dress the part. His sunglasses today were mirrored and he wore snazzy European driving gloves. To begin their evening drive they were travelling through the Mennonite farm country to the north and east of Waterloo Region. Small, neat farmhouses with good-sized barns and silos, well-kept and close together. Later he planned to take a longer trip south to Lake Erie and tobacco-growing land. "Almost down to the Point," he said, relishing the idea of the open road. "Long Point, it juts out into the lake for 40 or more kilometers. Fantastic beaches and sand dunes. Further south than half the northern states and ideal for the James and Fleur scene I have in mind."

"Why Long Point?" asked Myra. "Isn't it mainly a bird sanctuary ?"

"There are lots of campgrounds in the area as well," he explained. "And a Marina close by. Our Fleur is into boats. And it's not that far to go. Not for the extra-special scene I'm coming up with for her. James should have no problem talking her into joining him. She won't be able to resist."

"So why are we out here, in the Mennonite community?" Myra wanted to know.

"There are small towns dotted around," he said. "John Deere and TCS rural farm stores. I figure on checking out a Tim Hortons on Highway 10 just outside Tilverdale and maybe find a school setting for the scene with the Kid and Tiffany. You remember she wrote about her school days. I want her to feel right at home. Her idea, come back to haunt her, well, to lure her in. Q.E.D. as my housemaster at Upper Canada College used to say. "

Myra nodded. "Richard, did you ever watch an old TCM movie called Witness?" she asked, sitting back and admiring the immaculate fields and landscape. "Harrison Ford was a Pittsburgh cop who had to hide out with the local Amish. They're sort of the same as the Mennonites up here."

"I liked him in Raiders of the Lost Ark," he replied. "I saw that as a kid." He was in a positive, expansive mood. Tooling around in his bright red Mustang always gave him a lift. He seemed finally to have recovered from the Stratford funk, thought Myra. At times he was still confused about his multiplicity of internet identities, but right now he was riding high on the email Billie had received back from Tiffany, the 'ideal' new girl, as they called her.

"Thanks for saying such nice things about my story," Tiffany had written back. "It did me good to get it off my chest." It was nothing more than a courtesy acknowledgement but it was enough to reassure him that she was taking the bait. There was also a small personal note in it. She had signed off as 'Your friend, Tiffany.' That was more than enough to motivate Richard to overcome his aversion to Billie and get him to set about pinning down a possible meeting.

He tossed the sleek gloves and the red cap on the dash and shook his hair loosely down on his forehead, Billie's forehead. The mirrored glasses wound up on the cap and Billie's round glasses took their place. He winked a hello to Myra and soon they were cruising along at about 105 klicks an hour on the 80 klick two-lane road, with Billie lazily weaving between the white centre lines.

"Send this to Tiffany" he directed Myra, falling smoothly into dictating mode. *"Thanks for your email, Tiff,"* he began, totally at ease with himself and the newish girl he was writing to. "*Like I said the last time, I think we should set up a first negotiation meeting on neutral ground with scads of folks around. I was figuring on the Tim Hortons on Highway 10 just north of Tilverdale. I'm on my way to check it out right now."* He paused impatiently, waiting for Myra to catch up. *"I know it's kind of scary to come and meet someone you don't know really well, but it's just for coffee. Like I said before, there's no obligation.*"

Abruptly he tooted his horn loudly as they swerved past a Mennonite horse-and-buggy trotting sedately along the shoulder, the driver all in black except for a wide-brimmed straw hat. "Get off the goddamned road," Billie yelled out of the window. "What are you, crazy!" He shook his head disbelievingly. "No electricity, no TV, these fuckers are like the Muslim peasants around Kandahar. Only this lot chose the life. Stupid fuckers."

“I thought the Amish were cute,” said Myra, making conversation.

“I don’t reckon any of them ever go to Tim Hortons,” Billie snorted, slowing the Mustang. “Unlike me and the bimbo."

They had reached their first destination and he pulled off the highway into the usual, familiar Tim Hortons parking lot. He ignored the drive-thru lane, with too many idling cars inching forward, and brought the car to a screeching halt as close as he could get to the main entrance and still drive out forwards. He most often took such ingrained precautions. In a restaurant he would usually sit with his back to the wall, his dark eyes searching the room behind his glasses. “Bring the laptop inside, babe,” he ordered Myra, giving her one of his deceptively boyish smiles. “Tiffany will be waiting on tenterhooks for my reply.”

There were eleven people in the Tilverdale coffee shop. At the counter he ordered two Iced Capps, along with a Boston cream for himself and a Honey Glaze for Myra. “We’ll take the table by the washroom,” he said to Myra. “It’s always one of the last to go.” He angled the chair so he sat against the wall. “Did you know there are some two thousand Tim Hortons’ franchises in south-west Ontario,” he told her. “Everyone trusts Timmie’s. Ideal for casual meetings over coffee. Wear a baseball cap sideways and you blend right in. Or a business suit. Or a cop’s uniform if it comes to that." He grinned at her. "So how you been, sweet cheeks," he went on, "Still horny?"

Myra coloured, remembering how he had left her hanging at their last meeting. "I got over it, Sir" she said quietly. "I'll know better next time."

His grin widened. "Think there'll be a next time, do you ? Good, me too." He reached over the table and patted her hand possessively. "Just so you remember who's boss."

It was early evening, around 7:30. Most of the reconnaissance research was timed to take place at approximately the same hour as Billie or James would be meeting their marks. This seemed a perfectly sensible thing to do.

He barely gave Myra time to sit and open the laptop. "Tell her we'll try for a mutually convenient Friday in early-August. 7:30, 8:00 o'clock. Say I'll be a little early, sitting at this table, near the washrooms." He fluffed his hair. "*That way, Tiffany,* " he resumed dictating, then waited on Myra, taking a bite from his Boston Cream. "*That way, you can come in and head straight to the can, giving me the once-over on the way. When you come back you could just get a coffee to go and leave without me even being aware you'd been by. Mind you, I hope you'll stop and say hello. I'll be sipping coffee, wearing my reading glasses and skimming a MacLean's news magazine. Heck, I'll even wear a short-sleeved white shirt with a - what do you call them? - an ascot, a red ascot around my neck." He grinned at Myra. "In the heat of summer yet! It'll be well into August by the time we get young Tiffany to open her legs for me. But at least it ain't a red carnation."*

He really enjoyed this type of 'long-distance, internet manipulation.' He particularly liked the way that he could casually weave his words into a pretty, innocuous picture. In his mind's eye he saw Tiffany joining him at the table, the background tinged with a faint red glow. He liked visualizing the naïve new girl wreathed in red. "You'll get off on this chick, Myra," he assured her confidentially. "She comes off real innocent for someone asking for rough sex." He casually licked the cream out of his doughnut. "Plus, she has impeccable bone-structure for a person with your artistic talents. Just crying out for a tattoo." He whispered the last word, as Myra glanced around nervously. Not that anyone was listening. Tim Hortons had its own code of customer privacy.

"And you know what?" he said, with a boyish smirk. "I'd really like to see her when she finally makes it home. Peering in the bathroom mirror at the big, beautiful bunch of forget-me-nots on her forehead." He took a drink from the Iced Capp. "I'd bet she won't be in a hurry to come meet a stranger again. Silly young twat."

Myra nodded, slurping a drink herself. "I can see why you take so much time showing them how unthreatening you are. I have to admit I'd feel nervous. Real hesitant about agreeing to a first meeting."

"But that's exactly how you acted, Myra," Billie said, with a wicked grin. "All nerves, I mean. Which is why Dickie-Boy dropped into Igor's tattoo parlour. Though of course you were just another 'prospect' in those days. And how you can still be so obtuse is beyond me. Think about it. Even before the baby dragon tattoo Richard knew precisely what turned your crank." He finished his Iced Capp and stood up. "C'mon, slowpoke, time to hit the road."

Her face red, Myra followed him, the laptop in one hand, the Honey Dew doughnut in the other. She couldn't help wondering how she could have been so gullible as to think Richard's first visit to the tattoo parlour had been remotely accidental. Nothing he ever did was accidental. Except maybe the Stratford disaster, but that was Henry, she thought, clambering awkwardly into the Mustang. All the careful planning had gone sadly awry on that occasion.

The night air was cooling nicely. Not too far off the church clock in Tilverdale was chiming 8.00. A flock of swallows swooped and darted majestically overhead. The powerful engine revved and then purred as Billie turned back onto the Highway into town.

"Well, lookee here," Billie said, as St. Bernadette's hove into view on his left. "Do you see that Myra? The Fates align. It's a fucking conspiracy…. Just for Tiffany and Moi."

"The church ?" asked Myra, puzzled by his suddenly pleased reaction.

"A Catholic Church," he said, almost hugging himself with satisfaction. "Not five hundred metres from Timmie's. And Myra, do you see what's half a block past it?"

Her eyes widened. "A school," she said, marvelling at the way things came together for him. "A Catholic school."

"A boarded up Catholic school," he emphasized. "You really should pay attention to detail when you're out with Dickie-Boy on recci. Reconnaissance, a French military term," he added, in a very Richard reprimanding tone. “And, Myra, do you see the school signboard. Or are you blind as well as dumb ?” He could be very sadistic verbally as well as physically.

A large free-standing electric signboard was still positioned on the grass verge outside the venerable old school building, the black letters clear and readable even in the gathering dusk. St. BERNADETTE’S PRIVATE SCHOOL FOR GIRLS, it was headed. ‘WE BID A FINAL GOODBYE TO OUR FORMER STUDENTS’ it proclaimed. “GOOD FORTUNE, PEACE AND ETERNAL LOVE BE UNTO THEE.”

Billie laughed gleefully. “All this, just for sweet Tiffany,” he crowed. “I'll give her eternal love from now till Doomsday.” He was exultant at the way things were shaping up. “I’d lay odds the school fixtures and desks are still in there, ready and waiting.”

He had slowed down to the Tilverdale posted limit of 50 klicks. It was still on the outskirts of the small sprawling township and there were no houses or businesses nearby. Just the old church with its weather-beaten steeple and the granite, ivy-covered school nearby. “Exactly what the doctor ordered,” he said contentedly. “All those windows… A massive pillared entrance… And a single door on the side. Geez, I could break into this with my eyes closed. Thank you, St. Bernadette. Thank you, Tiffany.”

“Thank you, Richard," Myra breathed stubbornly, finishing her doughnut.

“I'll make her an offer she can’t refuse,” Billie said cheerfully. “I know she’ll come to Timmie’s and getting her down the road and into the old school should be a piece of cake. We've got history and religion on our side. What more can Tiff ask for? It’s a cinch.”

He turned businesslike again, or at least as businesslike as Billie was ever likely to be. ‘Let’s wrap up that email,” he said, taking a last quick look at the lie of the land and making a U-turn on the highway out of Tilverdale. “Just like with you, babe. We'll be sweet and cuddly, safe and familiar. A warm friendly guy on the other side of the coffee mug.”

He speeded up and the Mustang shocks bumped slickly over a yawning pothole in the road. This far out in rural Ontario not all the ravages of winter had been smoothly tarmacked over. And it had been a typical Canadian winter. Freeze and thaw, freeze and thaw again. Very tough on the roads.

“So Tiffany, my sweet” Billie started again, dictating happily. “I hope you’ll drop into Timmie’s one Friday quite soon, take a glance at this kind of sheepish looking guy and say ‘He doesn’t look too scary. Fairly good-looking, with a cute smile, though I say so as shouldn’t. Actually, that’s what my Mom says. I’m not so keen on the cute myself. The thing is, Tiff, since my last email I can't stop thinking about you in your school girl outfit hooking up with Monsieur Desjardin in the school building itself. In a cloakroom, say, or maybe in the night-school classroom. That's what fills my mind right now, an empty school after hours. And your mind too, I bet.

"Anyway, dear girl, I’ll be counting the days and then the hours till we meet. Oh, and that Questionnaire thingie I sent you. If you're hesitant about emailing it you can bring it to Timmie’s and we'll go over it there. TTFN, fondly, your new friend, Billie.”

“And a postscript?” she queried archly. .

“Warm and cuddly,” he said. “*PS. Maybe after the scene we could head back to Timmie’s for a nice chat and some gentle After-Care. . I think it’s real important after a scene like ours to have a comfortable place to unwind and good After-Care is real essential in my book. Also, it's one thing I specialise in, After Care that is. Be well, Billie*.” He was driving faster now. smoothing his hair, putting the red cap back on. He was in a hurry. “That should hook her,” he said, well satisfied with his efforts. “How can she not feel safe when I’m talking about After Care.? Capitalise that, Myra, and Send.”

He settled comfortably in his seat, steering smoothly with his knees as he changed eyeglasses, pulled on his sleek Swedish gloves and adjusted his cap jauntily. Richard was back at the wheel. “That looks after Tiffany baby, “ he said. “Now it’s Fleur’s turn. Gennifleur and James." His hands went to the classic ten to two position and he floored the accelerator. "Lake Erie, Long Point, here we come….. "

*

An hour and a few minutes later, Richard and Myra were sitting in the red Mustang in a discreet layaway on the shores of Lake Erie. They were into the second part of the double recci.

Myra had pulled the pashmina up over her cap, but there were still windblown tendrils of reddish hair peeping out. On the surface, Richard was relaxed and casual but his face was slightly feverish as he looked out over the all too familiar waters of the seemingly tranquil and peaceful lake. He had spent many summers here as a very young boy. Mostly unpleasant.

From the road they overlooked the entrance to Long Point Provincial Park. They had made excellent time. No Ontario Provincial Police had been disturbed. Richard was a lucky as well as a fast driver.

"We don't need to go in and reconnoitre around," he said, somewhat ambivalently. "I know this whole area like the back of my hand."

Myra looked at him questioningly. She remembered him saying much the same words about his knowledge of Stratford, with its Pet Shoppe of unfortunate memory.

"Back in the day, I came here a lot on every vacation with my mother," he went on, trying to sound cool and collected. "She was a professor of Ornithology at York University in Toronto. Sylvia Ostrowski. She penned scholarly and frankly weird tomes about birds, shot through with Lake Erie lore. Legends and stuff." His face clouded over at the memory. "Long Point was one of her main stomping grounds. And I was most often the one getting stomped," he added with a note of bitterness creeping into his voice. "She's always been a thoroughly nasty piece of work."

Myra could see that this bothered him. She deftly changed the subject. "That huge, curling sandy spit," she enquired cautiously. "It seems to go out in the lake for....must be kilometres."

He was relieved to drop his mother. "Over forty-two klicks all told. With some of the best beaches in Canada, outside maybe Tofino and the West Coast. I've ridden the waves there, too. The Pacific is spectacular, but cold and with giant rollers crashing in all the way from Japan. Here, to the south, there's nothing but Lake Erie and the States. It's the second smallest of the Great Lakes, but small is a relative term. Bigger than Holland and Denmark put together."

He was warming to his subject. As when talking about L Ron Hubbard, he liked to show off his knowledge. "Erie also has one of the most diverse and fascinating histories. Smugglers and shipwreckers. Fishermen and sailors of all ilks. Old time sailing schooners. Grain and supply vessels. And towering, almost hurricane force storms that can blow up out of nowhere. Many a good ship's gone down in a Lake Erie blow. Cleaned it up recently, have Canada and the Americans. The fish are spawning again. Skate's one of the biggies now."

He indicated the darkening sky to his left. "Over Eastward, farms and campgrounds run from here through to almost Niagara. One of the camps is Long Point Retreat, which you've probably heard about. It's the gay camp that Francis Dickie runs, the horse trainer. Every August it's home to Black Angel's BDSM camping convention. Four hundred kinksters from the States and Canada getting together for a week of fun and perversion. It's all over Kinklife.ca."

"Would we ever go to a camp like that, Master?" Myra asked, intrigued. She liked camping and couldn't help wondering what it would be like spending a week with four hundred wildly celebrating BDSMers.

"I prefer to do my own thing," Richard said curtly, not picking up on her query. "Too many rampant cocks spoil the gravy, if you know what I mean."

"There can't be four hundred Doms in one camp. That would never work."

"I gather it balances out. Maybe two hundred Doms and a hundred-fifty subs. Plus fifty genderqueers and I don't know what they are. Drop it, will you."

She smiled to herself, enjoying the odd twist to the travelogue. He gave her a searching look, but continued. "Closer towards us, in that small bay, is the Three Lakes Marina. James will probably rent a boat there. He says Fleur is right into sailing. Though he'll probably go for a cabin cruiser. He's an engineer after all."

"Why's it called Three Lakes, Master?" she wanted to know, quickly before James could appear on the scene. "There's only Lake Erie here, isn't there?"

Richard took the bit between his teeth. His mother had filled his boyhood with weird and fearful tales about Great Lakes history. "Not just Lake Erie, if you give any credence to the local legends," he said, reeling her in as his mother had done to him, time and again. "This Erie coastline can be, well, very eerie. Very deceptive. In the early 19th Century the fishermen from old Port Dover called it Three Lakes in One... Calm and peaceful, the way it is tonight with the sun going, going, gone and the wind turbines revolving in the offshore breeze. Sailing her is a gift on an evening like this."

He sat up straighter in the car seat, cracking his knuckles one at a time, a habit he had picked up from young Billie the Kid. "But in a storm, Lake Erie can be wild and tempestuous. It's shallow compared to, say, Lakes Superior or Huron, and the moon drags the waters over the bottom. That's the fishermen's second lake. Thirty, forty foot waves and monstrous breakers.... Then there's the Third Lake, the down-below-lake. Same as Davy Jones Locker in the oceans....All rocks, shape-shifting sands and clinging weed. A graveyard and nothing but."

"How do you know all this?" she asked.

"My fucking mother," he said, the dislike written on his face. "She collected old legends, tales of the bygone she called them. Used them to flesh out her bird books. Ships were always going down with all hands. Innocents getting drowned., My childhood bedtime stories. Like the Port Dover legend of Culotta Greyfrairs.

She was the local ship chandler's daughter, long fair hair and beautiful, or so they said."

His eyes clouded over. His mother had so relished frightening him with the legends. "It was during the American invasion of 1812," he went on to Myra. "Culotta was a sort of less well known Laura Secord, or the American Betsy Ross. She set out from Turkey Point, by rowboat yet, to warn the British who were gathering off Long Point. But the damned perfidious Yankees, they were always damned and perfidious, strung up all sorts of misleading lanterns along the coast. Like shipwreckers of old. Lured her onto the rocks, down into the Third Lake. As she told me this, my wretched mother always held up her hands helplessly, loosened her long blonde hair and rolled her eyes back in her head. I had nightmares for years."

He peered out into the lake, a summer mist drifting on the horizon, a flash of faraway lightning illuminating the distant sky. Overhead a flight of gulls were soaring inland to their nightly roosts.

"James brought this up with Fleur," he said, a touch hesitantly. "He figured she was looking for equal amounts of roughness and romance in her rape scene. He used the Culotta legend to show her that he wasn't all figures and cosines. I'm none too sure of Fleur myself. She's been around so much longer than the others. He thinks there's bloodlust in her.... I don't know exactly what he means"

"Why do you do it, Master?" she asked softly. It was something else she had always wanted to know. "All this involved set-up, James, Billie, the others? Even the scenes themselves? The violence. The rapes?"

He stared off into the gathering mist, his countenance wan and earnest. "It's what I do," he said, carefully sifting his words. "It's what James does. Or Billie, with Tiffany. It's who we are." He sat up very straight, his Richard shoulder almost touching his ear. "it's a fantasy world we live in, girl. Gennifleur, Tiffany, they're not regular people. They've made themselves over to fit their fantasies. They look on us, their so-called ravishers, as castrated

Service Tops. Well, I'm no service top, Myra. For my money, they're there to service ME."

There was an edge to his voice now. "Why do I do it, you ask? Because I'm what they really want and daren't admit. Because it gives me what I need. Total subjection."

He got out of the car and stood by the parapet, looking out into the mists. As she joined him, he pulled his eyes away from the lake and gave her a deeply searching look. It was as if he was aware he was saying too much, but the misty lake made it all right to speak. "At night, Myra," he said, his tone very serious. "I'm not the Richard you know. I'm not a 21st Century ex-soldier trying to cope with a mob of raging feminists. In my dreams, I'm Richard Crookback, Richard III, England's most vilified king."

His left shoulder had become even more pronounced. The was a beady flicker in his eyes. "At night I woo sweet Anne of Lancaster over her royal husband's bloodstained bier. In my dreams I despatch Tyrell, my always willing Sir James Tyrell, to the White Tower of London, where the boy princes await their doomed fate. I walk with dire determination in the footsteps of the king."

He had gone deathly pale, staring soulfully out into the gray mists forming over the lake. The visions, the dreams, the memories, had taken on a reality of their own. He was what he thought he saw.

With a great effort of will he returned to Myra and the present. "Gennifleur and Tiffany Purejoy," he said, forming the words slowly, with difficulty. "They're my two Princes in the Bloody Tower. The older of the two, Fleur, is going for a night-time cruise deep into the Three Lakes of legend. You understand?"

"The Three Lakes," Myra acknowledged, humouring him.

He was very firm, his voice stony. "It will be up to you and James, Sir James, to give her a cruise to remember. Am I clear?"

"Yes, Master. A cruise to remember."

"And young Tiffany," he went on, laying out the dispositions of his troops. "The girl in the school-girl outfit. You and Billie the

Kid will see she gets even more than she is asking for. Understood?"

"At St Bernadette's School for Girls," she assured him, knowing full well that where and how he placed his shadowy retinue was important to him. . .

His eyes were now back on the lake, the mist swirling in and reaching out to him on the parapet. "It's as if I can see myself and my followers in the mist," he said, marvelling at his special abilities. "Myself in the lead. You, dutiful Myra, at my Richard shoulder. Sir James, trustworthy and always weighing the odds, Even the shameless Billie, bringing up the rear with his devil-may-care laugh. I see you all in the mists, your faces forming and dissolving and forming again. I don't know what I'd do without you." .

Myra could see that he was on the verge of losing it again. She knew him well enough to feel the inchoate need just below the surface. She took his arm, gently. "It's time to leave this place, Master," she said quietly. "The Three Lakes are not good for you. You will find only pain and disaster here."

He was not listening, He was sniffing the air. "There's a storm coming," he said, his instincts keen. "From the Gulf. High winds and heavy rain."

She helped him into the car, unprotesting. He seemed relieved to be leaving Long Point. It was a place of unhappy memories, "Maybe with you at the wheel, we'll beat it home," she said.

"I love storms," he said. "And this is going to be a big one. Floods and road washouts all over. It will wrap up our terrific day very nicely"

"Great!" she said, a touch sarcastic.

What neither of them could even imagine was the effect the Great Summer Storm would have on their lives. The future is like that. Hidden from view. Until one day it isn't. And all hell breaks out.

Chapter 27 Voices in the Storm

It was the late evening of the reconnaissance day that the Great Summer Storm finally blew into K-W from the Southwest. For Richard it was to be the Storm of Storms, one that would affect the remainder of his life.

"It was a dark and stormy night" he said to Myra, giggling at his cliché. Richard III had been left behind with Culotta Greyfrairs in the mists of Lake Erie. He was back in the 21st Century now, dealing with his current over-abundance of names.

It wasn't enough that he was Richard with Myra, James with Gennifleur and Billie the Kid with the new chick Tiffany Purejoy. There are so many of me," he confided to Myra, only partly in admiration for his facility in handling it all. "I am also Rick and Rickie-Boy, or occasionally Billie's sad-sack avatar William-the-so-called-Conqueror. Till recently I was Henry with Carol and Edward with Dawn."

"Hank and Eddie," said Myra helpfully. "You had to delete them."

"They're still on the chicks' computers," he said gloomily. "Just no profiles or homepages to track them back to. Instead, I have George and Johnny setting up home pages, to say nothing of the kids...."Christ, Myra." he said, bringing another old chestnut into play. "My Names are Legion!" And he gave her a wan smile.

"Fucking hell," he thought, figuratively patting himself on the back. All these different names had become a big part of the daily grind. Keeping them straight in his brain was fast turning into a full-time job. "It's understandable," he reassured himself, "that sometimes I'm a tad confused by who was what and when and with whom."

He was standing on the balcony of his apartment in Uptown Waterloo, a stone's-throw across from the world renowned Perimeter Institute with its Stephen Hawking connection. Myra was huddled close by, nursing the laptop under a flowered rain cape. He didn't want her more customary home nudity drawing attention from the owners who lived downstairs, a snooty feminist librarian and her neatly bearded and brow-beaten husband. Or their accursed Scottish sheepdog, he thought bitterly, hating the dog, all dogs. He noted that Myra's glasses, which he permitted her to wear when she was on K.P. with the laptop, were already misting over as the storm rolled in from the Southwest.

His view of the black-painted Institute with its profusion of small windows was partly obscured by an ancient and gnarled Norwegian pine, now starting to sway in the rising wind. The Great Summer Storm was finally on its way: though a supercharged Mustang was definitely faster, particularly with Richard behind the wheel. Dark shapeless fingers of rain-drenched nimbostratus clouds were starting to roll ominously in toward Waterloo Region. He could feel the first drops of rain on his upturned face. Maybe the coming storm would clear his head. There were things to do, emails to send, ravishments to set up.

On the Fleur front, James had already received a number of emails back from her. They had even exchanged Questionnaires, highly edited and more than a little ridiculous since they originated from her. But he had played his hand effectively and it was now time, he believed, to initiate the final move on Ms. Gennifleur. Stupid name. Stupid woman, he was sure. Older than he liked them. Less suggestible.

"Master," Myra broke into his thoughts, anxiety on her face. "Shouldn't we go inside ? It'll pour down at any minute." She nervously indicated the huge tree with its heavy branches. "It could be dangerous."

"Of course it's dangerous," he responded unhelpfully. "It's a fucking storm." Ignoring the wind and the still light rain he stiffened his bearing, almost unconsciously losing his Richard identity and assuming the stance and style of James Renfrew, his most trusted sock puppet and correspondent with Fleur. Clearly a supremely efficient young man, a self-dubbed civil engineer in his late twenties. "*This is our fourth exchange of emails concerning the projected ravishment scene*," he dictated briskly. Very plain and businesslike. "*With this particular goal in mind*, comma, *I think it would be helpful if each party submits a brief statement of current conclusions, period. Like your splendid Questionnaires but perhaps a trifle more personal."*

He turned to Myra. "You fill in the punctuation. A lot more commas than usual and abbreviate where relevant." He cleared his throat and resumed. *"Earlier*, comma, *I suggested a preliminary interview at the Coffee Tyme Café in the Three Lakes Marina at Long Point. Second Friday from now, 8.00 PM. Pursuant to your posted desire re scene location, I have hired a cabin cruiser for the same date, 8.30 PM. For the record I wish to state that I believe our rape scene will be everything you expect, hopefully more. Do you approve? James*." He nodded, satisfied. "Send right away."

A sudden gust of wind swirled and whistled around him. The rainfall had picked up. The thunder was nearer now. Unlike most dogs, the Scottish shepherd in the downstairs apartment was beginning to bark, driven by inbred instinct to bring her charges into safety. "Blasted bitch," James cursed. "She should be cowering under the bed." He turned his face into the rain. James had his quirks. The storm was abating in the west, out Stratford way, its low roiling clouds reaching like gray tentacles toward K-W, Kitchener-Waterloo.

*

Thirty-five kilometers down Highway 7 from the apartment, in the township of Shakespeare, just outside Stratford, Fleur was already sitting at her computer when the email came in. She was at her computer most of the time she was at home in the 'condo.'. The Sexual Freedom coalition kept her good and busy. She scanned the KayJames16 email rapidly and decided on a prompt reply. She, too, thought it time to bring this spate of correspondence to a head.

Fleur had changed a lot recently. She was less highly strung, more tolerant of others. But she felt a certain responsibility for James, and good rape-tops were hard to find. Besides, her visceral hatred for actual rapists hadn't dissipated and there was always the off chance he had been Carol's attacker, Henry by name.

Her stubby fingers took over. *"I am in receipt of your notes regarding our upcoming ravishment scene,"* she wrote forthrightly. "*The proposed meeting at the Three Lakes Coffee Tyme is acceptable to me. I agree with the Marina setting for the actual rape. Also the rented cabin cruiser. Congratulations on deciphering my somewhat inarticulate wishes. BTW, I will go Dutch on the boat... Your submitted times and dates are approved."*

She paused for a moment, considering that perhaps she should soften the tone. Fleur, after all, was the now friendlier, more youthful side of Gennifleur's formerly totally abrasive personality, someone seemingly caring enough to risk being hurt. She continued, going for the lighter, slightly more sexy approach. "*As we enter the home stretch I feel it might help if I tell you why I chose my name Gennifleur and selected a pre-Raphaelite goddess as avatar. The name came into my head when I was very young. My Belgian grandmother always referred euphemistically to my genitals as my 'genni' or 'gennis.' I gather the term has a Walloon or Frisian origin. It works in both singular or plural. The French Les Fleurs came naturally."*

She debated how far she should go in the girly stakes. Decided civil engineer James most likely had a perverse sense of humour and could handle an unexpectedly lyrical writing style. "*From early childhood I have found the most delightful vista on earth to be a hilly bank of massed spring flowers expressing their joy in the sunlight. The luscious smell acts on my pheromones like a natural aphrodisiac. Daffodils, tulips, a wood-land carpeted by dancing trilliums in glorious bloom, affect me like intimations of the Infinite. Hence, Gennifleur. Colloquially I am a pussy in flower. (LOL)"*

She concluded her email with a slight flourish. "*I shall have more pertinent facts to relate in my next email, to follow shortly. I propose to clarify precisely why I am so interested in a ravishment scene, in slightly more detail than in 'our' questionnaire. Further, I shall have some comment on our age difference. Thank you, and goodbye for now, Fleur. P.S. We should be using MSN."*

*

Back in K-W, James was pacing to and fro on the now rain-swept third floor balcony. "Dirty-minded skag!" he said bleakly, unable to hear Myra clearly as she tried to read aloud through a clap of thunder. "Flowers in her pussy," for Christ's sake!" He snorted with irritation. "And who the hell does she think she is ? Telling me to use MSN. She'll have me texting next. Bitch!" "

Myra gave him a weak grin, as another flash of sheet lightning bathed the balcony in silvery white, almost unnatural in its eerie brightness. On the floor below them Clan Campbell, the shepherd's pedigree name, barked even louder, going about his appointed task. James was incensed. By his reckoning dogs hid from thunder. He remembered his mother's timorous Bulldog at home in his childhood. Rover had invariably slunk cravenly into the basement powder room and pushed the door shut behind him. Clan Campbell, on the other hand, was beginning to remind him of the damned Pet Shoppe in Stratford, the unmentionable Stratford. "We really ought to go in, Master," Myra pleaded with him.

"We'll go in when I say so," he snarled curtly, his hair plastered to his head. He looked up into the pelting rain, drawing energy from the storm, a strange sense of anticipation and purpose growing on his rain-soaked face. "Take this to Fleur and her pathetic Genni," he spat out, shaking the rain off his hair. "Thank you for your quality information. I await the reasons behind your choice of scene with some curiosity." He was in a hurry now.

*

Gennifleur smiled drily at his hasty response. The rape arrangements were moving along nicely. "*As indicated,*" she typed smoothly. *"I think we would benefit from comprehending my motives for wishing to experience a rape. I might caution you that I do not believe that when it is inevitable a girl should 'lie back and enjoy it.' I intend to resist, strenuously. Your job is to overcome my resistance. You should know that I have participated in two arduous take-down scenes with a vigorous young man. I greatly enjoyed the struggle and did not give in without a fight. Though 'fight' is actually the incorrect term. I am not looking for extreme violence."*

"Fair warning, Jimbo" she said sardonically to herself. "Anyway, I need the exercise. Been slacking off since that cathartic scene with Claire and Co." She decided against mentioning her many bouts on the grappling mats or the hours spent body building in the gym. Nor would she go into her recent Muay Thai training in Thailand and the victories it had brought her. He could find that out for himself, she thought, if it came to it. She still prayed that one day, soon she hoped, she would encounter the brute who had sadistically broken young Carol's jaw. "Probably not this one," she said out loud, with a trace of regret. "He sounds too mild-mannered and well-organised. Though he did get in touch off my 'Ask Madame Claire' podcast," she mused. "Maybe I'll strike lucky."

The weather was clearing over Stratford and Shakespeare. The late sun was starting to peep through. She thought about her next words for a moment before continuing. Her urge for rape play was still tricky to put into words. She elected to downplay her long ago rape and give him a simpler script to follow. It was to be his first ravishment she recalled.

"*I was a young, lonely teenager,*" she wrote at last. "*We spent the summers on a houseboat and I tended to lie awake late at night hoping that my stepbrother's footsteps would lead into my tiny sleeping quarters. They never did. I knew he could be very rough. He had little time for women in general and me in particular. But I felt I needed him. He was the only virile young man I knew. I wanted him to take me violently. Savagely, almost. Each of us in our own private hell of sexual hunger, matching souls of despair and deprivation.*" She struck the keys harder than usual. "*I want you to be my stepbrother. I want you to force me into unwilling submission. I want my own version of Nirvana.*"

A shiver passed through her taut body. It was so close to the truth. She wondered what KayJamesSixteen would make of it.

*

He was concise. "*Fleur, I fully grasp that you are not seeking extreme physical violence,*" he replied almost instantly. "*Neither am I, believe me. Nor have I ever participated in an actual take-*

down scene with a woman. I understand, of course, that such a scene is more akin to stand-up all-in wrestling and does not include, say, blood and gore. I would observe that if the latter is on your agenda I'm afraid you will not get it from me." He smiled mirthlessly as he wrote this. 'Believe this and you'll believe anything,' he thought. What he didn't know, couldn't know, was that Fleur had her own ideas about blood and gore. Quite the reverse of his.

"*Simply stated, Ms. Gennifleur,*" he went on, "*I have no objection to a fairly intense struggle. However turning our normal rape or ravishment play into a bloody spectacle is not my concept of how such a scene should shape out. Parenthetically, I do take the comment about your brother to heart. I understand the pain of societal attitudes and unrequited sexual attraction only too well. I shall do my best to be your stepbrother in a time of need. I fully comprehend how such powerful urges could have remained with you all these years... Most sincerely, James.*"

He peered up into the sky, as a sharp crack of lightning flashed and writhed almost in his face. "How do you like them apples?" he questioned the heavens with a smirk. He felt exhilarated that the rape scene with the Fleur babe was as good as confirmed. "Once we're alone on the cabin cruiser," he said in an aside to Myra, "I'll soon show her who's boss. Just not the way I showed you. Our Fleur will get raped good and proper"

The thunder cracked above his head. Below him, Clan Campbell added his throaty warning. James laughed a tad off-key. "Like the old Norse gods are doing to us right now," he snickered knowingly. "Showing us who's the real boss."

He blinked rain from his eyes. "Damn that fucking dog!" he cursed again. He was becoming impatient, irritable. "What about the other one? " he demanded abruptly of Myra. "Not Fleur, the other chick. What's her name - Tiffany. Yeah, Tiffany, how's that progressing. Goddamn it, Myra, do I have to think of everything? Show some initiative why don't you ?"

*

Off to the east of Waterloo, in Black Walnut Cottage on the side road halfway between Marybourne and Tilverdale, Madame Claire and her girl Leeza, now known as Tiffany, were watching the storm in awe. They were chatting about their response to Billie's earlier emails to 'Tiffany.' "Surely it's safe enough to go for a casual meeting at Tim Hortons," Leeza said blithely. "It's a perfectly okay place for a negotiation." She smiled fondly "You've even said so yourself."

"But not as a tethered goat," Claire rejoined simply.

Leeza coyly batted her eyelids. "No goat our sweet Tiffany," she said. "And my word, Claire, did he ever pick up on her fairy tale with the French teacher. And a school setting would be aces."

Claire shook her head in amused protest. "Quit playing with my head, darling girl. YOUR idea, Leeza, and yours alone. This Billie is merely feeding it back to you to win points."

"Billie's such a harmless name, "smiled Leeza. "And sure, it pleases me no end. I love it that this kind of nice, painfully shy guy gets off on my story. I may try some serious writing." She glanced outside as a massive clap of thunder made the window panes shake. "Thank you for the applause," she bowed, bubbling with life and good humour. "For all the.. er.. thunderous. claps," she joked.

"What about the Ravishee's Questionnaire?" Claire wanted to know.

"Kinda sweet, don't you think? I've already answered most of his questions. I'll polish it off and send it before I go to bed." She had entered fully into the hunt for the rapist, so much so that Madame Claire was growing apprehensive.

"You don't think he's the one we're after? The tiger, tiger, burning bright?

"I agree he talks about his Mom a lot. Billie this and Billie that. That's one reason we put him on the short list. So, yes, it's a little like Hank for Henry and Eddie for Edward. But it's just a pet name is all. I'm more concerned with him coming up with a school as a locale. Yes, it could be coincidence, but it might be the same overall M.O."

She leaned toward Claire, her expression earnest, almost pleading. "Claire sweetheart, what if he really is the one. I vote I drop him a line and go for a coffee and chat at Tim Hortons. At least he's a possible candidate, the best we have. I mean what earthly real danger can there be. Timmie's is nearly always packed."

“None, I suppose,” agreed Madame Claire, giving way gracefully as she so often did where Leeza was concerned. “And I'll be close by with my phone camera."

A loud peal of thunder reverberated through the cottage, shaking the dishes on the sideboard....

"Okay," said Claire, feeling they were too involved to do nothing. "Judging by his emails he's probably a mild enough play ravisher anyway. I doubt if the man we're really after even has a Mom " She was definite, committed. "Fair enough, Leeza-Tiffany. Billie at Timmie's it is. And I hope you realise what that makes you...?"

"What...?"

“You'll be a billy goat."

They laughed a trifle uncertainly, as a blinding flash of sheet lightning made its own illuminating statement. It seemed to be directly over Black Walnut Cottage. An omen, of sorts.

*

On the apartment balcony the rain was now falling in buckets. Businesslike James had reluctantly given way to the far more casual and youthful Billie. In the driving rain, neither of them was wearing glasses, any more than Richard had been wearing them earlier, though the curl of hair plastered to Billie's sopping forehead was definitely Billie. Not, strangely, that Richard fully believed he was Billie, or James, or indeed any of his diverse characters. In his still somewhat rational mind he appreciated that they were parts, facets, of his far-flung personality, accentuated in turn because they could write or talk to different prospects in different styles. At this point he still had a tenuous grasp of reality. Difficult as this sometimes was to maintain.

Myra was cowering under the rain cape, forlornly hoping to keep the laptop dry. “Please, Master…”she begged him humbly. "Let's go inside." But Richard, or James, simply weren't there anymore. And Billie was another Richard when it came to danger and violent storms. "Email to Tiffany," he instructed Myra. "Toute suite!" Disdaining the peril of lightning or falling branches, he deliberately moved into the half-shelter provided by the pine branches that reached hazardously over his exposed head. He was dripping wet from head to toe, but increasingly loose and shambly. He finally felt that everything was going his way.

When he spoke it was in Billie's easy-going, unassertive tones. *“Tiffany, I have to ask if you could do something special just for me. You see I been thinking about your school days and particularly the uniform you describe yourself wearing. The navy blue blazer and short skirt, with knee sox and cute tie. As you might have guessed I see it with two adorable little turned up braids sticking out from the beret, and well... Tiff, I have a sort of confession to make.*” He broke off, fascinated, as a bolt of lightning struck a utility pole near the Perimeter Institute. A loud crack and crackle and the street lights flickered and went out. “Ten bonus points to the gods of thunder and lightning," Billie said with a slightly nervous smile. “They just knocked out all the nerdy astrophysicists in Canada.”

He glanced a touch apprehensively at the looming sky, then returned to his dictation. *“Like I said earlier, Tiffany, I can just see you dressed like that. Braids and knee-socks and a white shirt with your school tie hanging out. A dark jacket with a smart gold crest and sensible shoes, you know the drill... And a backpack, there has to be a backpack. So, luv, here's my confession. Back in grade ten I figured the girls in the local private school were something real special. Like super cute, but kind of unattainable, you know what I mean?”* He moved from under the branches, back into the teeth of the wind and rain. “*Tiffany, captivating new friend, could you wear your high school costume to Tim Hortons? Just for me, like I said.”*

A piercing blast of thunder reverberated through the balcony. Myra gasped, as if in fear for her life. “A little thunder won’t hurt you, silly ninny,” he said coldly. “And if lightning strikes the tree we’ll both be toast.” He stepped closer to her and roughly tilted her head out of the flowered rain cape. “Concentrate on what the fuck I’ve told you to do,” he snarled in her face. “This storm is strictly for me and Dickey-Boy and James. The prehistoric weather gods ain’t remotely interested in the likes of you. We're the ones they want to talk to."

It was as if James heard his name. Quite suddenly Billie's callow features seemed to melt in the driving rain, his face disappearing before Myra's eyes. The hair plastered to his forehead was brushed back. James was almost literally butting in and taking over. Richard's personae were struggling among themselves.

"Fuck the new cunt," James said brusquely "How's about the Flowering Pussy?" It was definitely James on the balcony now, rainwater streaming down his tight-lipped face. A cruder, less self-contained James, who usually kept this side of his character well under wraps. "Did that stupid fucking cow say anything interesting about her cocksucking age?"

Myra was thoroughly confused by the suddenness of the switch from Billie to James and the language he was throwing out. Desperately she scrolled back to locate Fleur’s last email. “She was, well, sort of concerned about it, “ she said, doing her level best to ignore the rain and the danger and focus on fulfilling his instructions. “She’s a lot older than Tiffany or the others.”

James snorted derisively. “How did the silly bitch put it? Insecure, was she?”

"Um...er... I'm looking it up, Sir," Myra said, flustered and barely able to speak.

*

Unlike her regular style, Fleur had tended to beat around the bush. *“A question of age has come up,”* she had begun. *“Just because my home-page states I’m 37 doesn’t mean I look it. All my friends say I could be at least ten years or more younger. Besides, James, my calendar years in no way impinge on the purpose of our ravishment scene. In fact if you view it from the experience POV, it's good. It means I'm less likely to freak out."* She then Sent, without editing.

*

James spun on his heels, showering Myra with rainwater from the sodden deck. "She's likely in her forties," he commented caustically. He straightened up, brushing a hand across his forehead. "Set me up on MSN," he ordered in his business voice. "Less time for thinking but could be effective with the slower, more drawn out prospects." He resumed dictating. *"My final query is quite important, Fleur," he said bluntly. "Precisely how far do you want to go?"*

*

Thirty kilometers to the West, Fleur was watching the now distant storm, still raging over Kitchener-Waterloo. "How far do I want to go," she repeated reflectively, as the latest email came up on her screen. "As far as I can," she muttered to herself. She was fully committed now.

"As far as you, KayJamesSixteen - 'whatever your real name is' - dare to take me!"

Her fingers flew over the keys. "*I can better answer this question when we are face-to-face at the Three Lakes Coffee Tyme*.," she replied coolly. "*It's too easy to prevaricate online. I need to talk with you directly. We have some final negotiating to complete*."

*

James brought the exchange to a firm conclusion. She was beginning to bore him. "*Anything you say, Gennifleur*," he dictated impatiently. *"I'll see you at the Coffee Tyme Café. 8:00, Friday week."* Irritably, to Myra. "Send the fucking thing."

A squall of heavier rain drenched the balcony. The lightning, almost immediately overhead, lit up his sopping wet figure as he stared fixedly at the turbulent sky. His hair was plastered flat across his brow again. His eyes, screwed up against the now pelting rain. "And you.., Tiffany, how about you ?" he yelled up into the teeth of the howling gale. "How far do YOU want to go? You silly young bitch!"

"Billie, Master," Myra called out to him almost at the top of her voice. "You're Billie when you write to Tiffany. Billie."

"Of course I'm Billie!" he retorted savagely. "I know I'm fucking Billie with fucking Tiffany." He was petulant, incensed. His control of his personalities was slipping again. "I'm Billie the Kid!" he exclaimed wildly. "Young Billie. And James. And Richard. And George and ---- I'm everyone, you stupid twat." He raised both hands over his head. Made them into shaking fists. "I'm everyone there is!" He was becoming euphoric now, revelling in the nightmarish weirdness of his existence. "Everybody!" he bellowed.

Myra started automatically toward him, seeking to calm him, comfort him. Then she saw his face. She had seen that burning look before. In Stratford, at the Pet Shoppe. She stopped, gave up, gazing at him helplessly. The storm was at its peak. The rain poured down. The thunder pealed and thundered. The lightning flashed blindingly. The balcony groaned and swayed in the howling wind. Clan Campbell bayed desolately, inconsolably.

And suddenly, unexpectedly, as the storm reached its highest fury, a strange eerie calm came over Billie, James, Richard. They became aware that something indefinable had been set in motion. They were launched on a course they no longer understood. It was beyond their capacity to understand. But each knew that a barrier had been crossed. What they didn't know, couldn't know, was that there was a disaster in the making. A grim disaster beside which the ghastly scene in Stratford was a mere prelude. What they did know, what each sensed in every fibre of his being, was that something in the lightning was striving to make contact with them. To communicate with them. Someone, some THING, was reaching down and piercing through their very flesh and bone, searing into their souls.

The sky darkened, black as night. A sudden quiet descended. The dog had ceased its yowling. The thunder was in abeyance.

Anguished, yet strangely serene, Richard's black eyes fastened on Myra.

"Watch out, Myra," he said, in a voice she had never heard before. Deep, scary, sinister, alien. "It has been a dark and stormy night," he intoned hoarsely, as if speech was new to him. "Be afraid. Be terribly afraid. Something unbelievingly wicked this way comes."

Myra stared at him for a long moment, transfixed. Then turned and fled, terrified, into the apartment...

.......As the storm redoubled in unearthly, otherworldly violence and a sudden jagged bolt of lightning flashed down and struck the Norwegian pine. A branch broke off and grazed Richard's head and shoulder before coming to an agonising stop across his foot. "Goddammit all to hell," he swore as the blood trickled down his face and his ankle throbbed and pained. "Goddamn them all to hell!"

And Clan Campbell slunk fearfully into its cupboard under the stairs.

Chapter 28 Negotiations

In the Coffee Tyme Café at the Three Lakes Marina near Long Point a hasty deal was being struck. Myra had driven Richard, now almost permanently James since the lightning strike, south in the red Mustang for his meeting with Gennifleur and their final negotiation with, hopefully, their scene on a cabin cruiser to follow. James was not in the best of shape. He was in his favourite James attire; horn-rimmed glasses, dark-blue nautical jacket, regimental tie. Tallish, erect, military. He had planned to have an hour or more to rent a boat before Fleur arrived. With Myra's driving he had less than thirty minutes in hand.

"The Three Lakes Princess, that's your answer," said the scruffy, grizzled old salt they were drinking coffee with. He was wearing a dirty white turtleneck and a captain's cap. "Sure and didn't I design her meself from the Port Dover Ship Portfolio I did. An' I'll rent her only as often as me livin' supplies need replenishin' and that's the honest to god truth so it is." He fixed James with an earnest stare and topped up his coffee mug from a mickey in a crumpled paper bag. His softly musical Irish lilt seemed to have increased exponentially as he launched into his pitch.

He was an aging and colourful professional Irishman with a wickedly innocent twinkle in his eye., They had approached him ten minutes earlier on a tip from the red-haired waitress, who herself looked like a typecast barmaid from a Stratford Festival Elizabethan tavern. "Captain Seamus O'Rafferty," she had called him "He knows every boat and every owner in the Marina. He'll steer you right enough."

"Boat rentals on the Point are a bad business so they are, "the captain informed them seriously. "Ye can niver be sure who's after profiteering on a boat rental in these parts," he pontificated. "So maybe the Princess isn't as yare as ye'd fancy, but she has more foine cabin space than anything else the Eries have to offer so she does."

"What's yare?" asked Myra curiously. She was dressed casually, with a purple pashmina wrap around her shoulders. She was looking much better these days: her dull red hair less straggly and her complexion almost pimple-free.

James shifted uncomfortably in his booth seat. "A good-sized cabin is what I'm looking for," he said single-mindedly. His voice was clipped, very much the professional engineer. He was sitting with his right foot stuck out straight in front of him in the aisle. He was carrying a walking stick and the foot was encased in plaster-of-paris. It had three signatures scrawled on it, James, Myra and Richard. He had a small bandage round his head and two fingers on his right hand were pointing rigidly skywards from a bandaged wooden splint. He had ordered Myra to sharpen the business end.

"Tis a common sailin' term down Philadelphia way, missie" said Seamus O'Rafferty, who had picked it up from an old movie. "An' tell me, young sir. What was it after being like, struck by a wayward bolt of lightning as it were?"

"He was lucky not to have been killed," Myra piped up, shaking her head. She had been in her helpful mode since the accident on the apartment balcony. It was a relief to her that the worst of the stroke-like syndromes of slurred speech, confusion and roiling anxiety seemed to be clearing up. Though she missed Richard being around most of the time and thought it must be because James was the Gennifleur 'catfish,' a term she had picked up from the MTV series. She wasn't sure she really liked James. He was always so darned businesslike.

"Captain O'Rafferty," said James, in his brusque tone of voice. "I had intended to be here an hour earlier to rent a boat." He shot Myra a sidelong glance of disapproval. "The branch smashing down on my foot meant I needed a driver. We were 'lucky' not to be hauled in by the cops for driving too slow. The point is," he went on. "My good friend Fleur is meeting us here for her planned birthday celebration. In Fifteen Minutes," he emphasized, tapping his watch with his splint.

Seamus O'Rafferty took the hint and returned promptly to his closing oration. "Sure and to goodness, young sor, there's ample room on the Princess for yisselves and two or three ither couples if ye've a mind to party, and why shouldn't you if it's a friend's birthday and all. Lots of gleamin' woodwork and the melodic tones of John McCormick hisself waftin' out of the grandest Bose speakers on the Three Lakes." He added another nip from the paper bag to his mug. "Would you be after taking a wee drop yisself?" he asked ingratiatingly.

James put a hand over his coffee and shook his head, a gesture that made him wince visibly. He was really in a hurry now. "How much do you charge for a single night, O'Rafferty?" he asked, attempting to take charge.

'You can call me skipper, me boyo" replied the captain equably. "My regular summer rate is $250, but seeing as you're a wee bit banged up I'll turn over the keys for 20% off so I will. The Three Lakes Princess is yours till the crack of dawn for $200 even and not a penny more. No GST, no PST and no bleeding Marina fees, which is a big saving so it is"

"Can we inspect her?" asked Myra who of recent days was doing her very best to look out for James' and hence Richard's interests. Her former acquaintances would have been surprised and no doubt pleased to see how far she had come under her Master's tutelage.

The self-styled skipper waved his hand expansively. "Sure if you don't mind the slight Scottish mist fallin' you can come aboard right now. She's moored just off the marina, around yon low headland in Culotta Bay. You can for sure see her peeping through the Willows." He pointed her out to them. "Ye follow that wee path an' it will bring you smack to me private jetty and the gangplank itself so it will. An' fear not, the light drizzle will be evaporatin' within the half hour or less." He didn't add that the Princess was moored off the headland to keep her well away from the water-skiers and power boaters who paid the marina's way.

He straightened his cap and smiled at them confidentially. "Sure she's a grand lady for sure, is the Three Lakes Princess. `I'd not part with her for a quarter of a million an' that's the god honest truth so it is. The pride and joy of my old age she is."

Myra offered him a half smile. She didn't quite know how to handle his Irish blarney "You named her after the old legend?" she asked.

He gave her a broad wink. "Ah, lovey," he said. "It's after being a fantasy world we live in down here on the Point." He looked ready to launch forth into another grand Irish flow, but James stopped him with a raised hand. All HE had registered was the valuation. "I'll take her," he said abruptly. "She suits my purposes I'm sure."

"Without even a look-see?" queried O'Rafferty, feigning doubt.

'I can see her lines through the trees," James responded impatiently. "One hundred and seventy-five dollars cash." He nodded curtly to Myra. "Give it to O'Rafferty now."

She took out her pocketbook. "You're convinced Gennifleur is coming?"

He sniffed. "She's not the sort of woman to agree to a meeting and not show up. "$175 it is, Captain. Agreed?"

"Sure and you're a hard man to do business with," said O'Rafferty, as he smoothly took the money from Myra's hesitant grasp. "The keys are in and there's records on the stereo. I'll raise a glass to you at the Legion. But first," he said peremptorily, taking out a pen, "A final obligatory codicil to our negotiation. Lift yer foot." James did so, blankly, and with a rare old Irish flourish Seamus O'Rafferty scrawled a few words on the cast. "Any and all damages to be paid extra," he read off. "Now sign your name here," he said straight-faced. "Twill cover my ass if you young folks get carried away is all," he added with a wink at Myra.

"Happy to oblige," said James, on the verge of irritation but equally straight-faced. "And a very good night to you, Captain O'Rafferty."

The captain threw him a parting salute. "An' to you, sor and miss," he said. "My thanks for your helpful courtesy and all. A rare pleasure it has been." With a pronounced seaman's rolling gait he started out of the café, pausing only for a smack on the blowsy waitress' bum as he left. He was in good spirits, and intended shortly to be in better. It was not every day his job as live-in caretaker of the Three Lakes Princess paid so well. Not any day, in fact.

Behind him, James unbelievingly rapped his cane on the unusual inscription. "The man's a complete fucking moron," he said. "Can you see this in Court?"

Myra giggled. "I just hope Fleur turns up," she said, with a worried frown.

"She'll be here any moment," James said without a flicker of doubt. "This is my evening for supremely successful negotiations

*

The second negotiation kicked off right on time. As it happened, Gennifleur, Dana Van Lith, aka Fleur, arrived at the marina Coffee Tyme, one minute before the agreed hour. She was indeed not the sort of woman who agreed to a meeting and then didn't show up.

Her punctuality, however, did not prevent her being more than a little peeved. "I didn't realise I was getting a bloody ambulance case," she said bluntly. "Or a couple for heaven's sake. "Who the hell are you?" she asked Myra. Even the new, more relaxed Fleur did not believe in beating around the bush. She was even wearing a smart sailing outfit, with a cheeky dark blue cap complete with gold anchor. Her hair was cut short, very dark. Apart from a current deep frown she looked much younger than her actual age.

"I'm Myra, Master's chauffeur," Myra replied, nervous but well-schooled, straightening out the purple pashmina wrap around her shoulders. "His ankle, you see."

James hauled himself to his feet, standing almost to attention. His knuckles were white on the walking stick. "Good evening, Ms. Gennifleur," he said, hoarsely but with more vigour in his voice than he had shown negotiating with the alleged Captain O'Rafferty. "I'm James Renfrew, ex-2nd lieutenant in the Princess Pat's Light Infantry. Kandahar and Kabul. We corresponded at length." This was his usual James introduction, inaccurate as to details but suiting his spare, military look and manner.

Fleur looked him up and down. Caustically at first. He met her eyes without blinking. She eased off a touch. She wasn't a rude or unkind person by nature, just plain-spoken. "Been in the wars, have you?"

"Literally," he said. "And by your leave I'll call you Fleur. It's less of a mouthful." He smiled, though still tight-lipped. "And perhaps less suggestively physical," he added, referencing her email comments.

"But isn't that why we're here?" Fleur riposted, raising an innocent eyebrow.

Myra was a little lost at the exchange, but striving to be helpful. "Sir was struck by lightning," she said. "In the big storm last week." This time she gave the information with a note of pride in her voice. Not everybody was struck by lightning and still came out for a rape play scene. Whatever else he was, James was plenty tough.

"A falling branch hit my head and ankle," he clarified. "I had worse in Afghanistan. It didn't stop me then. This won't now. We'll have a solid, interesting scene."

Fleur gave him another keen, appraising look. "You're not exactly my ideal ravisher," she said. "Even in play."

"He's very good at what he does," Myra chipped in loyally. "And I think you're very brave, Gennifleur. To go after what you want the way you have."

"That's how you get what you want, girl," responded Fleur, flashing Myra a quick, friendly smile. "Have you known Sir James long?"

Myra beamed, remembering the back-story James had drilled into her in the Mustang. "Since I was a kid. Sir was my brother's best buddy in the Forces." Her face clouded over. "Colin never made it back. The Taliban."

Fleur reached out and gently touched her arm. "I'm so sorry, Myra," she said sympathetically, quite genuine

Myra bit her bottom lip. "Thank you, Gennifleur," she said bravely "It was a horrible time." A tear trickled down her cheek.

James interrupted coldly. "Myra, you talk too much." He ignored her and continued to the older woman. "So, Fleur, we have some final negotiations to complete. I'd say we covered quite a lot in our emails and I should thank you for the splendid questionnaires. Well done."

Myra hurriedly took some papers from the Osprey day pack by her chair and handed them to him. "To summarise," he went on, with a curt nod of acknowledgement. "I gather you're looking for no ropes, handcuffs or bondage of any kind. No blood or gore. No fisting or similar embellishments. Straight-forward Ravishment 101. Correct?"

Fleur had given Myra a consoling hug and a napkin as a Kleenex. "Businesslike, isn't he?" she drawled. She gave James her full attention. "I intend to get down to basics before we start," she told him. "Panties and T-shirt."

James nodded. "Agreed. I'll leave my shirt and pants on to begin with. I'll unzip when matters reach that point. Satisfactory, I trust."

She was as clipped as he was. In matters such as this, her bossy, Dana side tended to come through. "We'll have a short struggle. I'll go slightly easier on you than I had intended. I'd like a running commentary on your progress and a strict adherence to safewords. Red means stop. Instantly and without prevarication."

"Of course," he said without hesitation. Thinking all the while that she could be a real bitch if he let her get away with it.

"I'm glad we understand each other," she said, quite definite in her wants and feelings. At least, she thought, he seemed prepared to obey the BDSM maxim. Safe. Sane. Consensual. Part of her would have preferred not to be here, but he seemed harmless enough and she felt she owed him something. Judging from his responses to the questionnaire he was willing to learn.

There was a pause. A mutual assessment, though from widely divergent perspectives. They had both noticed a similar pause in earlier negotiations preceding an upcoming scene such as theirs. Even an experienced player like Gennifleur occasionally felt a slight awkwardness. Rape, or ravishment, was always a touchy subject to negotiate, even to talk about...

"Myra," James said, after a few seconds. "Time for another coffee. Take out, I think. Fleur, what about you?"

"Black. No sugar."

"No rush, Myra," James told her. "Fleur and I have some personal details to discuss." He was back to his controlling self.

"Thank you, Myra dear," Fleur said, watching the girl heading for the counter. "Cute." she remarked to James. "Becoming aware of who she is. Your sub, I presume?"

"I'm training her," he said, closing the subject.

"So, as I recall, you're a civil engineer these days," she said, making polite conversation. "Based on your army experience no doubt."

James was his formal self. "With my home town authorities, yes," he informed her crisply. He wasn't exactly stilted, she thought. Just excessively punctilious, military in speech and bearing. Regimented. No open necked shirt or casual runners for James. He certainly had presence and an innate air of command. Maybe this evening's rape session wouldn't be a complete washout in spite of his cuts and contusions. The ankle might reduce his mobility but it wasn't a major feature in deviant sex.

"And I see you are also very discreet," she said, still summing him up. He frowned, not quite following. "Your home town,' as you put it."

"Ah, yes. Waterloo Region," he said, more informatively. "I work for the regional government. I find it necessary to separate my business and personal lives." He returned to the affair at hand. "Incidentally, I have already leased a boat, the Three Lakes Princess by name. Regrettably I haven't yet had time to inspect her."

She shrugged. "We can check out the 'Princess' as well as each other. That is why we're here, after all."

"Precisely," he agreed. "Our purpose over coffee is to ascertain if we have sufficient mental and physical compatibility to conduct a viable fantasy rape-cum-ravishment scene. Q.E.D."

Gennifleur gazed at him for a moment with a glint of amused recognition. "You truly are a pompous ass, aren't you," she said pleasantly.

"Pompous? Yes, I suppose I am. My reading of you is that you prefer clarity. My point is, Fleur, we are engaged in setting up a highly personal and potentially embarrassing encounter." He was being utterly serious. James liked everything to be clear.

"Tell me about it," said Gennifleur, allowing her girlish, more frivolous mode to show through. She considered James' entire manner to be his way of assumptively taking control. It was an unusual reaction for her, she thought. In other circumstances she would find him annoyingly masculine. Normally she would throw a protective skein of competitiveness into the mix, but that was modifying since her cathartic drumming scene. Besides, in view of the forthcoming rape scene, he simply seemed to be more in character. Strong enough mentally and probably physically to be an actual dyed-in-the-wool rapist, she decided. But too damned meticulous and not threatening enough to be the brute who had abused poor dear Carol. That was definitely unlikely, she concluded with a trace of regret. She really had been hoping to have the opportunity to emasculate that bastard.

"Personally, I incline to using the specific word 'rape,'" he was saying as her attention returned to his words. "I know 'ravishment' is the preference in the BDSM Community, but in my opinion that's too mealy-mouthed. I lean toward calling a spade a spade. Mind you," he went on rather hastily, "I'm not what you might call a committed, violent rapist, not at all."

"Of course not," she agreed amiably.

"It's just that I was always intrigued by how many women fantasize about being treated so atrociously. A majority, in fact."

“Men as well,” she interjected helpfully. “In smaller, but still sizable proportions.”

“I am not bisexual,” he stated stiffly.

“If you say so,” she acknowledged equably, still vetting him in her mind. Pity about him being so beaten up in appearance. On the other hand, the cast and the bandage around his head, along with his army background, did give him a sort of Hemingway aura. A Farewell to Arms, or was it For Whom The Bell Tolls? She would have to be gentler with him than she had intended. Pity. But after all, he was still a rapist of sorts.

“Ahem,” she coughed, moving on. “Tell me, James, what does being zapped by lightning actually feel like?” she asked as a gambit.

He frowned. “Zapped was the correct word,” he replied. “A massive jolt. I literally felt shocked. Like old movies about being sentenced to death on the electric chair. Strangely, there was no pain”

“And afterwards?”

“Slept like a baby for fourteen hours straight. When I woke up my heart was still racing. Absolutely no feeling in my right arm or fingers. The broken finger tingled but didn’t hurt at all. It was hard to breathe. Think. Or remember anything. Vertigo, and my voice was even hoarser than it is now. Not recommended for electrical play…”

Gennifleur shook her head slowly. “Are you sure you’re up to ravishing me? You know I intend to resist”

“It wouldn’t seem like rape if you didn’t.” James said. “And by the way, the boat I’ve leased, the Princess, is moored in Culotta Bay just around that treed headland over there. The rain has virtually stopped so we can go aboard shortly. You will repair to the main cabin and pretend to be asleep. I’ll pace back and forth, briefly.” He was, she realised, describing the scene she had related in her emails. She was pleased. He had done his homework, she thought as he continued. “When I burst in, I’ll yank you around to face me, by your hair.”

Gennifleur snorted. It was a wig, after all. "Try that and I'm likely to spring out of bed and clobber you mighty hard."

James smirked. He was supremely confident in his martial arts abilities. He had swiftly dismissed any reservations he might have felt about his temporary handicaps. The lure of the rape scene was too strong. Anyway, he knew he could manhandle a mere woman.

He made a droll joke. "My ankle won't interfere too much. Just a slight impediment for my kick-boxing skills."

"But not my Muay Thai," Fleur responded sweetly, thinking she would give him a few hard jabs in the chops before letting him overpower her. Something to remember her by. He wouldn't think of rape as play ever again.

By this time Myra had returned with the take-out coffee and was hovering in the background. James beckoned her over with his sharply whittled splint. "You can sit," he told her. "We have nearly finished. Just a recap on the actual sex," he continued to Gennifleur. "More or less as covered in the questionnaire." James knew he had no real intention of following the questions and answers too closely. In his heart he believed in totally free-form and violent rape. Rape, not ravishment, as he put it.

Fleur smiled a welcome at Myra. "You're back at the best possible time, Myra" she said, with a sly wink. "This is when the negotiation gets good and titillating. Juicy, I'll bet."

James tapped the questionnaire forms and pressed resolutely ahead. "According to your answers, Fleur, you are not averse to having your nipples licked and sucked quite liberally. Along with a fair degree of pulling and twisting."

"Standard nipple torture," Gennifleur whispered to Myra, who was now sitting next to her. "I have highly educated nipples."

"Me, too," grinned Myra. "And I should warn you, Sir can be dreadfully sadistic."

Fleur laughed. "But you love it," she said. "It hurts so good."

'For Christ's sake," he burst out, seemingly ready to tear his hair. "This is an official negotiation not a budding orgy."

"Sorry, Sir J.," said Fleur, clutching Myra's arm and trying to be serious "It's just you bring out the masochist in us"

He glared at her for a moment. Then he unbent and smiled faintly. Fleur and Myra laughed and any residual awkwardness disappeared. It was almost as if the sex talk had made them into firm friends. James was smart like that. He knew how to reach people in all sorts of unexpected ways. He thought of it as reverse manipulation.

Gennifleur steered the discussion back into line. "In the interest of clarity," she said, in a suitably husky tone. "I don't mind being aroused by your fingers. You see, Myra," she went on, matter-of-factly. "I have an oversized clit. Over an inch when it's stimulated right. Correctly, as you'd say, James," she added, batting her eyelashes lasciviously.

James stayed doggedly on topic. "And if I'm correct," he said, "Two fingers in the vagina are okay preliminaries for you." He permitted himself a slight, redeeming smile. "Or so you indicated in the questionnaire."

"Oh my, I thought I was quite clear," Fleur said, chatting mainly to Myra. "Two, three, even four up the wazoo is fine with me. Just hit my G-spot is all I ask." At this point she seemed more interested in amusing Myra than negotiating with James about the soon-to-be ravishment scene. She, too, had complete confidence in her ability to control events, physically if need be. She had three Muay Thai victory ribbons on her wall. And that was serious combat with able-bodied opponents

"And a vibrator up your ass," James offered drily.

Myra giggled. "You guys are fabulous," she said, taking the opportunity to distribute the coffees. "Black for you, Fleur, no sugar. And yours, Master."

"Watch and learn, Myra," Gennifleur said. "Bet you didn't know negotiating could be so delightfully pornographic." She straightened up and looked directly at James. "A couple of points I want to make crystal clear, James," she said forthrightly. "I don't mind a finger or two, but no actual anal intercourse. Clear?"

"I registered that as verboten," said James smoothly... "Questions 47 and 49."

"And a condom on any toys and specifically on you," emphasized Gennifleur very firmly. "I don't propose to take any risks with an ex-soldier. Heterosexual or otherwise."

James folded the questionnaire document and passed it back to Myra. "Then, ladies, I think it's safe to assume we have the makings of a most agreeable scene," he said in his patented supervisory manner. "Shall we take our coffee and go round the headland. I'd say it's time we inspected the Three Lakes Princess."

"To the Three Lakes Princess," said Gennifleur, rising and ensuring the top was well fastened on the cup before toasting.

Myra joined in the jovial toast, but looked a bit disappointed at the thought of losing her new-found friend "I guess I should wait for you in the car," she said, disappointed but accepting the situation.

"Nonsense," said Fleur breezily. "As I understand it you haven't seen the Princess either. You can always come back to the café if you get bored. Or not."

Myra's eyes went as round and large as saucers. "I'd really, really love that, Fleur," she said excitedly. "Is it okay with you, Master ?"

James nodded pleasantly and picked up his cup and walking stick. Things were going exactly the way he had planned. Better than he had planned. "You girls can entertain yourselves while I stumble along behind," he said. "We follow that path… through the trees. It's not far according to O'Rafferty."

"We're not girls," Gennifleur said with a note of warning. "Or at least, I'm not."

Myra had slung her bulging Osprey day-pack over her shoulder. "This is gonna be awesome," she said happily. She was pleased to see James in such a buoyant mood. Things were going well for his scene, and she really liked Gennifleur. The older woman was a good match for James, she thought contentedly. Just as controlling as him, but in a nice I-know-who-you-are feminine kind of way.

"What's in the bag, luv?" Gennifleur asked casually, in a chatty manner. "Looks heavy."

"My tattoo kit," said Myra. "I'm a tattoo artist."

James spoke up easily "And some of my stuff," he said. "Rope, which I won't need. Lube, condoms, a couple of vibrators." He was making good progress clumping along the winding path The cast slowed him down, but that was all. He patted his upper arm. "Myra's pretty good with the needle," he added, pulling a face.

"What, did it hurt?" Gennifleur asked smilingly.

"I'm a Top through and through," he said "Pain ain't my bag."

" I was working at Mister Igor's Hespeler salon," Myra volunteered proudly. "But I got canned for holding out on him. Like sexually. Now I'm freelance. Master is helping."

"Even in restaurants folks get interested," James noted. "She can't make too many contacts."

Gennifleur said "I doubt there are many customers waiting on this Princess of yours. But who knows?" She glanced at Myra. "I could be up for another tattoo some time real soon."

They had reached the willows at the crest of the small headland. "Life's full of surprises," said James, a bead of perspiration on his forehead from the exertion.

"This is gonna be an awesome night," enthused Myra again. "Spectacular, I know!"

"Keep this up and she'll want to stay and watch," said James drily.

"Sounds kinky to me," Fleur said.

Even James laughed at that one. Not one of them had any real idea of what lay ahead.

The Three Lakes Princess was coming into view through the trees. She was not exactly what Seamus O'Rafferty had described. Not exactly? Not at all.

The drizzle had tapered off. Night was settling in. What awaited them was beyond their wildest imagination.

Chapter 29 The Three Lakes Princess

It was close to a kilometer from the Marina parking lot where they had left the cars, across the treed headland to the small adjacent cove where the Three Lakes Princess was moored. The Culotta Greyfriars bay according to the 1812 story.

It was plenty far enough for James, in his depleted physical condition, to regret setting out with such confidence. Far enough for voices to get lost in the trees, muted by the soft susurration of the gently lapping waves. At least, he thought, the Princess was moored in a private location, away from the marina vacationers and steady traffic.

"This takes me back to the rocky ground around Kabul," he said, clomping along with his stick, swiping at some tall Queen's Anne lace. "As far as walking goes anyway." There wasn't really any similarity but he was the only one who knew that. "More wild flowers out here as well," he added, just in case.

Fleur and Myra were a few steps ahead, strolling casually arm in arm, stopping from time to time to admire the dozens of wild flowers dotted by the path. Myra was enjoying being with the older woman, who seemed to understand what she was going through, learning to be a slave to a demanding Master. And such a different master since the lightning strike, she thought to herself. Richard could be less rational and more obviously sadistic, but James always seemed to calculate the odds and then act in accordance with some uncanny instinct. It was difficult serving different masters in the same body.

Gennifleur looked back over her shoulder. "You didn't have to be so masculine and stubbornly independent." she told James. "Myra said she'd give you a hand."

James gritted his teeth. "It's a working foot I need, not a hand" he said ruefully. "Fortunately, we're almost there. We should have a clear view of the Princess at any moment"

The woman and the girl, as he pigeonholed them now, were moving out of the trees and approaching the ramshackle, unpainted jetty. “Captain O’Rafferty said she was his pride and joy,” Myra said with girlish enthusiasm. I can’t wait to see her.”

“He would niver be takin’ three hundtred t’ousand dollars for her, so he would not,” said James in a very phoney Irish accent. “She’s after making his day so she is.”

Fleur and Myra had drawn to a halt on the steps leading down to the jetty and were now gazing incredulously at the dark gray vessel tied up in front of them. “Good goddess almighty!” exclaimed Gennifleur, staring blindly at the breathtakingly unexpected sight that met their eyes.

“THAT is the Three Lakes Princess?” Myra asked slowly, blankly. “That’s her?”

"She," said Fleur mechanically. "I think..."

The Princess was an impressively ugly, flat-bottomed barge, with a dirty orange sail and a jumbled mess of rusty cables and high ironwork looming above her prow. She was the only vessel of any kind in the Culotta Greyfriars Bay. She had a stumpy mast and a yawning, shallow after-hold beyond it. Her forward hold had been covered in by a plain gray-painted cabin with four chipped gun-metal portholes. The high steel arm of a digger or excavator rose up at an angle high over the cabin and the small ‘bridge’ area that jutted out from the cabin toward the gangplank at the end of the jetty. There were two small outboarded scows tied up amidships, one on each side. The farthest scow was piled high with rocks and seaweed.

James caught up with his two dumbfounded companions. “Don’t stop on the steps…” he started to say peevishly. Then he froze to an abrupt halt and his voice trailed away. The colour left his cheeks. He was utterly taken aback. “What the hell is that?” he burst out, as if he had once again been struck by lightning.

With less directly at stake, Fleur had quickly put two and two together. “That’s what you paid One Hundred and Seventy-Five dollars for,” she said, more than a little disbelieving herself. “And I’ll tell you what it ain't." She stared at him as if he was an absolute moron. “It ain't a luxury cabin cruiser. It’s a fucking calamity!”

“Fuck that blasted O’Rafferty!” spat out James, barely able to contain his wrath. “The mother-fucking con-man! I’ll cut his heart out with a fucking spoon!”

Myra hadn’t quite realized what had gone on. She was still trying to be helpful. “It’s the Princess all right,” she said, pointing to the squat, dirty vessel. “It says so, right on that signboard on the front. “The Three Lakes Princess.”

“The bow, Myra,” Gennifleur said, correcting her gently. “Ships have bows, even ones as plug-ugly as this abortion”

Indeed, the Princess was no fairy-tale beauty. She was a working girl. She was covered in mud and long strands of seaweed. A largish single digging bucket hung out over the water from the rusting excavator built into her bridge. Her sole mission in life was to keep the channels around Long Point clear of rocks and miscellaneous flotsam and jetsam and dump them further out in the lake. She desperately needed a coat of paint...

“Your opulent Princess is a goddamned dredge,” Fleur went on, turning back to James and starting to laugh a whit hysterically. “The luxury boat you’ve leased for our storied ravishment scene is a filthy, seaweed-infested, bucket-dipping, bottom-trawling fucking dredger!” She laughed in his face, her voice dripping with scorn and derision. “The way I see it, you’re the one who’s been raped, James my boyo. Your Irish seadog has taken you to the fucking cleaners, and then some.”

James shot her a look of pure hatred. “Shut the fuck up, you…you feminist… woman!“ He broke off, spluttering incoherently. For once in his life he was at a complete loss for words. “Jesus Christ!” he yelled impotently, and pounded his walking stick against the steps.

Myra attempted to come to his rescue again “It’s not exactly the way I pictured it,” she said. “But he, Captain O’Rafferty, never did actually say she was a cabin cruiser. He said he rented her to young couples who wanted a moonlit cruise on the lake. Big enough for two or three couples, he said.” She frowned, trying to remember his implied if somewhat misleading description. "What

I don't fully understand is what that excavator thingie is doing on the front. On the bow," she added with a smile at Fleur.

Fleur was patient with her. "Not the way I pictured it either, Myra" she said with a wry smile. "The Princess is a working boat. She's a dredge, or dredger, depending which books you read, English or American."

The 'excavator thingie' was the centerpiece of the bridge, or maybe the bridge had been built around it. It was a mechanical digger of the pre-all-hydraulics era. Thick hawsers and taut wire cables were the sinews and muscles of the high angled and jointed arm that manoeuvred the steel-toothed bucket suspended from the open end. "The bucket dips deep into the water," Gennifleur explained simply." She rarely missed an opportunity to be a mentor to worshipful young girls. Myra had struck her fancy. "The bucket comes up loaded with bottom rocks and sludge and the arm swings around and deposits it into those little scows alongside. Then it swings back to the Third Lake for more. Simple mechanics, I suspect, but messy as hell."

"A goddamned dredger," James said hollowly. It had sunk in by now. He rounded irately on Myra. "You gave O'Rafferty $175 for a fucking dredger."

"Only because you told me to, Master," Myra protested weakly.

Fleur chipped in sharply. "Don't take it out on poor Myra!" She started down the steps to the gangplank. "Come on, guys. We made it across the headland. We might as well explore while we're here." She had noticed what Myra had said about two or three couples. She wondered what the inside of the Princess was like.

"Is there any point?" James asked gloomily. "It baffles me how well-laid plans go awry like this, I was sure I had this evening, our rape scene, all lined up perfectly."

"In your dreams," said Fleur, with a sarcastic edge. She led the way down the steps and on to the swaying, creaky gangplank. "Careful, Myra, there's a missing plank or two. And the deck's piled high with junk."

*

James was still bleak and dejected. “As far as I can see the Three Lakes Princess is nothing but a deathtrap.” He followed Fleur and Myra off the gangplank and across the deck. "All these dangling wires and equipment. It’s a bloody disaster waiting to happen.”

“But it’s our disaster, Master,” said Myra, trying to be cheerful. “We might as well check it out. Just don’t trip over anything is all.”

The deck was a tangle of wires, cables and inexplicable pieces of equipment, seemingly cannibalized from a number of rusting sources. The arm suspending the bucket was jointed in the middle to another fifteen foot high metal arm, known in the trade as the stick. The support stick could swing right back over the cabin roof to above the scows secured to each side of the Princess. Close up it was a very Heath Robinson or Rube Goldberg piece of mechanical construction.

They entered the bridge through a low door. A ship’s wheel was offset among the digger’s levers and controls. James had perked up a bit by now. He was an engineer after all. Or professed to be. “These levers must control the bucket,” he said, with a spark of interest. “Forward to lower it. Back to drag it up.”

There was a key in what had to be the ignition and a big red starter button. He pushed it gingerly. An almighty clanking and whirring pierced the night. “It’s like an old digger I saw the ragtops using in Afghanistan,” he said. “O’Rafferty must have taken the housing apart and rejigged these levers. Not difficult with a wrench or two.”

“You know so much about machinery, Master” said Myra with a note of admiration in her voice.

“Doesn’t he just,” Fleur said dryly.

He flashed them both a quick look and engaged one of the levers. “This lever here brings the bucket back over our heads,” he added. “And this one. “He touched another lever but didn’t pull it. “This one probably dumps the whole load in the scows, if the bucket’s gone back that far. Which I guess it must.”

He switched off the key and the grinding and clanking came to an end. “Q.E.D,” he said, and gave them an almost sheepish grin. “I still can’t believe we rented a goddamn dredger. Must have been the blasted lightning,” he added, rather apologetically.

Gennifleur had gone to the back of the excavator housing and was looking down into the cabin directly beyond. “Your friend must have sprung the back off the digger and built the cabin between the bridge and the mast. It looks a fair size.”

James nodded. "Two steps down into the forward hold, the cabin" he said. "They run the length of the bridge, with only a curtain as a divider."

“A beaded curtain,” observed Gennifleur with a raised eyebrow. “I’d say your Captain Rafferty is a bit of as lady’s man.”

“The plump woman at the Coffee Tyme,” said Myra. “At the cash. She was very friendly with him. He patted her bum on the way out.”

“The barmaid type who told us to see him about boat rentals,” said James, with a doleful look again. “It was a conspiracy from the get-go. They were both in on it.”

Fleur had moved down the steps into the cabin. She pulled a cord hanging from a rattan-bladed fan with three light bulbs. “Definitely a lady’s man,” she said drily, as the lights came on and bathed the whole cabin in a soft red glow. “This was his own private bordello…..”

The cabin was an open, surprisingly roomy area, quite clean and well furnished with chairs and side tables. It extended a good ten feet from the bridge back to a large comfortable-looking bed covered by a plush hot pink comforter. A few feet in front of the bed the wrap-around steps led back up to the wheelhouse, separated only by the sparkly bead curtain and the offset levers and controls of the cannibalized excavator. A massive 5-ton counterweight to balance the digger passed through the cabin under the ceiling and ended directly above the king-sized bed.

“You want to know something weird,” said Fleur, suddenly thinking deeply. “This bordello has possibilities.”

James had started fiddling with the stereo. He too was revising his previous negative assessment. “Not a bad old sound system,” he said. “The stereo is fine, and those really are top-line, antique Bose speakers.” He switched on the stereo and the voice of John McCormick, a popular Irish tenor from the Thirties and Forties filled the cabin. He was belting out ‘O Danny Boy,’ an even older Irish staple.

“The pipes, the pipes are calling,” harmonized Fleur, in good spirits again. “I remember my grandmother singing this. She was from Brussels,” she told Myra. “In Belgium. But by some quirk she adored early Irish tenors.”

“No accounting for taste,” sniffed James, turning the volume down to background music. “We had to sing this at school. Upper Canada College,” he added for Flour’s benefit. He looked curiously around the cabin. “On the starboard side, a small head,” he pointed out. “To port, a tiny but functional galley. With running water if you want to clean up.”

He stepped up the two steps to the bridge and excavator area. He tested the wheel. It spun easily. He moved to the excavator levers. Turned the key and depressed the starter again. The bucket clanked and whirred noisily above the bridge roof.

Fleur had perched on a stuffed armchair. “James,” she said silkily. “Are you thinking what I’m thinking?”

He toyed with the open and close levers for a moment. The clanking, now directly above his head, intensified. “It couldn’t be more private,” he said thoughtfully. “We have lights, music, atmosphere.” He switched off the excavator and the bucket ground to a halt. ”I even have a crazy digger to play with. The Third Lake is literally at our fingertips.”

In the cabin, Myra had a question. “Master, there’s a great hole in the ceiling, covered by a black tarp” she said, pointing. “I wonder how that happened.”

James shook his head disparagingly. “That idiotic O’Rafferty likely dropped a load of sludge and rocks on it,” he suggested caustically. “Like I said, this insane dredger is a disaster waiting to happen.”

He looked meaningfully at Fleur for a moment. "Putting it poetically." he said, his eyes gazing into hers. "This whole cabin reeks of rape and ravishment."

Myra finally cottoned on to the change in attitudes. "You're going ahead with it," she said, marvelling. "You're gonna play out the scene..."

James had taken his cue from Gennifleur. He switched into organizing mode. "Myra," he ordered crisply. "Go back out on the headland and pick some flowers for Fleur. She really likes flowers and she might need them. Afterwards." He was fast becoming his normal, controlling self.

"Oh my," said Myra happily. "You guys are wonderful." She thought how nice it must be to have such self-confidence, to be able to make up their minds so quickly. "But it's getting dark out," she remembered. "Don't flowers, like, sleep at night?" Myra was quite simple about many things.

"Pick them anyway, Myra," Fleur said firmly. "See how many flowers you can gather in thirty minutes, eh?

"Forty minutes," snapped James.

"I came here to be raped," said Gennifleur. "And this is the exact sort of environment I'd expect to be raped in. An Irishman's passion pit on a rusty old dredger. Quick, Myra, shoo!"

"I'll be back with the flowers," laughed Myra. "Have a great scene, guys."

"That," said Gennifleur "Is entirely up to your Master. I'm just the virtuous victim. He's the vicious rapist." Not too vicious, I hope, she thought, as Myra made herself scarce. She decided she didn't like James very much, but he had spent all that money. Anyway, she could take care of herself. And he was rather crippled.

She rose smoothly to her feet. "I intend to resist, James," she said calmly. "Vigorously, remember."

Almost without thinking she aimed a couple of practise Muay Thai blows at the back of the armchair. Well balanced. Fast, hard, perfectly aimed strikes. With considerable force behind them.

James watched her hitting the chair. He was surprised how quickly she moved. How well she knew how to hit. He would have felt those blows, he thought. She was fast and athletic. She knew what she was doing. And his foot was still throbbing from all the walking. He would have to be careful. Fleur was no pushover.

He saw her deliver three more fast neck-level chops. Then a couple of spinning kicks to the top of the armchair.

“Jesus!” he said aloud.

Her eyes flashed. She smiled thinly. It was a confident, rather cruel smile. She wasn’t even breathing hard.

“You’re quite a handful,” he said, and began to cast around for an alternative.

Any alternative.

**

And so the critical rape scene between James, 27, and Gennifleur, 39, was set in motion. Aboard the Long Point dredger Three Lakes Princess at 8.30 P.M. on a Friday evening in July. Negotiations had included two questionnaires, six email exchanges and a face-to-face meeting. There was no great personal liking between James and Fleur but each felt bound by the conditions of the scene they had negotiated. As long as it served their purposes.

It was a momentous decision.

Fleur finished her warm-up with a flurry of short-arm punches and robust elbow jabs to the upper wings of the high-backed La-Z-Boy chair. She was ready.

James had closely witnessed her exercises. He was looking for an opening. Considering possibilities.

“Muay Thai,” he said, with a note of caution in his still raspy voice. “Martial Arts.”

“I mastered Muay Thai to defend myself against men,” Fleur said. She was stating a fact. “I trained in Toronto and Bangkok. I’m good.”

James spoke with seeming equal calm, though he was less calm below the surface. “My training was in the Army. Camp Borden and two tours in Afghanistan.” He flexed the knee of his crippled leg. “I am at some disadvantage.” He gave Fleur an appraising glance. He was still negotiating. “Nonetheless, I trust we can work up a fine sweat.”

“In the struggle…?”

“And in the ravishment to follow,” he replied. They were two ultra-competitive people. James was trash-talking, buying a few minutes while he searched for a possible alternative. Fleur was a much more skilled opponent than he had bargained on. Dangerous, even.

Nor was she averse to a dash of educated trash talk herself. “One of the things I most like about Muay Thai is that it’s intended to hurt,” she said. “Every blow, every action, is designed to inflict serious pain.”

“It’s the BDSM of martial arts,” James more or less agreed. “So, I gather you’re a switch. A full blown sadist at heart.”

She nodded earnestly. “There’s one man I hope to meet in a scene like ours. He mercilessly raped a friend of mine.” She showed her disappointment. “I don’t think you’re him.”

James blinked and cleared his throat. He covered up by examining the cabin layout. “Move that wing-chair over by the galley stove,” he instructed her crisply, slipping out of his dark blue jacket. “I’ll drag the other one out of our way.” He was trying to take charge again. The die was cast.

They cleared the furniture. Silently.

"I'll go up to the wheelhouse," he said next, setting the scene. You slip off your shorts and that sailor blouse and crawl under the comforter. I'll take a while coming back down the steps."

He stopped off by the stereo while she stripped. The record was changing. "More of the same ilk," he said, reading the label. "McCormick singing 'Mother Macree' and other Irish music hall favourites."

He used the cane to help him up the steps, then looked back through the beaded curtain. She was on the bed, hauling the comforter over her. She was wearing a brief thong and a sports singlet. Not a T-shirt, he noticed. She was almost chunky, powerfully muscled with heavy thighs. Not totally unattractive.

He switched on the excavator but left the levers alone. "Think of the buzzing and whirring as eerie accompaniment to your rape" he said. "John McCormick acapella with some preternatural, other worldly orchestra."

"Very poetic, I'm sure," said Gennifleur sarcastically. She was facing away from him, one naked arm and shoulder showing against the hot pink comforter. Its redness was highlighted by the three red bulbs.

He had returned to the top of the steps. He was still unexpectedly unsure of himself. Making conversation while he looked for a way to compensate for the handicap of his ankle. He smiled thinly at the heavy counterweight looming over the bed. "We'll have to hope that 5-ton weight isn't jarred lose by our sexual goings-on," he said forebodingly.

Gennifleur turned her head irritably. "It would hurtle right through the deck and sink the fucking Princess,' she said tersely. She was perhaps more nervous than she let on, even to herself. "Get on with it man!" She flounced back under the comforter.

He remembered that during the negotiations he had promised her an ongoing narration. "It's late night in the family houseboat," he began. "I'm starting down the companionway now. You're lying there, awake, pretending to be asleep. You're hot, wet between your legs. "

"For Christ's sake!" she snarled.

He ignored her impatience and came down the two steps, the clacking of his stick adding to the whirr of the machinery and McCormick's tenor. "Now I'm outside your cabin... I'm excited by your presence. I've had a beer or two. I'm sweaty. I want sex…"

Fleur was trying to get in the mood of their scene. She breathed deeply, remembering her girlhood. This was what this evening was intended to be about, wasn't it? At least he was doing his best, silly damned fool…

He paced back and forth outside her supposed door. Clack, clack, clack, went the cane. He resumed the narration. "I hesitate to break in. You're a relative, almost a half-sister. I don't know how you'll react…" He broke off, this was becoming a bore. "Ah, to hell with it!" he said, and limped quickly to the big bed and ripped the comforter off Fleur's near naked body. "Look at me!" he ordered brusquely.

She turned her head, making a pretense of waking up. It was a performance in itself. She was still feeling her way into her part, wondering at the back of her mind why she was doing this. For Carol, she thought, but dismissed it immediately. He's too prissy, she told herself, too calculating and logical.

Which was when James closed his hand on the naked flesh of her upper arm and jerked her around on the bed. It hurt. She actually felt violated, defenceless.

And more was to come. He dropped his stick on the sheets and knelt beside her, grasping her shoulders cruelly, his fingers digging painfully into her flesh. "You want me as much as I want you," he said coarsely, using the old familiar justification and meaning every word. In his mind, women were cowards who refused to admit their carnal urges. To him, most women were really asking for sex in Dress. Manner. Posture. They were begging for it.

He stared into her eyes for a long moment. Then suddenly, unexpectedly, swooped in and kissed her mouth, hard. His lips were wet.

“No kissing,” she mumbled, pulling away.

He let go of one shoulder and wrenched her arm tightly behind her back.

“Holy fuck, stop that!” she burst out, taken by surprise.

He twisted the wrist harder and kissed her again. Savagely. He pushed his tongue into her mouth. “Suck on this for starters,” he mumbled crudely, remembering his promise of narrative flow.

Gennifleur tried to bite him but failed and he ran his tongue wetly around the inside of her upper lip. “Ugh,” she groaned in disgust. “Let go of me.” .She was still trying to play her part as negotiated.

He dropped his free hand to her crotch. His first and middle fingers slithered under her flimsy thong and reached for her sex. He had the speed and dexterity of a striking cobra.

“Leave me the fuck alone!” she yelled out. The reality was less appealing that the teenage fantasy. She had taken enough of his nonsense. She jerked her wrist from his grasp and followed through with a lightning quick Muay Thai chop toward his throat. At the same time she wrenched loose from his shoulder grip and punched him forcibly in the belly.

James moved remarkably fluidly for a man in a cast. The sudden chop nearly caught him in the Adam’s apple but he swayed back just out of reach. His stomach muscles tightened protectively under the punch. No problem there. He grabbed both her wrists and pulled her upright. They stood face to face by the king-sized bed, nose to nose, not a hands-width between them.

For a moment they read each other. He saw a stubborn but wanton and wanting woman, asking for it. She saw a flint-eyed hard-ass, determined to take what he wanted, by force if necessary. The polite James she had met at the Coffee Tyme had vanished. In his place, a ravening male animal, demanding his due.

She threw up her hands and pushed him off. He staggered and nearly fell. She felt a wave of immense strength and competence flow through her. She aimed a swift knee feint at his genitals, backed off a pace or so, spun on her toes and threw a high kick at the side of his head. She had spent many hours practicing her Muay Thai, against men as well as women. Her last Thai sensei has been a saffron-clad monk, who gave no quarter. She knew she was invincible. Particularly against a guy with a cast on his foot and his fingers in a splint.

Again he swayed rapidly backwards and absorbed her blows. "I was in the military, remember?" he said coldly. "We had bitches like you for lunch."

She was misled by a recollection that this was only a scene after all. "Now you're talking," she said, with a touch of excitement. "And don't call me a bitch," she murmured, seemingly contradicting herself." Lithely she sprang to her left and went back on the attack, hands jabbing and chopping and her foot stamping down to his cast before she spun again and kicked for his head.

This time he was partly fooled by her changing attitude and her fist caught him right over the heart. Her flying foot practically tore the ear from his head. A trickle of blood oozed out.

He was righteously mad now. "Bitch! Bitch! Bitch!" he shouted at her, working himself into an adrenalin-fuelled high. He grabbed her arm and hauled her into a crushing bear-hug. There was no conscious thought left in his brain. He was James, the implacable soldier, reacting like an automaton to a Mujahadeen suicide bomber. He ignored the pain in his ankle, ignored the bleeding ear. He had been trained to fight to the death.

Gennifleur had been trained too. 'Go for the ears and nose,' her Muay Thai instructors had taught her. 'Hurt him more than he can hurt you.' She ruthlessly stamped on his cast and dropped suddenly in his grip, using his agonized surprise and her weight to break his hold. "Fuck you to hell!" she bellowed full blast, as her open hands flew to his ears with a resounding clap.

She seemed to have no fear, he thought backing away with his foot and ears on fire. Probably she hadn't yet latched on to the bigger picture. Blood trickled down his neck. His chest pounded. His eyes were bloodshot. By comparison she was untouched.

He used his voice again, even raspier now. He knew that trash-talking was a potent weapon in his arsenal. Especially against a woman. "I'm gonna rape your fucking cunt," he ground out brutally. "Just for starters! Then," he added cruelly, going for her most private phobia, revealed in her final negotiation, "Then my throbbing cock will fuck your tight female ass." His lips were bared over his teeth. "You're not in pissy Kansas anymore, cunt!" he growled menacingly, and lunged the sharpened splint viciously towards her eyes.

She swayed back and he missed by millimeters. For a timeless moment they stared, fixedly, into each other's eyes. His now appeared to have taken on a yellowish hue, with green-tinged floaters within them. She was deeply disturbed, discombobulated. She blinked numerous times. What she saw in his eyes was feral, not human. "That's what I said, bitch," he snarled at her. "This rape is for fuckin' real!"

He made to leap forward like a wild animal on its prey, but his ankle gave out and again he almost fell. He growled in unreasoning frustration. She registered the murderous intent behind his eyes, more mad beast than civilized man.

Fleur dropped her eyes, unable to look at what lived there. It was beyond her limited human comprehension. A wave of out-and-out fear and terror quivered through her body. Moving purely by instinct she ducked under his outstretched arm and summoned all her strength to smash her elbow into his nose with desperate power, once, twice. The blood spurted.

He had been half off balance from his slip. Under the sheer ferocity of her blows he stumbled backwards and the back of his knees caught the rim of the steps. He fell awkwardly back and landed, sprawling, amid the levers and controls of the excavator. It whirred and whistled. It was waiting…

He thrust out a hand and instinctively grabbed a lever to propel himself back to his feet. It was that simple.

Above the ceiling, above the tarp, above the yawning hole in the roofline, the dredging bucket teetered….

"You are utterly mad," she said. There was a sense of wonderment in her voice. Then horror, as the realization struck. "Good goddess almighty! You're HIM! THE RAPIST!" Grim determination flowed through her. She moved slowly towards him.

His yellowed eyes never left hers. He didn't even blink. With his free hand he beckoned her forward. She came. Till suddenly he held up his hand, palm out, the splint pointing straight up. She stopped. Their eyes remained locked.

There was an expression of raw triumph on his face. He shook the blood from his face and started to move forward. But again he seemed to trip, and again he had to grab another lever to right himself. He was gloating as he pulled himself upright.

What followed was instantaneous.

The girl Myra came bustling in through the low door to the bridge. "I picked lots of lovely flowers for Fleur," she started to say as she entered. A clanging, crunching din sounded from above the roof. A loud wheesh of tearing plastic. Metal screeching across metal.

"NO!" shrieked Myra. "PLEASE GOD NO!"

Life, death, seemed to flow into slow motion. Inevitably, inexorably, a three-quarter full bucket of Third Lake weed and rocks smashed down on Fleur's exposed head and shoulders.

"James was the one,' was the last clear thought to flash through her mind like jagged lightning. She knew instantly that she had uncovered Carol's rapist and that she must die. 'He'll be caught now," she started to think, as an even brighter flaring of white light suffused her last flicker of consciousness. In the light, a small boy, his hands extended in welcome. Diego,

The Three Lakes Princess had brought the rape scene to an unnegotiated end. Gennifleur was dead before her corpse hit the deck.

Behind her, Myra passed out cold and, on the stereo, the third John McCormick record dropped smoothly into place. "Too-rah-loo-rah-loo-lah," he sang mellifluously. "Too-rah-loo-lah-lie. Too-rah-loo-rah-loo-lah - It's an I-rish - lul-la-by….."

Darkly eternal forces were abroad in the Lake Erie night.

Chapter 30 AfterCare

The scene in the cabin had barely changed.

Gennifleur's battered and bloodied body lay on the deck at the foot of the steps, rocks around her and seaweed lying across her head. Her eyes were staring starkly up at James.

He was still standing in the wheelhouse, frozen among the levers and controls. His hand had reached out mechanically and switched off the machinery. He appeared to be in shock, not fully aware of what had gone down.

The excavator had whirred and whined to silence. On the Three Lakes Princess, the only sound was John McCormick still singing his tender rendition of an Irish lullaby.

Myra was gradually coming round from her fainting spell. Some colour had returned to her cheeks. The harsh reality of Fleur's death had been too much for her. There was a childish quality about her.

Somehow she clambered to her feet, pale and weak but trying to do right by Gennifleur. Her new friend was dead. She had gone away. They had known each other for such a short time and Myra had liked her very much. She had admired her. Respected her… Now all she felt was…acceptance.

Carefully she took the purple pashmina from her shoulders. "Fleur loved this colour," she said. Gently, smoothing it out as she did so, she draped it over the dead woman's head and torso. "It was the same colour as the loosestrife on the headland. The royal colour, she called it. Imperial purple. " The pashmina covered most of the worst injuries.

She turned to face James, at the top of the steps. "They'll say you did it, Sir," she said calmly, almost matter-of-fact. "Sir J." she said softly, smiling to herself as she remembered Gennifleur's sly contraction.

James hadn't moved. His hand was still on the digger. He was ashen-faced and empty of emotion or coherent thought. His brain was trying to comprehend what had happened. He knew that the woman Fleur was dead. He felt that in some way he was partly responsible. But he couldn't quite get to grips with the enormity of the event.

Myra extended a hand to help him down from the wheelhouse, away from the excavator controls. She knew that he was lost right now. But he was still her Master, her boy-friend. She accepted that the rape scene had gone terribly wrong. "Did you kill her, Master?" she asked him quietly, dispassionately. "Fleur?"

His eyes glittered like blood in the reddened glow of the Princess. The pupils were jet black pools, hugely dilated. The sole expression within was a bottomless, soulless pit, devoid of comprehension.

"Master," she asked him again. "Did you kill her?"

He stared at her, distantly. "It was an accident," he replied, his words hoarse and halting. "An accident in the dredging mechanism. One just waiting to happen."

Myra nodded evenly. She believed him. "But it wouldn't have happened if you hadn't brought her here. They'll say it was the ravishment scene that caused it."

If she could have commented, which of course she couldn't, Gennifleur might have regretted that she hadn't had time to kick James' ass as she had hoped. She hadn't been raped either. Now she was dead. All her hopes and plans, her dreams, her fears, were over and done with. Forever. She would for sure have hoped that the blinding white light her brain had last seen was a waiting universe welcoming her home.

It was a horrible way to go, thought Myra, but at least it was quick. Quick? It was instant. A ghastly accident. Sir James was right. Sir J. was right. Myra smiled again, faintly, at Fleur's remembered inflection.

"I liked her so much," she said sincerely. "I wanted her to be my best friend."

"She was too bossy," James said, with a touch of his old self. He still hadn't quite put things together, but he had thoughts, intimations, of the way the future might shape up. They were not comforting intimations. "She made me lose my temper," he said, working through his uncertainty. "My temper and myself. I lost control of myself. She broke my nose," he added plaintively. "She could really fight. Muay Thai. She was very fast."

His countenance took on a stubborn look. "It was an accident," he repeated more forcefully. "One minute she was alive and kicking and the next…." He smiled thinly. "She was a first-class kick-boxer," he said, with grudging admiration. "I didn't mean for her to die. It was a sudden, dreadful accident." He looked as if he might break down at any minute. Fear was beginning to show on his face.

Myra nodded. She was still calm, almost as if she were unconcerned. "I guess death is like that in real life," she said simply. "That's how a cousin of mine died. Johnny. He was run over by a school bus. He was five. Fleur was going to be forty in two weeks."

James seemed to understand why she was acting the way she was. She stared at him myopically. She was not uninvolved. In her own way she was trying to reach out… To him. To Fleur.

"We can't leave her lying like this, surrounded by rocks and blood," she said. "Fetch me some water from the galley." Myra had come to a decision. "I'll clean her where I can. We'll make her as comfortable as possible." She knew what she had to do. She had picked up a great deal from Fleur in their short acquaintance. She tore off the tattered, dirty sports singlet. "She'll never be able to wear this again. It's filthy," she said.

James watched as she went to work, only his eyes moving. They glittered less now. The pupils were shrinking back to normal size. He went over to the galley without protest.

"I know what we'll do," Myra said. Her calmness was eerie. "We'll cover her with flowers. Fleur loved flowers. She wrote about them in her emails. And we smelled them together crossing the headland. She was a flower person."

James returned to her side with a basin of warm water and a bunch of dishcloths and tea-towels. “A flower person?” he repeated, not quite sure where Myra was heading.

“Flowers for Gennifleur,” Myra said with a smile. “The ones I picked for her. St Anne’s Lace and purple loosestrife. Daisies and buttercups. Day lilies and golden dandelions. “

Myra was being very pro-active now. She had started washing the mud from Fleur’s body. She felt close to her. It was like a labour of love. Fleur had become her instant mentor.

In her own way, Myra was almost happy. Sad, but happy to be of use. “What we’ll do, Master, when I’ve washed her, we’ll make her beautiful. She can keep my pashmina and we’ll cover her in petals. She said day lilies were her most favourite flower. Here today and then gone to flower heaven.” She bent to her task, humming softly.

In the background, the John McCormick record had hit a flaw. It began clicking quietly.

James understood that the girl was still in a form of shock… Like with himself, her voice and actions were a defense against events that were beyond her. He watched as she carried out the tender act of aftercare, washing Fleur lovingly, reverently almost. For the first time since the accident he was conscious of coming back to himself. His mind was still cloudy, but beginning to contemplate what exactly had transpired.

He was still not quite sure how it had all taken place. If he had ever felt sorry for anyone, guilty about anyone’s fate, he felt sorry for Fleur, for Gennifleur. He couldn’t fully understand how the accident had actually occurred. She had irritated him when she was alive… Her femdom bossiness had riled him. But he hadn’t meant to kill her ----

Or had he?

A small part of him, quietly insistent, whispered that just maybe he had. From the very beginning of the evening, the whisperer said. He had introduced Myra to Fleur by her real name. No Sorry-Girl in between. He had been clear, too clear, about the tattoo kit and her freeform art. Crystal clear. Later, Fleur would have remembered his words. A crippled rapist with a tattoo artiste girl-friend. Not hard to trace…

'She had to die,' his inside voice prodded him. 'You know you planned to kill her all along. You had to kill her," it echoed in his mind. "The Princess of the Three Lakes merely did the job for you…'

The quiet, sibilant voice nudged away at his memory. 'And of course you knew how to run the digger. You had excavated trenches all over Helmand Province. You knew what lever did what….'

The words exploded in his mind. His culpability flooded through his brain the way the sludge and rocks had cascaded over Gennifleur's head. And, as if in recompense, the coldly logical, calculating James died and something monstrous appeared in his place. "Damn you, Fleur," he cried out, as his last drop of compassion and rationality fled. "Damn you all to hell!"

Without a conscious thought in his head he fell on her broken body. The flowers crushed between them.

Myra had taken out her tattoo kit.

Each in their own way, James and Myra paid their last respects.

As the Irish lullaby clicked-clicked-clicked-clicked----

It was terribly sad, and terribly terrible.

Book Two of "The BDSM Factor" is called "Predicament Bondage"

Turn the page to read the first chapter,
an article from the Times Dispatch Tabloid

Chapter 1 Ritual Rape/Murder at Long Point

Kitchener-Waterloo Times Dispatch

BIZARRE RITUAL MURDER AT LONG POINT

Culotta Bay Scene of Gruesome Crime

by Angele Del Zotto, roving reporter

Lovely Dana Gennifer Van Lith would have celebrated her 40th birthday two weeks from last Friday. She was a popular Canadian representative of the Washington based National Coalition for Sexual Freedom. She also went by the pet name Fleur, French for Flower.

Her savagely broken and violated body was discovered late Monday morning in the red-lighted and decorated main cabin of the Three Lakes Princess. The Princess is a private dredger working the sandspit waters of Lake Erie near Long Point, Ontario. The dredger was moored in picturesque Culotta Bay.

Dana Gennifer had been most foully raped and murdered. "Death was caused by extreme physical trauma to the head and shoulders," said Detective Horatio Bellingham of the Ontario Provincial Police Criminal Investigation Service. "Indignities," he pointed out, "were inflicted after death."

He spoke in a tightly controlled tone as he outlined the alleged weapon wielded in this cruel and brutal slaying. "Rocks," he told this reporter. "Her skull was crushed in by rocks. It was murder most foul."

SECRET RITUAL OF DEATH, SAYS FINDER

Ms. Van Lith's naked white body had been stripped, washed and ritually cleaned. She was laid out in a supine position on her back in the exact centre of the boat's main cabin floor. Her arms were splayed straight out from her shoulders as if they were nailed to a cross. A diaphanous silken purple scarf was draped loosely over her battered head. Police estimated the time of death to be between Eight o'clock and Midnight on Friday evening last.

The victim was discovered aboard the Princess late Monday morning by Sheamus O'Rafferty, 59, resident caretaker/master of the vessel. He said sadly that he "had been haunted ever since by the strange and terrible ritual events which appeared to have been deliberately staged and enacted in his living and sleeping quarters."

"It was like to a royal queen lying in state," Captain Rafferty stated. "The poor woman's body had not a single shred or stitch of clothing to mask it's pale nudity and the whole grisly setting was like to being veiled in a drooping cascade of limp white petals and wilted wild flowers, all of it backlit by a blood-red glow. A ritual of death is what it was after looking like to me."

DANA GENNIFER'S PET NAME WAS FLEUR

Captain O'Rafferty said that the wild flowers scattered over the corpse included daisies and day-lilies, purple loosestrife and Queen Anne's lace, among many others plucked from the Culotta Headland. "Sure it was a horrifying sight to be walking in on," he said to your reporter. "Even more since I'd been after being out of action for three days."

Barbaric and yet bizarrely entrancing," he said, groping for words. "It was all too sadly evident that some outlandish ritual had been performed here. I felt sick to my stomach for the poor lass, but what hit me the hardest was her face.

Calm and peaceful it was, even serene in a strange and wondrous way. I'll be after seeing that pallid face till my dying day so I will indeed."

PROBABLE SERIAL RAPES

Detective Bellingham of the OPP CIS said the results of DNA samples taken from the victim should be available to police within days. "We have DNA from a baseball cap found at a sexual assault case in Stratford," he said. A serial rapist is suspected.

The Police and Captain O'Rafferty revealed one monstrous and surreal aspect of this vile and shocking crime. Dana Gennifer's body had been tattooed on the upper right breast with a circlet of purple flowers,, matching the rich Tyrian purple scarf around her mangled head.

Detective Bellingham identified the flowers as forget-me-nots. Captain O'Rafferty opined that they were most likely part of the mysterious death cult perpetrated in the crimson-tinted ship's cabin. He said he would put nothing past the perpetrators of this weird and degenerate crime.

Professor Colin Hinckley, Anthropologist Emeritus of Grabel College at Laurier University, said that the tattooing of corpses and spreading of symbolic flowers over the cadavers are a secret mythological practice with Solomon Island and New Guinea death cults. "Even Neanderthal Man sprinkled buried bodies with flowers and petals," he said.

WHAT NEXT IN THIS VILE CRIME?

Police state they have no clear concept regarding the motivations for the horrendous rape and murder. "We are not even sure of the exact sequence," admitted Bellingham, his face drawn. "But it does appear that we have a serial rapist on our hands. We are appealing for the public's help in establishing a time-frame."

Captain O'Rafferty stated categorically that he had no idea when or how the doomed woman and her killer gained access to the Three Lakes Princess. He noted for the record that he had left the dredger after completing his work late Friday afternoon. "I can't remotely imagine how two strangers got access to La Princessa," he declared.

Police hope that a member of the public will have spotted the two people approaching or boarding the craft. Ms. Van Lith's white Honda Civic was still parked in the marina parking lot late Monday. "It may provide some clues as to what she was doing here," said Detective Bellingham. Captain O'Rafferty said that he had never seen the dead woman before finding her slain in his living quarters.

The Three Lakes Princess was tied up in Culotta Bay, a small cove in the broad reaches of Long Point Bay, which itself stretches for some 150 kilometres along the north-eastern shore of Lake Erie. It is partly enclosed by the 41 kilometre curve of the famed Long Point sandspit, a U.N. designated Wildlife sanctuary. Culotta Bay was where Culotta Greyfriars was drowned by Yankee freebooters during the War of 1812.

About the Author

Lord Peter Chalant (85) started on his BDSM journey in 2004, after a protracted bout with cancer. He was then 74 and says he has been researching The Madame Claire crime thrillers ever since.

"From the inside," as he puts it with a wry grin.

Back in the Sixties thru Eighties Peter was well known in the Toronto retail market as president of Mr. Gameways Ark, where he introduced Dungeons and Dragons and Trivial Pursuit to the Canadian scene.

Previous adventures included Wig Shoppes of Canada and a chain of Union Jack Boutiques. Even earlier he had run the first art-movie house In Vancouver and was artistic director of the Cambie Theatre. He also had more than 100 TV dramas produced by CBC Vancouver

For the past six years Lord and Lady Chalant have been hosts to the Kitchener-Waterloo monthly BDSM party FATMAN, (Friday At The Manse), featured in Predicament Bondage.

Made in the USA
Charleston, SC
24 September 2015